Silence

Book Five of the *Echoes* Series

by

Jamilah Kolocotronis

Muslim Writers Publishing
Tempe, Arizona

Published by Muslim Writers Publishing
P.O. Box 27362
Tempe, Arizona 85285
USA

www.MuslimWritersPublishing.com

ISBN 978-0-9793577-9-4

Cover Art by Shirley Gavin Anjum
Book design by Leila Joiner
Editing by S. E. Jihad Levine

Printed in the United States of America

To my sons, Ahmad Mujahid, Adam Umar, Ibrahim Abdullah, Musa AbdurRahman, Salahuddin Ayyub, and Nuruddin Isa,

May Allah always guide you to be righteous.

Author's Note

This, the last story in the *Echoes Series*, begins in January 2036. Contemplating life in the future is an interesting endeavor. I'm certain to have some things wrong, but I have enjoyed tracing the lives of my characters through the decades. I will especially miss Joshua.

Acknowledgements

First, I give thanks to Allah for the ability to write.

The person most instrumental in the completion of this book is my husband, Dr. Abdul-Mun'im Jitmoud. He encouraged me every step of the way and patiently tolerated the hours I spent working at my laptop. He has always been supportive of me, and I can't say how much I appreciate this.

My son, Musa Jitmoud, provided valuable editorial assistance with this book and offered advice as to the direction of the plot, as well as the execution of certain scenes.

For his technical input, I wish to thank my former student, Zaid Ian Patrick Andrews. He helped me write a difficult scene, using his own professional experience to guide me along the way.

I have special appreciation for my editor, S. E. Jihad Levine, who worked tirelessly on this manuscript and showed a great deal of patience in the process.

As always, I must thank my publisher, Linda Delgado, who committed her efforts to this book, and to the *Echoes Series* as a whole. She has always been both kind and professional, and I have learned a great deal while working with her.

Finally, I would like to thank my readers. You have strengthened me with your support for my books, and I want you to know that as I wrote, I often thought of you.

Luqman: Race

Men can starve from a lack of self-realization as much as they can from a lack of bread.

—Richard Wright

America was different, they say, before I was born. Barack Obama was in the White House and, for a while, people hoped again. They even tried to kill off racism. But it never died.

It's been nearly thirty years since the night a black man won the presidency. I've seen the videos, and I wish I had been there. The hope is gone now. The racism remains.

~

Race has always been an essential part of my identity. My mother, a black woman, married a white man. My brothers, my sister, and I all reflect the inherent dissonance of their union. Jamal, the oldest, looks very much like our mother. Muhammad, though, is as white as our father, with only the tight curl of his black hair betraying him. Everyone says I resemble my maternal grandfather, a strong and respected black man who died years before I was born. Our sister, Maryam, is a soft mixture of both races and often people think she's Hispanic. The four of us belong to each other, though we often disagree, but none of us fits into the narrow categories dictated by society.

~

In spite of their obvious differences, my parents seem to have a close bond. They support one another, and they always present a united front, especially when it comes to us kids. Over the last few years, I have worked very subtly to divide them where I am concerned. This gives me more leverage.

For the next few weeks, I won't have to worry what they think. This evening they're flying out of O'Hare on the first leg of their journey to Makkah. Making the pilgrimage should be a lifelong dream for every Muslim. I know they're very excited.

We're all expected to see them off at the airport. That's how our family is. Most men my age are on their own, without the restrictive demands of birth families. But I am not like most men.

~

"Hurry, Luqman." My dad calls up the stairs. "We don't want to miss our flight."

I certainly don't want them to miss it either. Throwing aside my book, I pull on some jeans and a sweat shirt and run down the steps. The rest of my family is in the van, with Muhammad in the driver's seat. He honks, just to annoy me. I slip on my shoes and slam the front door.

On the way to the airport, Mom and Dad give us last minute instructions. Dad goes first. "Muhammad will be in charge of everything that goes on in our house while we're gone. Jamal, I know you're busy, but I hope you'll check in often. Luqman and Maryam, listen to your older brothers. Help Muhammad around the house, and let him know where you'll be when you go out."

"I'll miss you all," says Mom. "Be good to each other and remember to pray for us. I'll pray for you when I'm standing next to the Ka'bah." She smiles. "I can't believe we're finally going."

At the airport, Mom hugs us. Dad shakes our hands and pats our shoulders. Only Maryam gets his hug. They wave while heading toward security.

"Let's go." I walk toward the terminal exit.

"Don't you want to wait until their plane leaves?" says Muhammad.

"I'm sure they'll be fine," says Jamal. "I need to get back home and grade papers."

Muhammad shakes his head and follows us out.

~

Dad always puts Muhammad in charge of me. He says it's because Muhammad is older, but I wonder if there's subtle racism involved. It doesn't matter. I'm twenty-four years old, and no one can tell me what to do.

When we get home, I dash from the family van to my blue compact. "Where are you going?" Muhammad calls after me.

I wave away his question and climb into my car. Muhammad stands in the front yard, his hands on the top of his head, looking helpless. I speed away, honking as I pass.

~

Most of the boys are here, standing around waiting for Malek who is usually late. I walk around, shaking hands and exchanging the greetings.

"Hey Hakeem, how's it?" We shake hands and hug.

He smiles. "Assalaamu alaikum brother. It's smooth."

"What's the plan?"

"Wait till Malek comes. You ready for them?"

"You know me. I'm always ready."

Rasheed walks over. "Luqman, what's the good word?"

"Fight. You know what Malek is planning?"

"Not yet. He should be here soon."

We're looking toward the door when our leader rushes in. "Assalaamu alaikum." He waves his hand and looks around. "Sorry I'm late. Is everyone here?"

"Everyone who's coming," says Hakeem.

"Let's get started then." That's the cue for us to form a casual circle. When we're in place, Malek lowers his head and recites the first verses of the Qur'an. After that, he says a prayer.

Normally, I avoid religious gatherings. These few minutes before we get down to business are tolerable, though. Some here in the FOM joined because they wanted to be a part of a Muslim brotherhood, but I joined because I wanted to fight. It's been two months since Hakeem first brought me in, and I have not been disappointed.

When the devotional is over, Malek gets to the point. "The Young Pilgrims are on the offensive again."

"You don't have to go into details." I speak up, knowing Malek can talk all night. "Tell us when and where."

He ignores me and starts his sermon about our motivations and intentions. By the time he gets to the details, I'm ready to fall asleep. He's not fit to be the leader of a Cub Scout pack, much less the FOM. The boys picked him because of his college degree. But none of them knows Malek the way I do.

~

The house is dark. Muhammad probably waited for me until midnight, but he never lasts much after that. My parents are gone, my brother can't control me, and we have another battle tomorrow. Quitting school was the best decision I ever made. Now I can concentrate on what's important in life.

Sacred Trust

*Surplus wealth is a sacred trust which its possessor is bound
to administer in his lifetime for the good of the community.*

—Andrew Carnegie

Joshua: Part One

For years Aisha and I dreamed of making the pilgrimage to
Makkah, and for years we put it off. Last summer, we decided to finally do it. Our debts are paid, and our kids are grown. This year it
was our turn.

We'll land in Chicago soon. I dread to think of what I'm coming
back to. A devastated economy, entire families homeless and camped
out in parks and alleys, an administrative budget that doesn't begin
to meet the needs. I wish we could have stayed in Makkah and prayed
next to the Ka'bah every day. When we get back to the house, I need
to make some calls. For a few days I forgot about the problems back
home, but as we approach Chicago my stomach tightens.

I wish I could retire. My brother must be enjoying retirement. It
took him months to sell his car repair shop, but now Brad and Beth
have the time and the money to do whatever they want. I'll call him
later.

～

As our plane prepares to land at O'Hare, I close my eyes and remember Makkah. Millions of pilgrims from throughout the world
were crowded into the city for the once-in-a-lifetime experience. Now
I have completed the Hajj, the Fifth Pillar of Islam, and I am about to
enter Chicago reborn.

Aisha is sleeping, her head resting on my shoulder. I shake her
gently. "We're home, hon."

She opens her eyes and smiles. "Back to everyday life," she murmurs. "Do you think the kids missed us?"

"They're not kids anymore. By the time you were Maryam's age,
you were married."

"By the time you were Luqman's age, you were divorced from
Heather and living in Pakistan."

"So why are they still living at home?" I laugh.

"Times are different. Even Muhammad hasn't been able to get out on his own. Everything has changed." She looks out the window and watches our descent.

"Not everything." I pull her closer. "You're still beautiful. That will never change."

The plane speeds down the runway before gradually slowing. I take a deep breath. I never feel completely comfortable on a plane.

Aisha turns back to the window. "It snowed again while we were gone. And look at the flurries. I love winter."

Not me. I'm ready to head back to the desert. I frown.

She stands and grabs my hand. "I'll keep you warm."

∽

Muhammad is waiting for us in the terminal. He hugs us tightly. "Alhamdulillah, it's good to have you home."

"How is everything? Any problems while we were gone?"

"No, nothing important. Maryam started her student teaching. I barely saw Luqman, but I guess he was working on his thesis. We all prayed together every morning. The only problem is my job."

Aisha sighs. "Don't tell me you were laid off."

"Not that, alhamdulillah, but my station manager keeps sending me on these ridiculous assignments. I've been with the station for six years. They should start treating me like a serious reporter."

I pat his shoulder. "Be patient. You have to work your way up."

He shakes his head. "You're right, but wait until you see tonight's broadcast. He sent me to interview a dog. It was humiliating."

"You should have come on the Hajj with us. You could have boosted your spirits and your iman."

"I wish I could have, Mom, but if I ask for an extended vacation, they will let me go. Insha Allah, I'll make Hajj one day before I'm old."

I grin. "Who are you calling old?"

"Not you, or Mom either." He chuckles. "Um, why don't I go get your bags? Sit here and relax. I'll be right back."

We find two chairs. I lean back and close my eyes. Aisha puts her head on my shoulder.

"I'm exhausted. I'm glad I don't have to teach this week, though I can't wait to tell the children about my experiences."

I don't respond. I will have to go into work tomorrow. Aisha doesn't know that yet. She'll tell me to take a few days off. I can't.

I'm half asleep when Muhammad returns with our luggage. "I'll get the car. Wait by the door, and I'll pick you up in five minutes, insha Allah."

This is O'Hare, one of the busiest airports in the world. It will take him at least fifteen. I close my eyes.

∼

We're waiting by the door when Muhammad pulls up. When we walk out into the cold, the wind slaps my face. I gag as freezing air pierces my lungs. Snow blows into my eyes. I hesitate, disoriented after two weeks in the desert. Aisha grabs my hand.

"You have to keep moving or you'll freeze."

We dash for the side door of the van, quickly climbing inside. Muhammad has the heat turned up full blast. I lean forward, toward the vent, and try to catch my breath.

"It snowed twice while you were gone," says Muhammad. "They say another blizzard may come through tonight."

Aisha puts her arms around me. We huddle in the backseat. Snow swirls around us. "Twelve hours ago, we were in air conditioning."

"Welcome to Chicago."

"We really should think about moving."

"Stop complaining, Isa." Aisha gently scolds me. "You've lived in Chicago all your life. You should be used to it."

"I'm old."

"Old and grumpy," she laughs.

"That's me." I close my eyes. My body aches. I can't wait to get home and crawl into our nice warm bed.

∼

I must have dozed. We're home. "Wake up, Isa. Or do you want to sleep out here?"

"Do I have to go back out into the cold?"

"Come with me." She grabs my hand and pulls me out of the van. "Hurry, we're almost there." She laughs. I hold onto her, racing to the warmth of our home as snow falls around us.

Joshua: Part Two

Maryam made beef stew, a recipe she learned from Aisha's mother. It warms me.

While we eat, Maryam reads. She always has a book in her hands. Muhammad concentrates on his beef stew. Luqman sulks.

Halfway through dinner Maryam looks up from her book, breaking the silence. "How was the Hajj?" she asks. "Was it exciting?"

"It was unbelievable," says Aisha. "Millions of Muslims from every part of the world. And the Ka'bah. You have to see it. It's so much more wonderful than the pictures."

"When I get married, insha Allah, I'll make my husband take me on Hajj. It will be part of my dowry."

I nod. "Smart girl. Do you have anyone in mind?"

She blushes. "We'll see."

What does she mean by that?

"Who would want to marry you?" says Luqman.

"None of your business." Maryam shoots him a look and keeps reading.

"How's your thesis coming, Luqman? Are you almost finished?"

He stares into his bowl. "Don't worry. It's coming."

"You will still graduate in May, won't you? Have you started looking for a job yet?"

"Stop badgering me, Dad. I know what I'm doing." He gets up, throws out the rest of his food, and stomps up the stairs.

I wince. When will Luqman grow up? He's still acting like a three-year old.

For a few minutes, we sit quietly. My stomach is in knots. Luqman's outbursts always get to me. I breathe deeply and think of the Ka'bah.

Aisha yawns before catching herself and covering her mouth. "You kids can clean up. I'll see you in the morning." She offers her hand. "Are you coming, Isa?"

"In a little while. There are some phone calls I need to make."

"We just got home. That can wait."

"No, it can't. We've been gone for nearly three weeks, and I need to make sure the center is still standing."

"All right, I'll see you soon."

The short naps I took in the airport and the van refreshed me. I go to our office—formerly the kids' rec room—and pick up the phone.

Four years ago, we finally opened the Jim Evans Memorial Center. I had planned it to be a youth center, but the economy has been bad and our donors couldn't afford to fund an expensive playground. Instead, Evans serves the homeless—housing families in 700 apartments, providing three meals a day in the soup kitchen, offering twenty-four hour daycare to parents who work, and giving job counseling services and GED instruction to those who don't.

Stuart Woodson, my assistant director, has an office over at Evans and keeps things running smoothly there while I oversee both centers from my office at Hope, which still serves as a general community center. I enter his number.

"Hey, Stu, this is Joshua. How is everything?"

"You're back from the desert. We're okay, how about you?"

"I heard Chicago had some nasty weather while we were gone. Any problems?"

"We ran out of space during that second storm. A family died of exposure in a park—mother, father, and three children. I wish we could take in more. Are you planning to come in tomorrow? We need to talk about the budget."

I still haven't told Aisha. "Sure, I'll be there."

"I won't keep you then. Welcome back. How was it?"

"It was awesome. I'll see you in the morning."

I haven't looked at the budget in three weeks, but I know things are tight. We're in the middle of winter and at this rate, we won't make it to spring. Five dead. How many more? I consult my directory and make another call.

"Doug. This is Joshua Adams. I'm sorry to bother you so late, but we need to talk. Can I meet with you tomorrow? It's urgent."

"I'll be over that way tomorrow afternoon. I could come around one. What's the problem?"

"The weather is bad, and I'm running out of options."

"You know I always support the work Stu and you do. I'll see you tomorrow."

It's good to feel productive again. Now I'm wired. If I go upstairs, I'll disturb Aisha. Instead I go to the couch in the family room and catch up on the news. City council is at an impasse again. They say that Khalif Amin, a council member, refuses to discuss issues calmly. That's why this city is in such bad shape. While people are dying from the cold, our leaders are playing petty politics.

There was a skirmish in Evanston a few days ago, a clash between a radical Muslim group and some fundamentalist Christians. The FOM versus the Young Pilgrims. We've got to stop this nonsense. The FOM gives all of us Muslims a bad name.

I watch Muhammad's piece with the dog. He really was sent to interview the animal. Apparently, the mutt was named as heir in a rich woman's will. Such a waste. She should have donated her wealth to homeless shelters.

My eyelids are heavy. I'll rest for a couple of minutes.

～

"Don't you want to come upstairs?"

I open my eyes. Aisha is sitting next to me on the couch.

"I guess I fell asleep."

"You must be exhausted. Come on up." She strokes my face.

"We need to get away, Aisha. I'm serious. We could move to Pakistan and stay with Jennifer, or maybe live in Mexico with Michael. I'm too old for all this."

"I'll keep you warm." She kisses my cheek.

"That sounds good, but it's not just the cold. I want to get away from everything—Chicago, my job, all my responsibilities. It's too much sometimes." I pull her closer.

"You'll feel better after a couple of days' rest. Let's go." She takes my hand.

"I can't rest. Stu and I need to meet tomorrow."

She sighs. "You're going back to work? Tell Stu you need a couple more days. He can manage."

"Evans Center was at full capacity while we were gone, and we're running short on funds. This wasn't the best time to take a vacation."

"It wasn't a vacation. It was the Hajj. There is a difference."

"I know that, hon. That's not what I meant. People are dying in this cold, and I need to do something."

"Right now, you need to relax. Come on. I'll help you."

I follow her up the stairs to our room.

Muhammad's Journal

In the name of Allah, the Most Gracious, the Most Merciful

Alhamdulillah, I'm glad Mom and Dad finally came home. It's been hard without them.

My sister didn't give me any trouble. Maryam takes after Mom. She's calm and mature. She'll make a great teacher.

But if Maryam is like Mom, Luqman is like Dad. Not the father who raised me, but the man Dad used to be before accepting Islam. I had to practically drag Luqman from his bed every morning to pray with us. And I never knew where he was. He said he was either on campus or at Zaid's place, but he could have been lying. He's done it before. He never seems to work on his thesis, either. Up until a couple of months ago, he spent nearly all of his time on the computer, surrounded by books and articles, but lately his computer has been collecting dust. He says he's almost finished. I hope so.

I never knew how hard it would be to run a household. Just making sure the trash got put out and getting laundry done kept me running. At my age, I should know how to do all that.

My biggest problem is my job. After six years, you'd think they would give me real assignments; instead, they send me to interview dogs. I need to get a different job, but the newspapers are nearly extinct, and TV news has too much fluff. Last week, I sent out resumes to independent media in Minneapolis, Detroit, Omaha, and St. Louis. So far, I've heard nothing back.

Joshua: Part Three

"Allahu akbar. Allahu akbar." The call to prayer invites me to bow down with my fellow hajjis. I open my eyes. We're not in Makkah. We're home.

Muhammad knocks. "Assalaamu alaikum. It's time for Fajr."

I stagger into the bathroom to wash up. The water revives me. Aisha is still sleeping. I kiss her cheek. "Wake up, hon. We need to pray."

She groans and holds out her hand so I can help her up.

By the time we get downstairs, all of the kids are waiting. Even Luqman. Waking him up can be Muhammad's job now. I'm tired of it.

After the prayer, Aisha goes back upstairs. She pauses on the third step. "Aren't you coming?"

"I need to eat breakfast and get to work."

She waves her hand. "Go ahead. I'm too tired to argue." She stumbles up the steps.

I walk slowly into the kitchen. Muhammad is opening a cabinet. "Sit down, Dad. I'll make your breakfast."

"Thanks. You grew up a little while we were gone."

"It's a little late, astagfirullah. I never realized how hard Mom and you worked to keep things running, and I still can't imagine how you managed when we were all little."

"Your mother and I were younger then, too."

He starts the coffee, fries my eggs, and toasts my bagel. This is nice. We should leave home more often. "I saw your dog interview last night. It was criminal."

"They need to start giving me real stories."

"Not that. How could that woman leave all her money for the dog when people are dying? Stu told me about the family found dead in the city park. Children are freezing to death while animals live in luxury."

"My station barely reported on those deaths. Dirk, our station manager, says people want to hear news that makes them feel good."

"I didn't feel very good about that skirmish over in Evanston. What was that all about?"

"That was their second fight in three weeks. This time it started when a young Muslim sister was assaulted in a grocery store parking lot last Wednesday. Some guys taunted her and grabbed her scarf. She fought them for it, and they got rough. It could have been a lot worse, but a man came along and broke it up while his wife called the police. The sister came out of it with a few stitches and a broken arm.

"By Friday, every Muslim in Chicago knew about the incident, and I imagine every imam talked about it in the sermon. The imam at our masjid encouraged us to protect our sisters and write letters to the editor. He and some others met with the police department. They were handling it, but the FOM decided to do things their way. Last Saturday, they marched to the grocery store with signs. A few had weapons. Then some Young Pilgrims challenged them and things got rough. No one was killed, alhamdulillah, but guys from both sides ended up in the hospital, and the FOM made all Muslims look bad."

"I've heard of the FOM. Who are they exactly?"

"FOM stands for 'Friends of Muhammad.' They're a vigilante group. They used to just hassle other Muslims, but lately they've gone after the Young Pilgrims, the youth branch of the New Pilgrims. This wasn't their first fight, but it was the largest."

"Stay away from them. They'll only bring trouble." Muhammad brings over my coffee, eggs, and bagel. I take a sip. He's a good son.

"Don't worry. I'll stay far away. I'm not sure about Luqman, though."

"Luqman? He's too smart to get mixed up in something like that. Don't tell me he was there."

"No, I don't think he was, but he has a lot of anger, and he'd be the perfect recruit for those guys."

Luqman does seem angry, but I don't know why. We never denied him anything. I'm too tired to deal with him right now. I nibble my bagel. "He wouldn't risk his entire future by hanging out with a bunch of losers."

"I hope not." Muhammad brings his own coffee and bagel to the table. "Bismillah," he says quietly before eating. A good son.

Joshua: Part Four

Before heading upstairs to get dressed, I turn on the TV to check the weather. The blizzard they were predicting hit last night, leaving nearly a foot of snow. It's 15 degrees outside, with a wind chill of -11. I peer out through the family room curtains. The neighbor's motorcycle is nearly buried. The snow plow hasn't been through here yet. It doesn't matter. I have to get to work.

I walk slowly up the stairs and go down the hall to knock on our youngest son's door. "Luqman. Luqman, wake up. I need your help." I don't know if I'll get it, though.

Luqman doesn't answer, but Maryam opens her door. "What do you need, Dad?"

"I want Luqman to get up and shovel out my car."

"He probably went back to sleep."

I bang on Luqman's door and shout. "I have to get to work." I'm proud of Luqman's academic achievements, but sometimes I wish he was toiling away at a 9 to 5 job like the rest of us. After he graduates, he'll have to learn the meaning of work.

"You should take the day off, Dad," says Maryam. "You just came back."

"Did hunger and poverty stop while we were gone?" I pound Luqman's door. "Why won't your brother wake up?"

"You don't need Luqman. I can do it."

You're a girl, I want to say. Aisha would have my head for that. Women are equal. But my young daughter shouldn't have to do the work while her lazy brother sleeps. "It's difficult, Maryam. The snow gets heavy, and it looks like there's a layer of ice over it."

"I can handle a little snow. I've done it before. You still keep the shovel on the north wall of the garage, right?"

This doesn't feel right, but Maryam can do it. And Luqman won't. "Yes, it's there. Dress warm." I walk back toward the bedroom. "Be careful out there."

"Don't worry, Dad. It'll be fun."

I should shovel the snow myself, but my arm never did heal properly and my back is bothering me. If I pull any muscles, Aisha will sentence me to bed rest, and I'll never get caught up on my work.

Aisha has gone back to sleep. She needs a break. I don't know how she's managed to keep up with those fourth graders all these years.

That snow plow had better come through soon. I don't want to be late. Looking out our bedroom window, I see both Maryam and Muhammad shoveling the snow. Maybe I did have two shovels out there. What will Luqman contribute to the effort? Sleep is a luxury few can afford these days.

The snow plow must be on its way. I pull on my thermal underwear and an extra pair of socks. It's unbearable outside when the wind blows off the lake, and the furnace at Hope Center is unpredictable.

Maryam and Muhammad have the driveway and sidewalk clear. Muhammad has started working on the street in front of our house. Here comes the snow plow. He steps aside and watches while the mammoth machine eats the snow.

I pull on another sweater and a third pair of socks. When I'm properly bundled, I kiss my sleeping wife.

She sighs. "Come back to bed."

"I have to get to work."

"Be careful out there."

"I will." One more kiss for the road. "I love you."

"I love you, too," she mumbles.

I could stay home today. The schools are closed, and the snow plows are behind schedule. But somebody has to make sure we don't lose another family to the cold. I trudge down the stairs and pull on my boots.

Joshua: Part Five

I've worked at Hope Center for over fifteen years. Six years ago, they made me the director. In the last eight years, our services have doubled. Our client load has tripled. These are the hardest times I have ever seen. Chicago's unemployment rate is nearing 30 percent across all segments of society. Makeshift villages for the homeless have been erected in city parks. We face starvation on a massive level in one of the largest cities in America.

When I walk into the office, I remember that I haven't called Brad yet. I doubt he misses me. They may have taken a trip of their own. Brad doesn't like the cold either.

First, I call Stu. "Would you like to come over and fill me in on what happened while I was gone?"

"Come over? Are you in your office?"

"Where else would I be? Where are you?"

"I can't get out of my driveway. The snow plow should show up sometime this week." He laughs. "I admire your dedication."

"I don't know if it's dedication or insanity. It took me two hours to get here."

"They say it's cold out there, too."

"It's brutal. Have you checked with Evans? Are there any problems?"

"I called. We're running at full capacity. Some of the workers couldn't make it, but Sophia said everything is under control. You might want to stop in before going home. Some local high schools ran a food drive and brought in enough to get us through the month.

We're running short on funds, though. I was hoping you'd bring back some money from the Middle East. From what I've heard, they can spare it."

"I didn't go to Makkah to raise funds, but I am working on it locally."

"Good luck. Most of our old donors didn't come through at Christmas. I don't know how it will be different now."

"Now we're desperate. Don't worry. Not yet." We have another two or three weeks before we panic.

"I hope you come up with something. You must still be tired from your trip, though."

"A little. Stay warm. I'll see you tomorrow."

"Drive carefully, Joshua."

Doug Barnett is next on my list. He owns one of the few successful corporations still standing in this part of the country, offering security to those who have something to lose. He's always been there when we've needed him, but I'm afraid of asking for too much. I plan to tell him we need a little more.

Before entering his number, I look over the budget. We've already cut back on programs and staff. There's nothing left to trim.

He picks up on the second ring. "Hi Doug. When are you coming?"

"You're in the office, Joshua? I couldn't get out of my neighborhood. Let's try again sometime next week. I'll call you after I've checked my schedule."

"I'll look forward to hearing from you." I prefer to deal with Doug face-to-face.

But I do have to work on getting these funds. I open my list of contacts. Amos Edmonds—Senator Edmonds now—always promises to help, but he's become just another politician. I try his DC office and get a recording. "Congressional offices are closed today. Please leave a message." The snowstorm hit the east coast, too.

What about Hiram Johnson? I don't like the man, but he preaches about charity and brotherly love. I call his office. "Reverend Johnson is away from his desk. Leave a message and he will get back to you soon, God willing."

Why am I here? I must be the only fool out in this storm. I could have worked from home.

I walk down the hall to the vending machines. Usually I call out for a sandwich, but they won't deliver in this mess. I bite into my chocolate almond candy bar. Lunch.

The building is in good shape. No frozen pipes. There's no use staying. I gather a few papers and CDs and put them into my briefcase. Suddenly, I want nothing more than to be home.

I walk through the building one more time, leaving water dripping from the faucets. There's nothing else for me to do. I lock up my office. A steady pounding noise starts up. The pipes? No. There's shouting. Is someone here?

I walk quickly to the front. A young woman is standing outside, carrying a baby. Three children huddle next to her. I let them in.

"Thank God you're here," she says. "My kids and me about froze to death. They put us out of our place three days ago."

"Where did you spend the night?"

"We was lucky enough to get into a shelter, but this morning, I went out to look for a job and lost my spot. I dragged my kids all over the city in this cold. There's hardly nothing open today."

"You're behind in the rent?"

"My husband ain't had work in almost two months. He's up in Milwaukee trying to get something. I don't know where we'll sleep tonight. If we have to stay outside again, my kids will freeze to death."

"Did you try Evans?"

"I just came from there. They got no more room."

I grind my teeth. "I'll find a place for you. Come with me." We walk back toward my office.

On our way down the hall, we pass the vending machine. I buy each of the children a candy bar. The oldest, a girl, looks down and smiles shyly. "Thank you."

I unlock my office door. "Wait in the hall while I make the call." Stu takes a long time to answer. "Joshua? Is everything okay?"

"Stu, I have a woman here with four children. She was just turned away at Evans. We don't do that."

"Sophia says every apartment is full. We'll have to let a few of the men sleep on the floor. I'm doing the best I can."

I take a deep breath. "I'll take care of it this time. Tomorrow, we need to start looking for cots and planning other strategies. No one is turned away in this cold. Make sure your staff understands."

He sighs. "Settle down, Joshua. I'll make the calls." He adds. "Make sure you don't lose your cell phone."

"Yeah Stu. I'll talk to you tomorrow."

After hanging up, I call the other shelters. Every one of them is full.

The woman stands outside in the hallway, listening to my calls. She starts wringing her hands and crying. "What will I do? Dear Lord, what will I do?"

It's time for Plan B. "You'll have to come with me. I found a place for you."

"Thank you," she says. "I'm so worried about the children." She tries to hug me. I pull away. She looks down. "Thank you."

I lock up the building and lead them to my car. "I'll take you somewhere safe. You'll have to squeeze in back. Sorry there's no car seat back there."

"That's okay," says the woman, "just as long as me and my children are warm tonight."

I slide down the side street, carefully making my way to the expressway.

"Where are you taking me? I got the right to know."

"My name is Joshua Adams." I hand her my card. "I'm the head of Hope Center. The homeless shelters are full, so I'm taking you and the children back to my house."

"No. Stop the car. I don't care how poor we are, you ain't gonna take advantage of me. Stop right here and let me out." She shakes her head and mumbles. "I'd sooner die."

I reach into the glove compartment and hand her the family picture I've kept in there since one woman hit me. "This is my wife and me, with our four children. I won't hurt you."

"A picture don't mean nothing. Let me out so I can call the police," she screams.

"That's enough," I shout. "Settle down." I reach into my pocket. "Here's my cell phone. If I do anything wrong, you can call the police."

She gets calmer. "Okay. I got my fingers ready so don't try nothing."

I nod, concentrating on my driving. The city has had hours to clear the expressway, but it's still icy. I crawl along at a steady twenty miles an hour, praying that we all make it home alive.

Aisha has taken it well in the past when I've brought someone home, but I should have called. It's too late now. The woman has my phone and, anyway, it isn't safe to make a call while driving in this mess.

We've been on the road for an hour. She asks me about Aisha and the kids. I follow with questions about her. Nicole's story sounds familiar. She dropped out of high school at sixteen and married at seventeen. She's only twenty-six now, two years younger than Muhammad. Her husband, Jesse, works construction and other odd jobs. She hasn't heard from him since he left for Wisconsin two weeks ago. In a city where less than a third of our children finish high school and unemployment is at record levels, there are many Nicoles.

We're near the exit. Another car comes up too fast in the left lane and slides in front of me. I push my brake softly while steering to my left. The other car hits the barrier on the right. I squeeze around him.

"My God, that coulda been us," says Nicole. She pulls her children to her.

"Call 911 and tell the police about the accident, will you?"

I glance in the rearview mirror. Her hands are shaking as she enters the numbers.

My shoulders are tense. Finally, I reach our street. Alhamdulillah, we made it back safely. I'm exhausted.

The snow plow did a second run, making it easy for me to pull into the driveway. Nicole and her children pile out of the backseat.

I unlock the front door and peek in. The house is warm and inviting. Something smells good. "Assalaamu alaikum Aisha. Are you down here?"

She walks out of the kitchen. "You're home." She kisses my cheek. "Ooh, you're cold. Come inside and warm up."

"I have someone with me."

She frowns for a second and then forces a smile. "Tell them to come in. Dinner is almost ready."

"Did you cook?" Aisha knows her way around the kitchen and can make wonderful meals, but she rarely does.

"Of course I cooked. Now come in out of that cold."

I lead Nicole and her children inside. The kids line up shyly. Aisha offers her hand.

"Welcome to our home."

"You wasn't lying." Nicole hands me the business card, the picture, and the phone. Aisha shakes her head. Like Stu, she expects someone to walk off with my phone one day.

"Come with me into the kitchen and we can talk." Aisha leads Nicole and her children. I struggle out of my boots and trudge upstairs to the bedroom where I peel off layers of clothes and throw them on the bed.

After slipping into my navy sweats, I sit in the blue easy chair by the window. Icicles hang from the eaves of our house. The snow glistens in the moonlight. The neighbor's kids made a snowman. The snow looks pretty if you don't have to drive in it. I wish I could get out there and have a snowball fight with my kids like I did when they were little, but these days, I don't really have time, even, to sit and stare out the window.

I close my eyes. I shouldn't have shouted at Stu. He works hard, and I know he cares as much as I do. He did a good job while I was gone, but we both need to do more. Was Nicole the only mother desperately seeking shelter, or are there others? How many dead bodies will they find in the morning?

"Dad, dinner's ready." Maryam raps at the door. I stand, feeling much older than my fifty-seven years, and trudge back down the stairs.

~

Aisha made spaghetti. I sit down, say Bismillah, and pick up my fork.

"How did the shoveling go, Maryam?"

"It was easy, except that it was really cold out there. I had to come in twice to warm up."

"Did you help your sister, Luqman?" I eye my son.

"Maryam got the job done. Lay off."

He's twenty-four years old and still acting like a teenager. We probably spoiled Luqman when he was little. I'll try to talk to him later.

"Nicole, why are you homeless?" Aisha asks.

"We ran on some hard times. My Jesse always took care of us, but there ain't no more jobs around here. The landlord put us out, and Jesse won't know where to find us."

Nicole's children concentrate on the food. Her oldest reaches timidly for another breadstick but pulls back. I put one on her plate.

"Thank you," she says softly, looking down.

"How old are you, Jessica?" Aisha asks her.

The girl finishes chewing before she answers. "I'm nine. My brother Jason is seven. Jocelyn is four. Joseph, the baby, ain't even a year yet."

"What grade are you in?"

"Fourth grade. I should be in fifth, but I got held back because of the tests."

Aisha nods. While she talks with Jessica, I briefly study Nicole. She's about the same age as my niece Martha, Chris's youngest daughter. Martha is in medical school. Why are these two young women's lives so different? Is it because of something their parents did or is it simply the choices they made? Nicole had a baby when she was only seventeen. Martha is single and focused. Is that why one is homeless and the other is on the road to success, or is there something more?

They shouldn't have turned her away from Evans. Some workers there think they're better than the people they serve. Stu needs to remind them of their duties. Hopefully, we won't have to fire anyone.

"What's your favorite subject?" Aisha asks Jessica.

"I don't really like school. I like to draw."

"That's all that girl ever wants to do," says Nicole. "Drawing and telling stories. I always got to yank her head out of the clouds so she can help me with the baby."

Jessica smiles. "Would you like to hear one of my stories?"

"Yes, I'd like that." Aisha leans a little closer.

We all listen, except Luqman, who takes his empty plate to the sink and heads for the stairs. I stop him. "Luqman, it's your turn to do the dishes."

He sighs loudly and tosses dishes into the sink. I'm too tired to deal with him. Let Aisha do it. "I'm going to catch up on the news, hon."

Aisha pats my arm. "Go relax."

I settle in on the family room couch and close my eyes.

～

Muhammad kisses me on the cheek, as he always does. "Assalaamu alaikum Dad. Are you okay?"

I open my eyes. "Where were you? We finished dinner. Mom probably saved you a plate."

"I was on assignment. The station sent me out by the lake to see how long it takes water to freeze. It was brutal. This is not why I went into journalism."

"You'll work your way up to more interesting stories."

"Frying eggs on the sidewalk in August, freezing water in January, and that's not the worst of it. Tomorrow, I have to go out to the zoo and report on how the penguins are enjoying the cold. Ya Allah, I wish they would give me a real assignment."

"Be patient, Muhammad. Your time will come."

"I hope so. Well, I'd better go see about those leftovers. I skipped lunch."

Muhammad still lives with us. Jamal was married and a father by the time he was twenty-eight. Muhammad says he hasn't found anyone yet. He's talking about looking for his own place in the spring, but after he leaves, when will I see him?

I almost never see Jamal these days. Teaching high school is demanding enough. On top of that, he has his family. He and Rabia just had another baby, my thirteenth grandchild. Each one is very precious to me.

I close my eyes again. It's been a long cold day. I should have stayed home. But what would have happened to Nicole?

～

Aisha kisses me and brushes back my graying hair. "Isa, wake up," she says softly.

I try to hold on to the last remnants of a pleasant dream. "What time is it?"

"You're late for the prayer. If you don't pray soon, you'll miss it."

"Did you pray?"

"Muhammad stood right next to you and called the adhan. We tried to wake you, but you wouldn't budge."

"I was dreaming." I try to sit up. My muscles ache.

She sits on the arm of the couch. "Nicole is settled in Jamal's old room. The house is quiet. Why don't you pray and come join me upstairs."

I put my arms around her waist. "I'm getting too old for this."

She strokes my face. "You're not old. You work too hard. How many more will you bring home?"

I pull my wife closer. "I couldn't turn her away."

"I know, hon, she's a nice young woman, but you can't carry the weight of the world on your shoulders."

"If I don't, who will?"

"Allah will, as He always has."

"I have to do my part."

"And I love you for that. But you're only one man."

I grunt and try to stand, but I don't have the energy.

"Let me help you." She pulls me to my feet. "You need to stay home tomorrow."

"I can't, hon. Imagine what would have happened to Nicole and those children if I hadn't gone in today. And I have meetings tomorrow. The center is short on funds. These times are harder than I've ever seen them."

"Half of the parents in our school are unemployed. Students can't afford even basic school supplies. The school board has decided to cut back on the teaching staff again next year. We haven't had a librarian or a physical education teacher for three years, and they're talking about closing the upper grades."

"Do you think your principal is relaxing at home?"

"I know she isn't. And I know why you have to work so hard, Isa, but I worry. You're tense and tired. We just came back from Hajj. You should be exhilarated."

"I was until our plane touched down. Maybe I shouldn't have left. The situation is worse than I imagined. If I hadn't brought Nicole and those kids home, there would have been five more deaths tonight."

She squeezes my hand. "Go pray and come upstairs." She kisses me on the cheek. "I'll see you soon."

I watch as she walks away. It's been over thirty years, and she's still beautiful.

I rub my eyes and stumble to the bathroom to wash up. When I bow down, I ask Allah to make me stronger.

～

In the middle of the night, a dream became a nightmare and I wake up suddenly. The familiarity of our bedroom—the blue easy chair next to the window, the Qur'an on my bedside table, my wife sleeping peacefully next to me—eases my fear. I lie back down and stare at the ceiling, hoping for sleep. There's too much to do tomorrow, and I can't tackle the problems with heavy eyes.

I lie on my back and wonder about all the other Nicoles, the other Jessicas, Jasons, Jocelyns and Josephs. How many of them don't have a place to sleep tonight?

In the morning, I'll call Barnett and present him with the facts. Unless people like him give more, we'll have to turn them all out on the streets. Everyone who is sleeping in a warm bed tonight needs to sacrifice for those who aren't. And no matter what Aisha says, I need to work harder and do more because I have a warm bed, too.

I didn't call Brad, did I? It's too late now. I'll check in with him tomorrow. Maybe I'll stop by after work, if I don't have to bring anyone home with me.

Right now, I need to sleep or I won't be able to function tomorrow. First, I wash up and pray. Then I read the Qur'an. I lie down again and close my eyes, trying to relax.

I'm nearly asleep when the phone rings. I jump up. "Hello?"

"Assalaamu alaikum Uncle Joshua." It's Kyle. "Dad's been rushed to the hospital. You need to come."

"I'll be right there." I hang up and throw on some clothes.

Aisha sits up. "What's wrong?"

"My brother's in the hospital."

"I'm coming with you."

Luqman: Conformity

With confidence, you have won before you have started.

—Marcus Garvey

My parents are all about conformity, especially my father. The White mentality has seeped into him, though he would never admit it. Follow the rules. Don't question authority. Early to bed and early to rise. The average man is brainwashed before he starts kindergarten.

For some reason, I was spared. I played their game and did what they expected, but I always knew there was something more. When I met Hakeem and joined the Friends of Muhammad, I found what I had been seeking. We stand shoulder to shoulder in prayer and back to back in warfare. These are my brothers, closer to me than my own brother Muhammad with his white skin and weak will.

They expect me to wash their dishes and shovel their snow as if I was a servant. They don't know I'm working on something greater. The details aren't yet clear to me, but it will cause a tremor throughout Chicago. Wrongs will be righted, and justice will prevail.

Every evening, I train with the boys, preparing for the next battle. Malek insists we also learn about Islam. The rest of them don't know what a hypocrite he is. Does he think I've forgotten all those years of torment? He's never apologized and barely even acknowledges me. He doesn't know his day of reckoning is coming.

Family Bonds

You don't choose your family.
They are God's gift to you, as you are to them.

—Desmond Tutu

Joshua: Part One

My nephew is waiting for us in the emergency room.

"What happened?"

"Dad's very sick. He's been running a fever for the last couple of days but refused to go to the doctor. A couple of hours ago when he got up to go to the bathroom, he fell and couldn't move. Mom called an ambulance."

"Have they been able to get the fever down? Was he hurt when he fell?"

"No, he wasn't hurt, alhamdulillah. In a way, I'm glad he fell because that's the only way he was going to get treatment." He shakes his head.

"What's wrong, Kyle?"

He swallows hard. "Dad's dying."

"What do you mean?"

"The leukemia is back. His blood counts are all out of whack. The doctor doesn't give him much time." Kyle stops and catches his breath, squinting to hold back the tears. "He's probably never going home."

I don't know what to say. Aisha squeezes my hand. "Where is he?" I whisper.

We follow Kyle through a labyrinth of halls to Brad's room in the intensive care unit. My brother is receiving oxygen. I've never seen him so pale. When we enter, Aisha goes to Beth and hugs her. I stand by my brother's side and take his hand. It's cold.

He opens his eyes. "Joshua," he whispers.

"Don't talk. You need to rest." I sit on the edge of his bed, still grasping his hand, and softly recite the Qur'an.

His eyes close. I study my brother. When did his face become gaunt? His hair never did grow back after chemotherapy. His beard is completely gray. His arms are half the size of mine, the same arms that used to carry me. I hadn't realized how sick he was. And he didn't tell me.

I choke a moment. His eyes open. I continue reciting and he relaxes.

Beth walks in with Aisha. My wife signals me. I kiss my brother on the forehead and leave. We speak in whispers in the hallway.

"The doctor told Beth she should put him in a hospice."

"How much time does he have?"

"Days or weeks. A month at the most. They're surprised he's made it this long."

"How could it happen this suddenly?"

"The doctor told Brad eight months ago that he was out of remission. He should have started treatment then, but he refused."

"Why didn't he say anything?"

"Beth says he didn't want us to worry."

How can we not worry? Don't leave us, Brad. I don't know what I'll do without you.

∾

We've taken turns sitting with him through the night. As the light outside turned from black to gray, we found a corner in the visitor's lounge and prayed with Kyle leading. Afterward, I went and woke Brad for the prayer. He recited softly, immobile in the hospital bed. His usual self-control failed him, and tears leaked from his eyes.

Chris calls. He and Melinda are on their way. They hope to be here soon. Kyle goes home to check on his family. I help Matt call everyone else while Aisha comforts Beth.

∾

Brad's sons are with him. They're too young to be going through this. Matt's life is just beginning—a wife, a new baby, a new job. Kyle's triplets are so young. They need to know their grandfather.

I should check in with the centers. Stu answers on the third ring.

"How is everything over there?"

"Busy. When do you want to meet?"

"I won't make it in today. My brother was rushed to the hospital last night. He's in the intensive care unit."

"I'm sorry to hear that."

"Call me if anything comes up. Do you have Doug Barnett's number?"

"It's back in the office. Right now, I'm handling a minor crisis in the dining room."

"I'll call Sandra then. See you later."

"I hope your brother gets better soon."

"Yeah, thanks." *If only that was possible.*

It's nearly eight. Muhammad doesn't know where we are. I call him at home.

"Assalaamu alaikum. Dad? What's going on? Is everything okay?"

"Uncle Brad is in the hospital. The cancer is back, and it doesn't look good. They're talking about putting him into a hospice." It's easier if I say it quickly. "I need you to take care of some things for me."

"I thought he'd beaten it," Muhammad says softly. "Um, what do you need?"

"Make sure Maryam gets to class on time. Tell Luqman I don't want him sleeping all day. And you'll need to drop Nicole and her children off at Evans."

"Maryam is eating breakfast. We all prayed together, then Luqman went back to sleep. He said he doesn't have classes today. I haven't seen Nicole yet this morning."

"Have Maryam wake her. She needs to spend the day at Evans." I'm trusting, but I have my limits. "Tell Stu you can bring her back to the house in the evening."

"Don't worry, Dad. I'll take care of it, insha Allah. I need to come see Uncle Brad, too."

"Take care of the family for now. I'll give Brad your salaams."

"Good. Tell him I'm praying for him and keep me posted."

Sometimes I don't know what I'd do without Muhammad.

I'd better call Barnett and make a short pitch for funds. And I need to check with Hope to make sure everything's running smoothly.

Sandra answers. "Hope Center. Working for a better world."

"Hi, Sandra. It's Joshua. Is everything okay?"

"Everything's just fine. Where are you?"

"I'm at the hospital with my brother. Could you contact Doug Barnett and ask him to call me? I won't be in the office today."

"I'll pray for your brother."

"I appreciate that." Sandra is a strong believing woman who goes to church at least twice a week. We don't worship in the same way, but her prayers can't hurt. Brad needs all the help he can get.

~

I've sat here next to Brad's bed for the last hour, reciting the Qur'an until my voice is hoarse. He's sleeping. I close my eyes a moment. It's been a long morning.

"Joshua. Joshua." He whispers.

His words jerk me out of half dreams. "I'm here, Brad. You need to rest."

He breathes deeply. "I want to talk."

"You're very sick."

"Listen. I heard Beth. And Kyle." He stops and catches his breath.

"They're worried about you."

"Hospice. They talked about a hospice."

I nod. Beth is making plans to have him transferred as soon as the fever is under control. He'll spend his last days in comfort, under the close supervision of trained medical professionals.

"I won't go."

How should I respond? It's time to face facts? You know this is the end? He knows it, but I can't say it. "Beth wants you to get the best possible care."

"I'm not dying here."

Didn't the doctor tell him? Beth showed us the test results. It was all there in black and white.

"I know what the doctor says. I want to go home."

"That's not possible. If you know, why are you fighting this?" I grasp his cold hands.

"The old man died. In a hospice. Alone." Brad stops again, breathing carefully. "I want to go home."

"Our father was angry and bitter. You have your family, Brad. You have friends. You'll never be alone." I gently squeeze his hands.

"No hospice. I'm going home."

"You're sick. How can Beth take care of you at home?"

"I'm not sick. I'm dying. At home."

"We have to do what's best for you."

His eyes fill with tears. "Please." His voice cracks. "Joshua, help me. No hospice." He pauses again for a breath. "I'm going home."

Brad almost never cries. He has never begged for anything. I touch his cheek. "We all want what's best."

"Home is best. No hospice." He stares at me, communicating with his eyes what he's too weak to voice.

"Beth and Kyle are making the arrangements."

"Talk to them. Please, Joshua."

I hold him as he sobs in my arms. Brad has always taken care of the rest of us. Now, he weeps like a child.

"I'll tell them."

He calms down. Gradually, his breathing slows. I gently ease him into the pillow.

"Thank you." He closes his eyes, his breathing becoming even though still too shallow.

I continue reciting the Qur'an with my brother's hand in mine.

Someone touches my shoulder. I jump.

"How is he?" It's Chris. We hug tightly.

Brad opens his eyes. "Why are you here?" he says slowly.

Chris sits on the edge of the bed. "Kyle called. We came as soon as we could. How are you feeling?"

"I'm dying. Didn't they tell you?" Brad manages a smirk.

"It's natural to want to cling to life," Chris says, slipping into his pastoral role. "We don't want to lose you, but we have to understand that this is God's will." He speaks the words calmly, without showing the emotion I know he feels. His composure must come from years of ministering to the sick and dying.

"I fell. Beth panicked. I shouldn't be here." Brad's voice is weak, but stubborn as always.

Chris lays his right hand on Brad's chest, as if to heal him. "Why didn't you tell us the cancer is back?" His voice betrays him now.

"Don't worry. I won't die yet." Brad strains to talk.

"Rest," says Chris. "Your family is here. We love you." He stops, his professional mask failing him.

I step out to give Brad and Chris time alone. They have been best friends for sixty-two years, since the day Chris was born. For the last thirty-something years they've included me, but at times, I still feel like an outsider.

I need to talk with my nephews about what Brad wants. Can we give him that much before he dies?

～

Aisha is in the visitor's room with Beth and Melinda. My sisters-in-law talk quietly. Aisha leans against the back of the chair, her eyes closed.

"Are you okay, hon?" I grip my wife's hand.

"I'm just a little tired. It must be jet lag."

"Do you want me to take you home?"

"No, I'll be fine."

"You do look tired," says Melinda. "Maybe you should rest."

Aisha shakes her head. "Don't worry about me. Maybe I'll take a walk. That should clear my head."

"I'll come with you," I say.

She stands slowly and walks with me out the doors of the intensive care unit. "Let's go sit in the garden."

We stroll quietly to the small sanctuary in the middle of the parking lot. It's January and the flowers are gone, but the place still feels peaceful. I wipe snow off one of the benches and sit down, pulling her onto my lap.

"Better now?"

"Much better. It's so sad, Isa. Brad went for a routine check-up last spring. They've known since then, but he wouldn't let Beth say anything. Can you imagine what she's been going through?"

"That's my brother. He refuses to surrender."

"He should have thought about Beth and how hard it was for her to keep his illness a secret."

The way she kept his alcoholism a secret for over twenty years. "He didn't do it to be selfish. It's hard for him too, you know."

Aisha strokes my cheek. "And it's hard for you. I can't imagine if one of my brothers was lying in that bed. Do you want to go back inside?"

"Yeah. I think I'd better."

The world looks bright and promising out here. In a few months, there will be leaves on the trees again, and the flowers will be blooming. But Brad won't be here to see them.

～

At noon, I excuse myself to attend the Friday prayer. Aisha stays at the hospital.

Walking into our little masjid, I feel happy and yet a little sad. Last Friday, I was praying next to the Ka'bah. It already feels like a lifetime ago. I face the direction of Makkah and try to picture the Ka'bah as I raise my hands.

After the prayer, the brothers greet me and congratulate me on making the Hajj. Imam Iyad says they'll have a dinner soon for returning hajjis. He'll call later to let me know the details.

This isn't the time to socialize or think about special dinners. I need to get back to the hospital. Before slipping out the door, I ask the imam to pray for Brad.

～

They come in the evening after work and dinner, paying their respects to their uncle. Jeremy and Raheema. Jamal and Rabia. Isaiah and Becky. Maryam. Muhammad's taking care of things at home. I have no idea where Luqman is or if he even knows Brad is in the hospital.

Beth is with Brad. Melinda, Aisha, and Maryam stay close to her, offering their support. I wait with Chris and our children. This is as good a time as any.

"Kyle, Matt, there's something we need to discuss." I stand. "All of you. Pull your chairs closer."

"What is it, Uncle Joshua?" says Kyle.

I sit down and look at each of them, finally focusing on Kyle. "Your father and I talked this morning. He asked me to tell you not to put him into a hospice. He wants to go home."

"But Dad," says Jeremy, "you have to be realistic. Did you look at Uncle Brad? I mean, really look at him?"

I nod, a lump in my throat.

"That's not possible," says Kyle. "Mom can't take care of him at home. He needs to be in a medical facility. It's better for everyone."

"You didn't see him this morning. He was begging me. Can you imagine? Your father never asks for anything. He was crying. Do you realize how much this means to him?"

"Are you trying to make me feel guilty? I need to do what's best for Dad, whether he likes it or not. He's done the same for me all these years, and now I have to take charge."

"It's not easy to admit that our brother is dying, Joshua," says Chris. "He's in denial, but we can't help him if we're in denial also."

"He was begging and crying. You know that's not Brad. He wants to die at home."

"If that's what he wants," says Becky, "then his wishes should be honored."

"Are you going to take care of him?" Kyle snaps.

"No. Becky can't, but I will," says Matt. "This afternoon I asked the doctor how soon Dad could go home. He looked at me like I was crazy, but when I pushed for an answer; he said Dad could probably leave the hospital in a week or two if he's stabilized. I saw Dad's desperation too. He wants to go home. Emily and I can help."

"Do you understand what's involved here? You would have to bathe Dad and dress him, and put him on the bedpan or change his diapers. He's totally helpless. What if he has a medical emergency? You couldn't get him into treatment fast enough. Besides, you have a new baby, and that's enough responsibility. How could Emily manage?"

"We talked about it," says Emily. "Matt and I can do this. We have to respect your father, especially in his last days, as Allah commanded us."

"I am respecting him." Kyle shouts. He takes a deep breath and starts again. "Dad doesn't know what he needs. We have to give him the best care we can. He couldn't possibly get that at home."

I touch my nephew's arm. "Let's think about this, Kyle. Your father is dying, and he wants to go home. Shouldn't we make his last days comfortable?"

"We should give him what he needs, not necessarily what he wants."

"What if we hired a round-the-clock nursing service? I could contact the agency where my mother-in-law worked. Wouldn't a nurse be able to take care of his immediate needs?"

"I could do the rest," says Matt. "Emily and I will sublet our apartment and move back into Mom and Dad's house. We'll take care of the meals and cleaning and whatever else needs to be done. We can sit with him and keep him company, and help Mom get through this too. If there's an emergency, we'll be right there, and we can get him to the hospital."

"We'll all pitch in," says Raheema. "My mother and I will be happy to help with meals. We can also run the errands and help with chores around the house. There are enough of us to do the work."

"We have to do what he wants," says Matt. "Dad will be with us only a short while." He stops and looks down. Emily comforts him.

Kyle throws his hands in the air. "If you all are that determined, I won't stop you. I can hire the nursing service and buy the equipment Dad will need, but you're forgetting two things. First, we have to ask Mom what she thinks. She's going through enough stress already, and I won't add to it. Second, Faiqa and I can't help much. The triplets are still small, and Nathifa may have special needs." He looks down.

"Matt and Emily, are you sure this is what you want to do? You're talking about a great deal of sacrifice," says Chris.

"We're sure," they answer.

"Becky and I will help too, Dad," says Isaiah.

Chris smiles a little. "I know you will."

"So the next step is to talk to your mother and see what she says."

Kyle looks up. "I'll do that, Uncle Joshua. But are you absolutely certain about this, Matt and Emily? You'll be giving up your privacy, and your lives will center on Dad's care."

"You don't have to keep asking," says Matt. He grasps his wife's hand. "We can do it."

"Okay. Mom is still with Dad. I'll talk with her later. Right now I need to go home and check on my family. Don't say anything to Mom. I'll take care of it."

Brad would be proud of his boys.

～

It's late. Aisha looks tired, and I could use some rest. Kyle hasn't come back yet.

Jeremy and Raheema have left. Isaiah and Becky are getting ready to leave, saying final goodbyes to Beth. Chris and Melinda will stay at their house.

Jamal walks over. "We need to go home, Dad. Rabia's mother is watching the kids, but she has to get ready for work tomorrow. Let me know what Aunt Beth says."

"Kiss them for me," says Aisha. "Tell little Amir that Grandma brought him something from Makkah."

"We'll do that," says Rabia. She hugs Aisha, and puts her arm around Jamal's waist. "Assalaamu alaikum. We'll see you tomorrow, insha Allah."

"Yeah, Dad," says Jamal. "Assalaamu alaikum." He pats my shoulder and walks away.

We don't see our oldest much anymore. He's busy with his job and, of course, I'm busy at Hope. I haven't seen their baby since the aqiqah. Even when I do see him, Jamal doesn't usually say much. He's always been the quietest of my children.

Aisha leans on me. "Would you like to go home?" I ask her.

"I hate leaving Beth alone. Maybe we should stay."

"You need to rest. Kyle will be back soon, and Matt and Emily are still here. Let's go say goodbye."

Brad is sleeping. Beth sits by his side. I walk in quietly. She stands when she sees me.

"You can sit down." I whisper. "We're leaving now. We'll be back in the morning, insha Allah. Will you be okay?"

She crosses her arms. "Kyle will come back to stay with me tonight. His mother-in-law, Hannah, will help Faiqa with the triplets."

"I won't wake Brad up. Tell him I'll be back."

Aisha hugs Beth. "Call if you need anything. Our prayers are with you."

Beth nods, her face wet with tears. She sits down again as we leave. I glance at my brother. Oh Allah, I'm not ready to lose him.

Maryam is sitting alone in the visitor's lounge. "We're leaving now. Did you drive here or get a ride?"

"I drove. I'd like to stay a little longer, Dad. Don't worry. I'll be home soon."

I do worry, of course. Maryam thinks she's an adult, but I know better. "Walk out with us. A dark parking garage is no place for a young woman alone."

Maryam shrugs and looks to Aisha for support. "Let's go," says Aisha.

"And as soon as you get in the car, remember to lock your doors."

My daughter gives me a look. I grin and, after a second, she does too. She may be old enough to go to college and shovel snow, but she's still my little girl. I wait until she starts her car, and then I drive home behind her.

～

The lights are on in the front part of our house. We can hear the noise from the porch.

Maryam unlocks the door. I call out, "Muhammad. Are you here? Muhammad. What's going on?"

He walks out of the family room, where the noise is. "Assalaamu alaikum Dad. How's Uncle Brad?"

"He's very weak. We'll go back again in the morning, insha Allah. What's all the commotion? I don't think you're having a party."

"It's the four men I brought home. When I went to Evans this evening, they said Nicole was with her husband. Then they asked me to bring some guys home instead. They all have wives and children staying at Evans."

"Where are you planning to put them all?"

"One or two can stay in my room. The others will sleep in the family room."

I'm not comfortable having four strange men in my home, especially when I have a young daughter sleeping upstairs, but I'm sure they're decent. Being homeless isn't a crime. With all the layoffs we've had recently, it seems like half of Chicago is homeless. "Have you eaten?"

"I ordered pizza for me and the guys, and saved one for Mom and you. It has extra cheese, black olives, green peppers, and mushrooms, just the way you like it. Hold on and I'll get it for you."

"Make sure you clean up. And don't stay up too late. Mom and I had a long day, and we'd appreciate a quiet house."

"I'm going upstairs," says Aisha. "You can stay down here and work things out with your friends." She sighs.

"Don't worry," says Muhammad. "I'll take care of everything, insha Allah." He ducks into the kitchen and hands me the pizza.

"I'm going upstairs, too. You're on your own." I follow Aisha to our room.

We pray before digging into the pizza and collapsing into bed. After a few minutes I'm out.

In the middle of the night, the fear returns. Again, I wake with a jolt and look around, taking in the familiarity of our room. I lie back down and close my eyes. Brad's face is what I see, gaunt and nearly lifeless.

I go downstairs and step into the family room. A man snores loudly.

I sit at the kitchen table and put my face in my hands. Tears run slowly down my cheeks as I fight the urge to sob. My brother is dying. What will I do without him?

Muhammad's Journal

In the name of Allah, the Most Gracious, the Most Merciful

It's been a busy day. I can barely keep my eyes open.

Alhamdulillah, the men are finally settled in. One, a guy named Cal, is snoring on the extra bed in my room. I put two more in Jamal's old room. Another guy is stretched out in the family room. As tired as I am, I won't sleep well tonight. They seem to be good men, who just happen to be homeless, but my little sister is asleep down the hall and I worry about her. I'll kill any man who tries to put his hands on her.

Uncle Brad did look pale the last time I saw him, but I thought if he was sick he would say something. I didn't want to ask. Tomorrow I need to go visit him, insha Allah.

I'm always whining about my job, but I need to think about what's important. My parents are healthy. I have my brothers and sisters. And at least I have a job. It could be worse.

I'll keep it short tonight. I'm too tired to think. Before I go to sleep, though, I'd better check downstairs and make sure our homeless guest is asleep. When you work in a newsroom, you're reminded every day of the evil in the world.

～

Dad was in the kitchen. I didn't say a word. He needs this time to grieve.

I'd cry, too, if one of my brothers was dying. Even Luqman.

Joshua: Part Two

After the morning prayer, Muhammad fixes a simple breakfast of eggs, toast, and coffee for our four homeless guests. Aisha and I get ready to go to the hospital.

As we head out, Muhammad calls us. "Mom and Dad, come eat breakfast before you go. There's plenty."

"Thanks, but I'm taking your mom out for breakfast. Make sure you take care of things here at home." *And get Luqman out of bed before noon.*

"Don't worry, Dad. I have it under control. Give my salaams to Uncle Brad and everybody. Maybe I can drop by the hospital sometime today."

"That would be good. Check with Evans this evening." They're predicting warmer temperatures for the next few days, so we probably won't have any guests tonight. In nicer weather, the homeless will be out in the parks and alleys rather than in the safety of the shelter. "I'm sure Uncle Brad would like to see you," I add. I'm glad we have Muhammad around to take care of things.

∾

"We should do this more often." I reach for Aisha's hand.

"There's never time. I'll go back to school on Monday, insha Allah, and we'll be back to our same old schedules."

I sigh. "I can't wait until retirement."

She laughs. "We're too young to retire. I hope to teach for another ten years, at least."

"Then I'll retire and you can support me."

She smiles and squeezes my hand.

We've had a leisurely breakfast at a coffee shop near the hospital. Soon, we'll need to go see Brad. It's easier to sit here and pretend everything is good rather than face my brother's impending death.

∾

Kyle sleeps in his wheelchair. He has matured so much in the last twenty years—from a high school dropout and drug abuser to a family man who is taking care of his parents.

Beth sits next to Brad's bed, gazing at him. She looks up when we walk in. "Assalaamu alaikum," she whispers. "Don't you think he looks a little better?"

He does have some color in his face. "Did he have a good night?"

"He woke up once and was a little disoriented. Kyle talked to him and read Qur'an. Other than that, he slept all night."

Aisha hugs Beth. "You look tired. You probably haven't eaten anything, have you? Come with me to the cafeteria. Joshua will stay here."

"I can't eat. I need to be here with Brad."

"You need to take care of yourself, Beth. At least have some juice. Let's go."

Beth reluctantly walks with Aisha while glancing back at Brad. "Call me if he needs me, Joshua."

"I will." I sit in the chair she just left and stare at my brother. He does look a little better.

Kyle stirs and opens his eyes. It takes him a moment to focus. "Uncle Joshua, you're here."

"You must be exhausted. Your mom said he slept well."

"He did, for most of the night. Once he woke up and thought he was home. He wanted to get out of bed, but he was too weak. That frustrated him. I'm glad I was here."

"I am too. You'd better go home, though, and freshen up. I'm sure you want to check on your family. I'll stay here with your dad. Chris will be coming soon, too, I imagine."

"Call me if anything happens. Where's Mom?"

"Aisha took her downstairs to get some breakfast."

"Okay. Good. Tell Dad I'll be back soon. Matt should be coming any minute. I don't want Dad to be alone."

"You're a good son, Kyle."

He looks away. "I do what I can," he says, wheeling out of the room.

∽

My brother opens his eyes and looks around. "I thought I was at home. You talked to them, didn't you?"

"We talked. Kyle said he'll discuss it with Beth. How are you feeling?"

"Better. I hope they let me out of here soon. I can't wait to wake up in my own bed."

"You sound a lot better. I was worried."

He tries to laugh, producing a weak grunt instead. "Don't worry. I'll be fine. Why aren't you at work?"

"It's Saturday."

"Really? I lost a day."

"You were very sick." I can't forget that he's still sick, but he is a little stronger.

Chris walks in and sits on the bed. "How are you, Brad?" he says softly.

"Speak up. This isn't a funeral parlor."

Chris shakes his head and smiles a little. "I'm glad to see you're feeling better."

"As soon as I get home, I plan to start training."

"Training? What do you mean?" Is he still feverish?

"I need to get in shape, Joshua. Fourth of July. Family picnic. I'll beat you then."

"Okay, Brad. Give it your best shot."

Chris stays quiet. We all know Brad won't be with us in July, but it won't hurt to let him dream.

～

Like yesterday, we take turns sitting with him. He stays awake much of the day. I'm beginning to wonder if the doctor was wrong.

After lunch, Brad talks about our July soccer game. "I figured out why you always beat me."

"Why is that?"

"You're in for a surprise next time. Don't say I didn't warn you."

"Why is this so important to you, Brad?"

He frowns and stares up at the ceiling. "I have accomplished everything I ever set out to do," he says quietly. "I earned a graduate degree, secured a job with a top engineering firm, and became a senior engineer. I could have become head of the firm if I'd wanted it badly enough. I opened my own business, fulfilling my dream of working on cars. I'm the father of two fantastic sons, and now I'm a grandfather. I quit drinking and quit smoking—twice. I became a Muslim, made Hajj, and learned to read the Qur'an in Arabic. I beat leukemia the first time. The only thing I haven't been able to do is beat you at soccer." He looks at me. "When a man is dying, things like that become important."

"Okay, Brad. You can beat me at soccer."

"But you have to give it your all. I don't want to win out of pity. I need to earn it."

It's easy to pretend that this conversation actually means something and that death isn't waiting for my brother. "You got it."

～

Beth is in the visitor's lounge, along with Aisha, Chris, Melinda, Kyle, and Faiqa. "Come sit with us, Joshua. We're talking about Brad."

"I just told Mom what you said, Uncle Joshua, about not putting Dad into a hospice. What do you think, Mom? Would it be too stressful having Dad at home?" Kyle holds his mother's hand.

Beth looks down. "My husband is dying. I can't think of anything more stressful." She pauses. We wait. "What exactly did he say to you, Joshua? Tell me."

"He was very weak but he kept saying, 'No hospice.' He wants to die at home. Brad was begging me, and you know he never begs."

A smile flashes briefly across Beth's face. "Not since he asked me to marry him. I wonder why he didn't tell me what he wanted."

"He was probably afraid of burdening you. But we talked about, it and I think it will work."

"Kyle told me. I'll talk with Brad. I want to do what's best for him, and if being at home will make him happy, then, I think that's what we should do."

Aisha touches Beth's hand. "You're very brave."

"I don't have a choice. Being surrounded by family makes it all a little easier. Thank you for everything."

Chris and I should be thanking Beth for giving Brad the last forty years of her life.

Luqman and Uncle Brad

A good head and a good heart are always a formidable combination.

—Nelson Mandela

In the evening, after Mom and Dad have left the hospital, I go to see Uncle Brad. Matt is in the room with him.

"Assalaamu alaikum," I whisper.

"Walaikum assalaam." He shakes my hand. "I'm glad you could come." He steps away, leaving me alone with my uncle.

His eyes are closed. I sit and stare at him. He does look sick.

He opens his eyes. "Luqman? How are you?" He smiles.

Uncle Brad is the only person in my family who still smiles when he sees me. "How are you feeling? I heard that you're dying."

"That's what they tell me. Death happens and there's not much we can do about it. I do want to spend the time I have left getting closer to Allah."

"I wish you didn't have to go." I pause, not wanting to let my feelings show. "Do you remember when you taught me how to defend myself against the bullies? It was during a family barbecue. I was eight. I've always been able to talk to you, since the time you stayed at our house."

"I was a mess in those days." He shakes his head. "Do any of your friends drink alcohol? Make sure you stay far away from the stuff."

"No, they don't." I want to tell him what I'm doing these days, but I'm afraid to say anything. "I met some Muslim guys on the South Side. They're good."

"Friends of Muhammad?"

How did he know? "Would you tell Dad?"

He studies my face. "You're too smart to get involved in a gang."

"This is different. We'll make things better for all Muslims."

"Don't you think there's a better way than fighting?"

"We only fight when it's necessary. The Prophet fought, too."

"I don't like it, but I won't tell your dad. That's up to you."

"I can't even talk to him about simple things. All he does is scream at me."

"You're the only boy I ever met who doesn't get along with Joshua. Maybe you're too much alike."

"I'm nothing like him." I answer quickly. "He doesn't understand."

My uncle nods. "That's what Kyle used to say about me, before his accident. Come to me anytime you need to talk."

"You listen. That helps."

"Is there anything else you want me to keep from telling your father?"

"You need to rest. After you die, I won't have anyone."

"You have your friends. Your family loves you, too, even when they yell and scream."

"I won't have anyone like you. Take care of yourself, Uncle Brad." I give him a quick hug.

He hugs me back, longer and harder. "Be careful. Don't do anything dangerous. I don't want anything to happen to you, either."

"Thanks. Assalaamu alaikum."

"Walaikum assalaam Luqman."

I slip into the hallway and out toward the exit.

Simple Blessings

Reflect upon your present blessings of which every man has many - not on your past misfortunes, of which all men have some.

—Charles Dickens

Joshua: Part One

Brad is coming home today. Kyle had to fight the doctor on the hospice issue, but the fever is gone and Brad's condition is stable, though still serious. We know he's not cured and there will be another crisis—sometime within the next two or three weeks, if the doctor is right—but my brother is well enough to come home. Right now, that's what matters.

This week hasn't been very productive for me. My meeting with Barnett was scheduled for Monday, but he had an unexpected problem at his company. On Tuesday morning, Brad's temperature spiked, and I rushed to the hospital. Barnett and I spent the rest of the week playing phone tag. Alhamdulillah, the snow is gone and temperatures were in the 40s all week, so things have gone smoothly at Evans. No unexpected guests this week.

This morning, my sons and I, along with Chris's son, Isaiah, helped Matt, Emily and baby Zakariya move into Brad's house. Muhammad will sublet their apartment. He'll probably still pop in for dinner most nights because that boy can hardly cook.

Kyle and Matt left nearly an hour ago to bring Brad back from the hospital. They should be here soon. We're all waiting.

Aisha sits on the arm of the easy chair where I'm relaxing with a root beer. "Don't you think Brad should come back to a quiet house? There are so many people here."

"I know my brother. He'll complain, but he'll love it. Don't worry, we won't stay long."

Umar and Safa walk in, both carrying large trays of food. Muhammad takes Safa's tray. "I got it." He glances back at Jamal and Luqman. "Come on, guys."

Jamal takes Umar's tray. Luqman slouches out to their car to get the rest of the food.

Aisha goes to help Safa in the kitchen. Umar approaches me. "Assalaamu alaikum. How are you, brother?" We hug.

"I'm good, alhamdulillah. Something smells delicious. Did Safa cook biriyani?"

"Brad's homecoming is a special occasion. They wouldn't let me visit him in the intensive care unit because I'm not, technically, his family. How is he?"

"He looks good. Much better than he did a week ago."

"How long does he have?"

"The doctor gives him a few weeks at best. Did he tell you? No one else knew."

"He didn't have to say anything. I could see it in his face."

I'm sure it was there, but when I look at Brad, I still hope to see the big brother who took care of me. "You should have told me you wanted to come. I could have snuck you in."

"You've been hard to reach. Aisha tells me you're still working too many hours. How is the center?"

"We're surviving, but I don't know if we'll make it through another blizzard. I thought about calling you one night to see if you had room."

"Sakeena, Na'im, and the kids spent a few nights with us during that last storm because their power went out. It's been a while since I've awoken to a crying baby."

The front door opens. We both turn to watch Brad walk in, supported by Matt. Kyle and Beth follow. Kyle bought my brother a wheelchair, but I don't know how he'll get him to use it.

Brad meets our stares. "What is this, a wake? I'm not dead yet."

Chris steps forward and takes his other arm. "Welcome home."

"What are you all waiting for? A speech?"

"Do you have one?" I quip.

"How about this: 'Pray, be careful, and be kind because you never know how long you have.' I smell biriyani. Let's eat."

Matt and Chris take Brad to his old green couch. That thing is ancient, but Brad won't let Beth get rid of it. They bought it when they lived in that big house up north, before Mom died and Brad's alcoholism spun out of control. He spent four months on that couch while trying to reconcile with Beth after his fourteen-month disappearance. Maybe that's why it's so important to him. It's faded now, and there are holes in one of the arms, but Brad will never let go of that couch.

Emily appears with a plate full of food. "Here you are, Dad. I hope you're hungry."

"I'm starved. That hospital food will kill you. Put more vegetables in there. I need all the nutrition I can get. Did you know I'm going to beat Joshua this July?"

"That's great." She smiles. "You'll need a lot of energy for that soccer match. I'll get more vegetables then."

She's a sweet girl, the perfect companion for Matt. I hope she's still this sweet and patient after living with my brother.

~

Brad looks tired. We've been here too long.

Chris is the first to leave. "I have to be in church early tomorrow. It's good to see you home, Brad," he says as they shake hands and hug.

"You need to come up here more often. The church can get by without you part of the time. Don't you have an assistant now?"

"That young preacher from the next town helps out. During this last week, my son-in-law Andrew took care of things. Jacob does what he can, though he's a businessman, not a preacher." Chris glances at Isaiah, who was expected to take over the family ministry. He became a Muslim instead. "I'll be back in another week or so."

"Come because you want to see me, not because you expect me to die soon. Doctors aren't perfect, you know."

"No one is perfect except our Lord," he says as they hug again. "Melinda and I had better get on the road. We'll see you soon."

Jamal and Rabia are next. "We need to go, Uncle Brad. Kamila is fussy." The baby whimpers. She's quieter than Amir was at that age.

Brad reaches for Amir. "Come here, little man." He holds my grandson for a few minutes, stroking his soft head. "Do you have a kiss for your uncle?"

Amir reaches for Rabia. "He's a little shy." She apologizes.

Brad kisses Amir on the cheek before releasing him to his mother.

When Jeremy and Raheema are ready to leave, Brad cradles their baby, Maha, in his arms. Before Isaiah and Becky go, he grabs their two youngest and holds them close. Their older daughter, Jenna, kisses her great uncle on the cheek. "Get well soon," she says sweetly.

"I intend to," he says, quietly adding, "Insha Allah."

I pat his shoulder. "Welcome back, brother."

"I'm not back yet. Give me a week or two." He grasps Kyle's hand and looks at Faiqa. "I need to stick around for my grandchildren. Where are they, Faiqa?"

"They're all asleep."

"What about Zakariya?"

"He's nursing," says Matt.

Brad smiles. "I can't wait to play ball with them."

We made the right decision. He deserves to be home.

Joshua: Part Two

My brother is out of the hospital, and I need to get back to business, though I'm tempted to forget it all and spend my days with him. He would chase me away, complaining that his doctor doesn't know anything. And he and Beth need their privacy.

Barnett will be here soon. I keep poring over the budget, trying to find something else to cut. We're down to the basics as it is. At the last meeting, one board member suggested cutting back on the health clinic, but we serve more clients than ever these days. We may have to eliminate the athletic program. Unfortunately, basketball is a luxury in times like these.

"Hi, Joshua. It looks like you're hard at work," Barnett says, suddenly appearing in front of my desk.

"Doug. You startled me. Have a seat. I'm trying to figure out where else to save money."

"How bad is it?"

"I'm afraid we're not going to make it through the winter. Donations have fallen sharply these last few months, even during the holiday season, and we're facing increased demands. Another blizzard like that last one may wipe us out."

"How did things get this bad?"

"You know how the economy is, especially with all the layoffs here in Chicago. Most of our usual Christmas donors didn't come through for us this year. And the weather has been especially severe. I'm sure you heard about the family found dead in a city park. Sometimes Evans was so crowded that I took some of the homeless back to my house for the night. When the weather isn't bad, of course, many spend the nights in the parks and alleys."

"I've noticed." He frowns. "We definitely have a problem. What are you doing about it? Besides opening up your home, I mean. Your wife must be a saint."

"You could say that."

"When is your next fundraiser?"

"I don't have time for a fundraiser. We're just trying to survive here."

"I realize that, but fundraisers are essential for non-profits. January definitely isn't a good time. Schedule something for May, when the city is thawed and donors are feeling more generous."

"That's a major undertaking. I don't have the extra staff to work on it."

"Find a way. I can help, but only if you're willing to do your part. I'll put in some phone calls and keep you solvent through May. Meanwhile, you need to put on a good show and get more donors to open up their bank accounts."

I sigh. "Maybe you're right."

"I didn't build my business by being wrong. We'll get you through this crisis, Joshua, but you need to do your part. Wine and dine the donors and they'll be glad to help you with whatever you need."

Wine and dine. "Are you sure that's what it takes?"

"Absolutely. I need to be going. I'll call you later this week with an update. We can do this. Don't worry. You're doing great work here, and I'll make sure Chicago knows it." He stands and lightly raps my desk. "Talk to you later." He's gone as quickly as he came.

We've had only one fundraiser since I took over as director, and that had already been scheduled. I know what it takes to convince people to give. Good food and better wine. I always said I wouldn't do it.

But what are my choices? I can tell Barnett that I refuse to hold a fundraiser. He'll withdraw his support, and the centers will close next month. We can hold a fundraiser without the wine, but few people will come. Or, I can play the game and raise the money so we won't have to worry about another family spending a frigid night in the park.

Is it more important for me to stand by my religious principles, even if it means the poor will die? Or should I give in, just this once, as long as I vow to never do it again?

I take out my prayer rug and bow down, asking Allah to strengthen me.

~

For the last few hours, I've thought about the fundraiser. I can't do this, but I must do this. If I don't, the poor will suffer. They'll go hungry. They'll die in the cold like that family of five. In the afternoon, I call Stu and tell him the news.

"That's great, Joshua. We have about three months to plan for the dinner. We'd better get busy."

"Yes, we should." My enthusiasm can't match his.

"Can you imagine? If we don't have to worry about money, we can take this whole operation to the next level."

For Stu, the next level means education through preschool and tutoring programs. My dream is to open a rehabilitation center for male addicts.

"That would be great."

Stu draws me into a conversation about what we could do with the extra money. He's in the middle of discussing his plans for vocational training when Sandra rushes into my office, interrupting the call. "Joshua, we need your help. Now," she says, waving me toward the door.

"Hold on, Stu. What's wrong, Sandra?" She doesn't usually get this excited.

"There's trouble at the clinic. You have to come."

"Stu, we have a crisis. I'll call you back," I end the call and follow Sandra down the hall.

"A woman came in screaming and crying. Something about how they killed her baby. Emma tried to settle her down, but the woman started beating on her. Do you want me to call the police?"

"No. Let's see if we can handle it. Call Stu and tell him to come quickly. I might need his help."

The woman is behind the receptionist's desk, screaming and kicking Emma, while the waiting patients huddle together. I grab the woman's left arm and pull her away. "Stop that. Calm down."

It's Nicole. She kicks me and struggles to get loose.

"Settle down. I'm Joshua, remember? What's the problem?"

She punches me in the chest. "You people killed my baby. It ain't right. You killed him." She screams and moans.

"What happened to your baby, Nicole?"

"My baby is dead, my little Joseph. They killed him. You all did," she sobs.

Stu rushes in. "What's wrong?"

Nicole turns on him. "Don't you ask what's wrong," she screams, shoving him. "You was there when they took my baby away. Where is he? I got the right to know what you did with my baby."

"Settle down. I didn't do anything to your baby."

"You're lying. You was there. I saw you. You said to take him away with the others."

Stu sighs and nods. "Now I remember. We had to remove the bodies from the shelter before the epidemic spread."

What epidemic? Why didn't Stu tell me? I'll talk to him later. "Where are your other children, Nicole?"

"I left them at the shelter. But I miss my baby so bad," she cries out as a nurse steps forward to embrace her.

She needs more help than I can give her. I duck out into the hallway and call Umar. "Are you still at the office?"

"I plan to go home soon. What do you need?"

"I have a patient for you. Can you drop by?" Years ago, Umar volunteered to serve as an on-call psychologist. I hope he'll be able to help Nicole.

"I'll be there in twenty minutes, insha Allah."

∼

While Umar sits with Nicole in the clinic, Stu and I go back to my office. I sit behind my desk. "Tell me what's going on."

"The flu is bad this year."

"There were other deaths? Why wasn't I told?"

"It started when you were overseas. We lost six during those three weeks. Four more died while you were at the hospital with your brother. The baby and two other children passed over the weekend. You saw the crowd in the waiting room. We're facing an epidemic."

"What are you doing about it? And why wasn't I told?"

"It's been chaotic. After the first two deaths, I had a special meeting with my staff. The apartments are scrubbed thoroughly at least once a week, and public areas are cleaned daily. The fatalities have decreased. We're getting it under control."

"Where did they take Nicole's baby?"

"The city is disposing of the bodies. They're trying to keep it quiet to avoid panic."

"Where is Ashleigh? I didn't see her today."

"She came to Evans last Wednesday to talk with our residents about hygiene. Wasn't she in the clinic?"

"I didn't see her. What is the city doing with the bodies?"

"They're incinerating them." He sees me wince. "It's the only way, Joshua."

～

Ashleigh Madison, our new clinic administrator, is out sick with the flu. Umar talked with Nicole for over an hour and arranged for her to share an apartment with an older woman who can help her get through this. Her husband left town again this morning, looking for work.

Before going home, I check back with Emma. She's closing up. "Are you okay? She didn't hurt you, did she?"

"No broken bones. I'm just a little shaken."

"Would you like me to take you to the emergency room to get checked out?"

"No, I'm fine. Don't worry about me." She sighs. "I have a little boy about that age, and I don't know what I'd do if I lost him."

"It's tough." I'm not sure what else to say. When Emma is finished, I walk out with her.

Umar meets us outside the clinic. "Her grief is unimaginable."

"Thanks for coming, brother."

"Call me anytime." He gives me a quick hug. "You had better go home. Aisha worries about you."

I forgot to let her know I'd be late. "I'm sure Safa is waiting for you, too. Assalaamu alaikum. I'll see you later."

We climb into our cars and go home to our wives. Umar and I used to have long conversations. Now life is too hectic. I miss the good old days.

～

By the time I pull into our driveway, it's nearly 7:00 pm. I walk into a quiet house. No one is in the kitchen. No aromas of food cooking on the stove. "Aisha," I call. "Aisha, where are you?" There's no answer.

Her note is on the refrigerator door. "Maryam and I are at a seminar. Remember? We should be home by eight."

Was that tonight? She must have told me about it. I have too much on my mind.

They won't be home for an hour. I'm hungry. I search the refrigerator for leftovers.

Up until a few years ago, I did much of the cooking. That was before I became the director at Hope. Now, I have no time for simple pleasures.

In the back left corner of the third shelf, I find a small bowl of leftover spaghetti. That's good enough. I pull out a pot and heat it up.

A salad would go well with this. I rummage through the vegetable drawer, finding a brown head of lettuce. After peeling off most of the outer leaves, I have enough for a small salad. I chop up a couple of carrots and a stalk of wilted celery. My spaghetti is done. I sit at the kitchen table alone and enjoy my feast.

Satisfied, I wash my dishes and go into the family room to catch up on the news. It relaxes me. Over the last several years, I've noticed an increasing amount of fluff in the broadcasts. The stuff Muhammad complains about. My son doesn't understand that nobody wants to hear of endless tragedy after a day of struggling to survive.

The bad news seems worse today. Casualties were high in the Middle East after a series of bombings. A middle-aged Hispanic man in Indianapolis held everyone in his office hostage during an eight-hour standoff, and managed to kill two of the hostages and a police officer before shooting himself. A racial confrontation at Northwestern University turned into a melee. Three were wounded. And at today's city council meeting, members narrowly avoided a fist fight. By the time Muhammad's piece about Valentine's Day candy airs, I'm ready for some good news.

A touch on my shoulder wakes me. "Assalaamu alaikum Dad. Are you okay?"

"Muhammad. Assalaamu alaikum. I saw your piece about chocolate."

He groans. "Don't remind me. I should have been out at Northwestern covering the fight, not eating candy hearts."

I sit up a little. "What happened out there? Did you hear anything?"

"Yesterday a black student got into a shouting match with a white professor. The professor threw the guy out of class. Today he and his friends slashed the professor's tires. Other students fought them. A few students from both sides were arrested, but most ran away."

"Does racism exist on college campuses these days?"

"Times are hard and people are tense."

"On a college campus? There must be another explanation. Did they catch the student who started it?"

"No, but it doesn't matter. He's not the ringleader. No one knows who is."

"You just told me twice as much as I heard on the news. Why don't they tell us the whole story?"

"It would take too long. On television, we have to present everything in sound bites."

I miss newspapers. "What time is it? Your mother and Maryam should be home by now."

"They're both upstairs. We talked and prayed together. You wouldn't wake up."

"We had a crisis over at the center today. Maybe you and I should switch jobs. I wouldn't mind reporting on candy for a change."

Muhammad laughs. "Thanks for the perspective. I'd better get going." He gives me a hug. "Take it easy, Dad. You work too hard."

"Until hunger and poverty take a vacation…"

"I know. But you can't save the world without taking care of yourself."

"You sound like your mother." I ease off the couch, groaning. "You'd better get ready for work tomorrow, and I'd better pray. It's good to see you."

"I'll talk to you later, Dad, insha Allah. Assalaamu alaikum." He hugs me again and leaves. I lock the door behind him and head for the bathroom to wash up.

I'm nearly finished praying when I hear the front door open. I thought everyone was home. I complete my prayer and turn to see Luqman walking in.

"Assalaamu alaikum Luqman," I call. "You're out late. How's your thesis?"

He stops for a moment, his face turned away. "Don't worry. I have everything under control."

"Did you pray?"

"Yeah, Zaid and I prayed together. I was over at his place."

"Come here. I hardly see you these days."

"I need to get to bed. We can talk in the morning."

"Is something wrong?" I approach him. He tries to turn away from me again, but I grab his shoulder. "What happened to your eye?"

He touches his left eye, which is bruised and swollen. "Zaid left a book in the middle of the room. I tripped on it and hit the wall."

"You need to put some ice on that to take care of the swelling. Let's go into the kitchen." I grab his arm.

He jerks away. "I can do it myself." He pauses. "I mean, thanks, Dad, but you don't need to worry. Go to bed. I'll be okay."

He isn't a little boy anymore. "Remember to put ice on that. Before you go to bed, make sure the doors are locked."

"Sure, Dad. Don't worry."

I climb the stairs and fall into bed next to Aisha. She's snoring softly. I kiss her cheek and lie down on my right side.

I forgot to ask Luqman if he knew anything about the fight. He may not have been on campus. His entire focus this semester is on finishing that thesis.

I wonder how Nicole is doing. I can't imagine her pain. Later I should tell Aisha, though I may spare her. We have been blessed, al-hamdulillah.

I need to go see Brad tomorrow. How much longer will he be with us?

What will I do about the fundraiser? There's no way I can get out of it but I can't do it, either.

I squirm as my mind races. Aisha pats my back. I close my eyes and wait for sleep to come.

After thirty minutes, I'm still waiting. I get up, make ablutions, and pray until I'm ready to drop.

Joshua: Part Three

All week, I've been too busy to visit Brad, or even call him. His time is running out and I should be there, but the center has taken all my time, leaving me with only enough energy to eat and sleep.

Sandra was sick on Monday. None of our volunteers could come in, so I sat in the front office, dealing with callers and visitors while doing my own work, too. I didn't leave until nearly eight. Sandra works harder than I realized.

On Tuesday afternoon, a fight broke out during a basketball game in the gym. Stu helped me break it up. He's younger—the same age as my son, Jeremy—and the kids respect him. After they settled down, Stu gathered them into a circle and talked it out. I noticed one kid cradling his arm and took him over to the clinic where they wrapped it up in a cast. Then, I drove the boy home and explained everything to his mother. She apologized for her son's part in the fight. Some parents would have threatened to shut us down.

On Wednesday morning, the Hope Center furnace died. I knew it would happen someday soon, but I hoped we could hold out until summer. I called Doug before contacting the repairman. He offered to buy us a new furnace. That was the good news. The bad news was that I didn't get home until 8:30 PM. Aisha had meatloaf waiting. I managed a few bites before praying and collapsing into bed.

On Wednesday night, Arctic air blew down from Canada. Wind chills dipped to thirty below. By Thursday afternoon, sixteen bodies had been found in parks and alleys and twenty-two more were discovered in unheated homes. Stu and I were on the phone all day begging for emergency supplies. We broke city codes Thursday night, crowding the halls of Evans with the homeless. They slept in the cafeteria, the lobby, and the hallways. We ran out of cots, but even those who slept on the floor were glad to be out of the cold. I took two women and their six children home with me and squeezed them all into Jamal's old room. Maryam helped Aisha put together a simple meal of soup and sandwiches.

It's still bitterly cold, and Evans is packed practically wall-to-wall. If a city inspector drops by, we'll be fined. I hold my breath and say short prayers throughout the day.

Students from three area colleges held emergency food drives for homeless shelters throughout Chicago. They dropped off our supplies about an hour ago. It's not enough, but it will get us through the day. According to the weatherman, this cold is expected to hold on for another three days. I hope we can make it.

This morning, I called Reverend Johnson and Senator Edmonds. Both made promises, but I won't hold my breath. I learned long ago not to trust people in positions of power. If we want to get anything done, we need to do it ourselves.

There is something I haven't tried. I pick up the phone and call my son, getting his voice mail. "Muhammad, call me. It's an emergency." I hope he checks his messages.

The minute I hang up, my phone rings. It's Gameel.

"Assalaamu alaikum Joshua. How are you managing over there?"

"Walaikum assalaam. It's tough. We're packed solid."

"I'm sending a truckload of food. Expect it later this afternoon."

"Subhanallah. I don't know what to say."

"Don't hesitate to call me if you need more."

"May Allah bless you."

"I can't talk now. I'll see you soon. Assalaamu alaikum."

"Walaikum assalaam." I call Stu with the news.

"That's the best news I've heard all month. I'll keep my eyes open."

"Call me when the truck arrives. I'll help you unload."

I've known Gameel for nearly twenty years, since I started working at Hope. He was on the board. Twelve years ago, he became family when his daughter, Faiqa, married my nephew, Kyle. Gameel's company, Naturally!, produces natural foods and other products made organically. Not only will our clients at Evans have food to eat, they'll have the kind of nutritious food they could never afford.

~

I'm unloading the truck with Stu and a few of his staff members when my phone rings. I duck inside to answer.

"Assalaamu alaikum Dad. What's wrong? Is anyone hurt?"

"No. I didn't mean to scare you but this is urgent. We're running low on food and supplies. Gameel just sent a truck over and that will help, but I wonder if you could ask your station manager to make an announcement on the news. We can use all the donations we can get."

"I don't think Dirk will go for that, but I will ask him if I can interview Gameel about his donation. Dirk likes the Good Samaritan angle. Thanks for the lead, Dad. I'll let you know how it goes."

"You sound like you're in a hurry."

"Brett and I are on our way to the zoo to do a story on a new baby giraffe. It's not where I want to be, but we have a deadline. I'll call Dirk and see what he says. Talk to you later. Assalaamu alaikum."

He hangs up before I can answer. Right now, I wouldn't mind seeing a story about a baby giraffe.

~

I just got home. It took us a few hours to unload the truck and get everything put away. We were just finishing up, a little after five, when more donations came in. A clothing store manager called and told us to expect a truckload of coats. A toy store pledged stuffed animals. And while I was still at Evans, an old man walked into Hope with five one hundred dollar bills. "He said he was saving the money for a special treat," Sandra said. "He decided that helping the children was what he really wanted."

This is the best I've felt all week, but I'm beat. I fumble with my keys, the cold wind blowing around me.

The house is warm and inviting. Aisha is in the kitchen. She hugs me.

"I'm glad you're home. Are you alone?"

I nod. "Evans is full, but it looks like we'll make it through the crisis, alhamdulillah. I need this weekend. Do you realize I haven't talked with my brother all week?"

"I went there after school today. Brad looks good. Much better than he did in the hospital."

"That's great. I'll go see him tomorrow, insha Allah. Did you make anything for dinner?"

"The pizza will be here soon. It's an extravagance, but I'm tired, too. Maybe we should hire someone to cook for us."

"Along with a maid, a butler, and a chauffeur. I wish I could help out, but I'm swamped."

"I saw Gameel's interview on the news. That was wonderful. Did you get any response?"

"That's why I'm late. We got toys, coats, and money. Tomorrow we're getting another shipment of food. I'll call Gameel later. His generosity started a movement."

"That's so good to hear." She helps me with my coat and leads me to the family room couch. "Close your eyes and relax." She massages my shoulders. My stress floats away.

Muhammad's Journal

In the name of Allah, the Most Gracious, the Most Merciful

When Dad called me with the lead on Gameel's donation, I thought it might be my big break. My interview with Gameel would be so successful that I could say goodbye to animal stories.

Dirk didn't see it that way. He sent another reporter to do the interview and told me to hurry up with the story on the baby giraffe. I am glad the word got out because that interview got the donations rolling. I just wish I had been the one to do it.

Usually I go on assignment with Brett, a cameraman. We both have dreams of making it big one day. He wants to film animals in the wild, not in zoos. I want to cover major conflicts and interview world leaders. We talk about our ideal assignments while we're on our way to the silly ones. They're only dreams, but one day, we just might make it.

I'm glad the weekend is here. I can imagine the cold weather stories Dirk could send me on, but I plan to stay warm and dry this weekend. By Monday, hopefully, this cold snap will have broken.

For six years, I've reported fluff. How much longer will I have to wait to become a real journalist?

Joshua: Part Four

After breakfast, I call Evans. A sporting goods store donated cots this morning. Two churches offered to send volunteers. The publicity we received yesterday was risky because we're so overcrowded, but no politician wants to be responsible for putting people out on the streets in this kind of weather, especially during an election year.

Aisha is working at the computer in our home office. I kiss her cheek. "I'm going to see Brad. Do you want to come?"

"I have a couple hours worth of school work here. Give Beth my salaams, and tell her I'll call later today."

I run upstairs to bundle up. The sun is out, but the wind chill still hovers at ten below. I pull on two pair of thermal underwear before grabbing my sweats.

By the time I get to Brad's house, I'm sweating in all my clothes. The moment I step out of my car, though, I'm glad for the protection.

Emily answers the door, the baby sleeping in a sling. The house is quiet. "Assalaamu alaikum Uncle Joshua." She smiles. "It's nice to see you."

"How is my brother?"

"You can ask him yourself. Follow me."

She doesn't lead me toward Brad's bedroom as I expected. Instead, she turns left into the kitchen and points to the doorway leading to the garage. "He's in there."

"Joshua. Assalaamu alaikum. How are you?" Brad has a box in his arms.

It's chilly out here, even with the space heaters he has going. "Let me help you with that. You need to sit down." I try to take the box from him, but he won't let go.

"I can handle it. Yesterday I came out here looking for my ankle weights, and it took me nearly two hours to find them. Today's a good day for cleaning, and this place is way overdue."

"You're cleaning the garage? You should be resting."

He laughs. "I'll have many years to rest. Look at this place. If you think it's bad now, you should have seen it yesterday. I'll probably be out here all weekend."

"Brad, you're sick."

"I'm dying. I know that. Is there a law that says a dying man can't clean his own garage? I don't want to leave this mess for Beth and the boys."

"Kyle and Matt will help you. I'll bring my boys over, too. We'll make a party out of it. Now sit down before you hurt yourself." I glance behind me, looking for a place to sit.

Brad snickers. "Have a seat over there on that box. Give me just a minute and we'll go into the living room to talk." He moves another box and glances back at me. "You don't look so good. What have you been eating?"

"I don't know, the usual. Last night, we had pizza."

"You'd better take care of yourself, Joshua, or people are going to start wondering which one of us is dying." He stands up straight. "Look at me. I haven't had red meat for over a week. Emily makes me fresh juice every morning. No coffee or sugar or salt or any of that poison. If you don't start taking care of yourself, you'll be lucky to make it to sixty."

"No one in our family has made it past seventy. But don't change the subject. You have to take care of yourself, or you'll end up back in the hospital. I know you don't want that."

"If I wanted to spend my last days in bed, I could have let them put me in the hospice." He wipes his hands on his jeans. "That will do for now. Let's go back inside." He leads me into the kitchen where his daughter-in-law is chopping vegetables. "Emily, would you bring us two glasses of juice? We'll be in the living room."

"I'll be right there, Dad."

"Where's Beth?"

"She's volunteering at Evans. We saw Gameel's interview on the news last night, and I convinced Beth she doesn't need to hover over me all day. It's good for her to get out."

I keep staring. "You look good, Brad."

"Sure I do, and I feel good, too. I'm still a little tired, but I'm working on that." He smirks. "If I'm going to be dead in a week, at least I'll be a good looking corpse."

His gallows humor makes me squirm. Maybe it makes him feel better.

Emily brings the juice and hands one glass to me. I sniff it. "What's in this?"

"Pineapple and mango. Both fresh and organic."

I take a sip. It's different. I put my glass on the coffee table.

"Drink up," says Brad. "It's good for you. Look at me." He holds out his arms. "Sixty-five and feeling great."

I take another sip, and a third. My brother insists. If I drink it slowly enough, maybe it will be more tolerable.

Brad chuckles and shakes his head. "My own son is a top executive in a natural food corporation. He's been after me for years to try his products, but I didn't want to give up my cheeseburgers. I wish I had started eating this way ten years ago. Who knows? I might have made it to seventy."

At the rate he's going, I can almost believe he will live another five years. He's still thin, but he has gained a little weight. His hair is gone and his beard is gray, but there's life in his eyes.

"We should train together," says Brad, interrupting my thoughts. "I don't want to have an unfair advantage. Have you thought about jogging?"

"Even if I did want to jog, it's frigid outside."

"That's why I was looking for the ankle weights. I'll start with those and by the time the weather warms up, I'll be ready to run. What do you think? Do you want to join me?"

I've never jogged. I never wanted to. "Why not?" I shrug. "It may help," I say as I pat my middle-age belly. I still don't think Brad will be in any shape to jog. He probably won't even live to see spring.

"Good. I figure it will be warm enough by March or April at the latest. Then we can both get into shape. I'll feel better about beating you if you're giving it your all."

Brad is pulling me into his fairy tale, and I can almost believe it. He will jog. We will play soccer this summer. He could beat me. But he's dying. I can't give in to false hopes.

"Assalaamu alaikum." Matt walks in through the front door carrying groceries. He takes them to the kitchen and comes back to hug his father. "How are you, Uncle Joshua? It's good to see you."

"How have you been, Matt?"

"I'm great. Emily and I are glad we moved back here. Did you know Dad has started cleaning the garage? Can you believe it?"

No, I can't. "Shouldn't we stop him? It's too much of a strain."

"I'm right here," says Brad. "Don't talk around me. Trust me to know when I need to rest. Can you do that, Joshua?"

"But don't you remember how sick you were?"

"Of course, I remember—most of it, anyway. That's why I have to take advantage of the time I have. You'll understand one day."

"Kyle doesn't like it either," Matt adds. "But if Dad is happy, isn't that what matters?"

I look at Brad. He stares back at me and smiles. "If you were in my shoes, you'd do exactly the same thing."

"Maybe you're right."

Emily rushes through the living room, hands the baby to Matt, and picks up her textbooks. "I need to get to class. Lunch is in the oven. It's nice to see you again, Uncle Joshua. Assalaamu alaikum." She stops and kisses Matt before hurrying out.

"She switched all her courses to evenings and weekends so she can be here with Dad while I'm at work," says Matt.

"Not that I need babysitting," says Brad, "but my family thinks I'm not ready to take care of myself yet." He winks.

"I hope you'll stay for lunch," says Matt. "Today is our one of vegetarian days."

"No meat?"

"Three days a week we have fish and on the other two days, we eat chicken or turkey. We plan to eat beef once or twice a month but not more than that. Emily has always believed in eating healthy and she's a great cook." Matt smiles.

"Most of this nation is still eating junk," Brad adds. "That's why everyone's sick. People are racing toward death. Some will probably get there before I do."

"Does dying make you philosophical?"

"I've had some time to think. Forget about everyone else, though. I'm worried about you, Joshua. You work too hard and don't eat right. Life is too valuable to be thrown away."

He knows that better than anyone. I pick up my pineapple-mango juice and take a larger sip. "Maybe I could get used to this."

"So you'll stay for lunch?" Matt asks.

"I'll give it a try."

"Great," says Brad, slapping my back. "Now you'll have some real food."

Matt puts the baby in his crib and sets the table. Brad offers me a seat. The food smells good. Brad passes me a hot dish. "Wait until you taste this."

I don't recognize it, but I spoon some onto my plate. As the other dishes make their way to me, I take a little of each. My brother is busy eating. He smiles. "This is great."

I start with the green salad. It has zucchini in it, but I don't mind a little zucchini. Brad has poured something over my brown rice. I taste it. "What is this?"

"Orange curry. Isn't it great?"

"There's no meat in it."

"Of course not. That's the point."

I slowly make my way through the herbed soybean casserole and the spinach provencale with help from Matt who identifies each dish. Brad smirks at me while enjoying his vegetables. I think this whole meal would taste better with a little beef.

"You're probably feeling better already, aren't you?" Brad asks.

I nod, my mouth full, and pretend to enjoy the food. Hopefully, he won't ask me any more questions.

~

Matt offers me fruit salad for dessert. "Emily made it this morning. Doesn't it look good?"

Brad is taking this health food thing seriously. "No thanks. I'm full." And I am, which is strange because I didn't eat nearly as much as I usually do.

Brad hands me a small bowl filled with fruit salad. "Eat it, Joshua. It's good for you." He fills his own bowl and digs in. "Fantastic."

I have nothing against fruit but after eating all those plants, I'm ready for something more substantial, like an apple pie. I pick up my spoon and try a mouthful of cantaloupe.

I'm nibbling my way through the fruit when the doorbell rings. "I'll get it," says Matt. He jumps up.

Chris is at the door. "How are you, Matt? Where's your dad?"

"Come in. You're just in time for dessert."

We greet Chris with hugs. "Sit down," says Brad. "It's good to see you." Matt brings over another bowl of fruit salad.

"How are you feeling?" Chris touches Brad's arm while studying his face.

"I was just telling Joshua how much better I feel now that I've changed my diet. Eat your fruit salad, both of you. I won't let you leave until you finish every bit of it, Joshua." He grins.

"What does the doctor say? Has there been any change in your condition?" Chris's voice is somber.

"I have to go back to see him in a week or two, but I don't know why I should bother. If it wasn't for Beth, I would cancel the appointment."

"This is serious, Brad. You have to get the best possible care."

"So I can live a few weeks longer? I'm done with doctors. They're all a bunch of quacks." He pauses. "Except Faiqa, of course."

"Chris, ask Brad how he's been spending his time." Chris is going to love this.

"You've been in bed, haven't you? Tell me you're not wearing yourself out."

"No, I'm not worn out. I'm cleaning the garage. Is that a problem?" Brad laughs.

I sit back and watch the show. Chris getting flustered. Brad coaxing Chris's reaction like a naughty child. Now I can see how useless it is. Brad will do what he wants to do. He always has. Why should we expect anything else?

Chris's face is red. "Aren't you worried about your father, Matt? You need to prevent him from jeopardizing his health."

"I'm right here, Chris. You don't need to talk over me."

Matt grins. "If Dad is happy, isn't that what matters?"

It sounds like they've rehearsed their routines. Beth was probably their first flustered victim. I pat Brad's shoulder. "I'd better get going. It's good to see you, Chris. How long can you stay?"

"As long as necessary. At least until Brad goes back to see the doctor."

"In that case," says Brad, "you can stay at Joshua's house. I don't want you hanging around here with your doom and gloom."

"Will you let me help you clean the garage?" Chris asks. "I'll tell Isaiah to come over, and I'm sure Joshua's sons would come too."

I feel dizzy with déjà vu. "Listen, Chris, it's no use. We need to let him do what he wants. I'm going home now. Feel free to come over. We have room."

"We're staying with Isaiah. Melinda is there now. Thanks for the offer." He pats my arm. "I'll see you later, Joshua."

"Take it easy, Brad." I lean over and hug him. "Enjoy your time in the garage. I'll see you tomorrow, insha Allah."

"Lay off the junk," Brad calls as Matt walks me to the front door.

"We'll see." I give a final wave and whisper to Matt. "You're doing a great job. Emily, too."

"What else can I do? He's my Dad."

Kyle's Family

Uncle Chris was at Dad's house yesterday. He waited for a time when Dad left the room to pull me aside.

"Your father is acting recklessly. You have to make him take his health seriously."

"I've tried. You know how Dad is."

"Melinda and I plan to stay in Chicago for a few weeks. We need to be here when the time comes." He looked down.

"I appreciate that. But don't keep telling Dad to take it easy. We brought him home because we want him to be happy."

"I'm sure you're worried about him."

"I'm beyond worried. I can't imagine him being gone. I don't want to think about it. Right now, the best thing I can do is make sure his last days are good."

My uncle nodded and patted me on the back. I'm not sure he understood what I was trying to say. I barely understand it myself. All I know is that we have to let Dad be Dad for as long as we can.

~

Every morning, I wake up before my wife and our children and take a moment to gaze at them. There was a time when I thought no woman could love me, and after twelve years, I still thank Allah for bringing Faiqa to me. I was more certain that I would never be a father but, through in vitro fertilization, Allah gave us not one baby, but three. Nashwa sleeps with her little fists pulled up tightly against her. Yusuf squirms, never staying in one position too long. Nathifa opens her eyes and reaches for me. She has always been our early bird.

They were born two weeks early but very healthy. My father beamed the first time he saw them. I'm not sure if I've ever seen him that happy. At the time, we didn't know he was dying, though he knew.

On their second day, he asked me, "Have you recited the adhan for them yet?"

I hadn't. I asked him to do it.

Dad lowered his mouth to each baby's right ear and softly recited the call to prayer. I watched, moved by the connection between the generations. In the last two weeks, I've often thought of that moment, especially in the morning. This is one of the stories I will tell my children about the grandfather they will never know.

Luqman: Ready for Action

If there is no struggle, there is no progress.

—Frederick Douglass

While my father has busied himself with flu epidemics, busted furnaces, and Arctic cold fronts, I have engaged in discussions and meditations aimed at understanding the greater purpose of life. Dad's work deals with the everyday nuisances of living, but I'm seeking the greater meanings of life.

Short, skinny, and uncoordinated, I was never good at sports. While other kids played baseball, football, and basketball, I found my solace in books. I started with the usual mysteries and fantasies, but while still in middle school, I discovered the thinkers. Frederick Douglass was my first. His ideas awakened in me a power I didn't know I had. Over the last ten years, I've devoured the writings of other men, and a few women, who have fought with bodies and minds to obliterate injustice and bring comfort to the oppressed.

My studies are done. I'm ready for action.

~

When Rasheed told me about his troubles with the professor, he was apologetic. "I'm always getting into trouble in that class. If I don't shape up, Dr. Knight could kick me out for good. I need those credits to graduate."

"Why do you let him treat you that way?" I got up in his face.

Rasheed shrugged. "I need the grade. My father always says we have to play the game."

"Your father's wrong. We don't have to play their game. We have to fight."

Rasheed almost hit me for criticizing his father, but after I quoted a few of my favorite authors, he started to see things my way. "Frederick Douglass basically taught himself to read. He fought with the word. But we need something stronger."

"What should I do to get back at Dr. Knight?"

"Hit him where it hurts."

Rasheed finally decided that slashing Dr. Knight's tires would rattle him. I wasn't sure that was the best way, but my man was adamant. We put out the call to a few of the boys and went to work.

I'm not surprised that the Young Pilgrims showed up. They seem to anticipate all our moves. If I ever learn that one of the boys is talking too much, I'll have to take care of him.

It was a good fight. We got the message across. The boys and I did most of the work, and no one could prove that Rasheed was behind it. Dr. Knight accepted him back into class and watched himself a little after that.

I picked up a black eye during the melee. My father asks too many questions. That whole story about the book and the wall was lame, but I hope he bought it.

Later, Dad and the rest of my family will know exactly what I'm doing. But not yet. I need more time.

Random Fears

Nothing in life is to be feared. It is only to be understood.

—Marie Curie

Joshua: Part One

On Monday morning, the temperature is in the twenties and the sun is shining. I hope we can get through the week without any crises.

Stu comes by early. "We need to talk about the fundraiser. Do you have a date in mind?"

"First, how are things over at Evans? Has it settled down?"

"We're much better off than we were Friday morning. We have twice the supplies and half the homeless. Two more offers came in this morning. We're getting more food and a shipment of toiletries. People don't realize how much a new toothbrush can mean to someone who has nothing."

"Great."

"But we need that fundraiser. Are we looking at late May?"

I consult my calendar. "How does the twenty-fourth sound? It's a Saturday night."

"Sounds good. We'll need to arrange for the catering, the publicity, and the speaker. Do you think the gym is big enough, or should we try to hold it in a hotel?"

"I'd rather hold it in the gym, but you know Barnett won't go for that."

"I'll check on the caterers. It will be hard to keep the price down, especially when we figure in the wine." He glances at my expression. "I know Muslims don't drink. Don't worry about it. Leave it to me."

"It's not just that. I feel like I'm betraying my religion by hosting a dinner with alcohol."

"Nobody will force you to drink it. All you have to do is show up and shake hands."

"Islam is more comprehensive than that. I shouldn't buy alcohol, sell it, serve it, transport it, or have anything to do with it."

"Loosen up, Joshua. We're talking about raising money for the centers. You know what will happen if this fundraiser isn't successful."

"I know."

"You won't have to do anything except put on a suit and smile. How hard can that be?"

He doesn't understand, and I don't expect him to. "Who do you have in mind for a speaker?"

Stu frowns. "Why are you changing the subject?"

"We have three months. You can start pricing caterers, and we'll talk later about the wine. What about a speaker?"

"Reverend Hiram Johnson can move a crowd. He's very popular. If we want him, we'll have to act quickly."

"Don't you think he's a little pretentious?"

"Some people say that. I think of it as religious enthusiasm. He's a very spiritual man."

"You sound as if you know him."

"He's a family friend. My father and Reverend Johnson went to school together. If you want, I can approach him."

"Let me think about it."

Stu shakes his head. "I respect you, Joshua, and I've learned quite a bit from you these last few years, but I don't understand your stubbornness. Usually you would do anything to help the homeless. Why are you holding back when we're so close to getting the funds we need?"

I've often asked myself that question late at night when I couldn't sleep. The truth is, I don't think I have a choice. "Give me until the end of the week. And answer this. Do you think our donors would respond to a Muslim speaker?"

"You can't bring your personal agenda into this."

"I know, but would they?"

"They might, depending on the speaker. But I'm certain Reverend Johnson would bring in the donations. I've seen him do it before."

I've seen it, too. The man has charisma, but he makes me uncomfortable. "I'd like to pray about this first."

Stu smiles. "Don't let the board hear you talk that way. We're supposed to be secular."

"What they don't know won't hurt them, will it?"

Stu laughs. "I need to get back to Evans. It's almost lunch time, and we have some new volunteers coming in today to help serve. It's always good talking to you, Joshua."

He walks out, and I lean back in my chair. There must be a way out of this. If I think hard enough, I should be able to find a compromise. It's been nearly thirty-five years since my conversion, and I'm tired of being in the minority. Even though thousands of Muslims live in Chicago, we are always outnumbered.

Could I find a Muslim speaker? He would have to be local and every bit as dynamic as Hiram Johnson. I can ask Umar if he knows anyone.

Stu's right. This isn't the time to promote my personal agenda. It's not so much that I feel the need to have a Muslim. I don't trust Hiram Johnson, though I can't say why.

I'm getting ready to leave for the day when Doug Barnett appears in my doorway.

"Joshua, I need to talk with you. Do you have time?"

"Sure. Come on in. Have a seat."

"This won't take long. I wanted to check with you on the fundraiser. How are the preparations?"

"Stu and I decided on the Saturday before Memorial Day. He's checking into hotels and caterers. Everything's on track."

"I was thinking you should contact Hiram Johnson to be the guest speaker. Have you considered that?"

"Stu said he's a family friend. He'll speak with him."

"Good. Very good." Barnett raps my desk. "My own efforts are coming along quite well. Oh, by the way, I saw that interview with Gameel. We need more publicity like that. Don't you have a son who works in TV news?"

"Yes. Muhammad arranged for that interview."

"Excellent. I'll talk to you later." He leaves as quickly as he came.

I call Stu. "Go ahead and talk to Reverend Johnson."

"That was quick. You must have done a lot of praying this afternoon."

"It was more like a little prayer and a lot of persuasion."

~

I stop to see Brad on my way home. Aisha's van is parked out front.

Brad opens the door. "Good. You're here." He grabs my arm and pulls me inside.

"Assalaamu alaikum Isa." Aisha is sitting on the couch with Beth and Melinda. "I was hoping you'd come by. You're in for a special treat."

An Islamic song starts playing. Brad points to the projection on a living room wall. "I put this together this afternoon."

I sit between Brad and Chris and enjoy the show. He starts with pictures of the triplets as newborns in their hospital bassinets. They look so much smaller. His presentation continues through the days and weeks of their short lives, and ends with Brad holding all three.

The presentation is over, and the room is still dark. Brad remains on the couch. "I never get tired of looking at them."

"That's how it is with grandchildren," I say.

"They're a miracle," says Chris.

Brad stands and turns on the light. "I can't wait until they start calling me Grandpa." He pauses briefly. "Look at me. Did you notice? I gained two pounds in the last week."

"You're doing great. How's the exercise coming?"

"I've started using the ankle weights around the house, just a few minutes at a time. Beth is afraid I'll overdo it."

"And you will," she says. "That's how you are."

Brad laughs again. "I'm the grandfather of triplets. What do you expect? I need to be healthy and strong for those little babies. I won't desert them."

"Insha Allah," I say under my breath.

It's great to see Brad so happy. I've been a grandfather for sixteen years, and Chris's oldest grandchild is nearly twelve, but it's been a hard road for Brad. None of us thought Kyle would ever be a father. And now they have Zakariya, too. We have to remember to leave these things up to Allah.

Muhammad's Journal

In the name of Allah, the Most Gracious, the Most Merciful

I can't sleep. Things keep going from bad to worse, and I don't know what to do about it.

My job is enough to keep me awake. I did get to talk to real people today, asking them how they plan to celebrate Valentine's Day, but that's not why I went into journalism. I want the real stories. Police chases. Hostage situations. Workplace massacres. If I can grab a few juicy assignments, I might catch the attention of the national networks. That's where I really want to be. Interviewing famous and influential people. Traveling to exotic locations. Reporting with bullets flying. After six years, I'm starting to wonder if it will ever happen.

But it's not my job I'm worried about. It's my older brother. I hardly see Jamal these days, and when I do, he doesn't say much. He's always been quiet, but I have the feeling there's something more going on.

And then there's my younger brother. Somebody told me he saw Luqman in the middle of that fight over at Northwestern. That wouldn't surprise me. I don't know what I can do to keep him out of trouble.

Joshua: Part Two

Aisha made meatloaf for dinner. It's great. This is the third time she's cooked in the last week.

Maryam eats with us. Luqman isn't home yet. I barely see him anymore. He must be nearly done with his thesis.

We're finishing up when Muhammad comes in through the front door. "Assalaamu alaikum."

"Walaikum assalaam," I call from the kitchen. "You're just in time. Mom made meatloaf and mashed potatoes."

"Masha Allah. What's the occasion?"

"There's no occasion. I simply decided to make a nice meal for my family." Aisha glances at me. "And, frankly, your father hasn't been eating well. I'm worried about him."

"You're the best cook in the family, Dad. After Mom, I mean." He grins. "Why don't you make your famous biriyani?"

"I'm too tired." I sigh. "It seems like the work never ends."

"You need to take a vacation." He pauses. "I know. When hunger and poverty do."

"That's right. How are things at the station?"

"This morning they sent me out to cover the birth of a baby gorilla. There wasn't much to tell. I did get to announce the 'Name the Gorilla' contest. It was one of the most exciting moments of my career."

Someone knocks. "I'll get it," says Maryam.

Jamal and Rabia walk in. Jamal is carrying Amir on his shoulders. Rabia cradles the baby.

"There are my grandbabies." Aisha jumps up from her chair and reaches for Amir. "You're getting so big. My little man." She kisses him noisily while he giggles.

"Assalaamu alaikum. It's good to see you. Have a seat. Mom made meatloaf."

"We already ate," says Rabia.

"How are you feeling?" Aisha asks. "Is the baby letting you sleep yet?"

"She's a better sleeper than Amir was. You still keep me busy, don't you, little guy?" She tickles her son.

"Let me know if you need some time to yourself. I'd be happy to take care of them for a few hours."

"Kamila needs to stay close to me. She's still so little. But you're welcome to take Amir."

"Good. I'll come get him this Saturday. We can go to the zoo."

"That would be great. Thanks."

"There's something we need to tell you." Jamal traces the pattern on the tablecloth.

"What's up?" Is there a problem?

"The school district has decided to lay off some teachers, but they haven't announced names. They won't let anyone know until May."

"They won't let you go, Jamal," says Aisha. "You're a wonderful teacher."

"That didn't stop them from axing some of my friends. I was at school until nine nearly every night last week. All my records are current, my lessons are creative, and I have good rapport with the students, but I don't know if that's enough."

"They're lucky to have someone that conscientious. What more do they need?"

"Dad, do you remember Seth Everett? We went to school together, and he came by the house a few times. Last November, he was fired because one student—one out of the nearly 300 he taught—complained that he graded unfairly. Can you imagine?"

This doesn't sound right. "Doesn't your union protect you from that kind of abuse?"

"The union contracts aren't worth the paper they're written on because the school district knows how to get around them. Former teachers are waiting in line to take our jobs, and they're so desperate they'll accept lower salaries without benefits. The district filled Seth's position three hours after they let him go. They can fire us all and replace us by the time school starts the next day."

"That isn't right." Muhammad shouts. "This is what I need to be reporting on, not baby gorillas. People need to know. Parents complain about not having good teachers for their kids, and they don't realize what's happening to the good teachers. I'll talk to Dirk on Monday. We can do an exposé."

"Don't bother," says Jamal. "You'll do more harm than good."

"Somebody needs to say something."

"If they find out my brother is making waves, they'll just move me up on the lay-off list. I need to remain anonymous and hold on. It's my best chance."

"We can't stay quiet."

"Muhammad, do you want to see me out of a job? Who's going to take care of my family? Keep your mouth shut, and let it go."

"He's right, Muhammad." I wince at the truth. "Sometimes it doesn't pay to make waves. Especially not these days." Whether it's holding on to a teaching job or serving wine at a fundraiser, you have to know when the fight is over. I haven't reached that point yet.

"I can't fight it. Rabia and I are talking about moving instead. I've heard the job situation is better out west. What do you think?"

He sounds like he's already made up his mind. "I don't know, Jamal. I can't imagine you living that far away. But you do need to support your family."

"I'm helping Jamal with his resume," says Rabia. "And in a year or two, I hope to get back into teaching, too."

"You're talking about moving hundreds of miles away," says Aisha. "When would I see my grandchildren?"

Jamal touches Aisha's hand. "You don't want to see your grandchildren without food or a decent place to live, do you?"

"You could always move back here with us. We have plenty of room."

"No, Dad. I need to take care of my family."

"Have you prayed about this?"

"Yes I have, Mom. Nothing is definite. Rabia will update my resume, and I'll start sending it out. I just wanted you to be prepared."

Aisha shakes her head. "There must be another way."

"Let me know if you come up with one. I've thought about this for weeks, and it's the only solution I can find."

"Rabia, how will you manage to take care of the children without the help of your family?"

Our daughter-in-law smiles. "My mother raised the five of us on her own. I'm sure I can handle it, insha Allah."

"But you'll be taking my grandchildren away from me."

"We'll visit, Mom. Maybe Dad and you can come out to see us, wherever we end up. I know Dad is getting tired of Chicago."

"Maybe we should move with you," I say. "As long as it's warm where you're going."

"I don't like this. There must be another way."

"I wish there was. But I won't be one of the homeless Dad takes care of over at Evans. The way things are going here in Chicago, that's a real possibility." Jamal stands and goes over to hug Aisha. "I'll miss you too."

"Isn't there anything we can say?" I ask.

"You know how things are, Dad, probably more than most people do. How is everything over at Hope and Evans? I saw the interview with Gameel."

"I wanted to do that interview. Dirk gave it to someone else," says Muhammad.

"The important thing, Muhammad, is that the word got out, and you were a part of that. We had a few rough days, but things are settling down. We're supposed to have a fundraiser in May."

"That should help. By the way, how's Uncle Brad? I haven't seen him since he got out of the hospital."

"He's cleaning his garage."

"Are you serious?"

"He's on a special diet now, and it seems to be working. And he spends as much time as he can with his grandchildren."

"I don't know how Faiqa manages with three babies," says Rabia. "I can barely keep up with these two."

"Do you give your mama a hard time?" Aisha squeezes Amir and kisses him. He laughs.

"We'd better go," says Jamal. "We haven't told Rabia's mother yet."

"Give her our salaams." I hug my son. "I am going to miss you."

After they leave, Aisha and I retreat upstairs. I hold her. "Are you okay?"

"No, not really." She sighs. "I don't know who I'll miss more—Jamal and Rabia,

or their children."

"I hope Jamal finds a way to stay here. It's great watching our grandkids grow."

Her nod is followed by silence. "What is it, Aisha?"

"I know I shouldn't say this, but Amir and Kamila are my first grandchildren. I love all of your grandchildren as if they were mine. They're not, though. That's a very selfish attitude, isn't it?"

I kiss her. "They're our first grandchildren. And wherever they live, I pray they'll be healthy and strong."

"Insha Allah." She leans against me, and I stroke her head.

Kids really do grow up too quickly.

Joshua: Part Three

On my way to the center this morning, I listened to the news. A pregnant black woman and her three kids disappeared yesterday. Police can't locate the husband. An Arab woman went berserk on a cross-country flight last night, and the plane was forced to make an emergency landing at O'Hare. Khalif Amin lost his temper at a city council meeting and had to be forcibly removed. The world is falling apart, and there's nothing I can do to stop it. I'm looking forward to Muhammad's next animal story.

～

Gameel walks into my office in the early afternoon while I'm working on payroll.

"Assalaamu alaikum Joshua. Are you busy?"

"Come on in. Brad showed us new pictures of your grandchildren. You must be very proud of them."

"I am, but I'm too young to be a grandfather. How do you handle it?"

"I enjoy them. I only have to look in the mirror and see the gray hairs to know I'm old. It's a fact of life."

"I admire your attitude. They are wonderful. Did Brad tell you that Yusuf rolled over?"

"No. That's great."

"How are things over at Evans? It looks like the weather is easing up."

"Alhamdulillah. I can't tell you how much your donation meant. Do you realize how many other donations your generosity inspired?"

"I'm glad we got through it. Hopefully things will get easier after the fundraiser. How is that going?"

"Stu is checking out caterers and hotels. Of course, I'd prefer to use the Hope Center gym and save the money."

"You know that's not how it's done. This has to be a major event. Putting up streamers in a gymnasium won't attract the money. Be sure to book the hotel soon because those spaces fill up quickly for May. Have them take care of catering and decorations. Don't forget the musicians."

"I'm not happy about the prospect of wining and dining our donors. I know how things are done, but how can a Muslim get involved with alcohol?"

"Be realistic, Joshua. This isn't an Islamic organization and, in fact, you're the only Muslim employed here."

"But as the director, I'm the one who takes responsibility for the decision."

"Don't take responsibility. Have Sandra or Stu make the arrangements or hand it off to the board."

"Do you realize I've avoided every Hope Center fundraiser for this very reason?"

"And you haven't held a fundraiser in five years. The board should have called you on it long ago, but we realized you had your hands full, especially after Evans opened up. You can't put it off any longer."

"You're a Muslim. Doesn't it bother you?"

"Being bothered is a luxury. Both centers will be forced to close their doors unless you do this. You and your staff will be out of work, and the homeless will have one less avenue for relief. Are you telling me you would allow your faith to get in the way of helping your fellow man? That's not Islam."

"Allah knows I want to help. During the winter storms, I took some of our clients home with me for the night. But why do we have to serve alcohol?"

"Why are you asking me? You know how things work here."

"I know that too well. Before I became a Muslim I was a drunk, like my brother and my father, and probably my grandfather. Islam has broken that cycle, alhamdulillah. Why would I want to go back to that?"

"I'm not asking you to drink. All you have to do is host the event. Are you telling me even that is too hard for you to do?"

"What would happen if I refuse?"

He takes off his glasses and rubs his eyes. "According to the latest statistics, Chicago has an unemployment rate of 33 percent. In times like these, no one is irreplaceable." He puts on his glasses but doesn't look at me.

What can I say? From anyone else I would take that as a threat, but I know it's the truth. "I understand."

"So you need to start looking into hotels," he says, changing the subject. "In terms of a speaker, I was thinking of Reverend Hiram Johnson. Have you ever heard him give a talk?"

He's trying to lighten the mood, but I still feel the tension. "I heard him once. He is dynamic. Stu knows him personally."

"A man like that should have no problem getting donations. Have Stu arrange it."

"It's already taken care of." I don't trust Hiram Johnson, and I know wine is the mother of all evils, but I'm out of options. I'm too young and too poor to retire.

"I'd better be going," Gameel says, standing.

"I'm glad you stopped by."

"I'll see you later, Joshua. Assalaamu alaikum."

We shake hands. "Walaikum assalaam." He walks out. I put my head in my hands.

⁓

I decide to leave work a little early. My desk is clear, and I need to see my brother.

Kyle's car is parked in Brad's driveway. I've hardly seen him since Brad came home.

Emily answers the door. "Assalaamu alaikum Uncle Joshua. I was just on my way to class. They're eating in the kitchen. I'm sure Dad will want you to join them."

"Joshua?" Brad calls from the kitchen. "Assalaamu alaikum. Come on in."

Emily gives me a little wave and heads for her car. I walk into the kitchen.

Brad, Beth, and Matt are in here, along with Kyle and Faiqa. "Assalaamu alaikum." I pat Kyle's shoulder. "Where are the babies?"

"The girls are taking their naps in the living room. Zakariya's sleeping in his crib," says Faiqa. "Yusuf is right here." He sits on her lap, reaching for her plate. I hadn't noticed him.

"Pull up a chair," says Brad. "Emily made vegetarian chili. It's delicious."

Before I can object, Matt brings me a chair, and Beth hands me a bowl. "Eat up," says Brad.

This looks more like food. I taste it. This is good. "Matt, did you know your wife was a good cook before you married her?"

"I didn't have a clue. Have you noticed the weight I've put on this last year? She knows all about eating healthy, too. She's never drunk coffee, and she refuses to add salt to the food she cooks."

This chili is great. "I do like vegetables, but I was never into the health food craze."

Brad nods. "That's what I always said. I thought carrot juice and tofu were for dying hippies. Then I realized death was waiting for me."

"You do look good." Not like a man who was supposed to be dead three weeks ago.

"I look damn good. Hospices are for people who are ready to die. I have too much life left in me."

"Thanks for the chili. I need to go home." I bend down to hug my brother. "I'm praying for you," I whisper.

"I'm counting on that."

Joshua: Part Four

Aisha and I eat breakfast together after Maryam leaves for class. I haven't seen much of Luqman for the last couple of weeks. He's usually either sleeping or out. I hope he's ready to graduate.

"You look serious. What are you thinking?" Aisha pats my hand.

"Nothing in particular. Have you talked with Luqman lately? Is his thesis finished?"

"I don't know. He seems to spend all of his time at Zaid's. Do you remember when he was little? He wouldn't let me out of his sight."

"I miss those days."

"I don't. It's wonderful to see our kids grow up and find their places in the world."

"Don't you miss their softness and the way they used to depend on us?"

"That's why we have grandchildren. I don't know what I'll do without my little Amir and baby Kamila. I wish they didn't have to leave."

I squeeze her hand. "We always have each other."

"You're sweet." She leans over and kisses me lightly. "We'd better get going, though, or we'll both be late for work."

I would be happy to sit with her like this all day. That will be one of the nicest things about retirement. If only I were a few years older. I could forget about the fundraiser and take an early retirement. We could move someplace warmer and spend our days together. I close my eyes and imagine it.

I haven't told Aisha about my troubles at Hope. There must be a way to work this out. She doesn't have to worry about it.

"Joshua. Are you daydreaming again?" She's standing at the kitchen door, briefcase in hand.

"You caught me."

"I need to get going. Have a good day."

I walk over and put my arm around her waist. "You too, hon." We kiss.

I stand at the back door and watch her pull out of the driveway before running upstairs to get dressed. Suddenly I don't feel like going to work. I could quit and let them worry about the fundraiser. There are other jobs.

But not for a fifty-seven year old man. I pull on my suit coat and knot my tie, wishing I could just forget it all.

∽

Things are quiet at Hope today. The weather has been good lately—highs in the forties and clear skies. All of our volunteers showed up. The flu season appears to be winding down, and the clinic is nearly empty. The snow is melting. Spring is coming. I can't wait.

Jamal and Rabia are planning to move. Why do Aisha and I need to stay in Chicago? Could I find another job in another city? There must be an organization somewhere that wouldn't ask me to betray my faith. I lean back in my chair and do a few searches.

I check some Islamic sites. An Islamic center in northern California needs an administrator. A service organization in Houston is looking for a director. In New York, a homeless shelter is advertising for a grant writer. I save the information. We could move.

Why not? Aisha could take a break from teaching. We might find a friendlier climate. There's nothing to keep us here in Chicago. Our kids are grown. It's our turn now.

I take a walk around the building, acting like an administrator. Sandra is drinking coffee in the front office. The gym is empty. Two old men sit in the waiting room of the clinic. Everything is under control.

When I return to my desk, I pull out my resume. This thing hasn't been updated in nearly twenty years. I'll freshen it up and try to start again in a new city.

Should I tell Aisha my plans? There's no use making her worry. It's just a thought. I'll send out my resume and see what happens. If I get a response, I'll have plenty of time to discuss it with her.

∽

When I get home, I find Aisha taking a nap upstairs. Her students wear her out.

Maryam's note is in the kitchen. She has to study and she'll eat on campus. I guess dinner is up to me. I open the cabinets. We don't have the ingredients for curry or biriyani, and I wouldn't have the energy to make them if we did. I fry myself a hamburger, adding tomato and lettuce in honor of Brad. In an hour, I'll wake Aisha for the prayer and fix her a hamburger, too.

While eating, I catch up on the news. Khalif Amin was in jail overnight. The FOM had another encounter with the Young Pilgrims, this time on the South Side, only a few blocks from Hope Center. No one was hurt, but property damage has been reported. I wonder where Luqman is.

When I'm finished eating, I go to the computer. We need to get out of Chicago. My son could be in trouble. My job is on the line. Jamal is leaving, and my brother could be dead soon. I can't keep ignoring the signs. I touch up my resume, adding my experience as director of Hope Center, and send it out.

Kyle's Family

Faiqa and I have a morning routine worked out. It's something like an assembly line. I bring her one baby at a time, usually starting with Nathifa. While she nurses, I play with the others and change their diapers.

After they're all fed and changed, we lay them on the bed and watch them play. Then I go to the kitchen to heat our bagels and pour our morning drinks—coffee for me, juice for Faiqa. We eat while watching our children. Yusuf practices rolling over. Nashwa babbles. Nathifa smiles and coos.

When breakfast is finished, I have to get dressed and leave for work. I kiss our children first. My last kiss is for my wife. "Have fun. I wish I didn't have to leave."

"Me too." She hugs me. "We'll see you tonight, insha Allah."

I take a final glance at our children before leaving the condo and heading for the parking garage.

Faiqa is scheduled to go back to work next month. Hannah will watch the babies. She's had experience with handling more than one. I'm sure Mom will be here, too, as often as she can.

But Dad's prognosis isn't good. Will he be alive even three weeks from now? The doctor gave him six weeks this time. I was there when he received the news, and it hurt to watch the light go out of his face. He really thought he had beaten the cancer. For a little while, he had me believing it too.

∾

I climb into my red sports car. Last fall, I bought a new van for Faiqa. She needed something bigger, something with enough room for three car seats. I'll keep my sports car. While listening to the Qur'an, I zip down the expressway.

When I arrive at the office, I have thirty minutes to catch up on my correspondence and prepare for a board meeting. Gameel is gradually giving me more control of the company. In five years, he plans to retire. I think I'll be ready.

Luqman: Politics

Nobody gives you freedom.
Nobody can give you justice or equality or anything.
If you're a man, you take it.

—Malek El-Shabbaz (Malcolm X)

Lately, I've tried to avoid my family. I stay out until the early hours and sneak into the house after I'm sure they're all asleep. But a few days ago, I ran into Muhammad on the front porch.

"What are you doing here? You have your own place now."

"I came over to do my laundry. All the washers at my place were being used. Why are you coming in so late?"

I shrugged. "Why not? You're out late yourself."

"What do you know about that fight over at Northwestern?"

"Whoa. You still don't pull any punches. I know as much as you do. Do you think I'm in on it?"

"That wouldn't surprise me."

"Sorry to disappoint you, but I don't have any scoops."

"Be careful, Luqman. They're looking for someone like you."

"Someone like me? Dark-skinned? Intelligent? Good-looking? What are you getting at?"

"Nothing. Just be careful." He threw his laundry bag over his shoulder and headed for his car. My brother thinks he knows everything. What a loser.

~

Last night, I was standing in front of the fridge when Maryam walked into the kitchen. "Could you pass me the milk?" she said.

"Sure. You can't sleep?"

"I'm thinking too much. There's my student teaching and getting ready for graduation. Then there's Jamal."

"What's up with Jamal?" I settled on chocolate fudge ice cream and went to get a bowl.

"They'll probably move this summer. The school district is making cutbacks, and he's afraid of being laid off. He's going to apply for a job out west."

I grin. "It sounds like you picked a good time to become a teacher."

She swats me. "I'll be okay. Some elementary schools are still hiring. But I'm going to miss them. Especially Amir. He's so sweet. And the baby's so small yet."

"That's rough." I lick the ice cream on my spoon. "You know whose fault it is, don't you?"

"Don't try to blame this on Muhammad."

"I'm serious, Maryam. It's the New Pilgrims. They think they own this town and everyone in it." Somebody needs to set them straight.

"I don't care about politics. I just wish Jamal and Rabia didn't have to leave."

My sister is smart enough to figure this out, but she has her head in the clouds and her eyes on Zaid. I wonder when he'll get up the nerve to approach my father.

∼

I don't know what the Young Pilgrims were doing on the South Side tonight, but we made sure they won't come back. I'm still pumped. They couldn't lay a hand on me.

Aziz put out the call that they were messing around his neighborhood. By the time our leader, Malek, showed up we had them on the run. What kind of leader arrives after the fight is over?

He impresses the brothers with his knowledge of the Qur'an and his pious ways. But I know Malek too well. It's all an act.

Death Threat

While I thought I was learning how to live,
I have been learning how to die.

—Leonardo Da Vinci

Joshua: Part One

Brad had a doctor's appointment yesterday afternoon. I wonder how it went. When I stop at his house after work, Beth answers the door.

"Assalaamu alaikum. How's Brad today? I hope he's not still out working in the garage."

"He's in bed."

"What's wrong? Does he have a fever? Have you called the doctor?"

She shakes her head. "Why don't you talk to him? Maybe he'll listen to you."

My brother is a lump under the covers. "Assalaamu alaikum Brad. How you doing? Is something wrong? I thought you'd be training for the soccer game."

He grunts.

"Hey, Brad, come out of there. What's going on, man?"

No answer.

I yank the covers off of him. "Come on, Brad. What's the problem? I bet that doctor got upset with you for proving him wrong."

My brother opens his eyes. "The doctor is right. He gives me six weeks. I don't think I'll make it that long."

"What happened? You were doing so well."

"I thought I was, but blood tests don't lie. I need to face the facts."

I look away. These past few weeks, I've begun to believe that Brad wasn't dying. He seemed so strong. I take a moment to recover and try to smile. "Then if you have six weeks, you'd better make the most of them."

"It's no use, Joshua. Who am I trying to fool?"

"But you were energetic and happy. Are you sure the blood tests are right?"

"Stop denying it. You should have let them put me in a hospice. That's the place for people like me."

"What about your grandchildren? Aren't you going to try, at least, for them?"

"I'll never see them walk or hear them talk. They won't remember me. I'll be just another face in a family picture to them." Tears slip down his cheeks, and he doesn't try to hide them.

The right words escape me. I talk anyway. "You can't give up, Brad. I won't let you."

"You don't have anything to say about it. Stop thinking you can fix things. That's one of your problems, do you know that? This can't be fixed, and it isn't going away." He lies down and pulls the blanket over his head.

"What about Kyle and Matt?"

"They have their families. They don't need me."

"You know that's not true. And what about Beth?"

He sits up, throwing off the blanket. "Don't start with me, Joshua. You know I can't control this. Aren't you the one who goes around preaching about life spans? This is all I have. Or, do you have some special connections with Allah?"

"No special connections. Just prayer." I touch his shoulder. "Maybe the doctor is right, and you only have six weeks. Maybe only four. Are you going to spend the rest of your time in bed?"

"You can't imagine how it feels to know you won't live to see April. I keep waiting for the spring, and it will never come." He stares into space. "I wasted all those years."

I pull him into a hug. He's not as bony as he was in the hospital, but he's still far too frail. "I can't imagine my life without you in it."

We cry together. I don't know how long. I try to memorize how he feels in my arms and how his voice sounds, taking a mental picture of this moment.

He pulls away. "I'll be okay. Thanks for coming."

"Do you need anything while I'm here?"

"Could you hand me the Qur'an?" He puts on his glasses and starts to read. His Arabic is slow but smooth.

"I'll see you later, insha Allah." He pauses briefly while I give him a quick hug. As I walk through the living room, I can hear his recitation.

~

In the evening, after Aisha has gone to bed, I go back to my job search. We're leaving Chicago. I don't want to stay here after Brad is gone.

I find two more job opportunities—one in Kentucky and one in Arizona. Chris's son, Benjamin, lives in Kentucky and he seems to like it there. Brad has always loved Arizona. Both should be warmer than Chicago. I send in my resume.

We have about three months before the fundraiser. I need to leave before then. That's my only way out. Brad will be dead, and Jamal and his family will probably be headed somewhere else. Maryam will be graduating, and Luqman will have finished graduate school. It's a good time to leave.

I need to talk with Aisha about this. I'm not sure what she'll say. She's lived in Chicago since she came here as a college freshman nearly forty years ago. Her mother still lives in Moline. Maybe I can convince Sharon to move with us. This cold weather can't be good for her, especially at her age.

I'll still be leaving behind some of the people I love. Jeremy and Muhammad. Umar, who is more like a brother than a brother-in-law. My nephews. But we can come back to visit, as long as we come in the summer. My job is in jeopardy. If I do what they're asking, my faith will be in jeopardy. We need to get out of here.

And I need to go to bed. It's late. These days, I rarely sleep more than five or six hours. There's too much on my mind.

I check the locks on the front door and turn off the lights before heading upstairs. My foot is on the first step when the phone rings.

I'm tired, and I don't feel like talking but it could be Beth. Maybe she had to put Brad back in the hospital. My heart is beating faster when I answer. "Hello?"

"Assalaamu alaikum Dad. How are you? Is everything okay? You sound worried."

"Michael? Masha Allah, it's good to hear your voice."

"What's wrong?"

"Uncle Brad is very sick. The doctor gives him six weeks. I was afraid he'd had a relapse."

"Six weeks? That would be the end of March. That's perfect."

"What?"

"What I mean is, I'll get to see him, insha Allah. We're coming, Dad. I'm bringing my family. Do you think you have enough room for all of us?"

"Of course we do." I laugh. "That's great, Michael. I can't wait to see you. And the kids. It's been so long. Ilyas must be getting tall now."

"He's nearly as tall as me. We're coming in the middle of March. I'll send you all the details." He pauses. "I hope we come in time to see Uncle Brad."

"I hope so. Pray for him. He's already lived longer than the doctor predicted."

"How is he feeling? Is he in pain?"

"I don't know. You know he wouldn't tell me. Chris is here in town, too. I guess he'll be here until, well, until the end." I gulp, nearly choking on the words.

We move on to routine matters, but it's not idle chit-chat when I'm speaking with Michael. He's been gone too long. I tell him about the troubles at my job and the lack of funds. He tells me about his work in the village. We talk about his children.

"You haven't seen Anna or Tariq yet. And Ilyas is nearly a man now. At least, he thinks he is."

"It's been six years, hasn't it? I wish we could have come last summer, but my work at the center held me back. I was able to get away for Hajj."

"That was last month, wasn't it? How was it? Gabriela and I hope to go when the children are a little older."

Was it only a month ago? "Don't wait too long. It's better if you go when you're still young, just as soon as you're able."

Michael laughs. "You're right, but I'll be forty in November, insha Allah. My youth is gone."

My son is nearly forty? How is that possible? "You make me feel old."

"Don't worry, Dad. You're doing great. I'd better go now. I'll contact you in a couple of days about our flight. I can't wait to see you again."

"Are you ready to finally come home?"

"To visit. Not to stay. My life is here. But I miss my country, and I think it's safe to come back. We'll see you soon, insha Allah. Assalaamu alaikum."

"Walaikum assalaam. I love you, Michael."

"Yes, Dad, I love you too."

He's gone. I stare at the phone for a moment, wishing I could hug him. One more month, insha Allah. I can't wait.

Now I can't sleep. I enter another number. A little girl answers. That must be Noora. How old is she? I've forgotten. "Assalaamu alaikum. Can I talk to your mommy?"

The phone hits the floor. A baby cries. A boy shouts. Jennifer scolds one of the children. I think Noora forgot about me. "Jennifer," I call. I hope she can hear me.

"Hello?" It's a boy.

"Assalaamu alaikum. This is Grandpa. How are you, Ahmed?"

"I'm Yunus."

"You sound so grown up. Can I talk with your mommy?"

Yunus shouts. Jennifer hushes him. The baby is still crying.

"Assalaamu alaikum. Who is this?"

It's Nuruddin, my son-in-law. "Walaikum assalaam. I'm glad you answered. Noora and Yunus forgot about me."

"Isa? Is that you? How are you? Is something wrong?"

"No, I just miss my daughter. And you. How is everything?"

"We're good. I need to go to work. Wait. I'll give the phone to Jenny."

The baby is still crying. Nuruddin says a few words, and the other children quiet down.

"Assalaamu alaikum Dad. How are you? I'm sorry you had to wait." She yells over the crying baby.

I yell, too. "It's okay. How are you, Jenny? It sounds like you have your hands full."

"Salma has teeth coming in. She hardly slept last night."

"Michael just called. He and his family are coming to Chicago in a month."

"Michael's coming? That's great. I wish I could see him."

"Could you?"

"I don't know, Dad. The kids have school. I'll talk with Nuruddin and see what he says."

"I'd better let you go. You need to take care of the baby."

"I'll call later when things are quiet. It's good to hear your voice."

"Assalaamu alaikum Jenny. I love you."

"I love you, too, Dad. Walaikum assalaam."

I end the call. Our house seems too quiet. I wish I could be with Jenny and her family on the other side of the world in a home where the children are still young and the rooms echo with their voices. I wish she could come. But the children have school.

I turn off the desk lamp and walk slowly up the stairs. It's late. I need to sleep. But sleep won't come easily. It never does.

Joshua: Part Two

Aisha and I have another quiet breakfast together. Luqman wouldn't get up for the prayer this morning, so I let him sleep. I'm tired of dealing with him. After he graduates in May, he needs to get a job and start taking care of himself.

I enjoy these times with my wife. We talk about the details of life. Her van needs an oil change. Her principal complimented her yesterday on her new classroom decorations. She asks about my work at Hope.

I haven't talked with her yet about the fundraiser, and I haven't told her about sending out my resume. Usually I share everything with Aisha, but I want to think it all through first. I'm starting to worry about her reaction.

While we eat our bagels, I say, "Michael called last night. They're coming next month."

"That's fantastic, masha Allah. How long can he stay?"

"I forgot to ask. I told him I'd like him to come back here to live, but he says his life is in Mexico."

"It will be wonderful to see them. Ilyas and Mariya were so small when we went there. That was nearly seven years ago. Ilyas must be almost fourteen. And we've never seen the youngest two. Will they be staying with us?"

"That's what Michael said. It will be great to have young children in the house again."

"It will. You'd better wait and see what Heather has to say about that, though. She may want them to stay at the condo."

"Can you imagine four kids running around her condo? I'm sure Michael's kids are all well-behaved, but they're kids. And the youngest is still a baby."

"Michael, Jeremy, and Jennifer all lived there once. Heather raised her daughter Brianna in the condo. I would love to have them here, but we always have to be prepared for what Heather wants."

How could I forget? I was married to Heather, and I know how she is. "We'll work it out," I sigh. Since Jenny moved to Pakistan, I've hardly seen Heather and I'd rather keep it that way.

~

It's been another slow day, alhamdulillah. I made my rounds and stopped over at Evans. Everything was running smoothly. In the afternoon, I had a short meeting with Ashleigh in the clinic. There were a few patients coughing in the waiting room, but she said the flu season is nearly over. We had eighteen deaths, but none recently. Umar tells me Nicole is making progress. Things are looking up. Spring will be here soon and so will Michael.

I should go see my brother on the way home. I don't like watching him slowly fade away, but Beth seems to handle it well, and Chris stays with him nearly every day. He's given up his work at the church and his life in Arkansas to be with Brad in his final days. How can I be so weak? I climb into my car and head for Brad's house.

Beth opens the front door and holds a finger to her lips.

Brad is sitting in the middle of the room, talking to no one. I notice the camera in Chris's hand.

"Always listen to your parents. You won't always agree with them, but everything they do is because they love you. Yusuf, when your father tells you to study hard, you need to listen. He knows what he's talking about. Nashwa, don't talk back to your mother or roll your eyes at her. She is a bright and capable woman. Nathifa, you were the smallest when you were born, and they worried about you the most. Be strong and make them proud. I want all of you to listen to them. Cherish them. Honor them. You can't imagine how much they wanted and hoped for you. You didn't see their joy when you arrived. I was there. I know. You three are a miracle from Allah. Be grateful. And always remember how much I love you."

He signals Chris, who turns off the camera. "I'm almost done," he says. "I'm up to their teen years. I've told them all about me, starting with my childhood. After it's all recorded, I plan to put together a photo presentation. If you have pictures of me, I'd like to borrow them."

"I'm sure Aisha knows where they are. How do you feel?"

"A little tired, but overall I feel great. Don't I look good? Be honest."

The color has returned to his face, and his eyes show a spark again. "You do look good. Has the doctor given you another reprieve?"

"I'm not going back. It's a waste of time and money."

"But, Brad, you should be receiving medical care."

"Why? So I can live longer?" He laughs.

"Doctors don't know everything, but they can help."

"Only Allah knows how long I have, how long any of us has. Why do I need a doctor to depress me with his predictions?" He puts the camera away. "After I finish this project, I plan to get back into training. I have less than five months before our soccer match, and I want to make sure I'm ready. This is it, Joshua. I won't die until I've beaten you."

Five months. One day he's ready to die, and the next he's convinced he'll live forever. I nod. "Michael's coming for a visit next month. He's anxious to see you."

"That's great. Is he bringing his family?"

"They'll all be here, insha Allah."

"Fantastic. Oh, Matt and Emily are moving out next week. They need their privacy."

"How will you manage?"

"I'm not an invalid. You just said I look good. I feel good."

"But the doctor said—."

"The doctor can say what he wants. I know my own body."

"At least you have the nurse to help you out."

"I contacted the agency this morning and told them we don't need their service."

"What are you doing?" I look to Chris. "Are you going to let him do this?"

"Don't talk around me," says Brad. "I'm still here."

Chris shrugs. "You're the one who said Brad has the right to make his own decisions."

"But Brad, what if you have a medical emergency?"

"We'll deal with it. I don't want to die in the hospital. I'd rather be in my own bed."

"How does Beth feel about that?"

"We've discussed it. She understands."

"You've always been so stubborn. I wish just this once you would listen to reason."

Brad smirks. "Why should I change now?"

"Relax, Joshua," says Chris. "Brad and I have had some long talks. I can see why he wants to do things this way, and I won't stop him. Neither should you." My brother stares at me, communicating with his eyes what he won't say. *Go along with Brad. We can give him that much.*

"You're right. There's no use trying to convince him when his mind is made up. So, Brad, when do you plan to start training? Do you still want me to join you?"

"Do you think you could keep up? I know you're a sprinter, not a long-distance runner."

"That's how you plan to beat me. I'd better get to work on my endurance."

"Let's start in the beginning of March, if the weather is good. I'm hoping for an early spring this year."

His last spring, if he makes it. "Sounds good."

We're old men, facing death, but we talk like children in a game of make-believe. Brad will train. He'll live to see spring and summer. He'll finally win a soccer game.

Chris glances at me and nods slightly. These are the roles we must play.

I hug Brad before I leave. "Keep training. I'm looking forward to that game."

～

When I walk into our house, Aisha is on her way out, followed by Sharon.

I greet my mother-in-law with a hug. "I didn't know you were coming. It's great to see you again. It's been months."

"I told you this morning, hon." Aisha gently scolds me. "Mom and I are going shopping."

"Are you spending the night, Sharon? I'll make something special."

"I'm sure it will be delicious. Let's go, Angela. We don't want to miss the sales."

Aisha gives me a quick kiss. "I'm coming, Mom."

Let's see. Maryam is attending an Islamic conference in Des Moines. Luqman is at Zaid's place or wherever Luqman goes. Muhammad has his own apartment. The house is quiet. I stretch out on the couch.

∼

By the time they come back, the biriyani is done. I had to cut my nap short to make a quick run to the store for the ingredients, but it felt good to be back in the kitchen.

Aisha takes a bite and smiles. "I wish you cooked like this more often."

"Maybe I will." It was more relaxing than I'd remembered.

After dinner, they show me what they bought.

"Look at this." Aisha holds up a pink baby outfit. "She'll look so sweet."

"Is that for one of Kyle's daughters?"

"No, I got them something else. This is for our Kamila."

"Didn't you just buy her some outfits?"

"I'm her grandmother. It's my job to spoil her."

"I bought her this blanket," says Sharon. "It's hand-woven."

"And wait until you see what I bought for Amir," says Aisha.

Maybe I should talk to my wife about my job problems. I'll do it sometime this weekend.

∼

On Saturday morning, Aisha tries to hustle me out of the house. "Aren't you finished with your breakfast yet? We need to go."

I sip my coffee. "What's your hurry?"

"We're going to visit Kyle and Faiqa. Remember? I can't wait to see those babies again."

"I'm tired. Why don't you go alone?"

"Oh, Isa, you need to come. Kyle is your nephew and I'm sure he'll be happy to see you."

My head hurts and the coffee hasn't helped. I don't feel like going anywhere. All those sleepless nights must be catching up with me. "Really, hon, I just want to go back to bed. Give them my salaams."

She sighs dramatically. "If you insist. Mom, you're coming, aren't you?"

"Of course I am. Just let me get my purse." Sharon washes her dishes and goes into the office for her purse. We have a fold-out bed for her in there so she won't have to climb the stairs.

Aisha kisses me on the cheek. "Have a nice rest. I wish you would change your mind."

"Sorry, hon. Tell them I'll come by later."

After they leave, I finish my breakfast and take an aspirin. I woke up with a headache, but I thought it would go away. It hasn't. I slowly climb the stairs and throw myself into bed. What I need is a good nap.

~

My throat is dry. I blink a few times until my eyes start to focus. It's nearly 2:00 PM. That was a long nap, but I still don't feel that great.

I need to pray. I try to sit up but fall back into my pillow. My body aches. Is Aisha home yet? "Aisha, where are you?" My voice comes out as a whisper.

I roll out of the bed. My head pounds. My legs are too heavy. I stagger, holding onto the bed as I make my way to the bathroom. My arms feel like rubber.

I manage to make my ablutions, so dizzy I can barely stand in front of the sink. The water chills me. I reach for my robe and pull it tightly around me before heading for the stairs. I stand at the top. My head swims. I try the first step, holding onto the banister with both hands. I don't think I can make it. I turn around and stumble back to our bedroom where I stand, facing northeast, and raise my hands. After a moment, I have to sit on the floor, remaining there while I finish my prayer. Every time I bow down, my head feels like it will explode.

I open the bedroom door. "Aisha. Are you here?" My call is weak, but it's all I can manage. I listen. No sound.

I fall back into bed and close my eyes. I need water. Can someone bring me a glass of water?

~

I'm cold. And wet. Drops of water trickle down my face.

"You're so hot," Aisha whispers. She wipes my face with a wet washcloth. "Here, drink some water. Can you sit up?"

I groan.

"I'll help you." She puts her hand behind my head and lifts me toward the glass. Drops of water ease the burning in my throat.

"What time is it?"

"Almost six. Have you been in bed all day?"

I groan again, moving my lips slightly. "I need to pray."

"You'll have to make tayammum. Do you want me to help you?" She pulls me into a seated position and holds me while I pat the mattress and wipe my hands, face, and arms. When I'm finished, she eases me back into my pillow and I pray with my mind, my body sore and nearly immobile.

After the prayer, she wipes me with the cloth and gives me a few more sips of water. I sleep.

~

Weak sunlight pours through our bedroom window. My head still hurts a little. I sit up and look around. Aisha is gone. I stand and walk to the bathroom. My legs barely carry me. Halfway there, I stop and rest.

I finish my ablutions and make my way back into the bedroom. Sitting on the floor, I raise my hands to Allah and begin my prayer.

When it's done, I lean against the bed. I'm still weak but not like I was yesterday. What was that?

The bedroom door creaks open. Aisha walks in. "You look better. How do you feel?"

"A little weak."

She touches my forehead. "You're still warm. You'd better get back in bed." She helps me. "I'll bring you some tea. Just let me get dressed first."

It looks like I'm grounded for the weekend. "Where are you going?"

"I have to get ready for school."

"On a Sunday?"

She helps me get back into bed. "It's Monday, hon. Don't you remember?"

I don't remember anything. "What happened to Sunday? Did I pray?"

"You managed, with Muhammad's help. You couldn't eat, though, and I had a hard time getting you to drink water or take aspirin. If you weren't better by this morning, I was planning to take you to the hospital. Mom said six people in Moline have died from the flu this year."

I can barely keep my eyes open. She strokes my face. "I'll go get your tea. Do you think you're ready to eat something yet?"

"No. Tea is good. Thanks."

She wakes me up a few minutes later. "Here, Isa, drink this." I take a few sips. The tea and honey soothe me. "Muhammad said he can go into work late today. He stayed here last night because he was worried about you. If you want, he can sit with you."

I nod.

She touches my arm. "I'll come home as soon as I can."

I remember something. "Stu?"

"I called Sandra. She said to make sure you rest. Don't worry about anything, hon. Drink a little tea, and go back to sleep. Do you need anything else?"

"No. I'm okay."

"I wish I could kiss you, but Mom warned me to keep my distance. I love you, Isa." She blows me a kiss and walks out. I fall back into my pillow.

∿

Muhammad is staring at me. I stare back. "How long have you been here?"

"Not long. How are you feeling, Dad? Can I get you anything?"

"I'd like some water. Don't get too close. I don't want you getting sick, too." I sit up a little. He holds the water to my lips. "Thanks. That was good."

"You need to eat. Grandma made chicken noodle soup. Do you want some?"

"Not now. Don't you have to go to work?"

"I told them I'd be late."

I'm tired. I need to sleep. But Muhammad is still staring at me. "You can go. I'll be okay."

"You were completely out of it yesterday. Mom was ready to call an ambulance."

"It's just the flu."

"But you never get sick."

"I guess it's my turn." The fact that I've barely slept and haven't eaten well since we came back from Hajj probably had something to do with it. And I should have kept my distance from the coughing patients in the waiting room on Friday. "After a day or two, I'll be fine. You can go on to work."

"There's a bell on the nightstand. You can use it to call Grandma and let her know if you need anything."

I'm not going to ring a bell to call my eighty-nine year old mother-in-law. But I don't feel like talking. I nod. "Bring me some soup before you go."

⁓

Today is Wednesday. I thought I would be at work by now, but I still don't have my strength. I haven't even attempted the stairs.

Aisha has been sleeping in Jamal's old room. Sharon insisted. This room is officially my sick room. And I haven't left it since Saturday. I'm getting tired of staring at the walls.

The house is quiet. Aisha left an hour ago, making sure I had water and tea before she took off. Muhammad brought me soup. Maryam peeked in before she left for school. I haven't seen Luqman. But that's nothing new.

I haven't talked with Brad since last week. Was that Friday when I went to visit? I can't remember. I pick up the phone and count eight rings, but there's no answer.

Brad probably went out. The sun is shining. He must be feeling cooped up.

I eat a spoonful of Sharon's soup and close my eyes. This flu has knocked me out.

⁓

I wake up in time to make the early afternoon prayer. Afterward, I try to call Brad. There's still no answer.

Where could he be? Maybe he went to see the triplets. I'll call in the evening. He should be home then.

I'm bored. I want to get out of this room. Slowly, I stand, pull on my robe, and go out into the hallway.

Years ago, I made my nightly rounds, peeking in on my sleeping children. That ended when they became teenagers. I've barely seen their rooms in the last ten years. A peek won't hurt.

Maryam's room is across from ours. The last time I was in here, everything was decorated in pink. Now it's a sensible beige. There's not much decoration of any kind, but she has books everywhere. I browse one of her bookshelves. I remember when she was in her Jane Austen phase. Jane was eventually followed by Isabel Allende and Toni Morrison, among others. I see names of Muslim writers also—Leila, Amina, Aisha. The top shelf is full of books by Jennifer Adams Ali. I wonder if Jennifer realizes how much her little sister admires her. When we met at Hajj, Jenny told me she has a new book coming out soon. I've only read her first two. I'm not much into fiction, but I am very proud of her.

I carefully close Maryam's door and go down the hall to the room that used to be Jamal's. Aisha has made herself comfortable in here, her magazines on the floor and her teaching books on Jamal's old desk. I hope she can move back into our room soon. I miss her.

Muhammad has the large room at the end of the hall. At one time, my son Michael and Aisha's little brother, Marcus, shared that room. Muhammad claimed it when he was ten, contending he needed more space for his collections. He especially liked this room because it has two windows looking out over the street. I remember ten-year old Muhammad reporting about the neighbors' comings and goings at the dinner table. We had to teach him the difference between reporting important news and just being nosy.

The room is nearly empty now. Just two unmade beds and empty shelves. Some of his clothes hang in the closet. Others are scattered on the floor.

Luqman's room is next to ours. When he was little, he needed the comfort of knowing we were close. I remember waking up to a small elbow in my face. For the last few years, this room has been his secret chamber. I turn the knob, feeling like an intruder.

Of all the rooms, his is the messiest. Clothes lay on his bed, some tumbling into a small pile on the floor. His desk is buried under papers, mostly handwritten notes. His two bookcases are full, but more books spill out into crooked stacks. Some have been left open; face down, on the floor.

I browse the books in one of his bookcases. Marcus Garvey, Richard Wright, Malcolm X, Eldridge Cleaver. I recognize those names. He also has Karl Marx, Che Guevera, and Syed Qutb. I pick up *Invisible Man* by Ralph Ellison and page through it. When Jamal was little, I read this book, even though it was already outdated. Being the white father of a black son, I wanted to see the world through different eyes. Most of the authors on Luqman's shelf are black, and many are revolutionary. I doubt he needs all these books for his thesis.

He's never told me the subject of his thesis. I look through the handwritten pages on his desk and spot my name near the bottom of a family tree. My father, Sam, and his brothers occupy an upper tier. Above them are more names, all unfamiliar to me. Luqman has drawn angry red marks through many of them. What has he been researching, and what has he found? Will he tell me?

I am an intruder. Luqman never meant for me to see this. I put everything back where I found it and make my escape, quietly closing the door behind me.

My snooping has tired me. I pray before lying down and closing my eyes. What did those names mean? I assume they're my ancestors and Luqman's too. What does he want to know about them? Why the angry red marks? Why hasn't he told me what he's learned? And what should I think about the books on his shelf? Is he angry, as some of those men were? His life is easy, much easier than many of the men he studies. What does he have to angry about?

∼

Aisha is sitting on the bed, looking at me. I smile. "How long have you been here?"

"Not long. How do you feel?"

"A little better. I'm still tired. Can you ask Sharon how long this is going to take?"

"She said you probably won't feel like yourself for another week or two."

"Great. I need to get back to work."

"You should be able to go back on Monday, insha Allah. You just won't feel like doing much."

"I don't feel like doing much of anything yet. This flu really knocks you out."

"You hardly ever get sick. You just don't know how to deal with it."

"I sure don't. I tried to call Brad today, but there was no answer. I wish I could go see him."

"Oh." Aisha frowns and looks away.

"What? Is there something I should know?"

She sighs. "He's in the hospital, Isa. He's very sick."

"When did this happen? Why didn't you tell me?"

"You were sick, and there was nothing you could do. I thought it would be better to wait."

"What happened?"

"He has the flu."

"The flu? Like me? So, he should be getting better soon. Why is he in the hospital?"

"His immune system is weak. He can't handle it."

This is serious. "Is he going to be okay?"

"I stopped at the hospital on the way home. Beth said his temperature has come down a little. Hopefully he'll pull through."

"I made him sick, didn't I?"

"You didn't know you were sick when you went to see him. And everything is from Allah. Right now we just need to pray."

"It's my fault. And if he dies from this …"

"Listen to me, Isa. Everything is from Allah. Just make du'a. That's what you can do for your brother."

"I need to go wash up."

"Do you need help?"

"No, I can do it. You'd better get out of here. I don't want to make you sick, too."

"Don't blame yourself. It's not your fault."

"Go on, Aisha. I'm full of germs. You're not safe around me."

"I love you, Isa."

"I know. Right now, I need to be alone."

After she walks out, I go into the bathroom and make ablutions. I sit on the floor in the northeast corner of our bedroom and make a long du'a for my brother. *Oh Allah, please don't take him. Not yet. Oh Allah, please make Brad strong again.*

I pray all evening, stopping only when Aisha brings me tea and soup. *Don't let him die, oh Allah. Not from this. Oh Allah, please let me see him again.*

I'd like to keep praying all night, but I can barely keep my eyes open. I crawl under the covers and murmur du'a while drifting to sleep.

~

I had a restless night.

When Aisha brings my tea, she tries to make me feel better. "It wasn't your fault, Isa. You know that."

"I should have been more careful. What if I never see him again?"

I want her to tell me he'll get well. He'll come home soon and be his usual grouchy self. We'll have many more days together. Instead, she just says, "Keep praying."

She sits with me for a few more minutes. Neither of us has anything to say. Just having her here makes me feel a little better. But I'm afraid.

Finally, she stands and blows a kiss. "I have to go, hon. I'll let you know if I hear anything."

"Did Sharon say how much longer you have to stay away? I miss you."

"I miss you, too. Drink your tea. That will make you stronger. Muhammad will bring your soup before he leaves."

"Is he here?"

"He's been here every night. You don't know how worried he is."

"Tell him I'm not the one he needs to worry about."

"Keep praying, hon. That's all we can do. I love you."

She leaves for another day of work. I'm stuck here looking at these four walls. I need to get out of here and go see my brother.

∼

Muhammad knocks. "Assalaamu alaikum Dad. Can I come in?"

"Yeah. Come in."

He brought my soup. "How are you feeling? Are you stronger now?"

"A little. Do you have a few minutes?"

"Sure, Dad." He sets the bowl on the table and sits in the blue easy chair. "You must get lonely in here."

"It's not just that. I'm worried about Brad. Have you gone to see him?"

"I was there last night."

"How bad is it? How soon can he come home?"

"He's very sick. They have him on life support."

"Did you talk to him? What did he say?"

"He's really out of it, Dad. The flu hit him hard. They're doing everything they can to keep him alive." He pauses while the words settle. "He might not be strong enough to fight it."

Muhammad reaches for me as my tears fall. "No." I shout. "Stay away. I don't want you to get sick, too."

For a moment, he just stands there. Then he picks up my Qur'an, sits down, and begins reciting. I concentrate on his deep voice and the words of Allah. I pray through my tears.

He stays with me for a while. It's good not to be alone. Finally he stands. "I have to get to work, Dad. I'll come home right away and keep you company."

"Visit Uncle Brad first. Give my salaams to everyone, and tell them I'm praying for him."

"I'll do that, insha Allah. Assalaamu alaikum." He pats my leg and leaves.

"Walaikum assalaam." Thank you for being a good son.

After Muhammad leaves, I say more prayers for Brad. I remember the hadith: "*The dua of a Muslim for his brother in his absence is readily accepted, an angel is appointed to his side, whenever he makes a beneficial dua for his brother, the appointed angels says 'amin and may you also be blessed with the same.*" I'm not doing this for myself though, except in the sense that I want to see my brother again.

～

I tried the stairs yesterday afternoon. Bad idea. It took me fifteen minutes to get back upstairs, stopping frequently to rest.

While I was down there, I got a hot bowl of soup. Sharon has kept it coming all week. I didn't talk to her. I don't want to pass on the flu to her, too.

I would be stronger if not for this cough. It won't stop. Aisha told me it will go away eventually. She said that while standing in the doorway. I don't want her to get too close.

Just as I'm finishing my soup, the phone rings. I pick it up eagerly, anxious to talk with someone.

"Assalaamu alaikum Uncle Joshua. How are you feeling?"

It's Kyle. "Don't worry about me. How is your father?"

"He's still in critical condition."

"I'm sorry it happened this way. I wish I could be there."

"Muhammad comes every day. We knew it would happen sometime soon."

"What does the doctor say? Is there any hope?"

"Dad's fever broke again last night and stayed down. But he's still unconscious. I don't know. He seemed so strong these last few weeks, but his immune system can't handle this. I think it's just a matter of time." His voice breaks.

"Tell him I'm praying for him."

"I will. Keep praying. I'll talk to you later, Uncle Joshua. Assalaamu alaikum."

He hangs up. I'm sure he has to get back to Beth.

Before I got sick, I was worried about my own pitiful life. The weather. The fundraiser. Luqman. None of that compares to what my brother and his family is going through.

Today is Friday, isn't it? Prophet Muhammad said, *"There is an hour on Friday and if a Muslim gets it while offering Salat and asks something from Allah then Allah will definitely meet his demand."* I hope I'm not too late. I sit on the bedroom floor and raise my hands, asking Allah to give my brother more time.

After a while, I glance at the clock. The Friday prayer will start in thirty minutes. Usually, by this time, I'm sitting in the front row, reading the Qur'an while waiting for the sermon to start. This week I'm stuck at home. I use my time to pray for my brother.

∼

I've prayed as much as I can, taking breaks only to eat and sleep. Brad's face fills my dreams. Sometimes he's young and strong again. Other times, he's nearly skeletal. I wake up and pray again.

I'm dozing on Saturday afternoon when Aisha walks in. "Isa. Wake up. You have a visitor."

"Who is it?"

"Why don't you go see? Are you strong enough to go down-stairs?"

"I don't know. I could try."

"Get dressed. I'll tell him you're coming."

I head for the bathroom and look at myself in the mirror. My hair needs combing. My face needs washing. I've worn the same t-shirt and sweat pants all week. I strip and climb into the shower.

When I'm clean again, I sit on the bed and catch my breath. A simple shower was almost too much for me. Will I be strong enough to go back to work on Monday?

It's been thirty minutes since Aisha woke me. I hope my visitor is still here. I check the mirror again before slowly making my way down the steps.

Chris is sitting in the family room with a cup of tea. He stands up when I walk in and reaches for me. "How are you feeling, Joshua?"

I step back. "Don't come too close. I could still be contagious." I cough.

He sits down. "Are you feeling better? Muhammad told me you were very sick."

"I'm okay. Muhammad was worried. How's Brad. That's who I'm worried about."

"He's better. His fever is staying down, and he's talking a little. It will take him a while, but the doctors expect him to recover."

I relax in my chair. "When Kyle called yesterday morning, he said this might be it."

"That's what we all thought. The doctor calls Brad's recovery a miracle."

Alhamdulillah. "How long will he be in the hospital?"

"They want to keep him for at least another two weeks. I don't know if he'll completely regain his health. The oncologist hasn't changed his prognosis."

"Four more weeks, right? So if it wasn't this, it will be something else."

"That's what the doctor says. I'm amazed at Brad's strength, though. On Monday, they didn't expect him to make it through the week."

"Thanks for telling me. I've been so worried about him, I could hardly sleep."

"Brad sends you his greetings. He doesn't want you to worry. Oh, and he told me you'd better get well so you can start training for the soccer game."

After this last week, the idea of Brad playing soccer sounds more ridiculous than ever. But I can't bring myself to laugh. "Tell him I'm going to need a couple more weeks, too. This flu really knocked me out."

"Brad will understand that." He fiddles with the spoon. "Death is a mystery. I've seen healthy young men die suddenly, and I've seen sick old men linger for weeks, months, or even years. No one can know the time of death except our Lord."

"Are you planning to stay up here or go back down to Arkansas?"

"After Brad is stable, I'll need to go home for a week or two. Melinda and I plan to return, though, and stay for as long as we're needed. I'll call some of my old contacts here in the city and see if I can start preaching again. I miss my work."

Over the last few years, my job has become the kind of task I dread returning to on a Monday morning. For Chris, his work has always been a calling. I envy my brother a little for that.

He interrupts my thoughts. "I'd better get back to the hospital. I knew you would want to hear the good news. In fact, Brad insisted I come." Chris smiles a little. "You know how he is."

"You can't imagine how worried I've been. It's good to hear that Brad is getting some of his spirit back."

"After lunch, he badgered the doctor to let him go home."

I can almost hear Brad's voice. "What will we do without him?"

"I don't know," Chris says quietly. "I accused him of being in denial, but the truth is I don't want to think about it either."

When Brad's gone, it will be just Chris and me. Brad has always been the glue holding us together. Without Brad, Chris will be all I have—the only one who's known me since I was a mischievous kid on the South Side of Chicago, and loved me anyway.

I look away. "Brad must be waiting. I don't want to keep you. Thanks again for coming." A cough hides my emotions.

"Have you tried lemon juice with fresh ginger? Melinda gives that to me when I have a cough. Some people swear by apple cider vinegar, too."

"I've been going with tea and chicken soup. I'll mention the ginger to Aisha. Thanks."

He reaches out as if to hug me, patting me on the arm instead. "Take care, Joshua. I hope you feel better soon. I'll tell Brad you said hi."

"And don't let him give the doctor a hard time."

Chris nods. "I'll try."

I walk him to the door and watch as he climbs into his car. A very special visitor.

~

By Sunday morning, I'm feeling well enough to get my own breakfast. Aisha smiles when she sees me in the kitchen.

"Do you think you'll go back to work tomorrow?"

"I have to. I just wish I could get rid of this cough." Another round starts up. I cover my mouth and wait for it to pass.

"That could take another two weeks," says Sharon. "Keep drinking the tea."

"Chris suggested ginger. Should I try that, too?"

"That's a good idea," says Sharon. "Angela, run to the store later today and buy ginger for your husband. Make sure it's fresh."

"Sharon, do you tell your patients to try the home remedies?"

"I wish I could, but the doctors wouldn't like it. If they ask, though, I make a suggestion. My mother grew up on the natural treatments, and she lived to be 112. I don't know if I'll make it for another twenty-three years."

"My brother is trying to go natural now. I don't know if it will help."

"You might be surprised. He made it through the flu, which few people do in his condition. We don't know what the Lord has planned for him."

I watch my mother-in-law as she takes her dishes to the sink, washes them, and comes back with the tea. "Keep drinking this if you want to get well. It always worked for me." She's nearly ninety. I can't imagine living that long.

"I plan to go home this afternoon," she says, "but I'll be back sometime next month. It will be nice to see Michael again, and I can't wait to meet his wife and children. Umar wants me to spend more time over at their house, and Marcus may fly in. You know how close he and Michael always were."

Aisha touches my hand. "Mom stayed here because you were sick." My wife laughs. "I don't think she trusted me to take care of you properly."

"Don't be silly, Angela," says Sharon. "Of course I didn't trust you. You never learned how to make chicken noodle soup. I tried to teach you how to cook years ago, but you never showed much interest."

"She can cook." I grin. "I just wish she did it more often. Anyway, thanks for staying. I hope I didn't keep you from anything."

"Not this time of year. You may not see me much in April, though. I'll be out working in my garden."

Maryam walks in, book in hand, and drops a bagel in the toaster. "It's good to see you down here, Dad. Are you feeling better?"

"A little."

"Great." She goes back to reading.

I lean back and observe these women in my life. My mother has been gone for nearly twenty years. Jennifer lives in Pakistan. At least I have these three.

~

After breakfast, Sharon tells Aisha to air out the bedroom and wash all my bedding. "Use plenty of hot water."

I stay downstairs, reading a little and watching the news. After lunch, I pull on a jacket and sit on the front porch. It's good to be part of the world again.

In the afternoon, Aisha and I say goodbye to Sharon, watching as she drives away.

"You were talking about leaving Chicago," says Aisha. "Would you be interested in moving to Moline? We could be close to Mom."

"I'd like that. But I'm still hoping for someplace warmer."

"You have me to keep you warm." She snuggles closer.

"Aren't you worried about catching the flu?"

"I think I'll be okay. Just don't cough in my face."

The kids are gone. I grab her hand. "Let's go upstairs."

~

Aisha hands me my tea and bagel. "Are you sure you're ready to go back to work today?"

"I feel much better. That flu gave me a chance to catch up on my sleep."

"You do look better."

"It was nice that your mom stayed here to take care of me. She didn't have to do that."

Aisha pats my hand. "We all love you. You know that. Or do you want me to keep saying it?"

I squeeze her hand. "I love you, too."

In a few years, we can retire and spend our days together. But in a few minutes, we both have to leave for work.

I'd better tell her about my job. I'll do it tonight.

Joshua: Part Three

It's good to be behind my desk again, but I can't concentrate. My mind flits through random thoughts and worries. I'll call Kyle later and see how my brother is doing. If anything was wrong, they would have called. Wouldn't they? Or would they be too wrapped up in the crisis?

And what am I going to do about Luqman? If I confront him, he'll be angry that I went into his room. But it is my house. I've respected the kids' privacy all these years. Maybe I should have gone snooping a long time ago. I need to know what's going on with him. The revolutionary literature. The family tree. The angry red lines. He'll say they tie in with his thesis, but I think it goes deeper than that.

And how will I tell Aisha about my job search? I had hoped she would enjoy a change of scenery. Now, I'm not so sure. Move to Moline? It's a nice town, but too small for me. I have to make her understand that a move will be good for both of us. For all of us. We're going to have to talk about Luqman. We've avoided the issue long enough.

And what am I going to do about the fundraiser? Ideally, I'll find a new job before May, and it will be someone else's problem. I can't leave, though, unless Aisha agrees. And what about my brother? Could he beat this? If he does, I can't turn my back on him.

I need some fresh air. Maybe that will help clear my mind. I push my chair away from my desk and walk out of the office. Halfway to Evans, I start coughing. I can't go over there like this. I go back, sit behind my desk, and stare into space, trying to remember what I need to do today.

$\sim$

I finally focused long enough to start catching up on phone calls and paperwork. Stu walks in just as I'm biting into my roast beef sandwich. The most solid food I've had in over a week.

"Hi Joshua. Do you have a minute?"

"Sure. Sit down." I put my sandwich aside.

"Keep eating. Don't let me stop you. I wanted to go over some of the details for the fundraiser. Hiram Johnson has agreed to be our speaker. I have quotes from three different hotels. Why don't you look them over and see what you think?"

I glance at the figures. "These are high. Isn't there anything cheaper?"

"Not on a Saturday in May. We're competing with graduation parties and wedding receptions. These three have the best quality for the money. The figures include food, drinks, and musicians, of course."

I nod, concentrating on my sandwich. "Of course."

"Is something wrong? Is your brother back in the hospital?"

I've worked with Stu for four years. We've visited each other's homes. He came to Luqman's college graduation. Aisha and I went to the hospital to see their newborn daughter. Our relationship goes beyond the office.

"He is, but it's not just that. Let me ask you something. Do you ever feel angry?"

"Sure I do. This morning, I nearly yelled at my son for spilling his cereal. It was an accident, but he almost missed the school bus."

"That's not what I mean. Do you ever feel angry as a black man?"

"That's an interesting question. It must have something to do with Luqman."

"Have you talked with him about this?"

"No, but I recognize the attitude. My parents wouldn't tolerate it. Besides, when I was ten years old, I saw Barack Obama go where no other black man had, and I knew there was no excuse for failure. So what's going on with Luqman?"

"I found some literature in his room. Mostly black revolutionary. And there was a family tree, but only of my side. Some of the names were crossed out in red."

"What were you doing in his room?"

"I was too sick to do much of anything and I felt bored."

"Luqman doesn't know you've seen all this, does he?"

"No. He's almost never home. Why do you think he's angry?"

"Reading literature doesn't mean he's angry. How does he act toward you?"

"Like a rebellious teenager. He's twenty-four years old."

"Maybe he's trying to define himself as a black man, and he decided to begin with the most radical voices. Have you ever discussed race with him?"

"By the time Luqman came along, I had five other kids and a demanding job. There wasn't time. And Luqman was a handful. He wasn't the kind of child you could sit down and discuss things with."

Stu nods. "I can see that. I'm wondering about the significance of the family tree. What do you know about your heritage?"

"Practically nothing. My father left when I was a baby. I never knew his family." I don't like talking about my background. "Luqman is working on his master's thesis, but he won't tell me his topic. Could it have something to do with what I found in his room?"

"You'll have to ask him."

"I should do that, shouldn't I?"

"It's always good to keep the lines of communication open."

"Lately, he's been impossible to talk to."

"My father still doesn't tolerate attitude. Sometimes you have to be tough."

"Won't that drive him away?"

"Listen, Joshua, I know you love your son, but you can't let him intimidate you. Don't allow him to talk back or pull any of that racial crap."

I raise my eyebrows. Stu isn't usually that direct. "You know boys like him, don't you?"

"A few hang around my neighborhood. I have no use for them. But I don't think that's where Luqman is. Talk to him, and remember which one of you is the father."

In spite of his youth, Stu often shows good insight. That's why we hired him. "Thanks. I'll think about it."

"My son, Travis, is nearly eleven. It doesn't get easier as they get older, does it?"

"No. Not yet."

∾

I'm still coughing so I won't go see Brad today. I need to get home. Luqman and I are overdue for a serious conversation.

So are Aisha and I. I should have told her when I first sent out my resume. We don't hide things from each other. I hope she won't be too upset.

She's in the office, working at the computer. I stand in the doorway. "Assalaamu alaikum. Are you busy?"

"I'm writing a letter to the parents. I thought the flu season was over but four of my students were out sick today. Two mothers told me they're afraid to send their kids to school tomorrow. Our classrooms are disinfected every night, and I make the kids wash their hands frequently. The principal said we would have to close the school if too many kids are absent."

"I won't bother you then. Let me know when you have some free time."

She looks up. "Is something wrong, Isa?"

"No. We just need to talk. Would you like me to put some dinner together?"

"That would be great. I brought a lot of work home tonight."

I go to the kitchen and find spaghetti noodles and a jar of spaghetti sauce. I used to cook from scratch, but I had more energy then. Jarred sauce is good enough, and it will give me time to catch up on the news.

Aisha sits in front of the computer all evening, even eating her spaghetti at the desk. I watch the news and doze a little. We pray. She's still typing when I trudge upstairs.

"I'll be there soon, hon, and we can talk."

By the time she walks into the room, I'm nearly asleep. She touches my shoulder. "Do you want to talk now?"

"Later," I groan.

Kyle's Family

Last week was rough. I really didn't think Dad would make it.

On Saturday evening, he had a slight fever. Mom wanted to call the doctor, but Dad just took some aspirin and went to bed, convinced he'd feel okay in the morning. On Sunday morning, he was burning up. Matt put Dad in the wheelchair and got him to the hospital.

All week, I split my time between work and the hospital. Faiqa was afraid I'd pass the flu to the babies. The few times I did come home she wouldn't let me hold them, not even after I showered. I spent every night in Dad's room, sleeping in my wheelchair. It was better for everybody, even though my shoulders ached from sitting up all night.

Dad's recovery came as quickly as his illness. The fever broke, and he opened his eyes. By the end of the day, he was starting to sound like himself. I don't want to overuse the word, but I look at that as a miracle.

Now Dad is bugging everybody to let him go home. He's still too weak, though. I'm tempted to raise the hospice suggestion because I want him to be somewhere safe and sanitary. Bacteria and viruses are everywhere. It would be better if he were in a controlled environment.

I mentioned my concerns to Mom last night while Dad slept.

"I agree," she said. "But you know what that would do to your father. As hard as it is, we have to let him be the one to make the decisions."

I always knew she was strong but, still, she amazes me.

〜

Now that Dad is getting better, I can concentrate on my family again. Nathifa is asleep. Nashwa smiles at me. "What are you looking at, little girl? Are you my baby? Are you?" I kiss her soft cheek. She grabs hold of my beard and won't let go. "Ouch! That hurts. Come on, Nashwa, I'm not kidding."

Faiqa laughs. "She loves to pull my hair."

"This little girl has a strong grip," I say, gently prying her fingers loose. "Maybe she'll be a tennis pro."

"Or a surgeon."

Yusuf is lying on a blanket on the floor, practicing rolling over. He rolls off the blanket. I hand Nashwa to Faiqa and scoop up my son. "Where are you going, little guy?"

He fusses, waving his little arms. I hold him on my shoulder, and he cries more. I bounce him. "What do you want?"

"He wants to go back on the floor."

I set him down on his blanket, and he starts scooting across the floor. "Keep going, Yusuf. One day you'll find the end zone."

Faiqa stares at me until I look at her. "What?"

"You really were a jock, weren't you?"

"Sure was. I had the jacket, the cheerleader, everything."

"I wouldn't have given you a second look back then."

"Well, I guess it's good that I have this old thing to slow me down." I pat my wheelchair.

"That's not what it is. You're just too smart to be a jock."

I'm not sure what she meant by that, but I lean over to kiss her anyway.

〜

Nathifa has just finished eating. Her brother and sister are asleep in their cribs. I change her diaper. She whimpers. "I know. Yusuf

doesn't like getting his diaper changed either. But we're almost done."
I finish up, pull on her clean clothes, and take her to Faiqa in the bedroom. We stare at our daughter.

"Do you think she'll be okay, Khalil? She's still so small."

"You're the doctor. What do you think?"

"I can't look at her case objectively. Next week, I'll talk with her
pediatrician and see what she says. What if she is developmentally dis-
abled? What will we do?"

"I have a little experience with disabilities, and I'm always willing to learn. Between the two of us, I'm sure we can get her through
this."

"You won't love her less than you love the others?"

"Are you kidding?" I grin. "Do you love me less? Maybe you'd like
to trade me in for another model. A jock, maybe."

She swats my arm. "Don't be silly. You know I'd never marry a
jock."

Nathifa coos. "Do you want some attention?" I nuzzle her cheek.

We snuggle in bed together—Faiqa, our littlest daughter, and
me.

Luqman: Dreams

To think is to differ.

—Clarence Darrow

I'm sorry my dad got sick, but the whole thing left me feeling disgusted. First, there was Muhammad. He had the perfect chance to reprise his role as "good son," sitting with Dad in the morning, bringing him soup, reading Qur'an to him. That's why I kept my distance. What chance did I have? Dad would simply compare us, like he always has, and conclude that no matter what I did, I could never measure up to my brother.

Muhammad rubbed it in, too. On Friday night, he was there in the kitchen when I walked in. "Where have you been?"

"I don't know why you would care."

"Dad's been really sick, and you haven't gone in to see him once. Don't you care about anybody except yourself?"

I walked away. There's no way to talk to that kind of ignorance.

That's not the only problem I had this week. I guess Dad got bored or something, so he went snooping around in my room. He moved my papers and some of my books. He probably didn't think I'd notice. As soon as he gets well, I'll get a lecture about my taste in literature, though he probably hasn't heard of half the books I read.

They think they know me, but they don't know anything. Neither of them knows that I've gone to see Uncle Brad in the hospital every night. Only Kyle and Matt know that. I sat by his bed, praying and hoping that he'd get better. I wanted to recite Qur'an for him because I think he would have liked it, but I've always had trouble memorizing the Qur'an, and I'm not that smooth in reading Arabic. I did talk to him though. I told him how much I needed him to get better. I think he heard me.

He's awake and talking now. Sometimes he's sleeping by the time I get there, but sometimes he's waiting for me. Tonight he asked me about my plans.

"What will you do with all that education? You could teach or even go into politics."

I didn't study political science to become a part of the system. I only wanted to understand it better. "I'm not sure yet. Whatever I do, I want to make a difference in the world."

"There are many ways to do that."

"I don't want to imitate what other people have done. It's not working. What I want is to find a solution to the most pressing problems of our society and then implement it."

"It sounds like you have big plans."

"No plans yet, but I have dreams. They're still taking shape."

He nodded and stifled a yawn. "Follow your dreams, Luqman. If I could go back to when I was your age, that's what I would have done."

He needed to rest. "I need to go. I'll see you tomorrow, Uncle Brad."

"I'm looking forward to it."

I touched his arm and then, because it seemed like I should, I kissed him on the forehead. Immediately, I felt embarrassed. Without looking back, I quickly left the room.

Work Challenges

Choose a job you love, and
you will never have to work a day in your life.

—Confucius

Joshua: Part One

The Islamic organization in Houston called this morning. They want me to fly out for an interview next Tuesday. Tonight, I must talk with Aisha.

During lunch, I search for information about Houston. It's much warmer than Chicago. They have Islamic schools. We would be close to the Gulf of Mexico, which sounds much more inviting than Lake Michigan. It's a big city, so they probably have the same traffic problems we have here, but I wouldn't have to drive in the snow and ice. And their economy is better. Maybe Jamal and his family could join us.

I call Aisha at 3:30 PM. Her students have gone home. She should be sitting at her desk, getting ready for tomorrow. But she doesn't answer.

I try again at four and call every fifteen minutes. She finally answers at 4:30 PM. "What's wrong, hon?"

"Where were you all this time?"

"We have teachers' meetings every Wednesday. What's so urgent? Is it Brad?"

"No. I'd just like to take my wife out for dinner tonight. What do you think?"

"In the middle of the week?" She pauses. "What did you do?"

"What are you talking about?"

"You wouldn't take me out for dinner on a weekday unless there's something to celebrate or you did something. Which is it?"

"It's a little of both. So what do you think?"

"I still have some work to do around my classroom, and I should do some grading this evening. Can it wait?"

"It could, but this is something I should have discussed with you a few weeks ago. I don't want to wait too long."

She sighs. "I can do the grading tomorrow during my free period. Okay, I'll be home around five. We can leave then."

Five is a little early for me, but I'd better grab this chance. "Okay, hon. I'll see you at five." Now that my cough has died down, I need to go see my brother. Maybe Aisha and I can visit together after dinner, if it's not too late.

~

I take her to an Italian restaurant not far from our home. It's one of her favorites. We give the waitress our orders.

"You can tell me now, Isa. What is it?"

All the way home, I thought about how to convince her. "You know I don't like the cold. It's not healthy for any of us. And I'm having troubles at work."

"Every job is difficult, especially these days. The economy is rough. You're not saying you want to retire, are you?"

"It's not a good time. I have a bigger problem. They're asking me to do something wrong, and I don't see any way out of it."

"What's going on, Isa. What are you hiding from me?" I don't like the way she said that.

"We've been busy. I haven't had time to talk with you about these things."

"You have time now."

First, I tell her about the fundraiser and Gameel's subtle ultimatum. "We've avoided fundraisers all these years because of the alcohol, but this time, there's no way out."

"Why didn't you tell me sooner? I could have helped you find a solution. At least, I could have made du'a."

"I know. So, between the fundraiser, the ultimatum, and the weather I decided to follow Jamal's example and look outside of Chicago for a job. I sent my resume to a few places, and this morning, I got a call from an Islamic organization in Houston. They want me to come for an interview next Tuesday."

"What?" Her voice is loud. A few people look over. "You decided we were going to move without consulting me? What were you thinking?"

"You were busy, and then I got sick. There was never the right time."

"You had plenty of time. We've always discussed things. Do you think you can move this family without first talking to me?"

"They have Islamic schools in Houston so you could keep teaching. The weather is warmer. The economy is better. Jamal may consider moving down there, too."

"I'm sure their schools are good, but I have been with my school for over twenty years. Do you want me to leave behind all my friends and former students? Not to mention our family. My brother is here. My mother is in Moline. And what about your brother? Will you abandon Brad when he needs you most?"

"Brad is dying. He made it through this last crisis, but we know he won't be around much longer. It will be easier for me to leave Chicago than stay here without my brother."

"We're going to walk out on Beth and the boys after they've lost their husband and father? What are you thinking, or are you even thinking at all?"

I close my eyes and try to find the right words. When I open my eyes, I reach for her hand. "I'm doing this for us, Aisha. In a few years, we can retire and have the life we've always wanted. We'll go to the beach and bask in the sun. No more snow. We've raised our family and paid our dues. It's our turn now."

She pulls away from me. "I never knew you could be so selfish. You're going to turn your back on your family, and my family, and think only of yourself. Go right ahead, Joshua. Move to Houston. I'm staying in Chicago." She crosses her arms and looks out the window at passing cars.

The waitress brings our food. I nod. She leaves quickly. I pick up my fork and try to get excited about my stuffed ravioli. It's no use. I lay the fork down and stare at the back of my wife's head.

After a minute or two, Aisha turns to her food and begins quietly eating. I do the same.

Three bites into my meal, I break the silence. "I'll give you another good reason for leaving Chicago. Luqman. Haven't you noticed his strange behavior? He's secretive, and his attitude is way out of line. And his room is full of revolutionary literature. I'm afraid he'll get himself into trouble, if he hasn't already. He could be a member of the FOM."

She doesn't look at me, but continues eating. "FOM? What's that?"

"It's in the news."

"I'm too busy working. I don't have time for the news."

That wasn't necessary. "They call themselves the 'Friends of Muhammad' but they don't promote Islam. They go around picking fights with anyone who doesn't agree with them. They started out agitating other Muslims. For the last couple of months, they've fought the Young Pilgrims. Some have been hurt, and others were arrested."

"That doesn't sound like something Luqman would do. He's busy writing his thesis."

"He came home one night with a black eye and some story about running into the wall at Zaid's place. And do you have any idea what his thesis is about? I'd sure like to know."

"It's about racism in early twentieth century Chicago. Umar helped guide his research. If you don't know what's going on with your son, I'd say that's your fault, not his."

"I try, but he always pulls that attitude on me."

"And you think forcing him to move to Houston will solve the problem? It would only make things worse. He's twenty-four years old. He can make his own decisions."

"He can't even support himself." I rub my forehead. "Listen, I don't want to argue about Luqman. This is a great opportunity for us, Aisha. I'd work with an Islamic organization and not worry about fundraisers with wine. We'd come back to see our friends and family." Not in the winter, though. "Houston has an active Muslim community. I'm not getting any younger, either. No one in my family has lived past seventy. In ten years, you could bury me and come back to Chicago if you want. Just give me this."

She shakes her head. "Joshua Adams, you are impossible. How long did it take you to come up with all these arguments?"

"I've been working on them since I got the phone call from Houston this morning. Why? Are you convinced?"

"No. And I'm not planning on becoming a widow, either, so you can forget about that. Why didn't you talk to me about this earlier?"

"Because I knew you'd disagree."

"You were right." She sighs heavily. "Let's pray about this. Go to the interview and see what happens. At least you'll get a short vacation out of it."

"You're not angry?"

"I'm upset that you didn't come to me. We're partners, Isa. You know that. But if I let little things like this upset me, I would have divorced you long ago."

I'm not sure how to take that. Did she just insult me? It doesn't matter. "Thanks for understanding, hon." She lets me hold her hand. "You won't be sorry."

"I got an Italian dinner out of it. Is there anything else you need to tell me?"

"No, that's it."

"Good. And don't make yourself crazy worrying about Luqman. He's not stupid. Trust him to make the right decisions."

I know he's not stupid, but I'm not sure I trust him these days. I stuff a ravioli in my mouth. I need to shut up and enjoy this time with my wife.

Joshua: Part Two

By Saturday, my cough is nearly gone. The ginger helped. Now I can visit Brad.

Aisha comes with me. "I wasn't much help to Beth this time. I'm glad she has Melinda." She shakes her head. "Can you imagine if we're in Houston when Brad dies?"

She's been doing that lately—making little disapproving comments. We're not arguing, but this isn't much better. I ignore her remark and keep walking toward the intensive care unit, stopping at the nurses' desk. "We're here to see Brad Adams. He's my brother."

A nurse smiles. "Does your brother always complain like that?"

"That's Brad. Which room is he in?"

"He's been moved out of the intensive care unit." She types his name into the computer. "You can find him in room 274. Tell him Mia said hi."

Mia can't be more than twenty-five. My brother must be feeling much better.

After a few twists and turns, we find the room. It sounds like there's a party going on.

Chris and Melinda are here. So are Kyle, Matt, and Emily. Beth is standing by Brad's side, as she always has. I knock and walk in.

"Assalaamu alaikum. It sounds like everyone is having a good time."

"Walaikum assalaam. Joshua! It's great to see you. Come over here for a hug."

"That had better wait, Brad. I don't want to make you sick again. How are you feeling?"

"I'm great. I hope you're here to help me escape. They're holding me hostage."

"You got out of the intensive care unit at least."

"Staying in the hospital will kill you. Tell Beth I need to go home."

"You don't remember how sick you were," says Beth, rolling her eyes.

Brad looks at me. "Do you see what I have to put up with? If I'm going to be dead in a few weeks, I might as well enjoy myself."

"Don't joke about that," says Chris. "We thought we'd lost you."

"You're not going to get rid of me that easily."

"So, Brad, are you still going to beat me at soccer this summer."

"If I make it that long."

"I plan to start training soon. You'd better be ready."

He snickers. "You won't beat me this time, Joshua, so you can keep on dreaming."

"What makes you think I'm going to let you break my record?"

"You don't have to let me do anything. You won't have a choice."

"At least you weren't training while I was sick. That wouldn't have been fair."

"Of course it would. You snooze, you lose."

I haven't heard that one in years. "So how are the grandkids?"

"I wish I could see them. Kyle says they're getting bigger every day."

"And active," says Kyle. "Even Nathifa is keeping us busy."

I breathe deeply, suppressing a cough. "I'm still worn out from that flu."

"I told you all that junk you eat would catch up with you."

"You were right." A cough escapes. Matt brings me a chair. I do need to sit. "Thanks."

"Do you want me to call the doctor and get you checked into the hospital?" Brad taunts.

"Why? So you can get out of here and start practicing behind my back? I'm not going to give you the edge."

It's good to be talking with my brother again. He looks good, too. In spite of everything, maybe he could beat me this summer.

Joshua: Part Three

Aisha didn't say much during breakfast. It wasn't until she was ready to leave for work that she gave me a hug and whispered, "Have a safe trip."

I don't have to be at the airport for another hour. I get dressed, carry my briefcase downstairs, and sit down to catch up on the news. It's all bad. I wish Muhammad's light-hearted reports aired in the morning. I could use a little entertainment.

I'll have to drive myself to the airport. No one knows about the interview except Aisha. Stu knows I'm going out of town, but I'll leave it to him to guess why.

I was born on Chicago's South Side. I've traveled to Pakistan, Mexico, and Makkah, but I've always returned to my hometown. I don't know how to live somewhere else. Am I too old to learn?

~

I don't really like flying, though I've done quite a bit of it. We should be landing soon. It will be nice to touch earth again.

I grip the armrest as the plane comes in for the landing. Nobody knows how uneasy I feel when I fly alone. When I took Jennifer to Pakistan, I was her brave, strong Dad. When Aisha and I fly together, I calmly grip her hand. I wasn't always this nervous. It must have started after my mother and stepfather died in a plane crash. I try not to think about their last moments.

When the plane stops, I catch my breath and stand to get my bag from the overhead compartment. While I wait for those in front of me, I have time to regain my composure and get ready for the interview. My first job interview in over fifteen years.

In the airport, I search for my contact, Basel Abbas. His name means "brave lion," but when I spot his sign, I'm surprised to see he's shorter than me and not much younger. I approach him. "Assalaamu alaikum Brother Basel. I'm Joshua Adams."

"Walaikum assalaam Brother Joshua." He greets me with a firm handshake. "It's good to meet you. Did you have an easy trip?"

"Alhamdulillah. No turbulence."

"That's good. You must be hungry. I'll take you to a Syrian restaurant. The rest of the board will meet us there."

"That's good. I like Syrian food."

"We won't spoil your appetite with an interview. That comes later. Have you ever been to Houston?"

"No, never."

While he drives to the restaurant, he asks about my wife and children. I'm tempted to tell him my life story, but I hold back, not even mentioning my three older children. This could be part of the interview.

Houston is another big city with miles of highway. And it is warm. I'm beginning to wish I'd worn a short-sleeved shirt.

Brother Basel doesn't tell me much about himself. I know he's married. There's a toddler's car seat in back. Is he an older father, or is that for a grandchild? I don't ask.

$\sim$

The restaurant is nearly twenty minutes from the airport. Cars fill the parking lot. "This is one of the best places in town," he says.

We walk to a room in the back. Six others sit around a table—four men and two women. The brothers stand and offer their hands. One sister, her hair casually falling out of her pink hijab, also offers her hand, but I politely decline. "I only shake hands with men." I hope I didn't offend her.

As soon as we sit down, the food arrives. First, the hummus and bread. Then, the salad. I especially enjoy the beef kebabs served with a special sauce.

Just when I'm sure I couldn't eat another bite, the baklava is served. I never pass up baklava. The waitress brings Syrian coffee to help wash it down. I'm wired now.

Dinner included polite conversation. Some of the brothers asked me about Chicago. A sister asked about my wife and children. I described the frigid Chicago winters. "It was twenty-five when I flew out this morning."

"You'll like Houston," says Brother Basel. "We don't usually go much below fifty or much above eighty-five."

"Yes," I smile. "That sounds nice." Very nice.

$\sim$

When the dishes are cleared, they start the interview. The first question is why I want to leave my current job. On the plane, I decided to emphasize my decision to leave Chicago. I also mention that I would prefer to work with an Islamic organization.

A brother asks about my imprisonment. He's thorough. I point out that the charges of terrorism were bogus, and they were dismissed nearly twenty years ago. It occurs to me that twenty years ago today, I was sitting in solitary.

$\sim$

The interview has gone on for over an hour, and I'm sweating. The sister in the pink scarf says, "I still don't understand why you want to leave your position in Chicago. Hope Center appears to be a very successful organization. What aren't you telling us?"

"I would like to work with an Islamic organization. At Hope, I'm the only Muslim, except for one brother on the board."

"But, have you ever run an Islamic organization?"

"My brother-in-law and I managed a center before, well, before the false charges shut us down. It wasn't explicitly Islamic, but we followed the principles of Islam."

"That was over twenty years ago, wasn't it?"

"Yes. After the charges were dropped, I worked at a restaurant for a while. Then Hope hired me as program developer."

"You've had a long career at Hope Center. Why exactly do you wish to leave?"

I tell them about our financial situation and the upcoming fundraiser. "I don't feel comfortable compromising my faith, but Hope can't continue without this fundraiser."

"This is the first fundraiser you've scheduled in nearly six years?"

"I've been busy with other concerns, such as the homeless shelter."

"I see."

It's hot in here. Right now, I would welcome one of those chilly Lake Michigan breezes.

A brother speaks. "Faith Foundation works with people of all backgrounds. Legally, we cannot discriminate against anyone. We don't serve wine at our fundraisers, but raising funds would be a major part of your responsibility at Faith. Am I to understand that you haven't raised any funds for Hope Center in your time as director?"

I don't like that question, but I feel more confident speaking with the brother. "I keep an active donor list. Some of our supporters have helped us through recent crises brought on by the severe Chicago winter. Between the harsh weather and high unemployment in Chicago, we've had a very rough year."

"And you want to walk away when the organization needs you?" the pink-scarved sister challenges me.

I've thought about this. "We have a very qualified individual who could take over."

The brother continues. "Do you have experience in applying for grants, and have you been successful in obtaining grant funds?"

"Absolutely. We wouldn't have survived without grants."

Brother Basel looks around the table. "Are there any more questions?" Everyone's quiet. "In that case, I'd like to thank you, Joshua, for coming to meet with us." He glances at his watch. "We don't need to be at the airport for another two hours. I'll take you to our offices and give you the tour." He dismisses the group. The men come to say goodbye. The woman in the pink scarf avoids me. I know where I stand with her. I'm not so sure about the others.

Brother Basel drives me to a two-story building in a commercial area about ten minutes away. "Welcome to Faith Foundation. Would you believe we started out in a brother's basement? We've come a long way in thirty years, and we hope to continue growing."

He leads me through a succession of offices. Workers stop to greet me. Not all are Muslim. It's nice and very professional, but it lacks the spirit of Hope Center.

I board the plane at 5:15 PM. In about two and a half hours, we'll arrive at O'Hare. I should be home by 8:30 PM or so, depending on the traffic.

It's been a long day. While we wait for take-off, I lean back and close my eyes.

Houston is nice, but I'm not going to get this job. Not if the woman in the pink scarf has anything to say about it, and I'm sure she will.

Do I want to go through this again? What would I do differently?

Aisha is standing by the front door when I walk in. She kisses me. "How did it go?"

"Were you waiting for me?"

"I missed you. How did it go?"

"I don't think they'll offer me the job. It doesn't seem like my kind of place."

"Alhamdulillah," she says softly.

"What should I do when my wife is rooting against me?" I laugh. "Did I mention that I sent my resume out to a few other places?"

"No, you didn't."

"If they call, would you mind if I went for an interview?"

"You can go if you want, but I still don't want to move. Are you hungry?"

Lunch was hours ago. "What do you have?"

"Spaghetti. Come with me." She takes my hand.

Chicago is cold, but I have a warm home to return to.

Joshua: Part Four

The place in Arizona just called and scheduled me for an interview. Dreaming of sunshine and cactuses—or is it cacti?—I turn to the computer to learn more about Flagstaff. They get snow there, and their winters are cold. If we're going to move, we have to go to someplace warm. I call back and cancel, telling them I have a job offer. It's a lie, and I don't like lying, but isn't it better than admitting that I didn't know Flagstaff is in the mountains?

∼

I don't have time to think about a new job right now. Michael and his family are coming next Wednesday. I don't have any vacation time left, and my sick days are nearly gone, but I will be at the airport to see my son. I'll work this weekend to make it up.

Jennifer never called back. She must be busy. I know what kind of chaos four children can bring to a household. On Friday night, I'll try calling again. It will be Saturday morning there, and things should be quieter.

Chris left for Arkansas yesterday. Brad is out of the hospital now. On my way home Thursday, I stop to see my brother.

Beth meets me at the door and hands me something that looks like a surgical mask. She's wearing one, too.

"Put this on. I'm not taking any more chances."

The white mask has loops that slip over my ears. It's a little uncomfortable, but I'd rather wear this than make my brother sick again.

Brad is sitting on his favorite couch, with carseats all around him. He has a baby in his arms.

"Assalaamu alaikum. Which one is that?"

"This is my little princess Nathifa. Isn't she beautiful?"

She's still very small, but she does have a sweet face, surrounded by curly black hair. I look closer and laugh.

"She looks like you, Brad. Without the beard and smirk, of course."

"See? I told you, Beth. We were looking at some of my baby pictures the other day, and that's exactly what I said."

"I hope her disposition is better than yours," Beth says quietly.

"I heard that," says Brad.

I look around. "Where are the others?"

"Faiqa is nursing Nashwa in the kitchen. Emily and Zakariya are at her parents' house. And Yusuf's over in the corner. He thinks he can crawl. We tried to make him stay on the blanket, but he scooted across the floor."

I walk over to the baby and pick him up. He squirms. "You're really going places, aren't you, buddy?"

Yusuf scowls for a moment, then lets loose with a scream. He wiggles, trying to get free.

"What does he want? Do you think he's hungry?"

"He wants to get back on the floor. Try it. You'll see."

I put the baby down on his stomach. He continues to scoot.

"It looks like Kyle got his football player."

"It's too early for that," says Faiqa, walking into the living room. She's wearing a mask, too. "How are you, Uncle Joshua? Are you feeling better?" She places a sleeping Nashwa in one of the car seats.

"Alhamdulillah, I'm much better now. I'm sorry I couldn't visit the babies. We'll come again soon, insha Allah.

"We hope the whole family can come for dinner a week from Saturday, including Michael and your other children."

"That sounds great. Michael will be happy to see everyone."

"I'm looking forward to meeting him and his wife. In Egypt, our families are very close. Kyle has met all of my relatives, but after twelve years of marriage, I still haven't met all of his. I understand, though, why Michael left. That was a very brave decision."

"It's hard to have him so far away."

"Michael always called me his favorite uncle," says Brad. "He only has two uncles, though. I'll never forget that time I spent with him in Worcester."

"He misses you as much as any of us," I say. "I know he's anxious to see you."

Brad kisses Nathifa and looks up at his daughter-in-law. "They grow up very quickly. Enjoy them."

We're all quiet for a moment. I don't know what everyone else is thinking. I'm remembering happier times with Brad. I hope we have a few more left.

Yusuf's cry breaks through the silence. He has lodged himself into a corner. Faiqa runs to him. "You silly boy. Don't cry. Mama's here." She kisses him and carries him into the kitchen.

I pat Brad's hand. "I'd better go. It's good to see you. You're looking good."

"I'd feel better if Beth didn't make everyone wear those ridiculous masks."

"Don't worry," she says. "When we go out, you'll be the one wearing the mask."

He scowls and mutters something under his breath. Brad is back.

≈

My work has suffered lately, and I'm not sure why. Before we went on Hajj, I was focused and determined. Everything has seemed harder since we came back. There was the severe weather and the budget crisis, and then Brad's illness. The fundraiser and Luqman added to the pile. Every morning, I sit in my chair for ten minutes, wondering where to start.

Stu's enthusiasm hasn't wavered, and I'm thankful for that. He keeps me going. If this fundraiser is successful, it will be due entirely to Stu's efforts.

He walks in on Friday morning with an update. "We need to book the hotel, Joshua. These are my figures. What do you think?"

I study the pages and wince. "We don't have this kind of money."

"Barnett will advance us the funds we need for expenses. He's sure we can raise five or six times this amount."

"I hope he's right. Call this one. It looks like it's the cheapest." It's still way too much. I wish Doug would just donate the money and forget about the fundraiser.

"You need to be in on the details. I'll use your phone and put it on speaker."

Stu barely states his request before the hotel manager cuts him off. "We're booked for that weekend."

"What about the weekend before? Could you check?"

"We're booked from the beginning of May through the end of September. You should have called earlier." There's a click.

Stu shrugs. "I'll have to call the next one."

We end up with the most expensive hotel. "We'll have to raise the price of the tickets," says Stu.

"Or, we could have it in the Hope Center gym."

"I know you're kidding. Besides, I just made the reservation. It will cost us to back out now. I'm glad we were able to get the twenty-fourth. Reverend Johnson may not be available on another date."

"What else needs to be done?"

"The hotel will take care of the entertainment and the decorations along with the food and drinks. That's major. Now we need to print up the tickets and get busy selling them."

"You wouldn't happen to know a cheap printer, would you?"

"My sister got a good deal on her wedding invitations two years ago. I'll ask her."

"I'll start making contacts. We're going to have to sell a lot of tickets."

"Stop worrying, Joshua. We can do this."

I'm worried about not doing the fundraiser, and I'm worried about doing it. Maybe I should call Flagstaff and tell them the "job offer" fell through.

"I appreciate your commitment on this, Stu. You're doing a good job."

"We don't have a choice, do we?"

No, we don't. That's what makes this so hard for me.

Luqman: Manifesto

Nothing could be worse than the fear that one had given up too soon, and left one unexpended effort that might have saved the world.

—Jane Addams

My parents are busy and distracted. I don't know what's going on with them, but they hardly notice me these days. I like the freedom.

Uncle Brad finally came home from the hospital. Every time I visit him, Aunt Beth makes me wear a mask. If it makes my uncle live longer, I'm all for it.

He doesn't like the mask, though. "I keep telling your aunt that I'm well now, but she won't believe me."

"She wants to keep you safe."

He grunts. "I'll remember you said that the next time you complain about your father's rules."

This is one of the things I love about Uncle Brad. Like Uncle Umar, nothing gets past him. But Uncle Psychologist is dark and grim. Uncle Brad is fun to be with.

≈

I've been out of school for nearly four months, and I haven't been able to come up with a plan. It's always been just around the corner, taunting me.

Last week, I had a dream. I don't remember the details, but when I woke up, my ideas began to solidify. I jumped out of bed and started writing them down.

Over the last few days, I've refined them. This is what I've come up with.

César Chávez stood up for the farm worker, and now the politicians are afraid of the Hispanics. It took longer for us blacks to make it, but we finally did, through a series of stops and starts and the leadership of a few men with real vision. Though it sounds stereotypical, you could say that the Asians conquered through technology, and the Jews took over the entertainment industry. As I read about the accomplishments of others, the question nagged me: What have Muslims done?

The answer? Nothing. We have doctors and lawyers and engineers who live in their big houses in the suburbs, and we have people like my father who struggle in non-profits and try to make a difference. We have writers, like my sister, Jennifer, and film directors. But we haven't made an impact. Not here in this country, and not anywhere on earth for the last five or six hundred years, though some have tried.

Muslims are weak. Petitions haven't worked. Neither have marches, meetings, or mind-numbing symposiums.

There is only one way to change our condition, and that is through armed struggle. I'll be the one leading the charge. The scientists, artists, and philanthropists may criticize me, but later they will follow the trail I blaze, grateful that somebody finally stood up and threw off the yoke of our oppression.

Parenting Nightmares

The joys of parents are secret, and so are their griefs and fears:
They cannot utter the one, nor will they utter the other.

—Francis Bacon

Joshua: Part One

Aisha and I spent a quiet weekend at home. Maryam was at the library most of the time. I haven't seen Luqman all week, and I have no idea what he's doing, but I'm trying not to care. I couldn't get hold of Jennifer. I called on Friday, but there was no answer. I miss my daughter.

After Aisha goes to bed on Sunday night, I stay up and watch the news. Muhammad's piece on baby rabbits airs. He told me about it on Friday. I know he wants to report on tragedy, but he doesn't understand how precious good news has become.

And there's enough tragedy in tonight's news. A train crash in Colorado killed at least twenty-three, with more still missing. A tornado touched down in Arkansas, wiping out an entire town. I hope Chris and Melinda are okay. It's too late to call.

Here in Chicago, seven African children died early this morning in a house fire while their immigrant mother was drunk at a bar. And there was another clash between the FOM and the Young Pilgrims. That makes four so far this year, and it's only March. Someone needs to stop the FOM.

Payroll needs to go out tomorrow, and I have to get busy selling tickets. Just thinking about it makes me tired.

~

I must have dozed off. The lights are on, and I haven't checked the doors. I'm tempted to stay downstairs tonight because the stairs look especially steep, but if I sleep on the couch, I'll wake up with a sore neck.

First, I check the back door, setting the deadbolt and slipping on the chain. We haven't been bothered, but in times like these, no one is safe. I make sure all the curtains are drawn and all the lights are out, except for the one in the front entryway that we keep burning all night. I'm locking the deadbolt on the front door when I hear footsteps on the front porch. I peek outside.

It's Luqman. I step aside and wait while he unlocks the door. He walks in quietly and turns around to engage the chain and deadbolt.

While he stands at the door, in the dark, I approach him silently and touch his shoulder.

He spins around, pulling something from his pocket as he turns. He shouts out and pokes me in the stomach.

Confused, I look down. He has a gun aimed at me. A gun? His finger is on the trigger.

"Luqman. Luqman! What are you doing?"

He startles and looks up. "Dad?" He quickly stuffs the gun in his pocket.

I gasp. My heart races. I stumble against the banister and try to catch my breath. "What are you doing? You could have killed me."

He looks down. "Sorry. I didn't know it was you." He turns toward the stairs. "Don't worry. I'll see you in the morning."

"What do you mean, don't worry? You nearly shot me. What's going on?"

He slouches, hands in his pockets, in his usual pose. "It's nothing, Dad. Don't worry about it. Why are you still awake?"

I close my eyes and remember the words of Prophet Muhammad. *"Don't be angry."* What would the Prophet do in a situation like this? "What do you mean it's nothing?" I try to stay calm, though my heart still beats wildly and all my muscles are tense. "How can you stand there and say it's nothing? Where did you get that gun?" I feel like screaming, but I need to stay calm. And I don't want to wake Aisha.

He sighs loudly. "I'm twenty-four years old, okay?"

What does that have to do with anything? "You didn't answer my question. Why do you have a gun? Where did you get it?"

"You know how it is, Dad. Times are rough. A couple weeks ago, I nearly got carjacked. I fought him off, but next time I might not be so lucky. I have to defend myself."

Is that true? "Are there carjackings at the university?"

"Sure there are. All the time. You know what I'm talking about. Don't act naïve."

I stare at his pocket. "Is it loaded?"

"Of course it's loaded. What kind of question is that?"

I try to catch his gaze, but he looks away. "You nearly killed me."

"You shouldn't go around sneaking up on people. I'm sorry, okay? Let's just forget about it. Don't say anything to Mom. You know how she is about guns."

That's all he has to say? Why can't I break through his attitude? "I still don't understand why you need a gun."

"You work on the South Side, and you don't understand? Then I'm not going to stand here and explain it to you. I've got to get to bed. Goodnight." He starts going up the stairs.

I'm angry and tense, and I need some answers. "What do you know about the FOM?"

He spins around. "I don't know anything about the FOM."

"What is going on with you, Luqman? You're out late at night, and we never know where you are. Now you're carrying a gun. If it's not the FOM, what is it?"

He shakes his head. "Stop with the accusations and get to bed. You've got to trust me. Can you do that?" He waves his hand, dismissing me. "I'm tired. See you later."

I go back to the family room and take a few minutes to calm myself. Before going to bed, I stand and pray again. Later, as I trudge up the stairs a verse of the Qur'an runs through my mind: *"Your Lord has decreed that you worship none but Him, and that you be kind to parents, whether one or both of them attain old age in your life, say not to them a word of contempt, nor repel them, but address them in terms of honor. And, out of kindness, lower to them the wing of humility, and say: My Lord! Bestow on them your Mercy even as they cherished me in childhood."* I quietly recite the verse from Surah al Isra.

When I was young, before becoming a Muslim, I caused my mother so much grief. Is this my punishment, after all these years?

Luqman

I almost shot my father.

My heart was beating furiously when I pulled out that gun, and I was ready to use it. But, I took a second to focus, and this time, that second saved my life. In another circumstance, that second could have killed me.

When Dad confronted me, I tried to play it cool. He doesn't know I was shaking inside. That whole thing could have gone wrong. I still shudder when I think of it.

My nerves were already tight. This afternoon, a group of Young Pilgrims attacked one of my boys. We came out in full force tonight. They didn't know what hit them. My strategy is what they used to call *Shock and Awe.* Not many people got hurt, but it taught them a lesson. I haven't had to shoot anybody yet, but I will if I need to.

I bought the gun back in January, after the Young Pilgrims harassed the Muslim sister. We taught them about mistreating our women. Some people in the Muslim community, especially the imams, are always criticizing us, but the women are glad that we brothers are finally standing up for them. Muslims have been too weak for too long. Talk of peace didn't get us anywhere. It's time for war.

My father is one of the weakest. He goes to his office and thinks he's helping people, but he has to beg for money to keep the centers running, crawling on his knees to people like Hiram Johnson. He can't help anybody until he starts fighting for them. But look where he came from. He's the son of scum and the grandson of scum. And he doesn't care. I never met anyone so clueless. Thank God I'm nothing like him. White and weak. A face that turns red when he's angry. A will that wilts in the face of opposition.

I didn't want to shoot him though. Before going to bed, I carefully unload the gun and place it in my dresser drawer. I turn off the lights and climb into bed, but the scene keeps playing in my mind. I don't think I'll sleep tonight.

Joshua: Part Two

During breakfast, I mentally replay my confrontation with Luqman. He didn't get up for the prayer. I hope he prays when he's on his own. I don't know.

"You're quiet this morning." Aisha hands me my bagel. "Is something wrong?"

Aisha doesn't like me to keep things from her, but this isn't the right time to talk about Luqman. We need to go to work soon, and

I still haven't decided if I'm going to tell her about the gun. It would upset her even more than it does me. But she needs to know.

Luqman isn't the only problem on my mind. "I'm worried about the fundraiser. I won't tell you how much it's going to cost us—the fancy hotel, the food, and the alcohol, astagfirullah. I don't see how anything good can come from it. Seriously, Aisha, I know you don't want to move, but can you give me any other suggestions?"

"Aren't there any other jobs in Chicago for you? There must be."

"Not in non-profits. They all have the same problems we do. And the main way they raise funds is to hold dinners for the wealthy. It would be the same thing all over again."

"What about the Muslim organizations?"

"None of them is hiring right now."

"Could you work in a restaurant again? I know it's a step down, but it's a job."

"I've thought about that, but there aren't too many restaurants still standing these days. You can drive down Devon and see all the boarded-up buildings. And if I have skills and experience working for non-profits, isn't that what I should be doing?"

She touches my cheek. "This is rough for you, isn't it? I agree with you about the fundraiser. We just need to keep on praying, and ask Allah for an answer."

"Would you mind if I send out my resume again?"

"Send it only to Islamic organizations. But, I hope we can stay here. This is our home."

"I know, hon." I hug her. After a moment I glance at the kitchen clock. "We'd better go. We're going to be late."

"Oh, I am late." She kisses me. "I'll see you tonight, insha Allah."

The Luqman talk can wait.

∼

All day, I've thought about it. Aisha should know about Luqman's gun. I can't afford to take her out for dinner tonight, so I leave work a little early and make a simple chicken dish with rice. By the time she walks in the door, the food is in the oven.

"Something smells great. Maryam, are you cooking? Don't you have an afternoon class?"

I stroll out of the kitchen with an apron tied around my waist. "Maryam's not here."

"Thank you, hon." She kisses me. Then she stares. "What did you do?

"Don't worry about it. We do need to talk, but that can wait. How was your day?"

She gives me one of her looks. "I don't know what you're hiding, but I guess it can wait until after dinner. Let me go change first."

That sounds good. After dinner, we'll be relaxed. She'll be somewhat prepared. We can sit down together and figure out what do to about Luqman's gun.

What can we do? He's not a child. We can't take it away from him. We won't notify the police. I don't have any proof that he's done anything wrong and, anyway, he's my son. Maybe all we need to do is talk about it.

∼

Maryam and Muhammad join us for dinner, which is all too rare these days.

Muhammad is enjoying his third chicken leg. "What do you eat when you don't come home?" I ask.

He shrugs. "I pick up a sandwich or heat a frozen pizza. Sometimes I just eat cereal."

"No wonder you're so thin," says Aisha. "Come home more often." She shakes her head. "One day you'll have to learn how to cook."

"Yeah, or I could just get married."

I raise my eyebrows. "Do you have anyone in mind?"

"No, it was just a thought."

"You won't make your wife do all the cooking, will you?" says Maryam. "The man I marry will be able to take care of himself."

"Good for you," says Aisha. "You don't need to think about marriage yet, though. Take your time. You're still young."

"You were younger than me when you got married, Mom."

"I remember those days—juggling a new marriage and my student teaching. I don't know how I managed."

"You don't regret it, do you?"

Aisha pats my hand. "Of course not. But, I hope Maryam waits a little longer. Once you have a husband and children, your life will never be the same."

"Don't worry. I won't get married until after I graduate."

"This is nice," says Aisha. "We don't eat together much anymore. I wonder where Luqman is. Do you know, Muhammad?"

"I saw him a couple days ago, but we didn't talk long. Maybe he's over at Zaid's."

"He wouldn't be there," says Maryam. "Zaid's out of town for a conference."

How would she know that? We all look at her.

"He's in St. Louis with other math geeks." She smiles. "Zaid is definitely a math geek." She finishes her food and takes her plate to the sink. "I have an observation on Thursday. Would you excuse me? I need to prepare."

"Muhammad, why don't you help me clean up?" I say. "You can go relax, Aisha. I'll talk with you after I'm finished."

"I do have some grading to do. Thanks for cooking tonight. You really should do it more often." She kisses my cheek and heads down the hallway to the office.

I quiz Muhammad while we clear the table. "You talked with Luqman? What did he say?"

"Nothing much. I came by here for some leftovers, and he was just getting in. Everyone was asleep."

"Did you ask him about that fight between the FOM and the Young Pilgrims?"

"Yeah, I asked him. He said he didn't know anything about it."

I stop and look at Muhammad. "Do you believe him?"

"I don't know, Dad. He's my brother and I don't want to believe anything bad about him, but things just don't add up."

"How long has he had a gun?"

Muhammad stops and looks at me. "About two months. How did you find out about that?"

"By accident. Did you ask him about it?"

"He said he needs it for protection. Something about an attempted carjacking."

"That's what he told me, too. Listen, Muhammad, if you know your brother is in trouble, you'd better tell me. I need to stop him before it gets any worse."

"I don't know anything for sure. It's all speculation."

"Okay. Keep talking to him. He's your little brother, and I need you to help him."

"Sure. I can do that."

As we finish cleaning Muhammad says, "Today, Dirk told me to go fly a kite."

"Seriously?"

"Yeah. I had to show our viewers how windy the Windy City was. Like they didn't know already. If he doesn't start giving me serious assignments soon, I'm out of there."

"A job is a job, Muhammad. And some people, like me, enjoy watching your pieces. It takes my mind off all the depressing news of the day."

"So you're against me now, too?"

"Do your best in whatever you have to do. That's what we've always taught you. How high were you able to get that kite?"

"It went high enough. You can watch my report on the 10:00 PM news."

"I'll do that, insha Allah."

～

Aisha is still grading papers. "I'm nearly done, hon. Why don't you watch the news while you wait? It's almost time for the prayer. After that, we can talk."

I settle into the couch and turn on the news. Muhammad's piece won't air for another two hours, but I can catch up on what's happening around the world. I plump up a cushion and lie down. The doorbell rings.

Who could that be? Do I have to get it? The bell rings again. And again.

"Okay. I'm coming." This had better be good.

I turn the knob. Heather pushes the door open.

"It's about time you answered. Were you going to leave me standing out in the cold?"

"Hi Heather. How's everything?" She still looks good. Age agrees with her.

"We need to make arrangements for Michael's visit. I was waiting for you to call and take care of it but, as usual, I had to take the initiative."

"Is Peter with you?" His presence usually calms her.

"No, he's at an art show in Denver. Are you going to invite me in, or do I have to stand out here and freeze?"

"Come on in, Heather. Sit down." *Go away and leave me alone.*

"Michael and his family will be here in less than two days. Are you aware of that?" She flounces onto the couch. "I can pick him up from the airport and take him to the condo, but I'm sure you'd like to see him also. Do you have any plans?"

"My plans are to meet him at the airport and bring him back here to stay with us."

"Are you crazy? He'll stay with me, of course. I'm his mother."

"What about his children? Aren't you worried they'll break one of your knick-knacks?"

"Those are expensive pieces of art, and Michael's children are very well behaved."

I take a deep breath. "He's my son, too, Heather, and I need to see him."

"Of course you do. That's why I came. We can work out a schedule."

Michael is a man and we shouldn't still be fighting over him. I'd better cooperate, though. It's the only way I'll get rid of Heather. "On Saturday, we're having a family dinner. Everyone is looking forward to seeing Michael."

"Saturday? You're going to take him away from me on his first weekend in town? Did it ever occur to you that I might have plans for him, too?"

"Your plans will have to wait. Kyle and his wife are hosting a dinner in honor of Michael and his family. Michael can see their triplets, too."

"Kyle? That nephew of yours? He's a father now? How did that happen?"

She always loved gossip. "Michael and his family need to be there."

"When were you planning on telling me this? You can't expect me to change everything to suit you and your family."

"Brad will be there. He's dying, Heather. Don't make this more difficult."

"That's a shame. I'm sure it's from all that drinking. He didn't fall off the wagon, did he? I wouldn't be at all surprised."

I bite my tongue and take a deep breath. "He has leukemia. It has nothing to do with his drinking. Can't we just enjoy having Michael here and take this one day at a time?"

She shakes her head and laughs. "You're the same old Joshua. I'm only trying to make this easier on everyone. Why do you always have to make everything so difficult?"

Aisha walks in—thank God she's here—and offers her hand. "Heather? I thought I heard your voice. It's so nice to see you. How have you been?"

"I'm wonderful. Peter is in Denver at an art show. Did you know our daughter Brianna runs a gallery out there? I thought about going too, but then Michael called. I can't wait to see him and his precious family."

"I can't, either. It's been years since we visited them in Mexico."

"I expected Joshua to contact me and make arrangements for Michael's visit, but I've waited for weeks without a word. Joshua just told me his family is expecting Michael at a function this weekend. It would have been nice to have advance notice."

"I hope it won't interfere with your plans, Heather. You can't imagine how important this is to Kyle, and to Brad. We don't know how much longer he'll be with us."

Heather sighs dramatically. "I'll rearrange my schedule." Her voice becomes acidic when she turns to me. "Are there any other dates I need to know about, Joshua?"

She does this just to get to me. "No, not as far as I know."

"We'll call you, Heather, and let you know." Aisha uses her teacher voice, sweet but very much in charge. "And if you have anything you'd like to discuss, you can call me. Do you still have my number?"

"Could you write that down for me again? So, Joshua, what have you been doing lately?"

"I'm working at Hope Center. Would you like to buy a ticket for our fundraiser in May?"

"You never did get a real job. Well, as long as Aisha can put up with you, I suppose it's not my place to say anything."

Aisha flashes me a look, reminding me to stay quiet. "Here's my number. Thank you for coming all this way, Heather. It was so nice to see you again. Please give my regards to Peter and Brianna. Maybe you can all come for dinner sometime while Michael's here."

"Let me know what date you have in mind. Peter won't be back for another week. He wanted to come home sooner, but that's the life of a famous artist. He has shows and interviews scheduled all week."

"I'll call you. Thank you for coming."

It takes Aisha another five minutes to get Heather out the door. My ex-wife goes on and on about her famous husband and successful daughter, and their exciting lifestyle. When she finally leaves, I collapse into the family room couch.

Aisha sits next to me, rubs my arm, and laughs a little. "She'll never change."

"Don't you want to divorce me and find a more successful husband?"

"You can't let Heather get to you, not after all these years. And you are successful, hon, in your own way. I'm very proud of you."

I close my eyes and relax in Aisha's love. She snuggles next to me. Why did I ever get mixed up with Heather?

～

After the prayer, we came upstairs. I'm nearly asleep, comforted by her closeness.

She breaks the silence. "What is it you needed to tell me?"

"Can't it wait?" I whisper.

"I don't know. Can it?"

Not really. I sit up, my arms still around her. "It's about Luqman. Don't you ever wonder where he is?"

"He says he's either at Zaid's or working on his thesis. I don't have any reason to doubt him."

"We know Zaid is out of town, so he's not there. The thing is, Aisha, I caught him coming in late last night."

"He's twenty-four years old. We can hardly hold him to a curfew."

"That's not the problem. I'd just woken up and went to check the door. When he walked in, I was standing there in the darkness and he didn't know it was me. I surprised him." I take a deep breath. The words have been running through my mind all day, but I never tried to say them out loud. "He pulled a gun on me, Aisha."

"What?" She screams and jerks out of my embrace. "A gun?"

"He was just coming in, and I surprised him."

"And he pulled a gun on you?"

"He could have shot me."

"He could have killed you." She's still screaming. "What was that boy thinking?"

"I don't know," I sigh. I wish I could understand.

"Alhamdulillah you weren't hurt." She pulls me close and hugs me tightly. "I can't believe it."

We're quiet for a few minutes. Her heart beats rapidly against my chest.

"He said he needs it for protection."

She gets out of bed, and starts shouting. "No. I don't believe a son of mine could be that stupid. That boy didn't grow up on the streets. He knows violence isn't the answer. Did you try talking to him?"

"Of course I did."

"Why didn't you take the gun away?"

"Do you want me to wrestle him for it? He's twenty-four years old, remember?"

She looks at the clock. "It's 10:30 PM. Where could he be?" She paces. "The university is closed, and Maryam said Zaid is out of town. Though I don't know how she would know that. I'll call Amal. Maybe Maryam was wrong."

"Isn't it too late to call anyone?"

"We're talking about our son. Think about it, Isa. What if someone else surprises him, like you did last night? I can't even imagine it. Let me get Amal's number. Here it is."

She takes a moment to catch her breath before entering the number. We wait.

"Assalaamu alaikum. Amal? I'm sorry to call you so late. I need to get in touch with Luqman, and I know he's usually at Zaid's apartment. What is Zaid's number?"

She nods. "Okay. Thanks for letting me know. I'm sorry to bother you. Walaikum assalaam." Aisha ends the call, sits on the bed, and grips my hand. "Her son is out of town. Where could Luqman be at this time of night?"

"I wish we could call him." He stopped carrying a phone a couple years ago. He said it interfered with his concentration.

"What should we do, Isa? Should we call the police? I'm scared."

"Let me call Muhammad."

The phone rings twice before he picks up. "Assalaamu alaikum, Dad. Is something wrong?"

"Mom and I are concerned about your brother. Could you go over to the station and see if there's been a fight?"

"I'll call over there and ask Blake. Give me a few minutes, and I'll get back to you, insha Allah. Tell Mom not to worry."

"Thanks, Muhammad." I hold my wife while we wait for his call.

～

There were no fights tonight. Muhammad offered to come and help us wait for Luqman.

At 2:30 AM, the doorknob twists as he uses his key. "Let me do the talking," says Aisha. She stands in the entry way, waiting for him. Muhammad and I look on from the family room.

The door opens. "Where have you been? It's about time you got home." She moves toward him.

"Mom. You startled me."

"Were you going to shoot me like you almost shot your father? Where's the gun, Luqman? Give it to me," she demands.

"What gun? I don't know what you're talking about,"

"Don't lie to me. Where is it?"

Luqman spots Muhammad and me. "Did Muhammad tell you I have a gun? He's always trying to get me in trouble. Muhammad, why are you telling lies on me?"

"Leave Muhammad out of this. Look at me when I talk to you, Luqman." He shrugs and raises his eyes. "I haven't checked your pockets since you were ten years old, but I'll do it if I have to. Where is the gun?"

He raises his arms. "Go ahead and search me, Mom. You won't find anything."

She stands there in her pink robe and pats him down. Her hands empty, she steps back. "Where were you?"

"I was hanging out with Zaid. What's with the questions? You can't tell me what to do."

Her hand comes across his cheek so fast that I think it surprises her. "Don't you ever think you can talk to me that way. And don't you stand there and lie to me. Where were you?"

He rubs his hand across his cheek. "Don't get upset, Mom. I was hanging out with some friends. That's all."

"Go upstairs. We'll talk about this in the morning. If I don't see you down here for Fajr, I will come up there and drag you down the steps."

"Okay." He whines. He looks like he wants to say more, but Aisha gives him her look, and he walks quickly up the stairs.

We're quiet. Muhammad breaks the silence. "What do you want me to do?"

We shouldn't have asked him to stay. We always disciplined our kids privately, away from the others. "It's late," I say. "You can sleep here if you want."

"I don't want you out on the road at this hour," says Aisha. "Go upstairs to your room."

When Muhammad's gone, I move toward Aisha. She backs away.

"I never hit any of the kids, and certainly not in the face. When I heard his back talk, I couldn't stop myself."

"Let's go get some sleep. We can deal with this in the morning."

"How will we deal with him, Isa? He's a grown man. We can't ban him from watching cartoons." She looks me right in the eye. "Are you sure you saw that gun?"

"I'm positive."

"I believe you. Maybe we should try to rest." She reaches for my hand.

We lie in bed and stare at the ceiling. What will we do about Luqman?

Luqman: Pride

I, too, sing America.
I am the darker brother.
They send me to eat in the kitchen
When company comes.
But I laugh,
And eat well,
And grow strong.

—Langston Hughes

Things are getting rough at home. I don't know how much longer I can take this.

Dad keeps badgering me. First, it was about the thesis. I finished the thesis four months ago. Then, after I was sure I had learned all I needed to know, I burned it. Somewhere in their university offices they have the diploma I never claimed. I'm finished playing their game.

Now he's all worked up over my gun. And tonight Dad dragged my brother into this. He's another loser. He looks like Dad, and thinks like Dad. He's the "good son." My father would never admit to being a racist, but it's evident in the way he treats Muhammad and me. Muhammad has always been the good one, and I've always been the trouble-maker. My brother enjoys the advantage of his white skin. We've never been close.

I knew Dad would go to Mom. He always does. He is nothing without her. He knows it, too. If not for her, he probably would have self-destructed long ago.

I refuse to bear the stain of my ancestors. I am the man my father could never be. Sometimes I actually feel sorry for him.

I hope to be like my mother. In her dark face, I see the pride of generations. She carries herself like a queen, sure of whom she is and where she wants to go. One day, when I trace her lineage back to Africa, I know I will find emperors. She's angry, but I respect that. She will not defer to me, as my father does. Confronting her is part of my growth, a necessary rite of passage as I move toward my larger purpose in life. Eventually, she will understand why I do what I must, and she will support me. Her acceptance is a prize I covet. We are of the same race, and we know each other.

She's told me the stories about her father. He had to work the system because that's what it took to survive in his day, but he also fought in his own way. This man went from the streets of East St. Louis, growing up without a father, and earned his doctorate. That took some kind of courage.

My other grandfather, on my father's side, is my enemy. He was already white, but he apparently didn't think he was white enough, so he put on some sheets and terrorized people like my mother's father. He's dead, too, but the hate didn't die with him. It's very much alive in the city of Chicago. My job is to kill it.

Tonight, I left the loaded gun in my glove compartment because I knew they would look for it. Tomorrow, they'll rush off to work and forget everything else.

Mom will lecture me before she leaves, but I need only to behave well for the next few days. If Mom knew what I was doing, she would secretly admire me for it.

I don't go looking for trouble, but I refuse to run away from it. If the Young Pilgrims or anyone else wants to mess with me, they'll get more back.

I don't sleep. There's no time. While the house is quiet, I plan my next move.

In the early morning hours, I call my main man, Hakeem. He's always awake at this time, getting ready for his job in sanitation. I whisper, not wanting my parents to hear.

"Hey, Hakeem, tell the boys I need to stay quiet for the next few days."

"Is something wrong?"

"Things are a little hot here at home. Don't worry. I got it under control."

"I know you do, man. Call me tomorrow, will you?"

"Sure I will. And kiss that little boy for me. We're doing this for him."

"That's right. I got to get to work, man. Talk to you later."

I go to the bathroom to do my business. When I'm done, I stand outside of my parents' bedroom door and make the call to prayer.

Balancing Act

Life is like riding a bicycle.
To keep your balance, you must keep moving.

—Albert Einstein

Joshua: Part One

Luqman's voice enters my dreams—not the ugly voice we heard last night, but the clear melody of his adhan. When he was young, he made the adhan all the time. He had the best voice in the family and one of the best in his school. It's been a very long time.

Aisha opens her eyes. "Is that Luqman?"

"It sounds like him." It couldn't be anybody else. Luqman's adhan is distinctive—rich and inspiring.

Before I get into the bathroom, he knocks on our door. "Assalaamu alaikum, Mom and Dad. It's time for the prayer." While I wash my face, I wonder if one lecture could bring these changes in him.

By the time we get downstairs, he's waiting, the prayer rugs lined up in the family room. I take my place in front, and Luqman makes the final call. We all bow down together.

∽

After the prayer, Luqman went back upstairs. He did wake up for Fajr, though, and without being reminded. "What do you think?" I ask Aisha.

"About what?"

"Luqman. He woke us up for the prayer. Do you think we'll see other changes?"

"It's too soon to tell. I hope he got rid of that gun. That worries me more than anything."

"Maybe he's just going through a phase."

"He's a little old for that, isn't he?"

I shrug. "When I was his age, I discovered Islam. I'm sure you remember that it took me a while to grow up. Maybe that's all this is."

"I hope so. He'd better grow up soon, before someone gets hurt."

"Stu asked me the other day when you stop worrying about your kids. His son is almost eleven."

"I hope you told him that you never stop worrying."

"Something like that." I shake my head. "Michael is nearly forty years old, and I keep thinking about his flight."

"I wish we could spend more time with him while he's here. Heather won't allow that, will she?"

"Probably not. Are you coming with me to the airport? His plane lands at 3:45 PM."

"We have teachers' meetings on Wednesdays, but I'll talk with the principal and see if I can be excused. I'll have to meet you there. You'd better take the van to work tomorrow morning in case I don't make it."

"Heather won't let Michael come back to our house. Why would I need the van?"

"I don't know, but I have a feeling you will."

I've learned to trust Aisha's intuition. "Okay. Sounds good. What about Luqman? Should we talk to him before we leave for work?"

"I don't know."

"What do your feelings tell you?"

"They're telling me we should step back a little. He got the message. Let's see what happens."

I'd rather wake him up and lay down the law, but Aisha knows better. "That's what we'll do then."

"I'd better go." She takes a last sip of her tea. "See you tonight, insha Allah."

I grab her for a quick kiss. "See you."

∼

Brad is sitting in a lawn chair on his front porch, reading. When I get out of my car, he looks up and takes off his glasses.

"Assalaamu alaikum. What are you doing out here?"

"It's a sunny day. I need to get my vitamin D."

"I thought maybe Beth kicked you out."

"She did, in a way. She's dusting, and she didn't want it to bother me."

"You're looking good."

"I haven't started exercising yet. I hope it stays warm. This is Chicago, though. We'll probably have another blizzard before we're done with it."

"Is Chris back?"

"He's coming in tomorrow. Why don't you bring Michael here on your way home from the airport? It will be great to see him."

"I'd like that, but Heather has her own ideas. Michael and his family will stay in her condo. Aisha did convince her to let Michael come to the dinner on Saturday."

"How is Heather? I haven't seen her in years."

"She looks good for her age. But she's still the same."

Brad laughs. "Still giving you a hard time, isn't she? I told you not to marry her. You wouldn't listen."

"What could I do? She was pregnant. Her father threatened to kill me. And I didn't know I'd still be paying for my mistake forty years later."

"That mistake did give you the three kids. How is Jenny? Do they plan to visit soon?"

"I called her over a month ago. The baby was screaming, and the other kids were making noise. She said she would call me back, but I haven't heard from her. I wish she could be here when Michael is."

"When I think of Michael, I still picture that young college student who helped out his old wandering uncle in Massachusetts. He's nearly forty, isn't he?"

"He's getting there."

"We're getting old, Joshua. There's no denying it."

"I don't know what happened to the years."

"Don't just stand there. Pull up a lawn chair. You're not in a hurry, are you?"

"No. I have time."

We sit and talk on his front porch until it's nearly dark. Just two old men.

~

When I walk in, Aisha is fixing dinner. Luqman is setting the table. I stare.

"Assalaamu alaikum, hon. Did you have a good day?" Aisha gives me a quick kiss. "Dinner will be ready soon. Why don't you go upstairs and change?"

Luqman is setting the table. And smiling. Am I in the right house?

~

As we're getting ready for bed, Aisha says she had a long talk with our son.

"He finally agreed to get rid of the gun. I can't blame him for wanting to defend himself, but I convinced him that it's simply too dangerous to carry a weapon. What if the carjacker got hold of it? He said he'll turn it over to the police tomorrow."

"Did he say where he got it?"

"He bought it from someone he knows at the university. He didn't say where he got the money, and I didn't press the issue."

"He didn't say anything about getting a job, did he?"

"Actually, he did. He's thinking about working with the city. He has a friend who might get him a job. Isn't that great?"

"That's one way to use his political science degree. I don't know. It all sounds good, but I'll believe it when I see it."

"Give him some credit, Isa. He's trying. I hate to see the wall that's built up between the two of you. Can't you at least meet him half-way?"

I roll over and pull my wife closer. "You're a great mother. Have I ever told you that?"

"I always like to hear it again."

We fall asleep with our arms around each other.

Joshua: Part Two

Luqman's adhan wakes me. I close my eyes and listen. What a beautiful awakening. Michael is coming today. He'll be here in about nine hours. I can't wait.

~

In the morning, I call Stu and tell him I have to leave early. "My oldest son and his family are flying in from Mexico."

"He's been gone for several years, hasn't he?"

"More than fifteen years now." I never told Stu why Michael settled there.

"I'm sure you're anxious to see him and his family. Tell Sandra to let me know if she needs anything while you're gone."

"I'll do that. Thanks, Stu."

"No problem. Talk to you later."

It's hard for me to concentrate. My most pressing task these days is selling tickets for the fundraiser. We have a little more than two months left and have sold only thirty-two tickets. We're aiming for 300. I open my list of numbers and pick up the phone.

∼

My stomach is growling. I order my sandwich and lean back in my chair. After nearly four hours of calling, I've sold only twelve tickets. Our old contacts used to come to every one of our fundraisers, and they know how much we need their support, but many can no longer afford to help.

I'll have to leave soon. O'Hare is clear across town. On my way out, I stop by to see Sandra.

"I hope you bring your family to visit us while they're here," she says. "I'd love to see your little Mexican grandchildren."

"I'll do that." If Heather agrees. "Call me if anything urgent comes up. Otherwise, I'll see you in the morning."

For two minutes, I search for my car in the parking lot before remembering that I brought Aisha's van. I climb in, adjust the mirrors, and glance at my watch. Michael will be here soon. My heart beats faster.

∼

Heather is here, carrying two shopping bags. A teddy bear peeks out from one. "I wondered if you would show up," she says. "You're cutting it close. They should be here any minute."

Their flight is due in ten minutes. They must be approaching Chicago now. I hope Aisha gets here soon. Her school isn't far away, but traffic is heavy.

"Didn't you bring something for the children?" It's Heather again, accusing as always. "They haven't seen you in years. What kind of grandfather are you?"

I walk away from her and study the arrival board. Eight more minutes.

"You sure are getting rude in your old age."

She asked for it. "Heather, I don't want to hear it. Can't you just lay off?"

"I was only making an observation. You're grouchy, too. I don't know how Aisha puts up with you."

I open my mouth, ready to let her have it. But a hand touches my shoulder.

"I was afraid we wouldn't get here in time. Four more minutes. I can't wait to see my favorite nephew."

"Brad. I'm so glad you're here." We hug. He's wearing a mask—not by choice, I'm sure. Beth stands beside him.

"Hello, Brad," says Heather. "How are you? I heard you're dying."

"We all are, Heather." He smirks from behind the mask.

She rolls her eyes.

I spot Jeremy and Nadia at the far end of the terminal. As they get closer, she runs to us. "Hi Grandma. Assalaamu alaikum Grandpa. Are they here yet?"

"Not yet, but soon."

"I can't wait."

"Do you remember Uncle Michael? You were very little when he left."

"No, but my dad talks about him all the time."

I glance at the arrival board. They're here. Just a few more minutes.

Aisha comes running up to us. "I came as soon as I could."

I put my arm around her shoulders. "You're just in time."

We wait. Even Heather is quiet, thankfully. After several minutes an old woman comes through the gate. Then a young man. My heart pounds as I stare at the door.

I hope they weren't held up by immigration. This is Michael's first trip to the U.S. since going AWOL to avoid fighting overseas. The president declared a general amnesty last November. I hope he meant it. We wait, watching as other passengers trickle out.

The children appear first. Ilyas looks a lot like Michael did when he was young. Mariya bounces next to him, as full of energy as she was six years ago. Gabriela is pushing a stroller. Michael carries a little boy in his arms.

Heather runs to them and grabs the youngest boy. He screams. She gives him a teddy bear.

I walk up slowly. "Assalaamu alaikum Michael. How are you?"

"Walaikum assalaam Dad." He releases his son to Heather and puts both arms around me. I hold on.

The next few minutes are a flurry of activity. I hug my daughter-in-law and their two oldest. The little guy holds back. I bend down to look at the baby. She's beautiful.

Michael is hugging Brad now. My brother is crying. I think Michael is, too. He's never seen his uncle so frail.

$$\sim$$

It's time to get the luggage. "Joshua, go help Michael." Heather holds Gabriela's hand. "You're all coming back to the condo with me."

"We can't leave the airport yet, Mom," says Michael. "Another flight is arriving in forty-five minutes, and I'm sure we'll want to be here for it."

"What are you talking about, Michael?"

He grins. "Jennifer and Nuruddin are coming. They wanted to surprise you."

Shock is more like it. "Did they bring the kids?"

"Of course they did. Now the two of you won't have to fight over who stays where." Michael laughs lightly.

"Are you serious? That's great." Brad laughs out loud. "You're not just doing this for your old dying uncle, are you?"

Michael isn't used to Brad's morbid jokes, but after a second he smiles. "We're all dying, Uncle Brad."

"Let's go get your luggage so we have enough time to find Jennifer's gate." Michael and I take off together. In the old days, Brad would have come with us.

When we're away from the group, Michael says, "I didn't think Uncle Brad would be so old."

"He's sixty-five. You know no one in our family makes it to seventy."

Michael winces. "Don't say that. That only gives me about thirty more years, you know."

"You're not old."

"Look at this." He holds up a small cluster of gray hairs, buried among the black. "I'm not a kid anymore."

I pat his back. "You're still my kid. It's great to see you. I wish you could stay."

"Our lives are in Mexico, but I'll do my best to make this a memorable month."

"I know it will be."

He lifts the bags onto the cart. I try, but my shoulder starts to hurt.

"Don't worry about it, Dad. I can do it."

"You'd better not wait fifteen years before your next visit. I may not be around that long."

He stops what he's doing and hugs me. "Don't leave me, Dad. I still need you."

              ~

Jennifer's flight has landed. It will probably take her longer to get through customs. While we wait, I talk with Ilyas.

"How old are you now? Fourteen?"

"Yes."

"What is your favorite sport?"

"I like soccer."

"We can have a family soccer game while you're here. Your dad started playing soccer when he was a little boy."

"Yes."

Mariya interrupts. "Will you take me to the top of the Willis Tower? Papa told me about it, but he keeps calling it the Sears Tower. I want to see Lake Michigan, too. My friend Yolanda didn't believe me when I told her that I was going to see a lake that's almost as big as Chiapas. Will it snow? I never saw snow before." She stops to take a breath.

"I'd like to take you to see the Willis Tower and Lake Michigan. It could snow." Michael's not the only one who still calls the Willis Tower the Sears Tower. Like most old-time Chicagoans, I have never gotten use to the name change. Anyway, it would be nice to see snow through a child's eyes again.

"Mariya, Ilyas, come here." Michael calls. "Aunt Jenny is coming."

A tall boy appears first. I recognize Ahmed. He's followed by Yunus, who stands out with the blonde hair he inherited from Heather and Jenny. Nuruddin and Jennifer follow. He's holding little Noora's hand. She's carrying the baby in her arms.

I greet my son-in-law first while Heather hugs Jenny.

"Did you have a good trip?"

"Alhamdulillah. The children were restless, though."

"Assalaamu alaikum Ahmed. I hope you remember me."

"Walaikum as salaam Grandpa. Yes, I remember you. How are you?" He offers his hand—such a young man.

Heather is holding the squirming, crying baby. "Calm down. You're with Grandma now."

I hug my Jennifer. "Why didn't you tell me you were coming?"

"Are you surprised?"

"Very. It's great to see you. How did you manage?"

"Michael and I arranged it. The kids have a break from school, and Nuruddin took a few weeks off. I even scheduled some book signings while we're here."

"It's great having my family together again."

"Where are the others?"

"Jamal and Muhammad are at work. Maryam's at school." Luqman could be anywhere. "You'll see all of them soon."

Heather claps her hands. "Listen, everybody." She pauses. "Quiet down. We need to make arrangements."

"I have a suggestion," says Aisha. "Michael can stay with us for two weeks, and Jenny with you, and then we'll switch. What do you think, Heather?"

"That sounds like a good idea, Mom," says Jenny.

Heather nods. "Okay, Jenny, Nuruddin, let's gather your things and go back to the condo."

"One more thing," says Brad.

The group is too noisy. Only a few of us heard him. Michael calls out, "Uncle Brad has something to say."

Heather stops in midstride. "What is it, Brad? Go on. We're in a hurry."

Brad clears his throat and makes Heather wait. She taps her foot impatiently. He says, slowly, "Kyle wants all of you to come to dinner on Saturday. Including you, Heather."

"I can't wait to see Kyle again," says Jennifer. "I can't believe he's the father of triplets."

"Let's go," says Heather. She waves. "I'll see you on Saturday." She walks proudly through the airport, with Jennifer, Nuruddin, and their kids in tow.

"Make sure we have all the luggage," says Michael. "Are we ready?"

"We're ready," says Mariya.

"Let's go."

We form our own parade, with Mariya in the lead. Aisha walks with Gabriela, who carries Tariq and his teddy bear. Michael walks with Brad, Beth, Jeremy, and Nadia, my two sons carrying the luggage. Mariya chatters while Ilyas looks around. I push the stroller, peering at little Anna who sleeps peacefully, missing all the excitement.

Kyle's Family

Our babies are growing every day. When we took them to the pediatrician last week, she was pleased with their progress. "They're all gaining weight and developing according to schedule."

I asked her about Nathifa. "You said earlier that she may have some problems."

"Some preemies display learning disabilities when they're older. I'll keep an eye on her to see if she needs any special intervention, but for now she's doing great. And so are the other two," she said.

That was a relief. I picked up Nathifa and held her close.

~

Michael calls on Thursday evening. "Assalaamu alaikum Kyle. Congratulations."

"It's great to hear your voice. You're coming for dinner on Saturday, aren't you?"

"We'll be there, insha Allah. Which masjid do you attend on Fridays?"

"The Lincoln masjid, on the north side." It's farther from work, but that's the masjid where I made my shahadah and the one that Dad still goes to.

"That's where Jeremy goes, too. I'll see you there."

"Do you need a ride?"

"No, Jeremy will take me. I'll see you tomorrow."

The whole family is in town. Dad tells me even Heather will be coming for the dinner. That should be interesting.

After the prayer on Friday, I plan to drive out to the country and slaughter two lambs. One will feed our guests on Saturday. I'll donate the meat from the other one to Evans. Uncle Joshua and I already made the arrangements.

We hired the Grand Caravan to prepare and serve the meal. Faiqa and her mother offered to cook, but it would have been difficult with the three babies. We're having the dinner at Gameel's house. He insisted.

~

Michael sees me first and calls outs. "Kyle. Assalaamu alaikum."
"Walaikum assalaam." We shake hands and hug.
"This is my oldest son, Ilyas."
"Ilyas, has anyone ever told you that you look just like your dad?"
"Yes." He smiles and looks down.
A quiet kid. "Well, let's go inside." I follow Michael, Jeremy, and Ilyas into the masjid. Mom and Dad are already here. My father sits in the front row, reading the Qur'an.

~

After the prayer, I invite Mom, Dad, Michael, Jeremy, and Ilyas for lunch at the Grand Caravan. More than half of Chicago's restaurants have shut down in the last several years, but Grand Caravan has managed to stay afloat. I support them whenever I can.
"You're looking good, Kyle," says Michael. "Marriage must agree with you."
"And fatherhood. You can see my little ones tomorrow. And you have four?"
"Yes. Two girls and two boys. Do you think you'll catch up with us?"
I shake my head vigorously. "Three is plenty for us."
"You two did it the hard way. How do you manage three babies?"
"We have a system. And our parents help. You should see my dad with the triplets."
"They're easy babies," says Dad. "Much easier than you were, Kyle."
"That's because you're not the one who feeds them or changes their diapers," says Mom.
We talk about children and Mexico and Chicago. "I noticed quite a few boarded up storefronts on our way to the masjid," says Michael. "Is it just this area of the city?"
"It's the entire city," says Jeremy. "Jamal and Rabia will probably move out west this summer because he's worried about his job. Raheema and I are getting by, but it's tight."

"Why is this happening?"

"There are different opinions," I say. "I think it's because of city corruption."

"Chicago has always been corrupt, hasn't it, Kyle?"

"It's worse now. Cases of bribery, patronage, and nepotism have increased dramatically. A religious sect, the New Pilgrims, controls many of the industries, and no one can do anything about it."

"Chiapas is more prosperous than ever. We have an active economy and our schools are strong." My cousin pauses. "Maybe you should all think of moving there."

Jeremy laughs. "Don't tempt me."

"I'm serious. What about you, Uncle Brad? Wouldn't you like to live someplace warmer? I know my dad would."

Dad nods. "That's an interesting thought."

According to the latest prognosis, Dad only has a very short time to live anywhere. But he's proven the doctors wrong before. I hope he can do it again.

~

Dad went with me to slaughter the lambs yesterday after lunch. He cringed. Thinking about death is never easy.

Kyle's Family: Part Two

The food has arrived from Grand Caravan, with servers ready. Uncle Chris, Aunt Melinda, Isaiah, and Becky are the first of our guests.

My uncle shakes my hand, and then Gameel's. "Thank you for inviting us."

"I'm very glad you could come," says Gameel. "Would you like some tea?"

"Not now," says Uncle Chris. "Thank you." He looks a little uncomfortable, definitely out of his element. He has made the effort to understand the Muslim side of the family, even coming to the aqiqah we held last November. He still disagrees with Islam, but he's become more tolerant, especially after learning about Dad's impending death.

"Where are the babies?" says Becky.

"Faiqa will bring them out soon," I say. "Come have a seat while you wait."

We escort them into the guest room. A moment later, Hannah appears with greetings and refreshments. My wife walks in behind her, pushing the triple stroller. Becky scoops Nathifa into her arms. "She is so precious." She kisses my daughter's soft cheek. "It makes me want to have another one."

Isaiah grins. "Four is enough for us."

~

Uncle Joshua and his family arrive nearly en masse, one after the other. By the time Jenny comes, with her family and her mother in tow, the guest room is vibrant and noisy. Nathifa cries a little. She never liked noise. Nashwa beams at our visitors and charms them. Yusuf begs to go down on the floor, fussing until Faiqa has to take him into another room to nurse him.

At seven, we escort everyone into the dining room. The servers come in and start feeding our guests. This lamb is delicious. I try not to think about the slaughter, when I put my hand on a living, breathing animal. One of the signs of Allah is the animals He gave us to eat.

Near the end of the dinner, Gameel stands. "I'm glad you could come tonight and bless us with your presence. Family is one of the greatest blessings we have been given from our Lord." The speech is surprisingly short for Gameel. "Would you like to say something, Brad?" Gameel turns to his right and whispers.

"Yes." Dad cradles Nashwa in his left arm, where she has snuggled contentedly all during the meal. "I feel very blessed to have my family around me. Even you, Heather." He smirks, and everyone except Heather laughs a little. "Pray for these children, and take good care of them after I am gone." He sits down and holds Nashwa close to him. Whether he does this out of love or to hide his tears, I'm not sure.

~

Faiqa kicks off her shoes as we walk into the condo. "It was a good evening. Your father's speech was really touching. I wish we had that on video."

"Matt recorded it."

"That's good. So who do you want to change first?"

"Nathifa is awake. Come here, baby. You look very pretty tonight. Do you know that?"

"What about me?" Faiqa hands me the baby.

"You always look good, honey."

She kisses me while Nathifa lies calmly in my arms. I finally have the life I always wanted. Allah is the Greatest.

Luqman: The Stranger

In this vast country that he had so loved, he was alone.

—Albert Camus

My father is happy with me again. It doesn't take much. He's such a simple man with simple needs. Eat, pray, sleep. The smallest of actions will win him to my side.

I promised Mom I would get rid of the gun, but I can't. I don't often lie to her. She is adamant about the gun, though, and she doesn't understand why I need to keep it. My safety goes far beyond the vague fear of a potential carjacking. When I'm in the battlefield against the Young Pilgrims, I must be prepared to protect myself at all times. She wouldn't yet understand or approve of my struggle against injustice, though, so it's easier to lie.

My oldest brother, Michael, is staying at our house, but he has barely spoken to me. He was fifteen when I was born of a different mother. All he knows of me are the early years I wasted on crying. I have spoken with his daughter, Mariya, who's one of the few people in this family who knows how to talk to me. That Mariya is one smart kid.

It's nice having the little kids around, too. Tariq plays ball with me. Anna let me hold her once. They're too young to have preconceived notions and prejudices. They accept me for who I am, and that's great.

But Michael couldn't care less about me. He's just like all the others.

∾

Last night, I went to Gameel's house with the rest of the family. His opulent lifestyle disturbs me. Doesn't he realize how much good he could do by living simply? He does give to charity, but he could be giving so much more if he wasn't living in a palace.

During dinner, I had a lively conversation with my cousin, Isaiah. We've read many of the same books, and his viewpoints aren't that different from mine. Our primary disagreements seem to come from our own personal experiences. Isaiah is white, and his main focus is to provide stability for his wife and children. As a single black man, I'm not tied down by external obligations, though I am sometimes hindered, still, by the color of my skin. Isaiah will never fully understand me, but he comes closer than most of the people in my family.

In general, even when I am with the people who should know me best, I feel like a stranger.

Building Connections

I am a part of all that I have met.

—Alfred Tennyson

Joshua: Part One

Last night was very special. It's not often that the entire family comes together these days.

The minute I walked into the house, my brother-in-law stopped me. "Where do you think you're going?"

I laughed and hugged him. "It's great to see you, brother."

"I'm serious, Isa. Where have you been? Is the center still keeping you that busy?"

"Busy enough. Michael and Jenny are in town now, and there's Brad, and Luqman. And the fundraiser, but that's another story."

"What happened with Luqman? Is he in some sort of trouble?"

"Not yet. Not that I know of. Things are getting a little better now, but it's been difficult. I don't want to go into it here."

"You know you can call me anytime. I miss talking with you."

"I don't know when things got so crazy. It must have started before we went for Hajj, but I didn't notice it then."

"It started long before then. You need to slow down, Isa, for your own good and the good of your family."

"Aisha said Luqman came to you for information about his thesis. What exactly is his topic? Why won't he talk to me about it?"

"Over a year ago, he asked for help with his research. Later, I wondered if I should have redirected him. He wanted to know about race relations in Chicago in the early twentieth century. Those were difficult times, with strict segregation and an active Ku Klux Klan."

"The Ku Klux Klan was in Chicago?"

"It certainly was, and for a number of years, it was quite effective. Racism was never confined to the South."

"I know that. I just didn't expect it to be so strong up here. Why do you say you should have redirected him?"

"Luqman is very sensitive. Information like that could stir strong emotions in a young man."

"Why don't you talk with him about his work?"

"I'll do that now." Umar put his hand on my shoulder. "You need to relax, brother. Think of your life as a test. You came back from the Hajj charged with renewed faith. The question is, can you keep it going?"

"I hope so."

"We'll talk again later, insha Allah. For now, I'd better speak with my nephew. It's good to see you, Isa."

He hugged me and headed toward my son, who was leaning up against the wall and staring into space.

Umar never got back to me, though Luqman seemed to be enjoying himself as the evening progressed. When we came home, he went straight to his room.

And this morning, he again woke us up with his beautiful adhan.

~

Sunday is nice—a blue sky with temperatures in the lower fifties—so I take Michael's family out for a walk along the lake. Afterward we have pizza.

"I like pizza," says Mariya. "Can we go to the top of the Willis Tower now?"

"Be polite," says Gabriela. "You're talking to your grandpa."

"We can go after lunch, insha Allah." It's still the Sears Tower to me.

"Good." Mariya puts her slice of pizza back. "I'm finished."

"Mariya. Eat your pizza." Michael gives her a look. Did he learn that somewhere, or does it come naturally to all parents?

"*¡Pórtate bien!*" ("Behave yourself!") Gabriela reminds her.

Ilyas and Tariq still seem a little afraid of me, and the baby is usually with Gabriela. I'm glad Mariya feels comfortable enough to say what she thinks.

When we walk outside she takes my hand. "Where is it, Grandpa?"

"Look over there." I point. "Can you see it? It's the tallest building in Chicago."

"I can't see. The sun hurts my eyes."

"Let's take a walk. We're not far away. When we get there we can ride up to the top."

"Good. I want to do that."

"Let's go. Come on, Ilyas. It's right down the street."

"You can go ahead," says Michael. "We'll follow."

Aisha takes one of my hands while Mariya holds the other. Ilyas walks beside us, keeping his distance.

≈

By the time we get there, about ten minutes later, I'm a little winded. Brad might beat me after all.

"Hurry, Grandpa," says Mariya. "I want to go inside."

"Let's wait for your Mama and Papa." I look back. They're still a block away.

"I like Chicago," says my granddaughter. "I want to live here when I grow up."

"I've lived in Chicago all my life. I like it here most of the time. But it's cold. Wouldn't you rather live someplace warm?"

"My village is always hot. I'm tired of it. I want to see snow."

"Chicago has lots of snow."

"Where is it? I want it to see snow now."

"Be patient. We could still get snow while you're here. If we don't, I'll have to send some down to Mexico for you," I tease.

"Would you do that? I would like that very much."

"But when the snow got to Mexico, it would melt."

She crosses her arms. "I hate Mexico. I want to live in Chicago with you."

"I hate Chicago," Ilyas mutters. "I want to go home."

"What's wrong, Ilyas?" Aisha puts her arm around his shoulders. He moves away from her. "I want to go home."

"It's hard to leave your friends," says Aisha. "You'll go back to Mexico and see them next month, insha Allah. Right now, I'm glad you're here with us."

Ilyas turns his back on her and sulks. Michael pulls him aside and speaks to him harshly in Spanish. Something along the lines of "you know better than that."

We're quiet while waiting for Gabriela to catch up. Even Mariya stops talking. Michael is angry, his face red. When we're all together, I lead my family inside and pay the admission.

≈

The elevator doors open and Mariya runs to look out over the city. Gabriela and Aisha walk with the other children while Ilyas sulks in a corner. I pull Michael aside.

"Do you think you were too rough on him?"

"I'm not rough enough, Dad. He acts like this all the time, and I'm tired of it."

"He is a teenager."

"You never made excuses for me when I was his age."

"I was your father and fathers have to be tough. Grandfathers don't."

"Don't spoil him. He has to learn to be a man."

"You wouldn't mind if I talk to him, would you?"

"Go ahead. I don't think you'll get anywhere."

"Relax a little. Enjoy the view." I pat his shoulder and approach my grandson. Ilyas stiffens and turns away.

"*Cuéntame de tus amigos*," I say in Spanish. "Tell me about your friends."

He looks at me. "Do you speak Spanish?"

I nod. He smiles.

His best friend, Musa, is the village soccer star. He enjoys math but doesn't like learning English. Chicago is too noisy, but he did like the plane ride. Pizza is good, but the tamales of Chiapas are much better. His sister talks too much, and his father yells too much.

Aisha interrupts. "The children are restless."

Michael walks over. Ilyas stops in mid-sentence. I understand. We'll talk later.

Joshua: Part Two

Luqman wakes us up with the call to prayer every morning. I worried over nothing.

After the prayer, Michael, Gabriela, Ilyas, and Mariya join us for breakfast. The younger children are still asleep.

"I wish I could stay home with you today, but I've already taken too many days off from work. I'll come back as soon as I can."

"Don't worry, Dad," says Michael. "We'll be fine."

"If you need to go anywhere, Luqman will be here at least part of the day. He usually goes back to sleep in the mornings. He's working on his thesis, so his hours are flexible."

"I'll remember that. We had a busy weekend, so I think we'll relax today."

Aisha finishes her breakfast and goes to the sink to wash her dishes. Gabriela stops her.

"I'll clean for you."

"Thank you. You don't have to do that. You're our guest."

"I'm part of the family, and I'm happy to help."

Aisha smiles. She's probably tempted to ask Gabriela to cook dinner, too.

I finish my coffee and run upstairs to get ready. Michael and Gabriela are still in the kitchen when I come back down. "Make yourselves at home. I'll see you this afternoon, insha Allah."

～

Hiram Johnson walks into my office soon after I arrive. "Good morning, Joshua. I wonder if I could speak with you."

"Sure. Have a seat. What's on your mind?" I'm never comfortable around the man, but I'm in a good mood this morning.

"We need to discuss the fundraiser. I was glad to accept Stuart's invitation. He's a fine young man. I did want to talk with you, though, about the topic."

"What do you have in mind?"

"People need spiritual uplifting these days. I don't need to tell you that times are hard. We are constantly tested and tempted. Evil lurks around every corner."

"I agree." With his ideas, though not completely with the way he expresses them. "What does that have to do with the fundraiser?"

"We live in dangerous times. Our youth are often difficult and rebellious. Crime is rising precipitously. Violence defines our earthly existence. We are close to the Last Days and life itself is fraught with peril. Can we meet for an evening of food and drink, turning our backs on the imminent disaster awaiting us? Or shall we use this event to awaken the sensibilities of our fellow man? What would you say?"

I can barely follow him. Now I remember one reason why I don't particularly like Johnson. "This is a secular non-profit agency serving the needs of the poor. We can't turn the fundraiser into a religious event."

"We most certainly cannot. How could you believe I was suggesting such a possibility? We must, however, retain some seriousness on a night promoting frivolity. I'm positive you agree with me."

I take a moment to dissect his words, making sure I do actually agree, before nodding. "Helping the poor is serious business."

"I'm talking not only of assisting the needy, but educating those to whom God has given much. Are they aware, do you think, that their very existence is in jeopardy? Do they fret over the conditions of their souls? Do they—"

I interrupt. "We can't use the fundraiser to promote religion."

"Not religion, Mr. Adams, but existence itself. I intend only to inform them of the hazards—"

My phone rings. A very welcome interruption. "What is it?"

"Joshua, we need your help here at Evans. We're having a problem with—"

"You don't need to explain, Stu. I'll be right there." I hang up and turn to Johnson. "I have an emergency. We don't need to talk about the speech, do we? You just need to inspire the people to support our centers. And, of course, we can't include religion. That would go against our bylaws and jeopardize our non-profit status." If he can use big words, I can throw in one or two of my own.

"I understand. Thank you for meeting with me." He offers his hand, which I accept. His handshake is weak.

"I'll walk you out. Stu needs my help over at Evans."

"So you wish to have no further input on my speech?"

"Bring in the money and stay away from religion, and I'm sure it will be great."

We walk silently to his car. I have to confess that I caught only half of what he said. Stu and all the others may feel inspired. To me, he's just another preacher—and not nearly as sincere as my brother Chris.

～

Stu's "emergency" was a minor plumbing problem in the kitchen, something I was able to fix myself. It's a good thing Stu called me, though. Hiram Johnson was getting on my nerves.

The rest of the day is less eventful. There are bills to pay and letters to send. I get on the phone for an hour and sell a few more tickets to the fundraiser. On my way out of the building, I stop by the gym and watch the boys play basketball for a few minutes before telling them they need to go home.

"Sorry, guys. We have to wrap it up."

"Aw, Joshua, we're just getting warmed up."

"I've got to close up. Consider this your two minute warning."

"Hey, man." Another boy calls. "Why don't you join us?"

I laugh. "You gotta be kidding."

"Come on. We'll go easy on you." One of them shouts. The others join in.

"Okay. Two minutes though." *If I last that long.* I put down my briefcase, take off my tie and suit coat, and roll up my sleeves.

They bring me in as a guard. I stay close to one of the boys— young, strong, and about six inches taller than me. When the ball comes my way, I wave my arms in front of his face and try to catch it. It bounces away. Another boy scoops it up easily and scores.

Darnell shakes his head. "Aw, Joshua, you can do better than that. I know you can."

I don't think so. I'm already panting. They put the ball in play again and I go back to guarding. I jump around a little. The boy I'm guarding accidentally bumps me while reaching for the ball, and I go sprawling onto the court.

Darnell runs over. "Are you okay? Here, let me help you up." He offers his hand.

Pain shoots through my left shoulder. I wince. "I can't get up."

Another boy shakes his head. "Man, you weren't joking. I hope I'm in better shape when I'm your age."

"Why don't you go get Stu?"

"He's gone already. I saw him leave. Do you need to get to the hospital? I can take you."

"No, just take me home. Can the rest of you boys help me up?"

～

Darnell has worked with us since he was fifteen, and he's our most popular volunteer. He's nineteen now, balancing work and school along with his volunteer hours at Hope.

"You took a nasty fall. Are you sure you don't want to go to the hospital?"

"I'll be okay. I hurt this shoulder years ago, and it still gives me trouble. It should be all right in the morning. Thanks for helping me."

"I'm glad to do it. I need to call home, though, and let them know I'll be late." He pulls out his phone. "I'm not supposed to drive and talk."

"Go ahead. I won't tell."

He punches a key. "Hey, Shauna, tell Mama I won't be there for dinner. No, there's no problem. Something came up. I'll tell you when I get home." He laughs. "No, it's not a girl. Just give Mama the message." He shakes his head. "My sister's always messing with me."

When we get to the house, Aisha invites him in. After we eat, Darnell takes Michael back to the center so he can get my car.

Aisha takes me to the bedroom and massages my shoulder. "A man your age trying to play basketball. What were you thinking?"

"I was thinking my wife would be proud of me."

"For making a fool of yourself? You're not a young man, Isa."

"I know." I know.

~

After Aisha medicates and bandages my shoulder, I go downstairs to stretch out on the couch. Ilyas is watching TV. "What happened to your arm, Grandpa?" He asks in Spanish.

I tell him the story, adding a little humor about my feeble attempts at basketball.

"I play basketball," he says. "Can I go play with you?"

I look at my injured shoulder. "Grandpa's too old. We'll find someone else you can play with."

He smiles. "I'd like that."

Michael sits on the couch with us. "What are you two talking about?"

"Nothing," says Ilyas.

"Michael, could you take me into work tomorrow? I won't be able to drive for a couple of days."

"Sure. I'm glad I have my international license."

"Do you think you'll have any trouble driving in Chicago traffic after all these years?"

"I drive up to Mexico City sometimes for conferences. Chicago is a small town compared to Mexico City."

"You can come, too, Ilyas, to see where your grandpa works and maybe play basketball."

"Good," he says in English. "I like that."

∾

Aisha props me up with extra pillows. "Take your pain pill so you can sleep."

"That's okay. I can stand it."

"Isa, you'll be awake all night if you don't take something. You're not planning to go to work tomorrow, are you?"

"Michael will take me. I'll be okay."

"Remember to stay off the basketball court. Leave that to the younger men."

That hurt. But she's right. Brad may be in better shape than I am for that soccer game. I'd better start training, one of these days.

I've joked for years about getting older, but I still felt young. The basketball court put me in my place. I'll be fifty-eight next month, insha Allah. Nearly sixty. I really am getting old.

Aisha gives me my pills and tucks me in.

∾

My shoulder hurts worse in the morning. I finish my coffee and take another pain pill.

Ilyas gobbles down his cereal. "Can we go now?"

"Wait. I'm not ready yet."

"I want to go, too," says Mariya. "Take me too, Grandpa."

"You can go later, insha Allah. Today it's your brother's turn." I should take her sometime while they're here, but with her chattering, I won't get any work done.

"Will you be able to work?" Gabriela asks. "Shouldn't you stay home and rest?"

"I'll be okay." I look to Aisha for words of sympathy, but she just grins and pretends to bounce a basketball. "That's enough out of you."

She kisses me. "Have a good day, hon, and stay out of the gym."

I smile. She's right. What can I say?

∾

First, I take Michael and Ilyas on a tour of Evans. "This is where we help people who don't have a place to live. Here is the dining hall where they eat." A few stragglers remain, eating breakfast, while the staff cleans up.

"Why don't they live in a house?" Ilyas asks. "I thought America was rich."

"America was rich, and some people still are, but many don't have jobs, and without jobs they can't buy houses. Here at Evans, we try to help them get jobs. We also give them a place to stay and food to eat until they can go live somewhere else."

"Mexico City has homeless people, but in Chiapas everyone has a house."

"In the villages, everyone helps everyone else. In a big city like Chicago or Mexico City, it's harder to find help."

I show them the residential wings and the recreation center. Children run through the gym. No adults are in sight. The parents are busy looking for work, and the center is understaffed. I hope no one gets hurt.

We end the tour at Stu's office. He looks up. "What happened, Joshua?"

"I pulled a muscle." Later, I'm sure he'll hear about me on the basketball court. "I'd like to introduce you to my son, Michael, and my grandson, Ilyas."

Stu offers his hand to Michael. "Welcome to Evans."

"Stu, Ilyas wants to play basketball. Do you remember what time Darnell comes in on Tuesdays?"

"I'm not sure. He may have classes all day. I'd like to play, but I'm swamped."

Ilyas pipes up. "I don't want you to get hurt like Grandpa did."

"Don't worry about that. Stu's a little younger than me." Stu raises his eyebrows. "I'll tell you about it later."

∼

At Hope, I show them the clinic and introduce them to everyone. Sandra offers Ilyas a piece of candy. "For a sweet boy," she says.

Ilyas looks down. "Thank you."

"We'd better go, Dad. I'm sure you need to get to work."

"Would you let Ilyas stay here? He can practice in the gym."

"Show me the way. I'll shoot some hoops with him."

"Do you play basketball, Papa?"

"I used to play when I was younger. I think I can still do it."

"Will you get hurt?"

"No, I won't get hurt, insha Allah."

"You'll need these." Sandra pulls out two pair of athletic shoes.

I peek behind the counter. "Where'd you get those?"

"You know these kids. Sometimes they leave their basketball shoes behind. Along with their backpacks, their coats, and anything else that isn't attached. I know they'll be back for them sooner or later. In the meantime, you two can use them."

"Thanks." Michael puts his hand on his son's shoulder. "Let's go play ball."

⁓

Three hours later, Ilyas bounces into my office. Michael limps, his face red.

"I beat my dad."

"He ran rings around me," Michael says as he plops down in one of my visitor's chairs. "I'm exhausted."

"You played for a long time."

"Your grandson is talented. If I send him here for high school, he could get a scholarship."

"That's great."

"Would you, Papa? I'd like to live here."

"I can't send you away, Ilyas. I would miss you too much." Michael catches his breath. "Are you hungry? Where would be a good place to eat around here, Dad? Can you get away?"

I thumb through papers on my desk. "I have some work to do. You two go on ahead. Drive north about five blocks, and you'll find a nice place on the left side of the street called Harry's Heroes. Bring me one of their turkey sandwiches."

"That sounds good. Let's go, Ilyas."

They walk out together, father and son. I don't really need to work through lunch, but they need this time for just the two of them.

⁓

Michael walks in a couple hours later with my sandwich. "I'm sorry we took so long. Ilyas and I had a good talk. There's isn't usually much time for that."

"I'm glad you enjoyed your lunch. Where's Ilyas?"

"The minute we came into the building, the secretary told him there were some boys playing in the gym. He'll be safe on his own, won't he?"

"Sure he will. Darnell's probably down there—you met him last night. Just about every day, some boys show up to shoot hoops. And occasionally an old man."

Michael frowns. "Are you feeling all right?"

"I'm good. The worst part of it was realizing how old I am."

He rubs his arms. "I'm already getting stiff from the little bit we did this morning. Tomorrow, I'll be very sore."

I pick up my sandwich. "Why don't you call Jenny and see if she'll let Yunus come over. Maybe he can spend the night. They're the same age. They'll have a good time together."

"That's a great idea. Can I borrow your phone?"

I could have called Jenny myself, but I didn't want to risk getting dragged into a conversation with Heather. She's Michael's mother. Let him handle her.

～

Michael went to the condo to pick up Yunus and spend some time with his sister and mother. Ilyas is still in the gym. I walk down the hall and peek in.

Most of the other boys are older and taller, but Ilyas is holding his own. He has good moves—better than I ever had. After he grows a few inches, he'll be a real competitor.

～

Michael arrives with Ahmed and Yunus just as I'm locking up.

Yunus protests. "I just got here. I want to play basketball, too."

"We need to go now. Do all of you want to come back tomorrow?"

Yunus and Ilyas shout, "Yes!" Ahmed just nods.

"After dinner, I'll take you boys shopping," says Michael. "You all need good athletic shoes."

"We have some at home," says Yunus. "Baba made us bring our dress shoes instead."

"Papa told me to bring my good shoes, too," says Ilyas.

Fathers and teenage sons and shoes. I remember those days.

~

After dinner, I feel like taking a nap. Michael can handle the shoe shopping. Before he leaves, I give him some money. "Get something nice for the boys."

During dinner, Mariya chatted about her day. Now she sits by my feet at the end of the couch while I stretch out and watch the news. Things have been a little quieter lately. Quiet is good.

Near the end of the broadcast, Muhammad comes on. "Look, Mariya, there's your Uncle Muhammad."

She laughs. He's surrounded by baby chicks in a story about Easter. Muhammad smiles and tries to look like he's enjoying himself, but I'm sure he'd rather be somewhere else.

When the news is over, I call him. "I just watched your interview."

"You can't call that an interview. They thought it would be cute to surround me with the animals. You didn't see what those chicks did to my pants. I was in the shower for forty minutes, and my slacks are ruined."

"But you made your niece laugh. Isn't that worth something?"

"She was laughing at me? Great."

"No. She enjoyed the story. Next time you see her, I'm sure she'll ask you all about it."

"I want to talk," says Mariya, reaching for the phone. She spends twenty minutes asking Muhammad about the chicks, and tells him she wants one. Finally she hands the phone back to me.

"She asks too many questions," says Muhammad.

"Yes. She reminds me of a little boy I used to know."

"Tell her not to go into reporting. It's not as much fun as it looks."

Luqman: Family

We do not judge the people we love.

—Jean Paul Sartre

One day, I printed out this quote by Sartre and taped it to my mirror. This, more than anything, describes the relationship I have with my family.

Uncle Psychologist came over to hassle me during the dinner. He acted like he cared, but I saw him talking to my father earlier. My uncle is my father's brain. He explains those things that Dad could never hope to understand on his own.

I should never have asked him for help with my thesis. He caught me in a moment of weakness, after I had spent hours in the library with little to show for my efforts, and pretended to be interested in my work. The information he gave me was valuable, but I shouldn't have let him get that close to me.

Now he's worried because, he says, someone like me with a sensitive soul may misinterpret what I learned about race relations. Does he think I'm emotionally deficient? I know exactly what I learned, not only about Chicago but about my own blood line. Anyone with half a brain should be upset. But Uncle Psychologist has played their game so long and so well that he's forgotten how to be proud of whom he is.

But he's not the one saddled with a horrible legacy. That was my father's gift to me and my siblings. And, as usual, he's clueless about what his ancestors and even his relatives have done. He walks through life like a zombie and thinks he's making a difference.

While we were at that dinner, I talked with Uncle Brad for a while. He's the only one who keeps me sane some days and the only one who makes me feel like someone cares if I'm around. He doesn't judge me, and I love him for that.

Reckless Consequences

While we are free to choose our actions,
we are not free to choose the consequences of our actions.

—Stephen Covey

Joshua: Part One

In a few days, Michael's family will move to Heather's condo, and Jenny will come here with her family. The month is passing too quickly.

Tonight, Ahmed, Yunus, and Daud are spending the night at our house. I'm surrendering the family room to the boys. The refrigerator is stocked with frozen pizza and ice cream, and our few breakable things are in the office. I think we're ready.

Twenty minutes after Daud arrives, I hear shouting. It sounds like boys having fun, but I decide to check.

Our family room has been transformed into a soccer field. I blink. Crowds of cheering supporters sit on the bleachers. Somewhere, someone is selling hot dogs. I can smell them. Small children play on the sidelines. Daud is kicking the ball toward the goal, while Yunus guards him and Ahmed acts as goalie. Other players are in our family room, too, all part of the game.

"What is this?"

"We're playing a video game." Daud points to the TV. "This one is 'Soccer Frenzy'."

I study the TV. It looks the same. Interesting. "How does it work?"

Daud stops and looks at me. "It's simple, Grandpa. I just put the game in and turned on the TV." He returns to the action.

There's a special slot on the front of our set. I didn't know our TV could do that.

∾

The boys were awake all night. I heard Michael go down once. Things got a little quieter, but that didn't last long. I barely slept, and neither did the other adults in the house. After the prayer, we struggle to our rooms. My grandsons are still going strong. Their noise fades into the background.

Suddenly a loud bang wakes me. I shake away my drowsiness and rush out into the hall. Someone is screaming.

"What happened?" I shout. No one answers.

I run down the steps and out the open front door. Michael and Aisha are right behind me.

"What happened here?" Michael shouts. *"Ilyas, ¿qué hiciste?"* ("What did you do?")

"I didn't mean to," Ilyas wails. He drops something on the ground.

I'm still trying to understand what's going on when I hear another scream of pain. Daud is lying on the grass, surrounded by blood. Aisha rushes to him. "What's wrong? How are you hurt?" She picks him up and cradles him to her chest. "Joshua, call 911."

I rush back into the house, passing Maryam and Gabriela on my way. When the dispatcher answers, I tell her that my grandson is injured, though I don't know what happened. "Please, send someone. He's bleeding."

"Why is he bleeding?"

"I don't know."

"Okay. Stay on the line."

Gabriela's voice rises above the others. *"¿Qué es esto? Contéstame Ilyas. ¿Qué pasó? ¿Porqué Daud está herido?"* ("What is this? Ilyas, answer me. What happened? Why is Daud hurt?") She grabs her son by the shoulders. He throws himself into her arms.

I take the phone outside. Some of the neighbors are in their yards. The guy next door is making a call. Daud is screaming. Ilyas is sobbing. Gabriela holds him and speaks to him softly.

"Joshua, get me a towel," Aisha yells. "Hurry."

I run to the linen closet upstairs. The 911 operator asks for our address and wants to know if we need an ambulance. I quickly rattle off the address. "Doesn't your computer show where we live? Yes, we need an ambulance. I told you that. Hurry."

When I run outside, Aisha grabs the towel and wraps it around Daud's leg. She rocks him and sings to him softly.

Ilyas screams and begins moaning. Gabriela holds and comforts him. *"Cálmate, mamá está aquí. Todo va a estar bien."* ("Be quiet. Mama's here. It will be okay.")

Michael walks over to the thing Ilyas dropped. "Dad, come here. Look at this." He points to a gun lying on the ground. The same one, as far as I can tell, that Luqman pulled on me that night. I notice his car door is open.

"Where is Luqman?" I look around. He must still be asleep. "Aisha, come with me." I shout.

"I can't leave Daud."

"I'll stay with him," says Maryam. She holds Daud gently and sings one of the lullabies Aisha taught her.

"Michael, stay here and take care of things. Watch the gun. We'll be back."

Luqman Interrupted

I'm trying to sleep, but Dad won't stop pounding. "Come out of there right now." What's his problem? I pull the covers over my head and try to ignore him.

He opens my door and stomps into my room. I should have locked the door.

"Get out of that bed!" He grabs my right leg and pulls me out. I fall to the floor, landing on my butt. That hurt.

He stands over me and screams. "What is wrong with you? What the hell did you think you were doing?"

I look up at him and blink. "What's the problem, Dad?"

He's breathing really hard. His mouth opens but nothing comes out. I've never seen his face that red.

"What's the problem?" Mom is shouting from the doorway. "An ambulance is coming for Daud. He's seriously hurt. You said you would get rid of that gun."

Oh, man. Those kids must have been playing around in my car. What the hell did they think they were doing?

I stand, tossing my blanket on the bed. "Take it easy, Mom. Everything will be okay. How did Daud get hurt? Wasn't anyone keeping an eye on him?"

Dad grabs my shoulder and talks in his low, quiet voice. "Ilyas found the gun in your car, and he accidentally shot Daud."

"My car? He's lying. I don't know where he got a gun, but it wasn't mine." *Think, man.* "It was probably Michael's. Everybody in Mexico has a gun, don't they?" That was weak. I'm too tired to think straight.

"Don't lie to us." Mom glares at me.

I look away. "I wouldn't lie to you, Mom."

"If it's not your gun, why was it in your car?"

"How am I supposed to know?" I throw my hands in the air. "Why aren't you asking those kids about the gun? I didn't shoot Daud, they did."

"Don't blame the boys. Aren't you worried about Daud?"

"What am I supposed to say? Of course I'm worried about Daud. He's not going to die, is he?" I can't handle a murder. And I like Daud. He's smart and kind of weird. I look at Mom and manage a tear. It's a trick I learned long ago.

"No, but he's seriously hurt. You still haven't told us why that gun was in your car."

With my dad, I can talk in circles until he forgets what he wanted to ask. That won't work with Mom.

"One of my classmates asked for a ride yesterday. Maybe it slipped out of his backpack."

"University students carry guns in their backpacks?"

"Sure they do. You know that. It's not against the law."

"You said you got rid of your gun."

I can go around with her for the next two hours, but eventually she'll wear me down. "I have to protect myself. Those kids shouldn't have been snooping around in my car."

"Why did you lie to me?"

The way she says it, it sounds like I cut her heart out. I sit on the bed and put my head in my hands. "You're not going to believe a word I say."

"Try me."

I stand up and walk over to her. "I know you don't approve of guns. You work with kids, and guns aren't safe around kids. But I'm not a kid, and I need the gun for my own protection. The world has changed, Mom. It's dangerous out there." I make eye contact. "I shouldn't have lied, but I didn't think you'd understand."

"So, that is your gun," Dad says softly. Isn't that what I said? Why does it take him so long to catch on?

Mom pierces me with her look. I turn away.

"I'm sure the police will be here to investigate. They have to look into any incident involving a gun, especially when a child is injured. You'll also have to answer to Allah."

Oh, man. How did everything get so complicated? I feel like hitting those kids for getting into my car. Not Daud, but the others. They should be old enough to know better.

"I'm going to the hospital with Daud. Isa, stay here until the police come. Luqman, you might want to go downstairs and talk to Ilyas. He thinks it's his fault that Daud is hurt."

That wasn't a suggestion. It was an order. "Sure."

I couldn't even handle my mother. How will I deal with the police?

Joshua: Part Two

We leave Luqman and run back outside just as the ambulance pulls up. We tell the paramedics what we know. They check Daud quickly before lifting him onto a stretcher. "How was he injured?" the blonde one asks.

"The gun," I say. "The boys found it. It was an accident."

"Where is the gun, sir?"

"It's, um, over there."

The other paramedic is on the radio. He calls over. "Ian, the police are delayed. Collect the weapon."

Ian puts on a pair of latex gloves and picks up the gun, slipping it into a bag. Then he pats Daud's arm. "Don't worry. We'll get you taken care of." The two of them put Daud into the back of the ambulance.

"I'm coming with him," says Aisha. She climbs in after Daud.

"It would be better if you follow in your car, ma'am."

"I'm not leaving my grandson." She stares them down. Ian climbs into the driver's seat while the other one stays with Daud. They take off, lights flashing and sirens blaring.

"I'm going to the hospital, too," says Michael. "I'll call Jeremy. Gabriela, take Ilyas upstairs. Keep them all in the room with you."

Gabriela puts her arms around Ilyas. I'm sure she would carry him if she could. "*Ven conmigo.*"("Come with me.") They walk into the house.

Yunus is hiding in the bushes. I call him. "Come here." He ducks down. "Come here, Yunus. You're not in trouble."

Slowly, he walks toward me, stopping a few feet away.

"Yunus, where did you boys find the gun?"

"I don't know," he says.

"You boys were in Uncle Luqman's car?"

"Yes."

"Was the gun in the car?"

Ahmed speaks up, stepping out from behind another bush. "It was in the glove box. We only wanted to look at it."

"Ilyas grabbed it from me," Yunus says quickly. "He shot Daud."

"It's not Ilyas's fault. Go inside and sit in the family room. I'll call your father to come get you."

Everyone's gone now, except our next door neighbor. He walks over. "Do you have it under control?"

Probably not. "I think so."

"Let me know if you need anything." He walks back toward his house.

"Go inside the house," I remind Ahmed and Yunus. I stay outside, staring in the direction of the ambulance, now long gone.

After a moment, I call Nuruddin. But Heather answers. "What is wrong with you?" Heather screams into my ear. "How could you stand by and let your son hurt my Daud? He may never walk again and it is all your fault. You and that devil spawn of yours."

"Heather. Calm down. Please."

She ignores me. "You've gone too far, Joshua. I'll do everything I can to keep you from my grandchildren. I always knew you were a terrorist. Why Daud? Why did you do this to him?"

"Can you send Nuruddin to come get the boys?"

"Those boys will never be allowed to come near you again. I'll make sure of that. What kind of grandfather are you?"

Too much has gone on today, and I can't deal with her right now. I hang up. When she calls again, thirty seconds later, I hurl the phone to the ground. It bursts into pieces. For a moment, I stare at the devastation and then crumple to the ground.

When Nuruddin pulls up in Heather's car, I'm still sitting, though my tears have dried.

"Assalaamu alaikum," he steps out and comes toward me.

"Walaikum assalaam. I'm glad you're here. The boys are inside."

"Are they okay? I should have come sooner but, as you know, Jenny's mother is very upset."

"Yes."

He walks into the house. "Ahmed. Yunus. Let's go to your grandma's house."

"It's not my fault," Yunus says quickly. "I didn't shoot Daud. Ilyas did."

Nuruddin pats his son's shoulder, though Yunus is as tall as his father. "It was an accident. Don't blame Ilyas." Nuruddin looks at me. "Where's Luqman?"

"He's in his room."

"What's wrong with him? Why did he do this?"

"I wish I knew."

"Let's go, boys." Nuruddin hustles his sons into Heather's car. "Grandma wants to see you."

He's driving away when a police car pulls up. It took them long enough. I walk over and greet the officers. "Hello. I'm Joshua Adams."

"We're here about the shooting incident. Who owns the gun?"

"My son. Come inside and I'll get him."

I trudge up the stairs. It isn't even noon, and already this day is too long. Luqman's door is closed. I knock. He doesn't answer. He never came downstairs to see Ilyas. I turn the knob, somehow knowing he's not inside.

Joshua: Part Three

I drink my third cup of coffee for the day. They've been at the hospital for hours. Someone should call soon.

While Aisha questioned Luqman in his bedroom, I listened with disbelief. He doesn't give a damn about Daud. He only wants to save himself. Now he's fled.

The police questioned me and searched Luqman's car. Later, they'll file a warrant for his arrest and send a tow truck to impound the car. They'll check the gun for registration. There is none, I'm sure. The evidence builds against my son.

Should I go to the hospital or stay here? Michael will be back soon. His family is here. I should comfort Ilyas, but he's upstairs with his mother.

Our home phone rings. I'm glad we've kept the landline all these years. "Hello?"

"Assalaamu alaikum Isa." It's Aisha. "I couldn't reach you on your phone. Daud is in surgery. The bullet fractured his leg. They say he'll be okay, but it will take a long time for his leg to heal. Have the police come yet?"

"By the time they got here, Luqman was gone."

"How could you let him go? You should have watched him. Do you have any idea where he is?"

"Zaid hasn't seen him in over a month. I don't know where else to look. Do you?"

"No. No I don't."

"I'm coming to the hospital."

"No. Don't."

"I want to be there for my grandson."

"Jeremy and Raheema are here now, and Umar and Safa. He has plenty of people looking out for him."

"But Aisha—"

"Here. Talk to Michael."

"Aisha? What's going on?"

"Dad, I need you to stay there and protect my family from Luqman."

"He's your brother. He won't hurt anyone."

"After what happened this morning, I can't be too sure. Mom's here, too. You don't want to see her right now. Believe me."

I know that. "Give everyone my salaams, and tell them I'm praying for Daud."

"How is Ilyas?"

"He's with Gabriela in the room. I don't want to disturb her."

"He needs to know it wasn't his fault."

They shouldn't have picked up the gun, but Luqman shouldn't have had the gun in the first place. "No. It wasn't."

∼

No one has called in over an hour. I hope Daud is out of surgery. I hurt for him.

It's time for the prayer. I stand at the foot of the stairs, make the adhan, and wait. Gabriela is still in the room with the children. Is she afraid to come out?

I go to the family room to make the prayer. When I bow down, I ask Allah to help Daud and Ilyas. And I ask Him to help Luqman. What happened to my son?

∼

Umar comes in the early afternoon. The front door is still open. It's chilly outside, but I don't want to close myself inside the house.

"Assalaamu alaikum." He calls out. "Isa? Are you all right?"

I stay in my chair at the kitchen table, drinking my sixth cup of coffee. "Come in."

He closes the door behind him and joins me in the kitchen. "You have no idea where he could be?"

"I don't know my son at all. So many times he said he was with Zaid. That was a lie. He told us he turned the gun into the police. Another lie. Where has he been all those times? Who was he with? What was he doing?" How did he get that black eye? Not from banging into the wall.

"I tried talking with him at the dinner. He was evasive. I should have pressed harder."

"It wouldn't have done any good. We've tried. After I caught him with the gun, Aisha and I both laid into him. The next morning, he stood outside our bedroom door and made the adhan, knowing that's what I needed from him. But it was all a lie. How could I have been so stupid?"

He touches my arm. "Don't blame yourself. Luqman is old enough to take responsibility for his actions."

"We loved him like the others. He demanded more from us, and we gave it to him. We taught him Islam. He had a good home. Why would he throw all that away?"

"You asked me about his thesis. He learned some things. He never told you, did he?"

"I went into his room once and found a chart—a family tree, I guess. His shelves are full of revolutionary literature." I study Umar's expression. "What didn't he tell me?"

"Why don't we go up to his room? I'd like to see that chart."

Luqman's room looks the same as it did this morning. Messy, as usual. I don't think anything's missing. Maybe he'll come back later.

Umar walks over to Luqman's desk and holds up the family tree. "Is this what you were talking about?"

"I don't recognize most of those names. Why are some of them crossed out?"

Umar studies the chart for a moment. "Sit down, Isa. There's something you need to know."

I clear a place on the bed. Umar sits next to me. "Luqman came to me over a year ago to talk about his thesis. I don't know why he chose to write about race relations. Perhaps a professor inspired him. I told him what I knew about the city at that time. Then he asked me about our family history.

"My paternal grandparents were born in Mississippi. Their grandparents had been slaves. Soon after my father was born, they moved up to East St. Louis, hoping for a better life outside of the Jim Crow south.

"Luqman asked if I knew anything about your family history, and I told him I didn't. He said he wanted to know where he came from.

"Apparently, this is what he found. Do you see the names he's crossed out? There's your father Sam, and his father, and his grandfather, and some uncles and cousins as well. You know your father was a racist. Do you remember when I told you that, at one time, the Ku Klux Klan was quite active in Chicago?"

What is he saying?

"Later, when I asked Luqman about his research, he said your family is full of bedsheets. I didn't take him seriously at the time, but that's what this is. Look at this chart. A third of the names are crossed off."

"Even if they were with the KKK, that's them, not me. Luqman knows that."

"Can you imagine a sensitive young man learning that members of his father's family had gone after people who looked like his mother? His mother's people were slaves and his father's people were, more than likely, cracking the whip."

"*Cracker.* I haven't heard that word in years." I pause a moment to let it all sink in. "So Luqman learned that my ancestors, including my own father, were members of the KKK. How does that explain his actions?"

"Are you familiar with a gang known as the Friends of Muhammad? They call themselves the FOM."

"They're a disgrace to Islam."

"All of their members are American born and the majority is black. Their goals are twofold: to strengthen the position of Muslims in this society, by force if necessary; and to advance the cause of black

Muslims. Luqman had a gun. What other suspicious behavior have you noticed?"

"Luqman is in graduate school. There's been a lot of suspicious behavior, but I can't believe he would join a gang. He's not a follower."

"Gangs need leaders, too. Think about it, Isa. Is it possible?"

The lies. The bruises. The gun. "It's possible."

"If he had stayed and talked with the police, they wouldn't have arrested him. The jails are bulging, and he has a clean record. Most likely, they would have fined him for possession of an unregistered weapon and let him off with a warning."

"Why did he run? There's a warrant out for his arrest."

"He wanted to avoid questioning. Whatever he's done thus far, I'm afraid he has plans for something bigger."

"What can I do to stop him? I don't even know where he is." I close my eyes and watch all of the pieces fall on top of me. "What am I going to do?"

∼

Umar stays with me, drinking coffee, until Aisha and Michael get back.

When they walk in, I jump up. "How is Daud?"

Aisha looks tired. "He came through the surgery. They'll keep him there for a few days. He may need more surgery later on."

Michael runs up the stairs.

"Umar, Safa went to Raheema and Jeremy's house. You two will stay with Nadia and the baby tonight. She wants you to get a few things from home and meet her there."

"Thanks for the message. I'll call her and see what she needs." He hugs his sister. "How are you holding up?"

Aisha sits down, stifling a yawn. "It's been a long day. Has Luqman come home?"

I look down. "No, and I don't know where he is."

"You two need to talk," says Umar. "Show her the chart. She'll understand." He pulls on his shoes and jacket. "Let me know if you need anything, and call me if you hear from Luqman. I'd like to talk with him."

Aisha gets up, pours a cup of coffee, and sighs. "What do you need to tell me?"

Luqman

The police were coming. I couldn't stay. That would have ruined my plans. Dad was sitting outside on the lawn when I called Hakeem.

"I'm in trouble. Can you be here in ten minutes?"

"I'm at work, man. What did you do?"

"I'll tell you later. We have to hurry."

"I'll meet you at the corner of Devon and California. Wait for me inside the bookstore. My shift is almost done, but I've got to make an excuse to my wife."

"I'll be there. Thanks."

"You owe me, man."

Dad was so upset and distracted that I was able to get away without trouble. I'm glad Mom went to the hospital.

The intersection of Devon and California is only about a mile from our house. I stayed on the side streets, watching for police cruisers. None came.

~

While waiting for Hakeem, I browse the shelves. When I was younger, I spent all my extra money on books. That lasted until about six months ago, when I learned the real focus of life.

"Don't move." A deep voice commands me. Before turning around, I know it's Hakeem, but for a second my heart stopped.

"Seriously, don't do that to people. Where have you been?"

"Fighting with my wife. What's going on, man?"

"Is your car parked out front?" I guide him to the door.

The guy at the checkout counter waves at me. "Assalaamu alaikum Luqman. How are you today? You're not going to buy anything?"

"Not this time. I'll be back, insha Allah."

We climb into Hakeem's old car. "What's this about?"

"Start driving."

He pulls into traffic. "Come on, man. I have to go home to an angry wife. You'd better make it worth the trouble."

I tell him about Daud, my parents, and the police. "They could be there by now. I wasn't going to take any chances."

"That would ruin everything. You have to go somewhere. Not my place. Why don't I drop you at my cousin's flat? He's not a Muslim, but he's cool. Tell him you got kicked out by your wife or something."

"Are you sure he's okay?"

"Positive. That will give you a place to land until things calm down."

"Why couldn't those kids have minded their own business?"

"Man, don't be too hard on them. Tell me you would have done something different."

"I wouldn't have gotten caught."

~

As Hakeem pulls up to his cousin's place, I caution him. "Your cousin doesn't need to know too much. Like my name. Call me Lucas."

"You don't have to worry about Darnell."

"Darnell doesn't need to get in the middle of anything. You know what I mean?"

Hakeem shrugs and leads me up to the second floor flat. "He lives here with his mother and sister. You'd better stay away from the sister, if you know what I mean."

"I have more important things on my mind. Come get me later tonight, so I can pick up my car."

"If my wife lets me. Don't smirk. You don't know what it's like." He knocks.

A woman answers. She's about my age and very fine. I try not to stare.

"Hey, Shauna. Is Darnell around?"

"He should be back soon. Jasmine just called here looking for you, and she's not happy."

Hakeem turns to me. "What you gonna do with these women?"

"Excuse me?"

"Not you. You cool, Shauna. My brother Lucas here just got thrown out on the street by his woman, and he needs a place. You think Darnell would mind?"

"Darnell won't, but you know Mama's not going to like it."

"I won't be no problem, Shauna. Just till I get things worked out with my woman."

She looks me up and down. "Come on in. Not you, Hakeem. You better get home to Jasmine. I'm not taking you both in." She gives him a dirty look.

"Don't get upset, Shauna. I'm just messing with you. Thanks for the help. See ya, Lucas." He waves, laughing as he runs down the stairs.

Shauna closes the door and points to her left. "That's Darnell's room. Go wait in there." She sighs and rolls her eyes. She bought the story.

~

Darnell walks in about fifteen minutes later and catches me stretched out on his bed.

"Who are you? What are you doing here?"

"Hakeem brought me after my woman kicked me out. I just need a place for a few days."

"Hakeem didn't say anything about you. What's your name?"

"Lucas A—" I hesitate a second. "Allen. Go ahead and check with Hakeem. He had to run home to his wife."

Darnell smiles. "That Jasmine is one tough woman. Okay, if you're a friend of Hakeem's, then I got to let you stay. But that's my bed. You can sleep on the floor."

"That woman of mine don't never let me rest. Always nag, nag, nag." The more I say it, the more I can believe I have a Jasmine of my own. But, I don't have the time. Let fools like Hakeem fall in love. I have more important things on my mind.

Darnell laughs. "What with school and work, I don't mess with that nonsense. In my spare time, I volunteer over at the Hope Center. Do you know the place?"

Yes, I know it. I'm glad I used an alias. "I heard of it."

"They do good work. I coach basketball. You should play with us sometime."

"Yeah, sometime." I close my eyes. I didn't get much sleep because of those kids.

He's quiet for a couple minutes. Then he pokes me. "Hey, Lucas, I set up your bedding. You can go sleep over there."

I groan and roll onto the floor.

~

When I open my eyes again, it's nearly dark. The room is empty and the apartment is quiet. I open the bedroom door. Voices come from the kitchen. They have one of those old phones in the living-room. Hakeem doesn't answer until the eighth ring.

"Are you coming to get me?"

"I'll be there, insha Allah, but I can't talk now."

"Your wife keeps you on a short leash."

"It's not her. I'm about to go over to the masjid for the prayer."

"Go ahead. But, I'll see you soon, right?"

"I'll be there, man. Don't worry. I have to go." He hangs up.

I should pray too. But, it's been a crazy day. Later, after the revolution is over, I'll have time to pray and read Qur'an and all that.

We have to plan carefully if we're going to pull this off. There won't be any room for error.

~

Darnell invites me to eat supper with them. His mother quizzes me while we eat fried chicken and greens. "Where do you work, Lucas? Do you go to school?"

"I'm between jobs. That's why my woman's mad at me. She won't believe me when I tell her it's only temporary."

"Jobs are hard to find these days. If you're serious, you'll have to get out there and start looking. It took Darnell six weeks to get his job."

"It better not take me that long. I got things to do."

"Where are you from? Maybe I know your family."

"You don't know them. They're up in Milwaukee. There aren't any more jobs up there, either. I looked."

"How did you meet Hakeem? He's never been outside of Chicago."

"It was just one of those things. I don't know him long. Just a few months." She better stop asking questions. I'm sweating. "Uh, this chicken is good. It reminds me of how my mother makes it."

"I learned that recipe from my mother and she learned it from her mother." She goes on about cooking. I'm off the hot seat.

After dinner, I take my plate to the sink and wash it, just like at home. "Don't worry about that, Lucas. You're company. You go sit down and relax." I like Darnell's mother.

~

We've watched TV for the last two hours. The writing on these shows is pitiful. But, I laughed anyway because everyone else did. It's getting late. Hakeem should be here. I yawn and stretch. "I need a little fresh air." I beat it out the door before anyone can question me.

Hakeem is waiting at the corner. I climb into his car.

"Your cousin is all right. But, his mother asks too many questions."

"That's my Aunt Denise. She doesn't mean anything by it."

"She knows how to cook, I can say that."

"You're right about that." He pulls out on the street and heads north.

～

The lights are off. Everyone's asleep.

My car is still sitting in the driveway. I was afraid the police would tow it.

"Wait here while I go to my room and pick up some things. I'll be right back."

"You have your car now. Why should I stick around?"

"In case something happens. Wait until I get myself together. It won't take long."

I use my key to open the front door. Dad put the chain on, but I know how to get past that. It's not hard.

I tiptoe up the steps. Dad is a light sleeper, but he should be knocked out after what he went through today. The fifth step always squeaks. I climb over it.

In my room, I gather my money, some clothes, and a couple of books. I'd like to take the computer, but I need to travel light. That should do it. I turn, my stuff in my arms.

The light comes on. Dad is standing in the doorway.

Joshua: Part Four

He's standing there with his arms full of stuff. I knew he'd be back.

"What do you think you're doing, Luqman?" I whisper. I feel like screaming, but I don't want to wake Aisha.

"Go back to bed. I can take care of myself."

"I'm not sure you can take care of anything. What's going on?"

"I need to get some of my things. Lay off."

I can't back down this time. "Are you involved with a gang?"

"Do you think everyone in Chicago who owns a gun belongs to a gang? You don't know anything. Get out of my way."

"The police have a warrant out for your arrest. All I need to do is call them."

"You won't do it. You're a coward, just like the other racists in your family."

"I barely knew my father, Luqman. You know that's not who I am. And I don't think this is who you are, either."

"You don't know me." He shoves past me and heads for the stairs.

I rush into my bedroom and grab the phone. All I need to do is push 9-1-1. Three simple digits. He slams the front door. His car starts up in the driveway. I put the phone down. I can't.

~

I can't sleep. Michael and Gabriela are still fighting. I try not to listen, but I know she's upset about what happened today. She doesn't trust Luqman, and she's worried about the safety of their children. I don't blame her.

In the darkness of my bedroom, I stare at the ceiling. Several years ago, my brother Chris could have called the police on his son, Isaiah. He didn't, and Isaiah is now a pillar of the community, a professor with a brilliant reputation and a good son, husband, and father.

Will Luqman pull out of this nonsense and take his place in society, or will he continue to shame me?

Joshua: Part Five

All night, I was haunted by restless dreams. It's time to pray. I stumble to the bathroom for my ablutions and go out to the hallway to make the call to prayer.

When we're done, everyone shuffles off to their rooms, still tired from yesterday. I pick up the Qur'an. Michael comes back and sits next to me.

"Was Luqman here last night? I thought I heard something."

"That was him."

"Why didn't you call the police?"

I put down the Qur'an and rub my eyes. "You're a father, Michael. You know it's not that easy."

"But if Ilyas or Tariq did something like this, I wouldn't protect them."

"You can say that when they're young, but you don't know what you would do. I don't know exactly what's going on with Luqman, but I can't give up on him. Not yet."

"Mom wants us all to live with her, and I agree. Her neighbors are traveling to Europe for a month, and Mom can sublet their condo."

I'm sure Gabriela has something to do with this. "Are you punishing me for what Luqman did?"

"Ilyas is still traumatized, and we don't know what Luqman might do. I need to protect my family."

"What about Jenny and Nuruddin?"

"Jenny wouldn't bring her kids here, and Mom won't allow it. We're all worried about what could happen."

"Luqman is your brother."

"No. Jamal and Muhammad are my brothers, but not Luqman. Not after what he's done."

"When will I see you?"

"We can arrange to meet each other at Hope Center or somewhere else. Not in this house. Not unless Luqman is locked up."

"We don't know he's a criminal. Owning an unregistered gun is only a misdemeanor."

"Can you tell me he's not involved in something worse? If you can do that, we'll stay."

I search for the words to convince Michael, and myself, that Luqman is innocent. Finally, I raise my hands in futility. "Do what you need to do."

Michael hugs me. "I'm sorry, Dad. You're a great father. It's too bad Luqman doesn't appreciate that."

He goes back to his family. I sit. My first three kids came from a broken home, shuttled back and forth between Heather and me. They went through times of real pain, hurt by the mess their mother and I had created. They had every excuse to fail, but they didn't. Unlike them, Luqman came from a stable two-parent home. I can't imagine a better mother than Aisha. He had everything. Somehow it wasn't enough.

I pick up the Qur'an again. The pages fall open to Surah Luqman. *"We bestowed wisdom on Luqman: 'Show gratitude to Allah.' Any who is grateful does so to the profit of his own soul; but if any is ungrateful, verily Allah is free of all wants, worthy of all praise."* We gave him a good name—Luqman, a man of wisdom. It wasn't enough.

Kyle's Family

Hannah and Gameel watch the triplets while we visit Jeremy's son. He's in so much pain that it hurts to look at him. I don't know how Faiqa can manage to treat sick and injured kids. She's tougher than I am.

Jeremy and Raheema plan to stay at the hospital until Daud can go home. Watching them, I feel anxious. When our babies were born, I thought that was the hard part. Then we had to wait for each one to get strong enough to come home. After that, I thought we were in for smooth sailing. But Daud is eleven and here they are, keeping watch over him at the hospital. When does it end?

When Daud is asleep, Jeremy talks about the accident. "Michael called this morning. Ilyas is still upset. That's hard to go through at his age. They're just kids. They really didn't know what they were doing. I thank Allah that one of them wasn't killed."

"Where did they get the gun?" I ask.

He pauses. After a minute he says, "Luqman left the gun in the glove compartment of his car. He said he needed it to protect himself. All the adults were asleep when the boys found it. Luqman fled before the police could question him. I hope he doesn't get himself in trouble."

"But his gun injured your son," says Faiqa. "Aren't you angry?"

Jeremy shakes his head. "I'm upset that the boys found the gun, but Luqman couldn't have known they would go in his car. I hope he contacts us soon. He'll need good representation."

For the last fifteen years or so, Jeremy has worked as a public defender even though he could be earning much more with his law degree. I admire my cousin for that. But if anyone, even my brother, hurt one of my children, I couldn't be as forgiving.

～

When we get to Gameel's house, I grab the nearest baby and hold her. "How's my Nathifa?" She coos and reaches for my beard.

May Allah protect them all. The world is way too dangerous for children.

Luqman: Preparations

Political power grows out of the barrel of a gun.

—Mao Tse-Tung

With my car and my cash, I'm back in business. For the next few days, I'll stay with Darnell while Hakeem makes other arrangements. We'll call a meeting with the boys soon. It would be best if I could stay with one of them.

We have to finalize our plans. As long as I had a base at my parents' house, we could take our time, but now we need to push it along. Each time we get into a skirmish, we risk the danger of injury or arrest. Already we've lost six of our members. It's time to move it to the next level and make a real impact.

Malek and I have argued about this for months. He's one of the founders of the FOM, but we're not getting anywhere under his leadership. The small advantages we gain through street fights are minimal. His strategy could ultimately destroy the FOM. I've challenged him on this, but he won't listen. This time, he'll regret not taking me seriously.

~

All day, I hang around Darnell's place. Hakeem comes back at night.

I'm sitting on the couch, watching a game show with Darnell and his mother. They wouldn't let up until I joined them.

Darnell's mother scoots over. "Sit here with us, Hakeem. We don't see much of you these days. How's your mother?"

"She's good. She says she'll come to visit on the weekend. By the time she gets home from work, her feet hurt so bad she can hardly walk."

"Don't I know it? A person has to work twice as hard these days for half the money, but it's still better than no job at all."

"That's what Mama always says."

"You don't remember your grandfather. He was the hardest working man I ever knew. If he saw any of us sitting around, that belt got whipped out so fast you hardly knew what hit you. Darnell and Shauna have it easy, but they're better than a lot of young folks I see around these days." She doesn't look at me, but her tone sounds insinuating.

"I'm sorry I can't stay, Aunt Denise. Lucas and I got some business to take care of. You coming, Lucas?"

We go to my car. "What do you have for me?"

"Aziz said he might be able to put you up for a couple of days. I haven't found anything long-term."

"Your cousin's family is nice, but I'm worried about Darnell. He works with my father, and he keeps asking me to go to the center with him."

"A lot of people around here know your father. He's done some good work."

"So they say. Are we set for the meeting on Friday?"

"Are you really going to do it?"

As long as I'm properly equipped. "You're with me, aren't you?"

"Sure. But once you do this, there's no going back."

"Every revolution faces a point in time when success or failure hinges on a single action. This is our time."

"Isn't there another way?"

"If I get the cooperation I need, I'll back off. But, I won't mess around with pleading and bargaining. We've done enough of that already."

"I still don't like it. He's a friend of mine. We go way back."

So do we. "Friendship is one thing. We're talking revolution, and revolution is dirty business. The question is if you're man enough."

"What you saying? Man enough. Hah! I'll show you who's a man, Mr. Luqmaan!"

"You won't regret it. We'll put this movement into high gear."

"All right!"

"You know, you can't run a revolution without weapons. Do you think you could hook me up again?"

"Absolutely. There's a pawn shop a couple of blocks over. You could go there yourself."

"I could, but I'll give you the money and 10 percent on top of that if you do it for me. They know you. I'm still a new face around here."

"Okay, Lincolnwood boy. Hand over the cash, and I'll have you armed and ready by this time tomorrow."

I reach into my pocket. "You think this will do it?"

"That will do it just fine. You never told me your plans yet. How are you gonna move us to that next level you keep talking about?"

"You'll know soon. I can tell you one thing. It's gonna shake this town upside down."

"Will it advance our cause?"

"Better than anything we've done so far. Soon, all of Chicago will be talking about us."

"They're already talking about us."

"But they don't fear us. When I'm done, they will take us seriously."

Hakeem nods and smiles. I know he's with me, but I like to keep checking. If I lose the support of any of my boys, my whole mission will be in jeopardy. After Friday, I don't think I'll have to worry about that.

Blame and Suspicion

O you who believe! Avoid suspicion as much (as possible):
for suspicion in some cases is a sin: and spy not on each other,
nor speak ill of each other behind their backs.
Would any of you like to eat the flesh of his dead brother?
No, you would abhor it ... But fear Allah:
For Allah is Oft-Returning, Most Merciful.

—Qur'an: Surah 49, verse 12

Joshua: Part One

I'd like to go to the hospital to see Daud, but I don't want to run into Heather. The last thing Jeremy needs right now is fighting parents. Aisha will go instead. Heather learned long ago not to mess with her.

I haven't seen my brother since the dinner at Gameel's house, so I climb into my car and drive over to his place. My last twenty-four hours have been rough, but they can't compare with what Brad goes through every day.

Emily answers the door, the baby in her arms. After Brad got sick that last time, they decided to stay. "Assalaamu alaikum Uncle Joshua. It's good to see you."

"Walaikum assalaam. Is my brother home?"

"Come inside and I'll tell him you're here. Don't forget your mask."

He's not in the living room. Could he be in the garage again? I hope he's not in bed.

Brad walks in, wearing a sweat suit, and gives me a quick hug. "How are you?"

"How are you? Are you feeling okay?"

"I'm feeling great. I was doing a little weight lifting in the library. Beth finally agreed to let me turn it into my exercise room."

"Are you sure you should be doing that? You don't want to get worn down."

"Stop worrying. It's not good for your health. I know when to stop. Trust me on that."

"Tomorrow is the end of the month."

"And I'm still here. I could die tomorrow—a meteor could fall on the house, or I could choke on my toothpaste—but it won't be from leukemia. No more doctors. I'll know when the time comes, and until then, I intend to enjoy life as much as I can."

"How's the workout coming?"

"Great. Will you be ready for me in July?"

"I hope so." I sigh.

"Oh, I heard what happened yesterday. How's Daud?"

"He's still in the hospital. I haven't gone yet. Heather's on the war-path."

"What else is new? Have you talked with Luqman?"

No. Not really. "When Kyle was going through his rebellion, how did you handle it?"

"Not very well. If not for the car accident, I'm not sure he could have been stopped. You were able to get through to him, though."

"Did you know that some of our relatives were in the KKK?"

"Some still are. Our half-sister Celia keeps me up to date. We have a cousin working for the Klan down in western Kentucky."

That explains a lot. "Luqman found out while working on his thesis. He holds me responsible."

"He has many questions these days about life and his own identity. Give him time, and he'll work through it."

"Have you been talking with him?"

"When I was in the hospital, he came to see me every day. He still visits often."

"He can talk to you but not to me?"

"When Kyle was troubled, he had an easier time talking with you."

"What kind of troubles does Luqman have? His life is easy."

"He has many questions. Do you remember when he was in middle school, and those kids beat him up?"

"It was a racial thing, wasn't it?"

"No, it was a bully thing. One of the kids was black. Luqman hasn't forgotten."

I nod, though I don't really understand. Why does Luqman talk to Brad and not me?

We chat a while longer before I climb into my car. Brad waves from the front door. The doctor predicted my brother would be dead by the end of this month, but today is March 30, and he's still very much alive. Alhamdulillah.

Joshua: Part Two

Somebody called me at work yesterday looking for Luqman. I don't know what kind of game my son is playing, but I don't like it.

Last night, I found Aisha crying while she graded papers. "What did we do wrong? Were we too strict or too permissive? I wish I knew."

I held her hand. "He's twenty-four years old, hon. He has to make his own decisions."

"But doesn't he realize what he's doing is wrong?"

"Maybe it's not as bad as it looks. He bought a gun for protection. The boys found it. Luqman got scared, and that's why he ran away."

"Then why did he leave again? And why didn't you stop him?"

Things have been tense around here these last few days. I hope they ease up soon.

≈

On Wednesday, there's a rap at my office door. No one ever knocks. "Come in. It's open," I call.

Michael walks in, followed by Ilyas. My grandson keeps his eyes to the floor.

"How are you, Dad?"

"How about you? I miss you."

"We miss you too, but, it's better this way. Has Luqman returned?"

"Not since you left. I don't know where he is."

"Jeremy says you haven't come to see Daud yet."

"I'm waiting until he's out of the hospital."

Michael nods. "He should go home tomorrow." He clears his throat. "Ilyas wanted to see you."

I walk over to my grandson. "How are you?"

"I'm okay." He doesn't look up.

"Darnell and the other boys will be here soon, if you want to play basketball with them."

"Maybe."

"Sit down, Michael. Let's talk."

"We can't stay long."

"This is ridiculous. Are we going to let one incident break up our family?"

"It wasn't a simple incident. My nephew was shot, and my son is traumatized. And who caused this chaos in our family? A stranger? No, it was my brother. My half brother. How could you let him do it, Dad?"

"What did I let him do? He's an adult, not a child. Do you know what this is doing to Aisha? I've never seen her so upset. Go ahead and get angry, Michael, but you're taking it out on the wrong person."

He sits down. "I'm sorry, Dad. You're right. I don't have anything against Aisha and you. But if I ever get my hands on Luqman—."

"He's your brother. Instead of cursing him, I wish you would pray for him. He's in some kind of trouble, and I don't know what to do about it."

We're quiet. This should be one of the happiest times of my life. All my children and grandchildren are here. They'll leave in two weeks, and I don't know when I'll see them again.

"We'd better go," says Michael. "Mom will wonder where we are."

"I can imagine what your mother is saying about Aisha and Luqman and me. But, Michael, don't turn your back on us."

He hugs me awkwardly. "I'll talk to you later, Dad. Let's go, Ilyas."

My grandson glances back in my direction. I smile. He turns away.

Joshua: Part Three

On Thursday night, I eat a quiet meal with Aisha. Maryam is out again. She knows I don't like her to be out late. It's not safe. After dinner, I call her.

"Don't worry, Dad," she says. "I'm finishing up some work at the library, and I'll be home in an hour, insha Allah."

"Ask someone to walk with you out to your car, and make sure you lock all your car doors. Keep your phone handy. And if anybody tries to hurt you, scream your lungs out."

"I'll be okay, Dad." She pauses. "I'll call you when I'm ready to leave the library. Will that make you feel better?"

"Yes, it will. I'll see you soon."

She won't understand until she has kids of her own. No one ever does.

Daud came home from the hospital today. I'd like to see him. But what if Heather is there? If she's there, I will deal with her. Daud is as much my grandson as he is hers. I poke my head into the office. "Aisha, would you like to go see Daud with me?"

"Give me five minutes."

~

Heather's silver car is parked out front. I can't avoid her forever.

On the way here, we stopped at a store. Daud can play with Legos for hours. I bought three sets. Aisha carries a cake. She rings the bell.

Heather answers. "What are you doing here? You didn't bring that son of yours, did you? I don't want him within five miles of my grandson."

"He's my grandson too, Heather. Let me in."

Raheema comes to the door. "Assalaamu alaikum Uncle Isa, Aunt Aisha. Please come in."

Daud is sitting in the middle of the room in a wheelchair, his leg supported in front of him. He smiles a little when he sees us. "Grandpa. You came."

"How are you, big guy? I brought you Legos."

"Thanks." He takes the boxes and looks them over. "These are the kind I wanted."

Raheema takes the cake from Aisha and asks us to sit down. "I'm glad you could come. Daud has been very strong. I'm so proud of him."

"How are you feeling, big guy?" I ask.

"It still hurts. I can't go to school yet. Mom will teach me at home."

Heather comes close to me and whispers under her breath. "He's in pain. He has to miss school. He can't run and jump like a normal boy can, and it's all your fault."

I ignore her. "I'm sure your mom is a good teacher. I'm sorry you got hurt. I wish I could fix it."

Heather starts up again. "What you can do is to stay away from my grandson."

Daud looks at me with his round eyes. "Mom says this is a test from Allah, and I have to be strong. She also says it's wrong to wish.

We have to trust in Allah. Don't worry, Grandpa. I'll be okay, insha Allah."

"You have a very smart mom."

Heather leans closer. "His grandfather is the stupid one."

Jeremy walks into the living room and looks right at Heather. "Mom, can you come into the kitchen? I need your help."

Despite her faults, Heather has always been a good mother. She gets up off the couch and goes to the kitchen with our son. I quietly breathe a sigh of relief.

~

When we're ready to leave, Jeremy walks out with us. "I have to talk to you, Dad."

"This has been hard on your family. Do you need money for the medical bills?"

"Not yet. I'll let you know. The thing is, I don't blame you and Aisha, and I don't really blame Luqman. Those boys should not have been in that car, and they knew better than to pick up a gun."

"But they are boys, and no one was watching them. In some way, we're all responsible."

"If Luqman needs legal help, I'll do what I can. I can't represent him, but I can make sure he gets a good defense. He's my brother. That hasn't changed."

"I wish the rest of the family felt like that."

"Don't worry, Dad. I'll talk to them. Michael and Jenny leave in ten days, and we can't let this separate us."

"You have enough to worry about."

"Daud is a real trooper. Raheema has a two-month paid leave so she can be with him. We'll get through it. It's just another test."

I pull him into a hug. "Take care of yourself. Let me know about the money, okay? I'll see you soon."

He walks us to the car and waits until I climb inside. "Assalaamu alaikum Dad. Thanks for coming." He closes the car door.

"Walaikum assalaam."

Aisha and I ride in silence. Halfway home, I ask her, "Did you hear what Jeremy said? He wants to help Luqman."

"I'm not surprised. The first time I met Jeremy, he was five years old, and even then he was a gentle soul."

I wish I could say the same for Luqman.

Luqman: Power

The revolution is not an apple that falls when it is ripe.
You have to make it fall.

—Ernesto Che Guevara

Darnell keeps asking me to come to Hope Center with him. "They need volunteers, especially these days. They're having a fundraising dinner at the end of May, and they need people to sell tickets. Hiram Johnson is the speaker. Joshua is giving free tickets to all the volunteers. If nothing else, you'll get a free meal at a fancy hotel."

"What's the date of the fundraiser?"

"I think it's the twenty-fourth. Are you coming to Hope with me?"

"Not this time. Maybe later."

He heads out the door and down the steps, whistling along the way. This guy is just too happy—like my dad. They must put something in the water over at that center.

May 24. That could work.

∽

Aziz's wife won't let me stay with them, and Hakeem doesn't know of another place. Darnell's mother hasn't said anything, but I can tell she doesn't want me around. I may have to go out and get a job. They're not easy to find, I hear—I never tried. Hakeem has a steady job hauling trash. I'll ask if he can get me in. No matter how hard times get, they'll always need someone to take care of their garbage.

Or, I could flip burgers. Most of the restaurants have closed, but people are still willing to throw away their money on a tasteless slab of meat. Flipping burgers is brainless, and it will give me a chance to get to know the people around here. When the revolution kicks into high gear, I'll need all the connections I can get.

I dig into my pocket, retrieving the small spiral notebook I always carry and a black pen, and write two items on my to-do list: get a job flipping burgers; prepare for Friday's meeting. Before putting the notebook back in my pocket, I decide to add a third: tell Hakeem to find me another place to live.

~

There's a burger place about half a mile from Darnell's flat. I walk in and ask for an application. As I browse over the paper, I'm concerned by the request for personal information. Name, address, Social Security number. I'll have to make a few adjustments.

My name and Social Security number must fit the government records. No fabrication there. I give them the Hope Center address and Dad's work phone. I'd like to be there when they call him asking about me. For education, I say that I have a high school diploma. Having a graduate degree is great if all you want to do is read and think, but it won't get you a job in today's economy. I create three previous jobs in junk food places near our house in Lincolnwood. They probably won't check. Hakeem is my reference. That should do it. Now, all I need to do is smile.

~

It's time to prepare for the meeting. First, I have to talk individually with my boys, starting with Aziz. He's been with FOM since he was fifteen. He's married now, with two kids, but he's loyal. I catch him during lunch break at the school where he works as a janitor.

"Hey, Aziz. Assalaamu alaikum. How you doing?"

"Luqman. Walaikum assalaam. What have you been up to, brother?"

"The same. How's the family?"

"They're good. Taught my little girl how to ride a bike over the weekend. You should have seen her."

"I bet she's something. You know, Aziz, you're the most loyal member of the group. That's why I came to you first."

"Is something wrong?"

"I could be worrying over nothing. But, last night when I was coming back from the masjid, I thought I saw Malek. It was dark, so I can't be sure, but it looked like him. Same broad shoulders. Same jacket."

"That Chicago Bears jacket. I know what you mean. Malek is crazy over that jacket. He won't go anywhere without it."

"That's what I'm saying. It had to be Malek."

"Didn't you talk to him?"

"I was about to give salaams when I heard a woman's voice. Some young thing was hanging all over him."

"Are you sure it wasn't his daughter?"

"She wasn't that young. Real fine. He had his arm around her waist."

"That couldn't have been Malek. He wouldn't step out on his wife. He's a true Muslim."

"Maybe. But it looked like him and sounded like him."

"You heard his voice?"

"He was saying, 'Oh Baby' and all that. It sounded like Malek."

Aziz is quiet for a moment. "He said they've been fighting a lot lately, but everybody fights. I didn't think anything of it. That's a real shame. He has a good woman and two nice kids. Why would he throw all that away?"

"I'm telling you this woman was fine. If you came across a woman like that, you might forget your wife, too."

"No brother, not me. I got the best woman there is." He takes a bite of his sandwich. "Those poor kids."

"A man like that doesn't deserve a good family."

Aziz shakes his head and sighs. "No. He sure doesn't."

By sunset, I've told the same story to Jaleel, Rasheed, and Abu Bakr. Before leaving Abu Bakr, I say, "I wonder how he can still hold his head up."

"It's dirty. If I'd done that, I would hide my face."

"In Islamic countries, an adulterer gets stoned. But we can't do that here, can we?"

"No. I guess we can't."

Tomorrow, I'll talk to the rest of the boys.

∼

When I walk up to Shareef, the first thing he says is, "Did you hear about Malek? He's been messing around."

"Really? Where did you hear that?"

"Jaleel told me. He saw them together with his own two eyes."

"Why do you think Malek would do something like that?"

"I don't know, but I don't have any use for a snake like him."

Siddiq and Mustafa already heard it, too. Bad news travels fast. Malek's reputation is quickly unraveling.

∼

In the afternoon, I check back with the manager at the burger place. "I'm ready to work."

"I tried calling you. Your father said he didn't know where you were."

"We don't see each other much. He gave me the message. So, where do you want me?"

"Come in tomorrow morning at eight for training." He offers his hand.

"I'll see you then."

Everything is falling into place. What can I say? I'm the man.

≈

During dinner, Darnell talks about Hope Center. "You should have been there, Lucas. That was a great game. One of the best."

"I'm not really into basketball."

"Are you serious? Everybody plays basketball. What are you into?"

"When I was a kid, I used to read a lot."

"Whatever makes you happy. Joshua wasn't very happy today. He yelled at me about not cleaning up the gym before I left. I heard he's having some family problems. He's such a nice guy. Something must really be bothering him."

Maybe Darnell wouldn't feel so sympathetic if he knew what Dad's family did to our people. I saw the newspaper article in the archives. My great-grandfather was part of a gang that lynched a black man for looking at a white woman. Thank God, I take after my mother's side of the family.

≈

At night, I meet Hakeem to go over our plans. "Phase One is complete. It went more smoothly than I expected. We are on our way."

"Leave me out of this. It's your plan, not mine."

"Why are you helping me?"

"Because I think you're right. We're headed in the wrong direction, and you're the one to straighten us out. But I don't like the way you're doing it."

"But the end justifies the means, right?"

"For Muslims, how we do something is more important than what happens in the end. I'm supporting you because I trust you. Pure and simple."

"Sounds good to me."

∼

There are two hours left on my shift. I can't wait to get out of here. Is this what having a job is all about?

First, they spent four hours training me to cook burgers and fry fries even though I could have learned it all in fifteen minutes. Then they gave me a ridiculous orange costume to wear. After I put it on, they handed me a mop and told me to go clean the dining area. Two minutes after I started mopping, some kid puked. I've got to kick the revolution into high gear. I can't take much more of this.

The meeting is tomorrow. My boys are pumped. Malek won't know what hit him.

∼

Our meeting place is the garage where Bilal, a low-ranking member, works as a manager. Bilal arranged it as a way to improve his status in the gang. There's nothing wrong with him, but he's too wrapped up in his family to be of much help.

I arrive first, ready and armed. Chances are slim that I'll have to use my weapon, but it's always good to be prepared. I'm waiting in the dark when Malek walks in.

"Assalaamu alaikum Brother Malek."

He jumps and turns on the light. "Oh, Luqman. Walaikum assalaam. You startled me."

What kind of gang leader gets startled? This is one of many reasons why he has to go. "What's the agenda for tonight, Brother Malek?"

He relaxes. "We must be vigilant. The Young Pilgrims are planning something. I can feel it. When they do, we need to be ready to respond."

Like me, Malek has a college degree. That's why he was chosen to lead. He lacks leadership skills, though. That's why he works in an office all day, managing accounts for Barnett Security. It's a secure job that requires absolutely no imagination.

"Respond? Don't you think it's time we took the initiative?"

"Islam is a peaceful religion. We don't attack. Our job is to defend the Muslims from the non-believers. We are the Friends, the Followers, of Muhammad. I refuse to take the terrorist route."

"Terrorist is a fighting word. You'd better be careful."

"What are you going to do, Luqman? Beat me up on the playground? We're grown now."

"Tell me more about your plan. Are we supposed to hide in our holes and wait for them to come after us? Shouldn't we uproot the enemy before they destroy us?"

"*Fight in the cause of Allah those who fight you, but do not transgress limits; for Allah loveth not transgressors.*' Surah al-Baqarah, verse 190. The words of Allah are clear. We must fight only in self-defense." He smirks.

When Malek recites the Qur'an, everyone else thinks he's pious. They don't know him like I do. "*Kill them wherever you find them.*' Allah said that too."

"Allah didn't mean for us to go around killing people. You're taking the verse out of context. Don't be fooled."

Nobody calls me a fool, especially not Malek. My right hand forms into a fist. "You think you're special. They don't know you."

He snickers. "They don't know you, either."

I'm about to grab him and shove him against the wall, but Hakeem walks in. "Assalaamu alaikum. Are we the only ones here?" He gives me a look, and I hold back.

"So far," says Malek. "The others will come soon, insha Allah."

I'm shaking. Hakeem pulls me aside.

"Take it easy, man. Remember the revolution."

That's easy for him to say. He hasn't known Malek as long as I have.

⁓

They all file in. Aziz, Rasheed, Jaleel, Abu Bakr, Mustapha, Siddiq, and Shareef. Bilal will probably show up later. His wife always makes him eat dinner with the family. I wonder if Yousef will come. He got married in January, and I haven't seen him since. I look around. This is pitiful. After I take over, I'm going to do a major membership drive.

Malek tells us to form a circle. Before starting, he recites Surah al-Fatihah. I know that one. I learned it in kindergarten. I feel like a kindergartener standing in this circle, waiting for my teacher to tell me what to do. Is this a gang or a Qur'an study group?

He looks around the circle, making eye contact with each member. "The Young Pilgrims are increasing their activity. We must be ready to meet them. Preparedness is key." I look away.

Shareef interrupts. "Hey, Malek, I heard you was going around with some woman."

"I don't know what you're talking about. Let's stay on track here, Shareef. You need to focus." Shareef dropped out of school in the middle of ninth grade. I'm surprised he made it that far. We're all used to his random outbursts.

"As I was saying, the Young Pilgrims are getting ready for a fight. I don't know where or when, but we need to be ready at a moment's notice."

"I saw you," says Jaleel, who often imagines things. "She was one fine woman. What you got going on there?"

Malek sighs. "Siddiq, remember that you're in charge of communication. When I send out the signal, you have to quickly alert all of our members."

"I should alert your wife," says Siddiq. "I'm sure she'd like to know what you're up to."

"Why are you talking nonsense about my wife? This is serious business. We have to be ready to defend the religion of Prophet Muhammad, peace be upon him."

Abu Bakr speaks up. "What we're talking about is very serious. Do you think Prophet Muhammad approved of cheating?"

"Let's get back to business. I believe the Young Pilgrims will act soon and we need to be ready."

"We're ready to get this out in the open," says Mustapha. "You can't go sneaking around and keep acting like a pious Muslim, brother. I don't buy it."

"How do you expect us to spread Islam when our own leader is going against the religion," says Rasheed. "I'd say it's time to root out the hypocrite. That's why we're not making any progress. The problem isn't with us, it's with our leader."

"I don't know what you all are talking about."

Hakeem steps up. "You can protest as much as you want, Malek. It won't change the facts. You were seen with a woman who was definitely not your wife. Do you deny it?"

"Oh, that. I can explain. It's not what it looks like. Ask Luqman. He knows."

I laugh. "Don't drag me into this. This is your problem. You'd better save your explaining for your wife."

"She knows all about it."

"Another lie," says Hakeem. "No woman would put up with that, and I don't think we should either. I say we give Malek two choices. Either he leaves on his own, or we use force. What will it be?"

As if on cue, the boys form a line and start bearing down on Malek, pushing him toward the door. "Yeah, Malek," shouts Abu Bakr. "What will it be?"

"You all are crazy."

"You have ten seconds," says Hakeem, coming closer to Malek until they're nearly nose-to-nose. "We don't want those children to lose their daddy, as rotten as he is."

"I'm leaving." He points at me. "You won't get away with this."

I snicker. "You're a good one to go around accusing. Who's gonna listen to an adulterer?" I stand behind the boys and open my jacket so he sees my gun.

He backs out, breathing heavily. "I'm going. Don't hurt me and, for Allah's sake, please don't hurt my family." It's nice to hear Malek pleading for a change.

"Get out of here," says Hakeem.

He glares at me and backs out through the door. As the boys shout, he takes off running.

He couldn't deny that he'd been with a woman. He introduced me to her. She was his eighteen year old niece, visiting from Philadelphia. The boys don't need to know the whole story. The nice thing about a rumor is that half the truth does the job very nicely.

∼

After Malek takes off, Hakeem takes over.

"We can't move forward without good leadership, and Malek went straying. The FOM started with Malek, Aziz, and me. We were looking for a way to promote Islam. Too many of our so-called Muslim leaders are weak. We need to move to the next level and wage jihad, like Prophet Muhammad, peace be upon him."

Abu Bakr shouts, "Takbir!"

The boys respond with "Allahu akbar!"

"I was the first leader of FOM. Last year, I handed it over to Malek cause he acted like he knew more. Now we need a new leader."

Siddiq shouts, "Hakeem. Hakeem." The boys all fall in, shouting his name.

My man lets them cheer for a minute or so before signaling them to stop. "We need new blood. If I agreed to be the leader again, my wife would make me sleep on the street." Everyone laughs. "We need someone who isn't tied down by a wife and children, someone who can give all of his time to the cause. We have two single brothers here, Luqman and Shareef. Which one do you choose?"

Shareef calls out, "I accept!"

He just lost. All Muslims know you're not supposed to ask to be the leader. At least not in public. Besides, Shareef is too dumb to be in charge of a house plant.

"I pick Luqman," says Rasheed.

"Me too," says Abu Bakr.

"Everyone who wants Luqman as our new leader say 'Allahu akbar.'"

The room echoes. Even Shareef joins in. Only Aziz is quiet.

Hakeem looks around. "Anyone opposed?"

Silence.

"Brother Luqman, you are the new leader of the Friends of Muhammad. Takbir!"

The boys respond with "Allahu akbar."

"Thank you," I say. "I didn't expect this."

Aziz is still leaning against the back wall, staring at me. I may need to keep an eye on him.

Embracing Dreams

Success is not final, failure is not fatal:
it is the courage to continue that counts.

—Winston Churchill

Joshua: Part One

On Friday morning, my phone rings soon after I sit behind my desk. "Joshua Adams."

"Assalaamu alaikum Mr. Adams. I'm Hanif Shalash from Lexington, Kentucky, and I have your resume right in front of me. Are you still interested in the position?"

Did I send a resume to Lexington? I quickly search my files for the job description. Director of social services for an Islamic organization. "Yes, I am."

"Good. We would like you to come for an interview. Would next weekend be convenient?"

Michael and Jenny are leaving next weekend. "I have a family event I can't miss."

"Let's plan for the following weekend then. We want you to come on a Friday and stay through Saturday night. Will that be a problem?"

"No. Not at all." Though I'm not sure what Aisha will say.

"I'll make the arrangements. I'm looking forward to meeting you, Joshua."

"Yes. I'm anxious to meet you, too."

Now I have something to take Aisha's mind of off Luqman.

This isn't a good time. Luqman is in some kind of trouble, and my brother is dying. But, I was worrying about those things when I went to Houston. Is there ever a good time?

～

The air is getting cooler. I zip up my jacket and pull on my gloves. Technically it's spring, but Chicago has been known to hold on to winter.

On the expressway, I think about how to tell Aisha. She won't like it. Lexington is closer than Houston—just six or seven hours by car. The temperatures are moderate they say—usually not lower than 25 even in January. The average January snowfall is six inches—and that's for the entire month. Those are the selling points. The problem is that it's not Chicago.

A few blocks from home, I stop and buy mint chocolate chip ice cream. After dinner, I'll fix her a bowl and tell her we need to talk. Maybe the ice cream will soften her up.

She's in the kitchen. I sneak up behind her and kiss her neck. She spins around, her hand to her chest.

"You startled me, Isa. Don't do that." She catches her breath.

"How's my favorite wife?"

"Is that why you bought ice cream? You're trying to tell me you got married over your lunch break?"

I kiss her cheek. "You know you're the only one for me."

She steps back. "You might as well tell me. What did you do this time?"

"Don't you want to wait until after dinner?"

"No, I do not want to wait until after dinner. Go ahead." She leans against the counter and folds her arms.

"In February, I sent my resume to Lexington, Kentucky. They called today and asked me to come for an interview. I'm going in two weeks."

"Kentucky? What would we do down there?"

"They want me to run an Islamic social services organization. I'm sure they have schools down there where you could teach."

"We've been through this before, Isa. Our lives are in Chicago. Why are you so anxious to uproot us? Don't we have enough to worry about?"

"I haven't sent out any resumes in over a month. This is the last one. I promise."

"You'll get a short vacation out of it. What about me, though? I don't like being here alone when you're gone."

"Why don't we drive down together? I'll call and tell them to forget the plane ticket. We can leave a little early and spend the night in a motel along the way. What do you think?"

"Two weeks? I don't know." She pauses. "My grades will be done for third quarter. The weather should be nice. We haven't taken a vacation without kids since Jamal was born. Do you know what? I think that's a good idea."

"And if you like it down there, you may decide you want to move."

"Or, if I hate it, I'll have enough ammunition for my argument."

"Either way," I pull her closer. "I can't wait."

Joshua: Part Two

On Saturday morning, I wake up and listen. Nothing. Our house used to be filled with the noise of children. Even when they were older, there were the sounds of slamming doors and footsteps running quickly down the stairs. Shouts and laughter and cars revving in the driveway drifted on the air outside our bedroom window. Now, there's only silence.

After making my ablutions, I knock on Maryam's door and stand at the top of the stairs while calling the adhan, as I have for years. Now, there's almost no one to hear me.

We used to have birds and cats, and even a snake for Luqman. Our house is cleaner now without the animals, the noise, and the chaos. It's also very lonely.

For a moment, the house was busy again. Ilyas talked excitedly about basketball and new shoes. Mariya talked about everything else. Tariq threw his ball down the stairs and sang little songs. Little Anna cried and cooed. Ahmed and Yunus and Daud came, and even though I was dead tired from lack of sleep, I loved to hear them play. Then one sound, louder than all the rest, brought tragedy to our family and silence back to our home.

Maryam and Aisha stand behind me as I lead the prayer. No son or grandson stands beside me. I ask Allah to ease my loneliness.

～

Now that April has arrived, it's time to start working outside. I'm anxious to see flowers and green grass again. It's still too early to plant anything, but I go out to prepare the ground. For the last several years, we've had a thriving vegetable garden. Our apple and pear trees give us fruit into the fall.

Aisha joins me. "Do you think it's too soon to start planting flowers?"

"Wait another couple of weeks."

"The daffodils should come up soon."

"Shouldn't you put on a jacket? It's chilly out here."

"Oh, you're always cold. Look at the sun, Isa. Listen to the birds. Isn't it wonderful?"

"There's still a chance of snow, you know."

"Then why are you out here getting ready for your vegetable garden?"

"A man can dream, can't he?"

~

There isn't too much we can do out here yet, but I've roped off my garden area and planned where to plant each crop. I want to grow more corn this year and not so many tomatoes. Aisha froze half of our tomato crop last year, after we'd given many away, and we just finished the last batch.

Aisha is on her knees digging up the earth, preparing it for her flowers. I'm sure she's dreaming too.

A car pulls into the driveway. Michael gets out and walks over.

"Assalaamu alaikum Dad. That's a big garden."

"Walaikum assalaam. You should see it when everything's growing. The corn is up to here." I gesture with my hand.

"As high as an elephant's eye, huh? What else do you plant?"

"You name it. Tomatoes, leeks, cucumbers, eggplant, zucchini. No guava, though. Our growing season is too short."

"That sounds good. I wanted to tell you I'm sorry, Dad. I overreacted."

I open my arms. "Come here." In my heart, I knew Michael wouldn't stay away.

After a short hug, he pulls away. "Hope you don't mind a little company." He waves toward the driveway.

Gabriela and the children come. Ilyas stands next to his father, too shy for a hug. Then I notice the van behind theirs. Jennifer and Nuruddin and their children approach. Aisha leaves her future flower bed and joins us for hugs and greetings.

Jeremy, Raheema, and their children follow, with Daud leading in his wheelchair. Then there's Brad and Beth, Chris and Melinda, Isaiah and Becky, Kyle and Faiqa and their triplets, and Matt, Emily, and Zakariya. Some carry food. Matt hauls a large bag of charcoal. Isaiah and his son, Mikhail, put up folding tables. Muhammad follows carrying an ice chest. Jamal carries two watermelons, one under each arm, with Amir perched on his shoulders. Rabia walks beside him, cradling Kamila. Sakeena and Na'im bring platters of sweets. And Umar and Marcus hold trays that must contain biriyani, with Safa and Sharon close behind.

Am I dreaming? This is the way I would dream it, with one exception. In my dream, Luqman would be at the head of the parade.

~

Umar has taken his place at the barbecue grill. I stand beside him. "Are you ready to pass on the secret family barbecue sauce yet?"

"My two sons know the secret. Derek said he would try to come today. They may be a little late."

"Are Tonya and Hafiz coming?"

"I hope so. It's been weeks since I've seen my little great-grand-daughter. Bilquis is walking now. Did I tell you?"

"That's great. So you're not going to tell me how to make the sauce?"

"You know, don't you? You helped me make it after my dad died."

"That was over thirty years ago. I may need a refresher."

"Okay, but listen closely. Whatever you do, keep it inside the family." As he shares the special recipe, I remember Aisha's father. That was so long ago, and I still miss him.

There's cheering on the other side of the yard. Matt shouts, "On your mark, get set, go!" Kyle and Daud are having a wheelchair race. Kyle has the advantage, but he pulls back and lets Daud win. At the finish line, the cousins and second cousins line up to give Daud high fives.

Muhammad and Jeremy are having a discussion at one of the tables. Muhammad is probably trying to get a scoop. He's still looking for the big story that will move his career forward.

Aisha, Beth, and Melinda are laughing about something. I enjoy seeing them together. My sisters-in-law accepted Aisha immediately after I married her. Considering they'd been friends with Heather, I've always appreciated that.

"I'm glad Heather didn't come." I say it more to myself than to Umar.

"She wanted to. Michael talked her out of it and, from what I heard, so did Peter. She's calmed down a little since the accident, but it would have been awkward."

"When did Marcus get into town?"

"He flew in yesterday morning, so he could see Michael before he left. This whole picnic was my brother's idea. He talked Michael into it, and together they did all the organizing."

In the middle of the yard, Umar's brother is kicking around a soccer ball. Michael enlists the help of Ahmed, Yunus, and Ilyas, and soon they have a field. They form teams, pulling Jeremy, Nuruddin, Jamal, Muhammad, Na'im, Matt, Isaiah, Ahmed, Yunus, and Ilyas into the game. Michael and Marcus declare themselves team captains. Kyle and Daud are appointed as referees.

It's a tough game. They did a good job of mixing up the teams, agewise, so no one has the advantage. I watch my oldest son run across the field, getting ready to score. Jamal blocks him. Michael stops and takes a deep breath. He's only eighteen years younger than me, and the years are starting to catch up with him.

Marcus's team wins. After the victory lap around the field, Marcus calls, "Now it's your turn, Umar. You and the other old guys. Come on."

There aren't too many of us old guys here—just Brad, Umar, Chris, and me. "We don't have enough for a team," I shout back.

"We'll help you. Come on over."

We all line up. Even Brad. "Are you sure you want to do this?" I ask.

"As long as you and I are on opposing teams."

"You haven't finished your training yet."

"Think of this as a warm-up."

Marcus is in the middle of arranging teams when Derek and his family arrive. Derek and his son-in-law Hafiz quickly receive their assignments.

Before we take the field, Umar warns the younger guys. "Go easy on us. We don't want any heart attacks out there."

Derek laughs. "I'm not that young myself anymore."

"Let's go, fellow grandpas." Marcus became a grandfather two years ago. "We can do this."

The younger guys are worn out from the first game. Everything is a little slower now. Even so, I find myself gasping after a run down the field. I'm really out of shape.

Marcus just scored for our team. Umar puts the ball into play. Brad is on top of it. I run after him, but his herbed soybean casseroles are beating my roast beef sandwiches. He gets into position in front of the goal. Nuruddin is ready to block him, but Brad is faster. He aims, shoots, and scores.

After that play, Brad slows down a little, but his team goes on to victory, winning by one point. The yard erupts into a cheer. Matt and Isaiah rush to Brad. "It's time for your victory lap," says Matt. They hoist Brad into the air and carry him around the field. I've rarely seen my brother look so happy.

∾

We moved inside an hour ago to make the evening prayer. The party continues.

"I told you I would do it, Joshua. Didn't I? It's only April. Just wait. I'll get three goals against you in July."

"You did it. And I wasn't holding back."

"I know you weren't. You were barely walking by the end of the game. You have to start eating better."

"I will. One of these days."

"Don't wait too long." He breathes deeply. "Take advantage of your health before you get sick."

He should know.

∾

Everyone is gone. Jenny enlisted all the kids in a clean-up effort, but there will be more to do tomorrow. From the backyard to the family room to the kitchen, there are signs of family.

I didn't have much chance to talk to Jenny today. She was busy with the kids. She said she'll come see us tomorrow. I'm looking forward to it.

My whole family was here. My kids. My grandkids. My brothers. Many of my nieces and nephews. It was great.

The only one missing was Luqman. As much as I wish he'd been here, I think he's the one who missed the most.

I hope he stays out of trouble.

Joshua: Part Three

In the morning, I wake up in the fetal position, huddled next to Aisha. It's cold in here. Did someone leave a window open?

My bare feet touch the floor. Quickly, I search for my robe and slippers. In the bathroom, I make my ablutions with warm water—as hot as I can stand it. When I go back to wake up Aisha, she mutters and pulls the covers up around her.

"Come on, Aisha. We need to pray. It's nearly sunrise."

"Why is it so cold in here?"

"I don't know. After the prayer, I'll check all the windows."

On her way to the bathroom, she stops and peeks out our bedroom window. "Isa, look."

Snow. I should have known. We're in Chicago. And it's still falling.

"I'll go down and turn on the heat. Hurry up. We need to pray."

She steps into the bathroom. I look out the window again. Four inches at least, maybe more. My Pakistani and Mexican grandkids are going to love this.

~

Jenny calls a little after nine, just as we're finishing up a leisurely breakfast. "Assalaamu alaikum Dad. Are you ready for a houseful again today?"

"Sure. What's up?"

"All the kids want to play in the snow, and there are no green places near the condo. They want to build a snow family in your yard."

"That sounds great. Bring them over."

"One more thing. Mom wants to come with us."

I knew there had to be a catch. "Sure, Jenny. Tell her she's welcome. Is Peter coming?"

"No. He flew to Santa Fe for an art show." She pauses. "I thought you two were getting along now." She must have heard the strain in my voice. "Did something happen?"

"Daud got hurt." That was part of it. As for the rest, well, there are good reasons why we couldn't stay married.

"Okay, we'll be there in about an hour. First, we have to go out and buy coats and gloves for all the kids. I hope we can find some in April."

"I'll see you in about an hour then." I can't wait.

I open the kitchen cabinets. No hot chocolate. I grab my keys and make a run to the store.

~

When they pull up in front of the house, I'm waiting on the front porch. As they pile out of the vans, I shout, "Who wants to build a snowman?"

"I do," says Mariya. "But I don't know how."

"Come here. I'll teach you."

Mariya and I get to work forming snowballs and building our snowman. A snow ball whizzes a few feet away as Ahmed goes after Yunus. Before long, the boys have a snow fort built. There are about seven inches on the ground, not four, and it's the wet stuff. Perfect for a day in the snow.

Someone's crying. It's Tariq. Michael holds him, trying to get him to play, but Tariq clings to his father. He screams, "It's dirty." The whole thing would be overwhelming for a four year old who has never seen snow before.

Heather walks around the yard taking pictures of our grandchildren. She avoids me, which is great. Michael and Jenny must have said something to her.

~

Our first snowman is finished. All the kids join in to complete the family. Maryam coaxes little Tariq into the snow. Soon he's playing along with the others.

Aisha walks out onto the porch. "Come out here with us, hon," I call.

"You said you didn't like the cold."

"I don't. But this is snow. That's different."

"I'll come out after lunch. First, I think we'd better eat."

"Do you hear that, guys? Lunch time. Let's go inside."

"I want to stay out here," says Ilyas.

"We'll come back after lunch. Now let's go in and warm up."

Aisha has grilled cheese sandwiches and homemade chicken soup waiting for us. Homemade? She must have learned how to make it while Sharon was here. It's good, too.

Kids and adults grab the food and scatter throughout the house. Aisha and I sit at the kitchen table. Heather perches on a stool.

"You can sit here with us," says Aisha. "It would be more comfortable."

"That's okay. I'm fine here."

"Come sit at the table, Heather."

She carries her dishes over and pulls out a chair. "After everything I said, I didn't think you'd want to talk to me."

"I'm used to it."

"Michael and I talked this morning." She leaves it at that. It's enough.

After lunch, Jeremy stands up and makes the call to prayer. It takes a good twenty minutes to get all the kids cleaned up and lined up. I ask Michael to lead us while I stand between two of my grandsons.

As soon as the prayer is done, Yunus pops up. "Let's go outside."

"Don't you want hot chocolate first?" says Aisha. "It will keep you warm."

"That sounds good," says Jenny. "I'll help you make it."

Warm and full, we're all soon outside again. I'm helping Mariya decorate our snowman when a snowball hits my back. "Hey. Who did that?"

"Catch me if you can," says Aisha.

I retaliate, hitting Heather by mistake. She responds. The yard erupts. This is great.

I wish it didn't have to end.

Kyle's Family

The picnic was great. By the time we get home, the babies are all asleep. They were passed around and admired all day, and they enjoyed the attention. Especially Nashwa, who cooed and smiled at every one of her fans.

We take them out of their car seats and change their diapers. I change two in the time it takes Faiqa to change one. "I beat you!"

"I had Yusuf. You know how much he wiggles."

Yusuf is wide awake now and ready to play. Faiqa puts him on his blanket on the floor. "Maybe if we let him scoot, he'll wear himself out."

I pick up Nathifa and gently place her in her crib, taking a moment to stare at my sweet littlest daughter before going to get my other little girl. I'm still looking at them when Faiqa calls me. "Khalil. Can you come get Yusuf? I'm too tired."

"He's asleep already? That was fast."

"Nursing calmed him, alhamdulillah. I was afraid he'd be up all night."

Carefully, I pick him up and carry him to his crib. He wakes up easily, but I've learned that if I move very slowly, he'll stay asleep.

By the time I get back into our bedroom, Faiqa is sleeping, too. I kiss her before turning off the light. "Goodnight, honey."

She murmurs a reply.

～

On Sunday morning, we wake up to snow. We were planning to take the babies to the lake, but not today.

After the prayer, I stare out the window at the swirling snow. It was cold when I woke up. I had to turn on the heat again. I'm glad the babies were covered.

Last month, Dad told me his furnace was on its last legs. They need to get a new one, but I thought it could wait. I'd better go check.

It takes me fifteen minutes to find my coat, hat, and gloves. Faiqa put away all the winter wear last week, except for a few things for the babies. She's in bed, surrounded by the three of them.

"I have to go, honey. I won't be long. Are you planning to stay in bed all day?"

"That sounds nice. Do you remember when I used to spend a day in bed reading? I don't think they'll let me read, will they?"

"With these three around, you don't need books." I kiss each of them. "Daddy will be back soon."

"What about me?" says Faiqa.

I take her in my arms. "I'll be back very soon."

～

Matt answers the door. "I was just about to call you."

"It's cold in here. I guess the furnace finally died." A second later, we both wince at my choice of words. "Um, anyway, where is Dad? Is he staying warm?"

"He's in bed. Go on in. He'll be happy to see you."

I knock on the bedroom door. "Assalaamu alaikum. It's Kyle. Are you okay?"

Mom opens the door. Dad is in bed, reading. "Walaikum assalaam Kyle. Come in. How are my grandchildren?"

"How are you, Dad? We need to get you out of here. It's too cold."

"I'll be okay. I sure didn't expect another snowfall. Isn't it great?"

That's one way of looking at it. "You need to stay with us until I can get the furnace replaced. All of you. We have room."

"Don't worry about me, Kyle. I'll be fine. Did you see the way I beat Uncle Joshua yesterday? He didn't know that was coming."

"Yeah, Dad, that was great. But you can't stay here. Mom, help me out."

She sighs in a way I've heard many times before. "That's what I've been telling you, Brad. You'll get sick staying in this cold house."

"Can't a man spend the day in bed without being nagged by his family? I have three covers on top of me, and I'm wearing sweat pants. That should be enough."

"Okay, Dad, you can stay if you want. But Zakariya might get sick. And wait until I tell you what Nashwa did this morning."

He stares at me and shakes his head. "I didn't send you to school so you could outsmart your old man. Get out of here so I can get dressed."

While they get ready, I call Faiqa and tell her to make sure the beds in the guest rooms have clean sheets. "We won't be able to get a new furnace put in until tomorrow. I hope you don't mind."

"Are you kidding? Of course I don't mind. Guess what. Nashwa started crawling. Isn't that amazing?"

When I told Dad about Nashwa, I was bluffing. Alhamdulillah, she came through for me.

~

Dad is walking slower than usual. "Are you sore from yesterday?"

"A little. I need to exercise more."

His face is pale and his eyes are dull. "Right now you need to rest. Would you like to go in the room and take a nap?"

"And miss watching my grandchildren?" Nashwa is practicing her new skill. Yusuf is scooting toward the nearest corner. Nathifa is swatting at a toy. Zakariya chews on a rattle.

"Why don't you rest here on the couch? I'll bring you a pillow and blanket."

"Leave me alone so I can watch the babies."

When I bring him a pillow and blanket, he smirks. "All right, I'll lie down, but only to make you happy."

Fifteen minutes later, he's asleep. I should have stopped him from playing soccer yesterday. With all his bold talk, I sometimes forget how frail he really is.

∼

It's good having my family here. Mom and Faiqa look after the babies, and Emily does most of the cooking. Dad rests much of the time. Matt and I decide to drive in to work together. I insist on driving. Matt holds on to the dashboard. He's always been the cautious one.

This was a good idea. Maybe we can take a vacation together sometime. Matt and I didn't get along very well while we were growing up. I'm glad we're past all that.

∼

The new furnace is in. As I negotiated with the repair service, I remembered that Dad probably won't live to see next winter. But he's made it this long, and that's a miracle.

They took three full days to get the job done. This morning, I went over to check their workmanship and make sure the furnace was working. Everything looked good.

After work, I go back to the house with Mom, Dad, Matt, Emily, and their baby.

Dad walks in and smiles. "It feels good in here." He looks around a moment. Then he goes into his bedroom.

When I leave, he's sound asleep. He's slept a lot these last few days. I hope he's feeling okay.

He did finally beat Uncle Joshua at soccer. But was it worth it?

Luqman: Finishing Touches

When I discover who I am, I'll be free.

—Ralph Ellison

Now that I'm officially in charge, I spend hours each day working on my plans. We have to do everything just right. The revolution depends on it.

I know the who, the what, the when, and the where. The why is the most obvious of all. Paper after paper goes into the trash while I work on developing the how.

~

On Saturday, a week after my coup, I hold my first meeting. I tried to be the first one at the garage, but Bilal is here waiting. He must have heard how much he missed last time.

"Assalaamu alaikum Brother Bilal."

"Walaikum assalaam. I heard you're the one in charge now."

"That's what the brothers decided."

"Malek was a good leader."

"It's too bad he was brought down by his weaknesses."

"I heard he denied it."

"It's hard for some people to admit their mistakes."

"What are you trying to pull, man?"

"We have much work ahead of us. Wait until the rest of the brothers come, and I'll lay out my plans. We will move this struggle to the next level."

"I heard enough. Save it for the others." He walks out.

I add Bilal to my list of the brothers I have to watch.

~

The boys are all here. I give them a few minutes to talk before calling the meeting. "Okay. Listen up. We have a lot to discuss tonight."

"Aren't we going to start with Al-Fatihah?" Abu Bakr asks.

"Of course we are. Why don't you recite it this time?"

Abu Bakr recites with feeling. He has a good voice.

"Amin," I say as he finishes. "Okay. Assalaamu alaikum brothers. Let's get down to business. First, I want you to look around. Would you be afraid of a group this size?"

"Malek is gone, and Rasheed couldn't come because his kid is sick," says Shareef.

"That's right. But that's not what I mean. We need to recruit new members. You remember back in January, don't you, when those Young Pilgrims harassed our Muslim sister? There must have been fifty of us fighting back. The brothers will come out if they know there's something worth fighting for; we need to invite them back into the group."

Siddiq speaks up. "Brother Malek always said it was good to keep the group small. That way we know each other, and we don't have to worry about being carjacked."

"What he said," adds Mustapha "is that if the group gets too big, our mission could be hijacked. We don't want to forget our purpose."

"I agree completely. That's why we need to be careful in our re-cruiting. Choose only the brothers who share our vision. There are many brothers in Chicago, but it takes someone special to be a Friend of Muhammad."

"FOM!" Jaleel shouts, his fist raised. We all join in.

This is good.

After they settle down, I start to reveal my plan. They don't have all the details yet. I'll release those gradually. As the time gets closer, I'll call smaller meetings with select members—those I know I can trust. We'll be the core of the action.

Before breaking up, I remind them to bring in new members. "But, only the best for FOM." Jaleel leads us in another cheer. Everyone leaves feeling good, having completely forgotten about Malek.

Except for Aziz, I guess, who stands in the corner and silently watches me.

$\sim$

What's with the snow? It's April. All the way to work, cars around me are slipping and sliding. I nearly get rear-ended.

For the last couple of days, I've carefully watched my co-workers, looking for new recruits. We only accept Muslims, though. A new guy started yesterday. Later, I caught him praying in the break room.

His name is Conner. Blonde hair and blue eyes. I never would have guessed.

After lunch, we have a lull. We're both on the burger assembly line. I ask him, "Are you a Muslim? I saw you praying."

"Yes. I converted three months ago."

"That's interesting. How much do you know about Islam?"

"I read the Qur'an daily. I don't know much yet, but I'm learning. Why do you ask?"

"I'm a Muslim, too. Assalaamu alaikum."

"Walaikum assalaam." He glances at my name tag. "Luqman. I should have known."

"I'd like to talk to you. When is your shift over?"

"At six."

"Mine too. Do you have the time?"

"Sure. I'd like that."

A woman walks in, surrounded by hungry kids. The order will be coming any minute. "Good."

"Insha Allah," he says.

"Yeah." I put Conner in the back of my mind and concentrate on assembling five double cheeseburgers.

～

After we clock out, I ask Conner to come sit in my car. I'm not sure he'll fit into the gang, but I want to check him out. "Why did you convert?"

"I never agreed with what I heard in church. Two years ago, I saw a documentary about Muslims, and I was impressed. I found the closest mosque—I mean, masjid—and talked to some people. I like the way everything in Islam comes together. It's a very sane way to live."

"Don't take this the wrong way, but I always want to know why a white guy chooses Islam. You're not the first white Muslim I met." *Not by a long shot.* "But I'm still curious. I mean, to me, the most important part is the message of liberation."

He nods slowly. "I never looked at it that way. I'm more into spirituality than social justice."

No, he's not what I'm looking for. He sounds like my dad. When I was in high school, I tried to discuss social and political issues at the dinner table. Dad's reply was he didn't care much about politics. End of discussion.

"That's interesting. You know, I just remembered I have to meet someone. It's good talking to you, Conner. I'll see you at work tomorrow."

"I'd better go, too. It's nice meeting you. Assalaamu alaikum."

Yeah. "Walaikum assalaam."

I'd better stick with the brothers. They know what I'm talking about.

~

When I get back to the flat, Darnell's mom is waiting for me. "I'm sorry, Lucas, but you can't stay here no more. It's hard enough taking care of my family. Tomorrow, I want you to find a place of your own."

No problem. I have a little cash now. "That's okay, Mrs. Jones. I understand." I never much liked it here anyway. Darnell is always bugging me about going to the center, and Shauna has an attitude. It'll be good to get out on my own.

~

I have a few hours before work to go look for an apartment. There's a place down the street with a "For Rent" sign. I'll be set in no time.

It's a flat, like Darnell's place. The landlady lives downstairs. I ring her bell. She takes long enough to answer.

"What is it?" She's an old lady, still walking around in her robe and slippers. Hopefully, I won't have to look at her too often.

"I'd like to rent the flat upstairs."

"Here are my terms. You need to pay the first and last month's rent, and I'll need a security deposit. If you smoke or drink, you can forget about it."

I look over the paper she handed me. Just moving in would cost me a full month's salary, and I don't have it.

"You pay your own heat and electricity, too. I'll provide the water."

I hand back the paper. "Thanks, ma'am. I can't afford it."

"Then you shouldn't have come here and bothered me. I'm missing my show." She slams the door in my face.

I wouldn't have liked it here, anyway. There are lots of other places.

~

While I'm at work, I ask around. Nobody knows of a place for rent. That doesn't mean anything. These people probably don't get out much.

Conner and I barely say two words to each other. We're too different. I don't know if it's skin color or just attitude. Whatever it is, I'm glad I take after my mother.

At the end of my shift, I clock out and rush to my car. I have a couple of hours before sunset to look for a place. But there's nothing. Is this why there's so many homeless at Evans?

I could check into Evans. That would be interesting. Stu has probably gone home for the night. Their staff changes all the time. It's possible no one would recognize me.

But, I'm not a beggar. If I'm going to lead a revolution, I have to be self-sufficient. Tonight, I'll sleep in my car. No problem.

∾

My neck hurts, and I'm cold. I hardly slept last night because of all the noise on the street. I have to find a place to stay.

On my way to work, I scan the streets, looking for a sign. There's nothing. No wonder that woman could charge so much. High demand and low availability. She probably never went to college, but she understands economics.

My back hurts while I stand on the burger assembly line. I hope it's a little warmer tonight. Last night, I had to curl up into a ball to stay warm. It's hot back here, with the boiling oil and the burgers on the grill, but when I step outside, that cold wind will creep under my clothes and stay there.

Hakeem will help me out. He has to. After work, I go over to his place.

"Hey, Luqman, assalaamu alaikum. How is everything?"

"Darnell's mother won't let me stay with them anymore, and last night, I had to sleep in my car. Do you know how cold it was out there?"

"That's tough. I'm sorry Aunt Denise threw you out. Do you want me to talk to her?"

"No, I just need a place to stay. What about your couch?"

"You know I'd like to help you, brother, but Jasmine and I are working things out, and this isn't a good time. Do you know what I mean?"

"But all I'm asking for is your couch, man. Or if you want, I'll sleep on the floor."

"Jasmine wouldn't like it. She keeps talking about our privacy. She wouldn't even let my sister spend the night on Saturday when her car broke down. She made me get out in the snow to take Lena home."

"That's the trouble with being married. Some woman is always bossing you."

"Quiet. She's in the next room. I can give you a blanket. That should get you through the night. There are some benefits to being married, too. At least I have someone to keep me warm. Hold on."

He shuts the door. What will Jasmine do to him if she sees me? He needs to man up and show her who's boss. Marriage sounds like too much trouble.

He comes back a few minutes later and hands me a blanket. "Stay warm out there. I'll see you on Friday."

Before I can say anything, he shuts the door. He has to get back to Jasmine.

~

Last night was better. The blanket helped. I should have asked for a pillow, too.

This is actually a good experience. A revolutionary has to be tough. First, I will conquer the cold. That will put me in better shape to conquer the racist, Islamophobic society I live in.

Plots and Plans

When evil men plot, good men must plan.
When evil men burn and bomb, good men must build and bind.
When evil men shout ugly words of hatred,
good men must commit themselves to the glories of love.

—Martin Luther King, Jr.

Luqman: Part One

This week, I'm meeting with only a few of my boys. They will be my lieutenants.

Hakeem was the first one I asked to join me, of course. I decided to include Aziz because he is one of the three founders. Abu Bakr, Mustapha, and Rasheed round out the group. The others don't need to be in on this mission. For now, I don't even want them to know much about it.

We meet at the lake a little after sunset. It's a public place, but in a city like Chicago, no one pays attention. We can't use the garage because I don't want Bilal involved.

~

We huddle together near the shore. The lake ebbs and flows. Not many people are out tonight. A police car sits in the parking lot. We'll break it up if we're approached.

Abu Bakr recites Surah al-Fatihah. It seems like a meaningless ritual to me, but the boys appreciate it.

"This is one of the most important meetings FOM has ever had. Remember that whatever is said here stays here. Don't even tell the other brothers. I chose you five because I know you have what it takes to get the job done. Involving too many people could jeopardize the mission."

"At the last meeting, you said you wanted to recruit new members," says Mustapha.

"I do, but not for this particular mission. Did you recruit anyone?"

"Not yet, but my cousin may join. I can bring him around next week."

"Good. Does anyone else have a new recruit?"

"My brother is sixteen. He'd like to join," says Rasheed.

"Bring him next week, too."

"What's the mission?" Abu Bakr asks.

"Listen closely. I don't want to repeat myself. Remember, this stays here with us. Not a word to your wives or anyone else. Understand?"

I glance at Aziz. He nods.

~

When I'm finished, they're all quiet. I use the silence to make my final point. "So far, we've concentrated on random skirmishes. Even when we win, we don't make progress. This time, we will strike at the root."

"Do you really think this will work?" says Abu Bakr.

"If each of us completes his assigned task, I don't know how we can miss. It will need teamwork and intelligence, but I know we have that. How can we fail?"

Aziz leans forward. "This could push our movement to new levels, but it's risky. If we're caught, we won't just spend the night in the Cook County jail. You're talking about time in the federal prison."

"*If* we're caught. But, if we work together and work carefully, we can do this."

"Are you talking about murder?" asks Rasheed.

"Only if necessary. We don't want to kill anyone, but if we have to in order to serve the mission, we can't hesitate. How many of you are armed?"

Only Hakeem and Aziz nod.

"The rest of you have two weeks. Make sure you know how to use it properly. We don't need any stupid accidents."

"I have a little boy at home," says Mustapha. "What if he gets hold of it?"

"My wife would kick me out if she saw me carrying," says Abu Bakr.

"Act smart. Don't leave it out where anyone can see it. Aziz has kids, and Hakeem has a bossy wife. They manage."

"And don't leave the gun in your glove compartment if there's any chance kids are going to go looking there," says Hakeem.

"Yeah. That too. Any more questions?"

Rasheed glances back. "Someone's coming."

The officer has stepped out of the car. "Next Friday, by the Field Museum," I remind them.

Each of us walks off in a different direction. My heart beats a little faster, but by the time he gets there he won't find anyone to question, and I don't think he'll bother chasing us. We just need to be careful.

~

Everyone has an assignment. Mine is to move back in with my parents. Unless I can get my father to help me, the mission will fail.

Tomorrow, I'll pay a visit to my brother Muhammad. If I ask him to help me reconcile with Mom and Dad, I know he won't refuse.

Joshua: Part One

Michael and Jenny and their families are leaving tomorrow. Heather and Peter have invited us to dinner at their condo.

I haven't been here since we had the going-away party for Jennifer, the first time she went to Pakistan. Heather serves a catered buffet meal with four types of salads, chicken, steak, three kinds of potatoes, and cheesecake for dessert. I eat until I can barely move. Brad wouldn't approve, would he?

We're nearly finished eating when Peter stands up. "I don't like giving speeches, but I wanted to say it's been fantastic having you here again. Michael and Jenny, you've both grown up quite a bit since I married your mother, and I'm very proud of you. We will miss you very much." When he sits down, everyone looks at me.

I don't like giving speeches either. "You know how much I love you. It's been great having you here, and it would be even greater if you didn't have to leave. Remember that family is more important than anything, except faith. If you have those two, you'll never go wrong." I pause. "Oh, and thanks for a great weekend. A barbecue and a snow ball fight. I couldn't ask for more."

The room is quiet. Then Daud speaks up. "Even though I got hurt, I had one of my best times ever." His leg is still stretched out in front of him, but his spirit hasn't been broken.

Before we leave, there are hugs and last words. We'll do it all again at the airport tomorrow. It's been quite a month, and not always easy, but, as Daud said, I had one of my best times ever.

Muhammad and Maryam ride with Aisha and me in the van. We're almost home when Muhammad says, "I heard from Luqman today. He wants to see me."

Aisha turns to look at him. "What did he say?"

"He just said that he wants to talk."

"When are you going to see him?" I ask.

"Tomorrow."

I almost ask Muhammad to tell him I miss him. But, I'd better wait to see what happens.

≈

They planned their flights to leave within an hour of each other. Jenny's is first.

We get to the airport early and wait in the Pakistani Air departure terminal. There aren't many travelers this morning. It's quiet until our family arrives, large and noisy. Other passengers give us disapproving stares.

I hug each of my grandchildren before moving on to Jenny and Nuruddin.

"Did I ever tell you I'm proud of you?" I ask Jenny.

"I always like to hear it again. I love you, Dad. Come visit us sometime."

"What if we decide to move there?"

"You would be very welcome," says Nuruddin.

Ahmed and Yunus won't let me hug them. Little Noora lets me hold her for a minute. Salma is crying. Almost every time I see her, she is crying. Once she starts talking, she'll probably never stop.

Kyle races up in his wheelchair. "Good. I didn't miss you."

"You haven't insulted me once this month," says Jenny. "Have you lost your edge?"

"Maybe," he grins. "But at least I haven't lost my waistline."

"And I haven't lost my hair," Jenny replies. Kyle's hairline has receded a little, hasn't it?

"Just don't lose your way back to Chicago," he says. "It's been great seeing you."

It's time for them to board their flight. Jenny hugs her mother and me one last time. Her final words are for Maryam. "You really need to tell Dad what's going on."

Maryam smiles. "Okay. I will."

What is going on? I don't have time to ask. But I do give Maryam a look. She grins and turns away.

~

We race to a different terminal and go through our goodbyes one more time. "I want to write to you," says Mariya.

"I would like that very much."

Ilyas won't let me hug him either. But he does come close and say, "Thank you for taking me to play basketball."

Their plane has started boarding. Michael gives me a quick hug. "Come to Mexico, Dad. I know you like it there."

"Yes, I do." He doesn't know how tempting that is.

He saves his final hug for Heather. We watch as their family disappears around a corner. Everything is quiet again.

Heather and Peter drift away. Aisha, Maryam, and I start walking toward the parking lot. Halfway there, I confront my daughter. "What do you need to tell me?"

"Can you wait until tonight? I think you'll like it. I hope you will."

When they were small, I thought things would be easier when my kids grew up. But these kids of mine are wearing me out.

Luqman: Part Two

I pull up to Muhammad's apartment building at 8:00 PM. Before getting out of my car, I review my lines. I'll need to show regret for my actions, and express the intention to do everything right. We should pray together before I leave. Muhammad is very much like Dad. If it works with him, I shouldn't have any problems.

Mom will be tougher, but I'll appeal to her emotions. It sounds rotten, and I don't feel good about playing her, but I need to do this for the good of the revolution. One day she'll understand.

On my way over, I pick up a pizza with all of Muhammad's favorite toppings, including pineapple. Who decided to put fruit on top of pizza?

I knock and wait. He opens the door nearly a minute later and stares at me. "I wasn't sure you would come."

"I can leave if you like."

"No, that's not what I meant. Assalaamu alaikum. It's good to see you. How have you been?" He gives me an awkward hug and nudges me into the apartment.

"Walaikum assalaam. Here. I remembered the pineapple."

"Thanks. So, where have you been? What's going on? Mom and Dad are worried about you."

"I shouldn't have taken off like that, but I got scared. I have a job now. That should make them happy."

"That's good. So you want me to talk to them for you?"

We barely know how to talk to each other. Muhammad never understood me. He was my first tormentor. Others followed. "Sure, if you want. But if they're planning to call the police, I'll just disappear again."

"I'll tell them that."

"If you want, I can call tomorrow and see how it went." I stand and face the door.

"Don't leave. Sit down and have some pizza. Why don't you stay here tonight?"

I look around at the dirty clothes on the floor and dirty dishes in the sink. Even I'm not this messy. I hope he doesn't have roaches. "Are you going to talk to them tonight?"

"I'll go after I finish the pizza, okay? Don't hassle me, Luqman. You're asking a lot of this family, do you know that? It's your fault Daud was hurt, and that poor kid is still in a wheelchair. They should call the police, or maybe I should. You broke the law. Doesn't that mean anything to you?"

"You're still 'Righteous Muhammad,' the 'Good One'. Forget it. I don't need your help." I throw my slice of pizza in the box and walk toward the door.

"Wait. Dad knows you're coming, and he wants to work things out with you."

"You're willing to do this for Dad, is that what you're saying?"

"I said you can sleep on my damn couch. What more do you want?"

"You curse? Do Mom and Dad know that? They would be shocked."

"Shut up and finish your pizza."

Nothing has changed. Strangely, I find some comfort in that. If Muhammad had sincerely hugged me and welcomed me back, I probably would have run away.

∼

After a few bites of pizza, he grabbed his keys and walked out. I won't lose any sleep over my brother. He's hated me for as long as I can remember, and he's just clever enough to hide it from everybody except me.

This place is a pig sty. He probably hasn't taken the garbage out for two weeks. I wash the dishes and get rid of the trash. Just enough to make the place livable. He can pick up his own stinking clothes.

He's been gone for an hour. Are they all sitting around laughing at me? I wouldn't be surprised.

That's okay. I have plans, and I know they'll be impressed when they see what I'm capable of doing.

Joshua: Part Two

At 8:00 PM the doorbell rings. Maryam practically flies down the stairs. "I'll get it." Does this have to do with her surprise?

Zaid walks in. "Assalaamu alaikum Uncle Isa. How are you this evening?"

"Walaikum assalaam Zaid. How have you been?" He's not technically my nephew, but his father, Ismail, has been my friend for over thirty years. Ismail's the one who arranged for me to meet Aisha. "How are your parents?"

"Alhamdulillah, we're all good. May I talk with you?" He fidgets, shifting from one leg to the other. Zaid never could stay still.

"Of course. Come into the family room. Maryam, could you bring some refreshments?" I have no idea what we have in the house, but she should be able to find something. "And tell your mother Zaid is here."

"Actually," says Zaid, "I need to talk with you first, Uncle Isa. How are you?"

He already asked that. "I'm fine. What do you need to talk about?"

We sit. He looks away and taps his right knee. "This is something I've thought about for a long time now. You know I'm teaching at the university, uh, in the math department. I just learned I'm being promoted to full professor."

"Masha Allah, that's great news. Congratulations."

"Thank you. That's not what I wanted to say, though. I only want you to understand that I'm building my career and making a good salary." He taps his knee to a faster beat. "The reason I'm here, Uncle Isa, is that, um, it's because I would like to marry Maryam." He sighs. His beat slows down.

Zaid was always a good kid, though a little mischievous. He earned his doctorate at a young age and immediately began teaching at Northwestern. "Have you and Maryam talked about this?"

He blushes. "Yes, we communicate. I hope you don't mind. She's nearly finished with her degree. I'm renting an apartment near the university. Later, we hope to buy a house through a non-interest program." He glances at me. "Yes, we've talked."

I lean back in my easy chair. Thirty-three years ago, I was the young man begging Dr. James Evans, a very imposing figure, to let me marry his daughter. He grilled me about my children and my failed marriage to Heather. I was a nervous wreck.

My father-in-law had never met me before the day I asked to marry his daughter. But, I've known Zaid since he was a baby. We went to his aqiqah. He was seven days old when I first held him in my arms. I've watched him grow and mature all these years. And his father is one of my oldest friends. Of course, he can marry Maryam. But I don't want to make it too easy for him.

"Why didn't you come to me earlier?"

He looks down. "Forgive me for that. I wanted to wait until after my promotion, so I could prove to you that I'm worthy of her."

Worthy of her? I didn't know he was so poetic. "Are you aware that Maryam is a very lively young lady who gets easily bored? I can't imagine her being tied down to a husband, certainly not one who expects her to fit the profile of a professor's wife."

He smiles. "I'm sure you know, Uncle Isa, that I can be lively myself. I would never ask Maryam to give up who she is. Her spirit and determination are two things I love about her." He blushes again and looks down.

I didn't expect Maryam to get married this soon, but she is twenty-one and not really my little girl anymore. If I was to sit down and try to choose someone for her to marry, I'm sure Zaid would be at the top of my list. It's tempting to string him along, but that wouldn't be fair. I offer my hand. "I will be happy to have you as my son-in-law."

Maryam and Aisha walk in with the refreshments. I was wondering what took them so long. Maryam hugs me. "Thanks, Dad."

"You should have told me." I try to sound stern.

"No wonder you knew that Zaid was in St. Louis," says Aisha.

My daughter looks down. "I'm sorry."

"Don't worry about it. Soon you'll have to answer to Zaid."

She hugs me again. This is my baby girl, who was born in my car the day before they hauled me off to prison. I held her the second she came into this world. Where have the years gone?

~

Muhammad walks in a few minutes later. Zaid is relaxed now, listening as Aisha and Maryam discuss wedding plans.

"Muhammad, you came at the right time. Zaid just asked to marry your sister."

"Really? Congratulations, dude." They shake hands. He grins. "Or maybe I should say lots of luck."

Maryam swats him.

He ignores her. "Dad, I need to talk with you."

"Let's go in the kitchen." This must be about Luqman.

He goes to the refrigerator and pours himself a glass of orange juice. "Do you want some?"

"No. Sit down and tell me about your brother."

"There's not too much to tell. He wants to come back home. He has a job."

"That's good."

"Yeah. And he doesn't want you to call the police."

That's why he stayed away. "Where does he work? Did he tell you? Where is he now?"

"He didn't say where he works. I left him at my place. He can spend the night there."

"I'm glad to see you boys are getting along. You two always used to fight so much."

He nods. "So what should I tell him? Will you call the police?"

"If I had wanted to turn him in, I could have done it when he came back for his car. Let me talk with your mother, but as far as I'm concerned, he can come back tonight as long as he doesn't bring another gun around here. I'm sure his case isn't a top priority for the police. Did you hear about the shootings on the West Side?"

"Yeah, that was awful. All those kids caught in the cross-fire. And somehow nobody saw anything. Anyway, I'd better get back. I'll tell Luqman what you said."

"Don't you want to stay and celebrate? This is an important moment for your little sister."

"No, I'd better go. I'll give Luqman your message."

"Tell him not to disappear again. In fact, ask him to come to the house tomorrow after work. Tell him we'll both be happy to see him."

"I'll tell him." Muhammad leaves quickly, not even stopping to say goodbye to Aisha and Maryam. I wonder what's bothering him.

Muhammad's Journal

In the name of Allah, the Most Gracious, the Most Merciful

My brother is asleep on my couch. I can't sleep.

I've heard the story of the prodigal son, but I didn't really expect it to work that way. What is going on with my father? I'm the one who has always been there for him. Have I ever talked back or made him worry? Have I ever broken the law? He calls me a good son, but he's willing to take back my brother, no questions asked.

How do we know what Luqman has been doing this past month? Does he really have a job? Is he stealing? Has he assaulted anyone? There must be some reason to explain his sudden reappearance. Luqman knows how to lie better than anyone. We still don't know if he's part of the FOM, but I sure wouldn't put it past him.

And what's with that 'Righteous Muhammad' talk? It's not the first time he's called me that, but I wish he would stop. I don't act all holy. I only do what Allah and His Prophet, peace be upon him, have commanded. I'm a Muslim. At least one of us is.

Mom is one of the smartest women I've met, but she has a weak spot where Luqman is concerned. He always went crying to her, and she always tried to fix it for him. That's another thing I can't stand about my brother. He acts so tough, but he's really a coward.

Luqman is a liar and a hypocrite. He prayed with me before going to sleep tonight, but it was all an act. I wish Mom and Dad could see it, too.

I need to pray. Then I'll read some Qur'an. I'm going to have a hard time sleeping tonight.

Luqman: Part Three

Muhammad makes the call to prayer. I struggle out of my dreams and stumble to the bathroom, so I can show him what a good Muslim I am.

After the prayer, he makes coffee. "Thanks for washing the dishes. Do you want breakfast?"

"Do you have any bagels?"

"Yeah, they're somewhere in the fridge. Go ahead and look."

The bag of bagels is on the bottom shelf. They're moldy. "I'll just have coffee."

"Did you sleep well?"

"Yeah. The couch is comfortable." I wish he would stop trying to make conversation. We both know we can't stand each other. Why pretend that we do?

It's like he reads my thoughts because he sits down and drinks his coffee in silence. When he's done, he leaves his mug in the sink. "I need to take a shower. When do you go to work?"

"I start at ten. Go ahead and take your shower."

He backs out of the kitchen, watching me. He's probably worried I'll stab him in the shower, like a scene from a movie. I could walk into the bathroom with a butter knife in my hand and watch him have a heart attack. That would be fun. But I need to be good for the next few weeks. I wash his mug instead.

I'm watching TV when he walks out of his bedroom, dressed in clean but wrinkled clothes. "I'm leaving for work now, Luqman."

"Go ahead. I can let myself out."

"You need to leave now, too. It's the lock. It's weird. Um, remember that Dad wants you to go to their house after work today. I'll see you later. Thanks for coming by."

Thanks for not stealing my stuff. Thanks for not stabbing me in the shower. My brother is pitiful. No wonder they don't trust him with the important news stories. "Thanks for letting me stay with you. It's been great. We'll have to do this more often." I like to watch him squirm.

"Yeah. Well, I'll see you later. At Dad's house. Assalaamu alaikum."

"Walaikum assalaam." He watches me as I walk to my car. He probably wants to make sure I don't stay and break into his apartment. The funny thing is that even if I wanted to steal something from him, he doesn't have anything worth taking.

∽

After work, I drive over to Mom and Dad's house. Both of their cars are in the driveway. This won't be easy, but I have to do it.

I knock. Dad answers. "Luqman. Assalaamu alaikum." He reaches out to hug me. His hug is sincere. "Come inside. We're just about to eat. Mom made meatloaf."

And mashed potatoes. One of my favorites. Mom's standing in front of the stove. I walk over and put my hand on her shoulder. "How are you?"

She turns around. "What about you? Where have you been?"

"I stayed with somebody for a couple of weeks, but I'd like to come home if it's okay."

"Let's eat. Get the biscuits out of the oven, will you?"

We sit down, just the three of us, and act like a normal family. "Where's Maryam?"

"She had to do some work at the library," says Dad. "Did Muhammad tell you she's getting married?"

Not a word. "No. Is it Zaid?"

"He came here last night to talk to me."

"That's good. Zaid always liked Maryam, even when they were little."

"Luqman, where were you all of those times when you said you were with Zaid?" Mom stares at me with that look of hers.

There's no use trying to get around her. She'll know. "I was with some friends over on the South Side. For a while, I stayed with my friend's cousin. You know him, Dad."

"Who is it?"

"Darnell Jones. He volunteers at Hope Center."

"Yeah, I know Darnell. He's a great volunteer, and I'm glad to hear he's one of your friends."

That's not exactly what I said, but I don't correct him. "Darnell talked about you all the time. He tried to get me to come to Hope

Center with him, but I wasn't ready to see you yet. He doesn't know I'm your son." I'm about to tell Dad my alias, but that's probably not a good idea.

"Somebody called my office once, looking for you. What was that about?"

"When I applied for my job, they needed a phone number. That's the first one I thought of. I went back the next day and they hired me."

"What kind of job is it?" Mom asks.

"Flipping burgers. I can get something better later on. For now, I just need some cash."

"Have you finished your thesis?" Dad asks.

If I confess to smaller lies, they won't worry about the big ones. "That's something else I need to tell you. I finished it last fall. They have a diploma for me. I haven't gone to pick it up yet."

"You already graduated?" Mom asks. "Why didn't you say anything? That's a great accomplishment. We should have celebrated."

"After I finished my degree, I wasn't sure what I wanted to do with it. I needed time to think things through. Now, I'm ready to get back on track. You know what I mean, Dad. Didn't you feel like that when you were my age?"

"I was a little younger than you, but I know what you mean. What was the title of your thesis?"

"'An Historical Analysis of the Role of the Ku Klux Klan in Early 20th Century Race Relations in the City of Chicago.' It's a mouthful, isn't it?"

"Listen, Luqman, Uncle Umar told me about your research on the day you ran away. I didn't know my family was in the Klan, though I should have guessed. You don't still blame me for what they did, do you? I'm not responsible for the actions of my ancestors."

Right. Tell me you didn't stain my heritage with that racist feculence. "It's not just your ancestors. Did you know that one of your cousins works with the Klan at its Kentucky headquarters?"

"Brad mentioned that a couple of week ago, but I never knew my cousins. Sam left, and I had no contact with his family. Brad still keeps in touch with our half-sister. That's how he knows."

"How is Uncle Brad? I haven't seen him for a while."

"He'll be happy to see you. The whole family came over here for a picnic about a week ago, and Brad finally beat me at soccer. The last time I saw him, he was very happy."

"That's good."

"Speaking of Kentucky, your mom and I are going down there this weekend. I've been offered a job in Lexington, working with an Islamic social services organization. Wouldn't it be nice to live someplace warmer?"

If he's not connected with the racists in his family, why would he go down there? He'd better not expect me to go to Kentucky with them. That won't happen. "That sounds good. You never liked the cold."

We spend the rest of the meal talking about normal, everyday things. My confessions seemed to satisfy them. Now, I'm free to move on to the next level.

Joshua: Part Three

Luqman opened up to us and told the truth, so we were able to talk things through. I hope he learned something from that.

Last December, I gave him money for this semester's college expenses. It wasn't much, because he had a graduate assistantship, but it was enough. While we were sitting at the table, I thought about mentioning the money. He probably wasted it. But, as long as he's willing to learn from his mistakes, I should just let it go.

This last month has had some real twists and turns but, alhamdulillah, things are settling down. Now I can concentrate on our trip to Lexington.

Aisha will make sure I have the right clothes and shoes for the interview. She's also checking out Lexington's attractions. I don't know if I'll have time for sight-seeing, but I want her to enjoy herself.

Today I told Stu where I was going. "You know I don't like the cold. Maybe we can settle down someplace warmer."

"That sounds like a good place to retire. I hope you don't leave us, though. You're a major part of our success."

"If I do accept another job, I'll recommend you to take my place."

"They wouldn't hire someone as young as me, but thanks for the compliment."

"I mean it, Stu. You have a lot going for you. Oh, don't tell anyone else where I've gone. They don't need to know I'm looking for another job."

"Is it the fundraiser?"

"That's one reason. There are others. The cold is getting to me. And after my brother dies, I'm not sure I want to stick around."

"Don't you have quite a bit of family here though?"

"Four sons and a daughter. A niece and some nephews. One of my sons will probably move soon because of the Chicago job market. We can always come to visit. It's less than 400 miles away. Anyhow, I haven't been offered the job yet, and if my wife gets her way, we'll stay in Chicago, so I wouldn't worry about it."

"Have a good trip. Let me know how it goes."

"I'll do that." I laugh. "Maybe I can sell some tickets to the fundraiser this weekend."

"We're doing well on sales now. Gameel bought twenty to give to his top employees, and your nephew, Kyle, just sold twenty more."

"No wonder their company is so successful." I pack up my briefcase. "Have a good weekend, Stu. I'll see you on Monday."

Driving down the expressway, I begin to feel excited.

~

Aisha has everything packed. Luqman helps me load the van before dinner. We'll eat and leave, stopping at a motel somewhere in Indiana.

During dinner, I give Luqman last minute instructions. "Make sure you lock all the doors at night. Mom stocked the refrigerator, so you should be okay for food. And no friends."

Luqman laughs. "Those are the same rules you gave me in high school."

"You've changed, but the rules haven't. That's the way it is."

"That's fine. I'll probably spend the weekend reading."

"You have quite a collection of books. I'd like to read some of those."

"You're welcome to them."

Luqman has behaved better this week than he has in years. I hope this means he has finally grown up.

~

Last night, we stopped just south of Indianapolis. We leave the motel after breakfast. This is nice. No jobs. No deadlines. No interruptions. We are on a schedule, though. I told the brother I'd meet him at the masjid for the Friday prayer. He asked me to give the sermon today, but I declined. I've never been much of a speaker.

After crossing the bridge over the Ohio River, we pass through Louisville, which is much smaller than Chicago. "This is nice," says Aisha. "It's a pretty city."

Several miles later, we go through a tunnel and enter a land of rolling green hills. Aisha opens her window and takes a deep breath. "The air is cleaner here."

She's right. I hate to think of how dirty our lungs have become in all the years of big city living. I breathe in the difference.

∼

I follow the directions to the masjid, arriving about forty minutes before the prayer. Aisha and I walk inside and go our separate directions.

Only a few men are in the prayer area. I bow down in prayer and sit quietly, remembering Allah. Every few minutes, I look around for Brother Hanif, though I don't know how he looks.

I pick up a copy of the Qur'an and begin softly reciting. About ten minutes into my recitation, I'm aware of someone sitting next to me. I finish the verse and look up.

"Assalaamu alaikum. Are you Brother Joshua?"

"Yes. Walaikum assalaam. You must be Brother Hanif."

"Welcome to Lexington. I hope you had a pleasant trip."

"The Kentucky scenery was beautiful. You can call me Isa. I've used that name since shortly after my conversion."

"How long have you been a Muslim?"

"Thirty-five years."

"Masha Allah, that's wonderful. I'll let you get back to your reading. We'll talk after the prayer, insha Allah."

I continue to recite as the masjid fills up around me.

∼

The sermon is about the relationship between parents and children. I've heard sermons like this many times, but I always learn something new. It's the most important, and sometimes the most difficult, of all relationships. I hope Luqman stays out of trouble while we're gone.

After the prayer Brother Hanif approaches me, along with two other men. "Assalaamu alaikum. I'd like to introduce you to Hisham and Zulfiqar."

I stand and shake their hands. "Walaikum assalaam. It's very nice to meet you."

"We would like to take you and your wife out for lunch. Is she in the women's section?" I nod. He calls a young boy. "Ashraf, go to the sisters and ask for Brother Isa's wife."

"She's wearing a blue hijab."

"How do you like Lexington?" Hisham asks.

"We haven't seen the city yet. We drove straight to the masjid. How old is this building?"

"We built the masjid nearly twenty years ago. The community has grown quite a bit since then. Do you see that old man over there? The one reading the Qur'an?" He points to a man with white hair under his kufi. "That's Dr. Abdul-Mun'im. He came to Lexington thirty years ago to be the principal of our school. He's been retired for many years. One of his sons now teaches in the school."

"My wife is a teacher, too. How long have you offered social services?"

"We opened Caring House eleven years ago. Our current director is moving to Florida soon, and we're anxious to find someone to replace him."

I spot Aisha in the doorway. "My wife is ready."

We walk out together and put on our shoes. I make the introductions. "This is Aisha. And this is Hanif, Hisham, and Zulfiqar."

Hisham smiles. "You're good at remembering names."

"I have seven children and thirteen grandchildren."

"Let's go to our cars," says Hanif. "You can follow me to the restaurant."

On our way, I ask Aisha, "What do you think?"

"The sisters are nice. Two of them introduced themselves to me and showed me around the masjid. We'll see."

∾

Lunch is friendly. They don't question me like they did in Houston. We talk about our families. And they tell Aisha about the Islamic school here. "We would be fortunate to have a teacher with so much experience," says Hanif.

I ask about the social services they offer. "Caring House was founded with two purposes," says Hisham. "First, we hoped to provide community service in terms of education, recreation, and economic assistance. Second, we planned to make da'wah through our efforts. We don't actively try to convert anyone, but they are exposed to a full Islamic environment. Most of the members of our staff are Muslims, though we do have some non-Muslim employees also."

I nod, smiling and listening carefully. That sounds like the kind of place for me.

After lunch, Hanif leads us to a hotel. "You can rest here. This evening, we'll have a dinner where you will meet the other leaders of the Muslim community. I'll take you there, insha Allah."

When we walk into the hotel room, I collapse on the bed. "I need a nap."

"How can you think of sleeping? I don't have anything to wear to the dinner."

"Just wear what you have on. It's nice."

"Not nice enough for a formal dinner."

"They know we're traveling. Don't worry about it, Aisha. Come rest with me."

She sits on the edge of the bed. I pull her into my arms. "What do you think?"

"I like it, but I don't know if I'm ready to leave Chicago."

～

The dinner is a blur of faces. I try to remember everyone's name. They're all very friendly. Maybe this is how people are outside of big cities.

As the evening continues, Aisha is pulled away from me by curious sisters. While I chat with the brothers, I catch occasional glimpses of her on the other side of the room. We don't have the chance to talk again until after Hanif drops us off at the hotel.

I'm beat. My wife is smiling. "Did you have a good time?" I ask her.

"Very nice. One of the sisters, Lubna, said she'll take me out tomorrow and show me the town. Hopefully, we can tour the school too. Everyone was so welcoming."

"I noticed that. Do you think it's because we're in a smaller town?"

"We're in the south now. There's a courtesy here that I've never found in Chicago."

"The South wasn't always this courteous."

"Times have changed, Isa. I thank Allah for that."

"So what do you think?"

"I'll let you know." She's smiling broadly. Is it possible she's ready to move?

∽

While she spends the day touring the area, I'm in meetings and interviews. Everyone is friendly, but I still have to answer the tough questions. When I tell them why I want to leave Chicago, some of them nod.

"Caring House has a distinctive Islamic character," says Zulfiqar. "I'm certain you would appreciate that."

They don't flinch when I describe my months in the federal prison. "I remember those times," says Brother Massoud, the prison chaplain. "Many brothers were unfairly arrested and some were tortured. Alhamdulillah, our country was able to move past that."

There will be another dinner tonight, smaller than last night's event. Hanif takes me back to the hotel in the afternoon.

I'm resting when Aisha walks into the hotel room, humming.

"Did you have a good time?"

"It was so nice, Isa. Lubna took me practically everywhere. The reason the air is so fresh, she said, is the horse farms. They have some industry but not nearly as much as most cities. The downtown area is manageable, and there are areas right outside the city that are absolutely beautiful."

"What do you think?"

She laughs. "They haven't offered you the job yet. Let's wait and see."

∽

Hanif and his wife, Nada, invite us for breakfast at their house in the morning. Before we leave, Nada packs some of the food to send with us. "In case you get hungry on the way."

Reluctantly, we say goodbye to them and to Lexington. We don't want to get back to Chicago too late because we both have to work tomorrow.

Halfway through Indiana, Aisha takes over driving while I nap. I'm exhausted. But, this was one great weekend.

Kyle's Family

The soccer game was two weeks ago, and Dad is still worn out. He spends much of his time in bed or napping on the couch. He looks pale, too.

"You need to go to the doctor, Dad. He might be able to help you."

"Or he might not. What if he wants to put me in a hospice? You know I won't go. Will he give me two more weeks, or six or twelve? I don't need that stress."

"But what if the doctor can treat you and make you stronger?"

"What if he can't? No, Kyle. No more doctors." He takes a deep breath and looks at me. "You know I don't want to die in a hospice. Maybe I don't even want to die in Chicago. Lately, I've had dreams of Arizona. Can you imagine?"

"What are you saying?"

He doesn't answer. I wait. Finally he says, "Let me talk with your mother first. But, I need to ask you something. Would you do anything for me?"

What kind of question is that? "Sure I would."

"If your mother agrees, I'm going to ask you and your brother, and your wives, to do something very special for me. It will require some sacrifice, but I swear it will be the last thing I ever ask of you."

What do I say to that? "What is it, Dad? What do you need? Is it money?"

"No. It's more important than money. Remember what I said, and be ready."

"Ready for what?"

"I'll tell you when the time is right."

"Why don't you just go to the doctor? That would make Mom happy, too."

"No. If I'm going to die soon, I need to do it in my own way. Both Matt and you have been great sons, especially these last few months. Just give me this."

"You're not going to tell me what it is?"

"Go home to your wife and children. Don't worry about me, Kyle. I'll be okay."

What is he talking about?

Luqman: Part Four

Mom and Dad are coming home tonight. I mopped the kitchen floor, washed the dirty clothes, and even organized my books. After spending the night at Muhammad's place, I'm going to stop being so messy.

They'll be surprised that I took such good care of the house. I have many more surprises for them.

$\sim$

When they pull into the driveway at around sunset, I go out to meet them.

"Assalaamu alaikum. How was it?"

Dad stretches. "It was good, but I'm tired. We had a busy weekend."

Mom studies me. "How was your weekend, Luqman?"

"I'm good. Go inside. I'll carry in your suitcases."

The two of them walk up the porch and into the house. They're starting to look old.

When I walk in with the suitcases, Mom hugs me. "Thank you, Luqman, for cleaning up. You even have dinner waiting. That's wonderful."

Dinner is two pizzas sitting on the kitchen table. Maryam is the only one of us who learned how to cook, and she's been gone with friends all weekend. Oddly, I don't think they mind that nearly as much as they did when I was out with my friends.

After they get cleaned up, we pray and sit down to eat. After they finish telling me about Lexington, I lay one on them. "I'm off from work tomorrow, Dad. Could I come into Hope Center and volunteer for a few hours?"

He stops eating. "Are you serious? That would be great. We can always use extra help."

"Good. Why don't I drive into work with you?"

He grins all evening. My credibility just rose another ten points. I am on my way.

Joshua: Part Four

At first, I was skeptical about the changes in Luqman. Knowing his past history, I thought he was probably just playing us again. But when he said he wanted to volunteer at Hope, I started seeing him in a new light. He really has changed.

≈

Luqman drives us to the center. I'm worn out from the trip. It's Monday morning, and I can't wait until the weekend.

"I'm glad you offered to volunteer. Stu could probably use help over at Evans, especially during meal times."

"That sounds good. I'd also like to help with the fundraiser. Isn't that coming up soon?"

"It's near the end of May. We have about a month left."

"How are ticket sales? I'm good at persuading people."

"Kyle and Gameel have helped a lot, but we need to sell more. Why don't you work at Evans until the end of lunch, and then come over to Hope and sell tickets? You can use the phone in my office."

"I'm looking forward to it."

Most of my kids have made the transition smoothly into adulthood. But I didn't, and neither did Jenny. With her, the problem was boys. Even her relationship with Nuruddin started off wrong. Alhamdulillah, they have a great family now. It looks like Luqman is following in our footsteps. If he succeeds nearly as well as Jenny has, I will be very proud.

≈

He has been on the phone for an hour and has sold ten tickets. He's good. When he was little, he was painfully shy. The other kids bullied him almost daily. I'm glad he's outgrown that phase. It's nice to hear him speaking confidently, as a man.

On the way home, he asks me questions about the fundraiser. He says he'll volunteer at the center again on Friday, when he has another day off. We can attend the Jummah prayer together.

Luqman: Part Five

Moving back home was one of the best ideas I've ever had. I confessed to a couple of lies, leaving my parents satisfied that everything else was true. I'm doing my best to please them and convince them that I've become the perfect son. Let's see how Muhammad likes being dethroned.

After this afternoon's performance, Dad will let me become more involved with the fundraiser. I sold twenty-eight tickets in three hours. Now, I have some questions for him.

"While I was on the phone, Dad, some people asked about the speaker. It's Hiram Johnson, right? What is his topic?"

"The title of his speech is 'Finding Hope in Dangerous Times.'"

"That's interesting. Do you know exactly what he plans to talk about?"

"It's hard to tell with Hiram. I never liked the man, but he's a popular speaker and the leader of the largest religious organization in Chicago. Have you ever seen their church over in Oak Park? It's like a fortress."

"No, I haven't." I should check that out. "How long will the fundraiser last?"

"We'll start at 7:00 PM. Including dinner, a short presentation about the centers, and Hiram's speech, the whole thing should last around two and a half or three hours. Make sure to point out that we're having a silent auction, too."

"The dinner is being catered by the hotel, right?"

"I would have preferred giving the job to Grand Caravan, but everyone insisted we serve alcohol. The hotel will take care of that."

"Will you be there? I thought you avoided those kinds of dinners."

Dad sighs. "I'm not sure what to do. As the director, I should show up. But, I don't want to be in a place where alcohol is served. That's the main reason I started looking for another job."

"Maybe Lexington will hire you. Otherwise, you should make an appearance. Allah knows your intention, and it will be better for the centers if you're there." I remember something else. "Hiram Johnson doesn't drink, does he?"

"Not as far as I know. The New Pilgrims preach abstinence."

"He doesn't seem to have any problem being at a dinner with alcohol. Maybe it's not such a big deal."

"I don't know, Luqman. I have been praying about this since January, and I still don't have an answer. If I weren't the director, I wouldn't go. But would my absence hurt the fundraiser? That's the question I can't answer."

"It could. You know the people rely on the centers. They're an important part of the community."

"We're doing our best."

"You are making a difference." At least he thinks he is. "In case someone asks, what's on the menu for the fundraiser?"

"The usual. A tossed salad, chicken, rice, and vegetables. The dessert will be cheesecake, I think. I hope no one is coming just for the food. That's not what this is about."

"I'm sure they're coming to donate." That's all the questions I have for now. Dad is helping me more than he realizes.

Change of Scenery

Travel and change of place impart new vigor to the mind.

—Seneca

Kyle's Family

Dad called me at the office this morning. "Come to the house tonight. Bring Faiqa and the babies. This concerns you all."

"Does this have to do with our conversation the other day?"

"Your mother and I talked, and we've made a decision. I'll see you tonight, insha Allah."

After we hang up, I let Faiqa know. "Make sure to have the triplets ready. We'll have to eat a quick dinner and go."

"He didn't tell you what this is about?"

"No." But I have an idea, and I don't think I like it.

∾

They're all sitting in the living room, waiting for us. Emily skipped her class this evening. This is serious.

Dad looks at each of us. "You know I wouldn't have asked you to come if it wasn't important. It's time to make a decision, and what I've decided will affect each of you."

He closes his eyes and keeps on speaking. "I hoped I could beat the leukemia this time, just as I did before. The diet and the exercise helped at first, but I can feel myself getting weaker. Too many years of bad habits have caught up with me."

"Have you talked with the doctor, Dad? There are other treatments."

"No, Kyle. I don't want to spend the rest of my life being poked and prodded and experimented on like a lab animal. Sometimes the treatments work, and sometimes they don't. That's a risk I'm not willing to take."

"But we're talking about your life."

"Yes, we are. I want to spend my last days enjoying life with my family. I can't do that in a hospital bed."

"What are you going to do then? What's your decision?"

He smiles. "I've been many places, and my favorite place on earth is the Grand Canyon. It's the most beautiful place I've ever seen, and that's where I've decided to die."

I don't know what to say. We all stare at Dad. Emily breaks the silence.

"That sounds beautiful, Dad, but what exactly are you saying?"

"We found a furnished house for rent in Flagstaff. It's big—four bedrooms and four baths—so we'll all have privacy. This morning, I sent in the deposit. They're expecting us in three weeks."

He's serious. I'm still trying to digest everything when Mom speaks up. "We need all of you to be there with us. Emily is nearly done with school. Kyle, Matt, and Faiqa, you will have to arrange for time off from work."

"How long should we plan to be gone?" Matt asks.

"As long as it takes," says Dad. He stops and waits for his words to sink in.

How do I respond? Gameel will give me the time off, but I'm not sure if Faiqa can be away from her practice. The practical world collides with my love for my father. I'll do anything I can to make his last days happy, but how do I live with the thought that after all these months of fighting and complaining, my father is preparing to die?

I look down and rub my forehead with my right hand. It's a good way to hide the tears.

∽

Everyone else has spoken. Faiqa will make arrangements. Matt is sure he can leave his work. Emily inspires us all with a simple observation. "How can we possibly consider not doing this?"

It's my turn. I wipe my eyes and clear my throat. "Gameel will give me six months off if I ask him. That's not a problem. But why are you ready to give up, Dad? You were doing so well. Why can't you keep fighting?" My mind flashes back nearly thirty years, when I was a little boy trying to wake up my drunken father. I feel as helpless now as I did then.

He's crying too. He comes to sit next to me and pats my back. "This is the will of Allah, Kyle. We all will die when our time comes. Be grateful that I still have time to be with you."

We hug. It's hard to believe that there was a time in my life when I never wanted to see him again.

~

Before we leave the house, Dad lays out a few more instructions. "First, you have to let me deal with my brothers. I won't tell them why we're going to Arizona, only that we're planning a family vacation. Dying will be harder, I think, if I have to say goodbye to them. Kyle and Matt, you will contact them after I'm gone.

"Second, I will be buried in Flagstaff. I spoke with the imam at the masjid there, and he agreed to my requests. My two sons will wash my body and prepare it for burial. Kyle, you will lead the janazah.

"Third, you will take care of your mother. Whatever she wants, whatever she needs, you will help her. Don't let her be alone." He grasps her hand. She looks down. I know this is hard for her although she hardly ever shows it.

We all agree. I don't know how I'll be able to wash my father's body, so I put the thought out of my mind. When it happens, I'll deal with it.

We have to go home. It's nearly midnight. The babies fell asleep long ago. Not only that. The emotions in this room are too big. I want to get away and think things over. "Um, I need to go to work tomorrow. I'll talk with Gameel."

"Don't be too specific," says Dad. "Gameel can't know more than my own brothers. I've asked you to come to Arizona for a family vacation. You don't know how long you'll be gone."

I'm sure he knows how hard that will be. Gameel never accepts a simple explanation. Besides, I'll be taking his daughter and grandchildren with me. "Why won't you tell Uncle Chris and Uncle Joshua? They would want to know."

"Leave that to me," says Dad. "I'm not gone yet, and I'm still in charge."

By the time we say our awkward goodbyes, it's after midnight. I feel like I should stay with Dad tonight, like I may never see him again. But practical concerns take over. I'll go to work tomorrow and talk with Gameel and pretend that my life isn't about to change very dramatically.

"Assalaamu alaikum Dad. I'll see you tomorrow, insha Allah." We hug. He kisses my cheek. I kiss his forehead. It feels like the right thing to do.

Joshua: Part One

Today is my birthday. It's not a big deal. Even when I was a kid, my mother never threw a party or baked a cake. I couldn't understand why. Later it all became clear. On the day I was born, she was hovering between life and death after having been pushed down the stairs by my father. My birthday brought back the awful memories. We had many good years before her death, and that's what I usually remember about her.

Fifty-eight isn't a milestone—just another year added to my life. Aisha and I don't celebrate birthdays because Prophet Muhammad, peace upon him, didn't celebrate them. So I'm surprised to walk into the kitchen and find a birthday card sitting on the table, next to a plate piled high with pancakes.

Luqman is standing at the sink, washing dishes. "I burnt one of the pancakes. I'm still learning how to cook."

"You did this? Thank you, Luqman. The card, breakfast. It's great."

"Your coffee is almost done."

I walk over and hug him. He stiffens at first, and then relaxes in my arms. "How did you remember?"

"I always remember important dates. This is a special day, isn't it?"

"Yes, I guess it is." Special because of what my son has done for me. Fifty-eight isn't a milestone, but I will always remember this birthday.

∾

Ten minutes after I walk into the office, my phone rings. I glance at the caller ID. An 859 area code. Where is that?

"Hello?"

"Assalaamu alaikum, Brother Isa. This is Hanif Shalash from Lexington. How are you?"

"Walaikum assalaam. Alhamdulillah, I'm fine. How is everyone in Lexington? My wife and I enjoyed our visit."

"We were very glad you both came to see our community. Would you and your wife be interested in moving here? The board of Caring House has asked me to offer you the job as director of our center."

I got the job? That's great. I think. Do we want to move? "Thank you for your offer." Thank you very much. "Could you give me a few days to think about it? I need to talk with my wife and make salatul istikhara before deciding."

"I understand. I'll send you the details of the offer and you can go home and discuss it with your family. Would you be able to let me know by Friday?"

"Yes, I can do that. Thank you for contacting me. I'll call you on Friday, insha Allah."

"Good. I'll send you details the minute I hang up. I'm looking forward to hearing from you, Brother Isa."

I got the job! I start to call Aisha, but maybe I should wait. This is special. We should go out for dinner. I send her a message. "Come home early so we can spend the evening together. Don't worry about cooking."

She responds a few minutes later. "I'll see you tonight, hon."

Lexington. It's smaller than Chicago and much quieter. The air is fresh and clear. The people are friendly. I would be working in an Islamic organization. It sounds too good to pass up, especially after I look at the offer Hanif sent.

We would be leaving our family and friends, though Chris's son Benjamin teaches at a university there. We would have to move out of our house, where we've lived for the last thirty-two years. I've never lived anywhere besides Chicago, except for those months in Pakistan when I was twenty-four.

It will be an adventure. I'm ready for something new.

∼

Doug Barnett dropped in to discuss final details for the fundraiser just as I was leaving the office. Later, I met Gameel in the hallway. He asked me why Brad was taking his family to Arizona.

"He is?"

"This morning Kyle told me he would need to take some time off, but he didn't know exactly how long he'd be gone. Brad didn't say anything to you?"

"No, nothing."

"I don't mind giving Kyle the extra time, but I was surprised that Brad would be taking a trip like that in his condition."

"Would you believe he beat me in a soccer game a couple of weeks ago? Brad is probably in better shape than I am. I'm sure it's just a little family vacation."

"I hope so. When I saw him last week, he looked very tired. If he's playing soccer, he would be tired."

Who knows what's going on with my brother? All I know is that he's fooled the doctors twice. Three times, if you count his battle with the flu. If lifespans were determined by strong will, Brad would live forever.

～

It's getting late. We'll have to pray before going to the restaurant. I hope Aisha is ready.

Umar's car is parked in front of our house. Why is he here? There are cars in the driveway too. Is something wrong? I run up the porch steps and open the door.

Aisha is waiting for me. "You're late. Everyone's getting hungry."

"What do you mean?"

"Chris and Melinda are going back to Arkansas tomorrow, and we decided to have dinner together before they leave. Don't tell me you forgot."

I shrug. "What should I tell you then?"

"Let's go. We have reservations for 6:30 PM."

"I need to pray first."

She looks at her watch. "Go ahead."

When we're in the car I ask, "Didn't you get my message?"

"I wondered what you meant by that. Were you going to take me out for dinner?"

"That was my plan."

"So it worked out anyway."

"But I wanted to have dinner with just the two of us."

"You won't see your brother for another month, and I know how close you've been lately. You see me every day."

But, I have something important to tell you, Aisha. I should have called her.

～

We don't get home until after 10:00 PM. It was a nice evening with my favorite people, but I couldn't wait to be home alone with my wife.

When we're in bed, she asks, "Why did you want to take me out for dinner?" She laughs. "What did you do?"

"Do you remember Hanif Shalash from Lexington? He called me this morning."

"How is he? Did you ask about his wife, Nada? She's so nice."

Why didn't she ask me the obvious question? "He offered me the job."

"He did?" She doesn't sound too surprised. "What did you tell him?"

"That I needed to discuss it with you and make istikhara. I'll let him know by Friday. What do you think?"

"It was a nice weekend. What do you think about the organization?"

"They're doing a lot of what I've worked on through the years, and they have a strong Islamic identity. Let me show you their offer." I take the paper from my nightstand.

"Lubna told me things don't cost as much there. They're offering you a retirement package, too?"

"I could retire in eight or ten years, and we wouldn't have to worry about money."

"What about Chicago? Jeremy's here, and all of our kids. Maryam is getting married soon. We couldn't leave until after the wedding. What about this house? Can you imagine living anywhere else?"

"I wouldn't want to sell it. Muhammad and Luqman could live here. Maybe Muhammad will decide to get married soon. He's nearly thirty."

"I'm not sure if it would be such a good idea to have Muhammad and Luqman living together. Maybe we could persuade Maryam and Zaid to move here. If they want to start a family, they'll need a house."

"Does that mean you're ready to move?"

"It means I'm ready to think about it. I'll call Mom tomorrow and see what she says. I'd hate to be so far away from her. Maybe we could get her to move with us."

"Maybe. We'd better get to sleep. Think about it. Talk to whoever you want. We both need to pray. We have two more days to make a decision."

We turn off our lights and lie on our right sides. Two minutes later, she turns on her lamp. "I can't sleep, Isa. Can you?"

"No." I turn on my lamp.

At 3:00 AM, we finally settle down, too tired to keep our eyes open. We still haven't decided.

~

In the morning, I remember that I forgot to ask Brad about his trip. According to Gameel, they won't be leaving for a few weeks. I have time.

Luqman has the coffee ready. "It smells great. Thanks." I'm going to need a lot of caffeine to get me through the day.

All day, I struggle to stay awake. And I think about the Lexington job offer. I would be working in an Islamic organization. I could pray with my coworkers, and wouldn't be forced into situations like I'm in now with this fundraiser.

But what will this mean for our family? Jamal landed a job in Salt Lake City. Muhammad is on his own. Maryam is getting married. And Luqman is finally becoming a man. The kids are all grown now, and Aisha and I can start thinking about our own wants and needs.

Brad must be doing well, too, if he's traveling to Arizona. If there is an emergency, we can be at his bedside in six hours—or even less if we fly. After we get settled, I'll ask him and Beth to come visit us. I'm sure he'll enjoy breathing in the clear air.

As far as I can tell, there's no reason not to accept this job. I can't wait to go home and find out what Aisha is thinking.

Kyle's Family

This is different than any vacation. Instead of the usual excitement, I approach it with a sense of dread. Dad is going to Arizona to die. I don't understand how he knows the time is coming, but I trust his instincts.

Faiqa just went back to work. Tomorrow she'll ask for another leave. The parents and kids all love her, so I'm sure she'll have a job to come back to. She's being great about this. I know I'll need her support to get through it.

Today she started checking out pediatricians in Flagstaff. She'll also arrange back-up care for Dad. He doesn't want to see any more doctors, but we still need a plan. I hope he'll change his mind once he gets really sick.

I told Gameel I would need a month or two. It was hard to convince him that this is a simple vacation. He kept pushing for information. I've always been direct with my father-in-law, but I need to obey Dad's wishes.

We have an office in Phoenix, and Gameel wants me to work from there, but it will just be an occasional meeting or conference call. Nothing heavy duty.

There are so many considerations: the condo, the cars, the babies' things. I'm glad for all the minute details of daily life. They keep my mind off the larger truth facing our family.

~

We eat dinner with Mom and Dad. I want to spend every minute I can with him.

"Last night, I talked to Uncle Chris," says Dad. "I told him we're going on a vacation in Arizona. He didn't like it, but I convinced him that I'm strong enough for the trip. They left this morning for Arkansas." Dad stops and puts down his fork. "I'll never see him again."

"Why don't you tell them what's going on, Dad? I'm sure they'd want to know."

"No, Kyle. I'm the oldest. They depend on me, and I don't want their pity. That's not the way it works." He picks up his fork. "They have their families to worry about. They don't need to worry about me."

I should be used to Dad's stubborn determination, but sometimes he still frustrates me.

Joshua: Part Two

Aisha is in the office, working at the computer. The minute I walk in, I ask her, "What do you think?"

"Assalaamu alaikum to you, too. You sure are anxious."

I kiss her cheek. "Walaikum assalaam. Did you have a good day?"

"Yes, I did. During science class, I took my students outside to plant seeds. It was so sunny and warm. I wish we could have had all our classes outside, but I don't think the children would have learned much."

"That sounds nice. Is that all you did today?"

"No. I called my mother. She didn't answer—she was probably working in her garden—so I left a message. I thought about calling Umar, but I thought you may have already talked to him."

"Not yet. So, what do you think?"

"I think we should pray about it. Do you still want to take me out for dinner?"

"We just ate out last night."

"I thought you were trying to soften me up."

"Go get your purse. Do you want Italian?"

"No, I think I'd like the Grand Caravan tonight. I can practically taste their kebabs."

≈

During dinner, we talked about everything except Lexington. Is she teasing me, or has she decided to stay in Chicago?

Sharon calls while we're on the way home, but Aisha just says she'll call her back.

"Why didn't you tell her?"

"I'll call her when we get home. Don't worry."

First we pray. After the prayer, I pick up the Qur'an. I just remembered a verse. I think it's in Surah An-Nisa. Here it is. *"When angels take the souls of those who die in sin against their own souls, they say: 'In what (plight) were you?' They reply: 'Weak and oppressed were we in the earth.' They say: 'Was not the earth of Allah spacious enough for you to move yourselves away (from evil)?' Such men will find their abode in Hell—What an evil refuge!"*

I have a choice now—to stay here in Chicago and throw fundraisers with wine, or to work with Muslims. Whatever I choose, I'll be held accountable. How can I possibly turn down this opportunity?

My mind is made up. I stand and pray, asking Allah to help me in my decision.

≈

Aisha walks into the room as I'm finishing my prayer. "I just got off the phone with Mom."

"What did Sharon say?"

"What do you think she said?"

Aisha is having a lot of fun with this. I'm in a good mood, so I play along. "She probably said she'll support whatever decision we make."

"You're right. It's not what I expected. I feel guilty at the thought of moving further away from her, but she said she would come visit us. And we could still visit her, couldn't we? It's not like we're moving to Pakistan or Mexico."

"Are you ready to say yes, then?"

"Not yet. I need to pray about it. I have until Friday."

"While you're praying, think about this." I show her the verse. "Doesn't that sound like we're meant to be there?"

"Maybe. Now be quiet. I want to pray."

I leave her alone in the family room. I think she will say yes if I give her time.

I stand by the staircase and look at our house. This place has been home for so long. Will I really be able to leave it?

∼

I haven't said another word to Aisha about the job. She needs her time to think it through.

On Thursday night, after I'm in bed and half asleep, she turns on her light. "Isa, we need to do this. You're having a hard time at your job, and you hate the cold. They have an Islamic school where I could teach. Our kids are grown. You're right. It's our turn now."

I turn on my lamp. "Are you sure?"

"Yes. Let's do this. Now, what should we do about the house?"

We talk for hours. There are so many details to consider. The most daunting is the move itself. I never expected to be taking on this kind of challenge at my age, but why not?

At around 2:00 AM, I close my eyes for a moment and drift off into easy dreams.

∼

I just finished talking to Hanif. They want me to begin as soon as possible. I'll need a month to wrap things up here. We agreed on a starting date of June 2.

On Monday, I'll contact the board. I hope they hire Stu as my replacement. He still has time to take over before the fundraiser. He's more involved with the details, anyway, so it will just be a formality.

My last day will be May 19, the Monday before the event. Aisha will wrap up the school year on May 16. That gives us nearly two weeks to finish packing and say goodbye to Chicago.

Maryam graduates on May 8, and we've arranged for an engagement party on May 9. The wedding is on July 5. We're going to have a very busy summer.

Luqman: Part One

On Friday, I go to Hope Center with Dad and sell more tickets. A little after noon, we head to the masjid. On the way there, he talks about what a good son I am. I'm the good one now. Hah!

In the afternoon, while running an errand for Dad, I bump into Darnell in the hallway.

"Hey there, Lucas," he says. "You finally made it over here."

If he calls me Lucas around my dad, I'll have too much explaining to do. "Listen, Darnell, I need to tell you something. My name isn't Lucas. I'm Luqman, Joshua's son."

He frowns. "Why did you lie to my family and me?"

"My dad and I weren't getting along, and I needed a place to cool off. I hope you're not mad."

"No, I guess I understand. But, do you know how lucky you are to have a father like Joshua? My dad died when I was ten."

I pat his shoulder. "Yeah, you're right. Anyway, thanks for helping me out."

"You would have done the same for me."

He gives me too much credit.

~

On Friday night, I go to the lake to meet with the boys and give them their instructions.

"Rasheed, do you think you could get a kitchen job at the Elegance Hotel? That's where they're holding the fundraiser."

He smiles. "One of my cousins works at the front desk there. She can help me."

"Great. Abu Bakr, we'll need your work van. Make sure you have all the tools cleaned up, and don't accept any jobs for at least a week after the mission."

"That gives me nearly four weeks of solid work. Okay. That's my busy season, but we have to sacrifice, don't we?"

"That's the spirit, Abu Bakr. Now, Mustapha, you'll need to load up on medical supplies. You can do that, can't you?"

"An LPN doesn't have access to the medications, but I'm sure I can find a way."

"Put together a first aid kit. We'll need sedatives, too. Could you nab some antibiotics and painkillers?"

"I can get whatever we need. Don't worry about it."

We're set. Hakeem and Aziz will do the heavy-duty work. My job is to make sure everything goes smoothly.

I glance at the police car in the parking lot. We'd better cut it short. "I'll see you next Friday, insha Allah. We need to write our list of demands and decide how we're going to get them into the right hands."

We break and go our separate ways. I return to my role as the good son. It's too bad it has to end.

～

After the prayer on Saturday morning, I get up to head for the kitchen, and Maryam heads for the stairs. Dad stops us.

"We have something important to tell you. Sit down."

What's this about? They don't look angry.

"Earlier this year, I started having troubles at my job, so I decided to send out my resume. Yesterday, I accepted a position with an Islamic organization."

"That sounds good. Which organization is it?" I ask.

"It's called the Caring House, in Lexington, Kentucky. Do you remember when Mom and I drove down there?"

Kentucky? Will he be working with the Caring House or the KKK? "Why would you want to move down there? Aren't they all racists?"

"There may be racists in Kentucky, but we didn't meet any."

"Don't you think I would have noticed racist behavior?" says Mom. "I'm sure there is just as much racism in Chicago as there is in Lexington."

"Would you like to move down there with us? I told them we'd be there by the end of May."

That's good. He'll be here for the fundraiser. But will they still be willing to give him the job by the end of May? "No. I'd rather stay here." There's no way I would live in Kentucky. "What about the house?"

"What about my wedding?" Maryam whines.

"We'll be here for the wedding," says Mom. "Lexington's not that far away. What do you think we should do about the house, Maryam? Would Zaid and you like to live here?"

"I don't know. I would have to talk with him. You're not going to sell it, are you?"

"No, we don't want to sell it. Zaid and you could stay here, or Muhammad and Luqman."

I'm supposed to live here with Muhammad? "Maryam and Zaid should have it."

"We can decide all that later," says Dad. "We just wanted to let you know. And don't worry about your wedding, Maryam. Your mom will be here to help you get ready, and you know I wouldn't miss it."

"You two are the first ones we've told, except your grandma. On Monday, we'll let the school and the center know. We'll spend the weekend telling the family." Mom stands. "I think I'll go make French toast. You'd like that for breakfast, wouldn't you?"

Mom almost never makes French toast anymore. She's in a very good mood, and so is Dad. Let them have their happiness. By the end of May, they will feel very differently.

Brad

*Everyone should know that most cancer research is largely a fraud
and that the major cancer research organisations are derelict
in their duties to the people who support them.*

—Linus Pauling

Before the picnic, I kept telling myself that if I rested and ate well,
I would regain my energy. Soon, I would lift weights regularly and go
jogging. Through my will power alone, I would defeat the cancer.

While standing on that makeshift soccer field, energy surged
through me. I seized the moment, stole the ball, and beat Joshua at
soccer. My final goal was completed.

Since that day, I've tried to regain my strength. Life spins around
me, and I sit on my green couch, drinking my freshly-squeezed juice.
Every night, I hope that in the morning I will wake up refreshed, but
it hasn't happened. This last week, I've sat on my green couch and
wondered how many more days I have.

My problem isn't the nutritional program I'm following now. I
should have started eating like this decades ago. My problem is the
chemicals I let them use on me the first time I was diagnosed. Everyone
said that chemotherapy was the way to beat the cancer. By the time I
started questioning this conventional wisdom, it was too late.

I won't last much longer. Not long enough to see my sixty-sixth
birthday. But I won't sit on this couch and waste my remaining days.

Beth agreed to let me die in Arizona. She's being very brave, and I
often don't have the words to say what her courage and strength mean
to me. She should have left me long ago, but she has always stood by
me. I pray that Allah rewards her with a place in the highest heaven.

This plan of mine will be hard on all of them. At least Kyle and
Faiqa will have jobs to come back to. Matt says he will, but I'm not
so sure. Our house is paid for, and they can stay here as long as they
want—for the rest of their lives if they like. He and Emily have helped
me in so many ways. I've talked with my lawyer to make sure both my
sons are taken care of after my death. My wealth will be distributed
according to Islamic teaching.

My brothers don't know how sick I am. I prefer to keep it that way.
There will be no emotional goodbyes. It's better to leave them now,

while I still have some life in me. Chris asked too many questions, but I was able to put him off. Joshua will be easier. He rarely questions anything. Life must be more pleasant for people like him.

I wish I didn't have to leave any of them, but I don't have a choice. I'm enjoying my life more than I ever have. Beth and I spend our days together, no longer running to jobs and appointments. Kyle and Faiqa bring my grandchildren here almost every day, so I can watch them grow. Zakariya brightens my every moment. My boys are men now who are better than I ever hoped they could be. In my last days on this earth, Allah has given me a taste of paradise.

~

I'm dozing on my green couch when there's a rap at the door. "Assalaamu alaikum," a voice calls. It's Joshua.

"Hold on. I'm coming." Beth is out running errands. Matt and Emily are visiting her parents. I struggle off the couch. The nap did me no good.

"Assalaamu alaikum." Joshua hugs me. Is it my imagination or is he even happier than usual? "How are you, Brad? You look good."

People usually see what they want to see, especially people like Joshua. "I'm great. Have a seat. Everyone's gone. It's just me." As I walk back to the couch, I concentrate on showing him how strong I am.

"I have something to tell you. It's important."

"I have something to tell you, too. But you go first."

"Aisha and I had to make a decision. And since you're looking so good lately, I decided it was time to take the opportunity."

"What are you talking about, Joshua?"

"Okay, you know how much I hate the cold. I'm also having trouble at work. So I started looking for another job in a warmer place. Yesterday I accepted a job offer from an Islamic organization in Kentucky."

"That's great. Congratulations on the new job. I've never been to Kentucky, but they say it's pretty down there. I know how much you've wanted to work with Muslims. I'm happy for you." It's good that he's moving on. Chicago is wearing him down.

"We don't like leaving our family behind, but it's not that far. It would be great if Beth and you could come down after we get settled. I start my job at the beginning of June, but we'll be back, of course, for Maryam's wedding. Maybe we can have a rematch in July."

"If I'm still here." His expression changes. I laugh. "My news is that we're going down to Arizona. The whole family. The kids were able to get time off from their jobs. We're renting a house in Flagstaff."

"Gameel mentioned that to me. How long will you be gone?"

Me? I'll be gone forever. "We don't know yet. We decided to play it by ear. Life is short, and we have to live it. I can't wait to see the Grand Canyon again." The last two nights, I've dreamed about it.

"You must be feeling well if you're up to making a trip like that. You will be here for Maryam's wedding, won't you?"

Do I lie to him outright or just play with my words a little? "I'll do my best to be there." In spirit, at least.

"So, we both have good news. Isn't it great when your kids are grown, and you're able to look at life in new ways?"

I can't argue with that.

Final Arrangements

First say to yourself what you would be;
and then do what you have to do.

—Epicetus

Joshua: Part One

Our family members all supported our decision, but it's still hard to think about leaving them. I'm sure we'll be making frequent trips to Chicago and even Salt Lake City.

Jamal and Rabia plan to leave after Maryam's wedding. "You're the one who gave me the idea." I confess to my son.

"It sounds good, Dad. I'm glad you'll be less stressed."

That's what everyone has said. If my stress is that obvious, I really do need to leave Chicago.

～

On Monday, I settle behind my desk and call Stu. "Do you have a few minutes?"

"We're nearly finished with the breakfast crowd. Let me make sure everything is on track, and I'll be right there."

While waiting for Stu, I turn on my computer and start writing my letter to the board. How do I tell them I'm leaving after more than fifteen years?

Stu knocks. I jump. "Hi Joshua. What's up?"

"Sit down. Do you remember when I went to Lexington for an interview?"

"Don't tell me they offered you the job."

"I'll start in June. I'm writing the letter to the board."

"I didn't expect this." He's quiet a moment. "That won't give them much time to look for a new executive director."

"I'm recommending you for the job."

He shakes his head. "They'll want someone older and more experienced."

"You can do it, Stu. My resignation will be effective on May 19."

"Before the fundraiser? So you're throwing me into the fire."

"You put the fundraiser together. All you'll need to do that night is greet people and introduce yourself. Gameel will emcee. You'll be fine."

"Aren't you going to be there?"

"You know how I feel about this. I hope you raise millions of dollars for the centers, and I think you can do it without my help."

"I knew you were looking for a way out, but I didn't expect anything this drastic." He shrugs. "Thanks for the vote of confidence. I'll do my best."

"I've enjoyed working with you."

"If I am ready to be executive director, it's because of what you have taught me."

We're both quiet a minute. He smiles. "I'd better get back to work before this gets too sentimental. I'll talk to you later, Joshua. Congratulations." He quickly leaves my office.

I am going to miss Hope Center, and I've enjoyed these four years with Stu. But I can't wait to get started in Lexington.

~

We have a busy weekend planned. Tonight Maryam is graduating. Tomorrow night we're having an engagement party at the Grand Caravan. And on Saturday, Aisha and I plan to drive down to Lexington to look for a place to stay.

We need to leave for the graduation soon. Maryam is still getting ready. Zaid and his parents will meet us there. Umar and Safa have invited us all to their house for a small party after the graduation.

Out of my seven children, two are most special to me. Michael, my oldest, came along when I wasn't yet ready to be a father. His birth changed my life in many ways. Maryam, my youngest, was born in the back seat of my car because we couldn't make it to the hospital in time. A day later, I was hauled off to federal prison. All those months, I dreamed of my baby girl.

She's not a baby anymore. In July, she'll be a wife. In August, she'll be a teacher, like Jamal, both following in their mother's footsteps. She walks down the steps in her cap and gown, and I nearly cry.

~

I've been to many graduations over the years, and I get excited every time. Tonight when they announced "Maryam Aisha Adams," a chill ran through me. As I watched her walk across the stage, I knew it was the end of something. The next graduate will be my oldest grand-child, Nadia.

Jeremy and Jamal and their families are here, along with Muhammad and Luqman, and Zaid. Daud is still in a wheelchair, but they hope to get him on crutches soon. The doctor says his leg should be fully healed by July.

Sharon is in town. She rides with us to Umar's house. "Are you getting ready for your move?" she asks.

"It's so much work," says Aisha. "We don't know who's going to stay in our house or what furniture we should take with us. There are so many details."

"You don't have much time left. Would you like me to help you?"

"Don't worry, Mom. You must be anxious to get back to your garden."

"I would rather help you organize. Would you mind?"

"No, of course I wouldn't."

"Tomorrow I'll call your cousin Jerome and ask him to look after my house. I can stay all month if you like."

"Thanks, Mom. That will be great." Aisha sighs. Moving is harder than either of us imagined.

Sharon just turned ninety, and she's still taking care of her daughter. It really doesn't end, does it?

～

Umar and Safa's house smells great, as always. We enjoy biriyani and Safa's famous sweets.

During the evening, I have a chance to talk with Umar. "How is Luqman these days?" he asks.

"Haven't you noticed? A month or two ago, he wouldn't even have bothered with his sister's graduation. He prays regularly and wakes us up for Fajr. And he volunteers over at Hope one or two days a week."

Umar nods. "That's good, but I find it hard to believe he could have changed that easily. Do you have any idea what brought about the change?"

"No. I'm just glad it happened."

Umar shrugs and goes over to talk to Luqman. Being a psychologist, I guess he has to be cynical. If Luqman is trying anything, he won't be able to trick Umar.

Before we leave I ask my brother-in-law, "Did you find out anything about Luqman?"

"I'm not sure." He leaves it at that.

"Isa." Aisha calls from the door. "We need to go. You'll see Umar again tomorrow."

It is late, and we have to work tomorrow. As I leave, I glance back at Umar. He's frowning. But that's not unusual.

Joshua: Part Two

Coffee kept me going today. At five, I leave work so I can go home and change before heading out to the restaurant. Aisha and the kids are waiting for me.

"Let's go," says Aisha as I walk in and slip off my shoes. "We're late."

"Don't I have a little time to relax?"

"You don't even have time to change. The kids are in the van."

I slip my shoes back on.

Ismail and Amal are waiting for us at the restaurant. My old friend holds out his hand and pulls me into a hug.

"Assalaamu alaikum, man. How's the father of the bride?"

"I'm great. We'll finally be related, dude." I've rarely used that word in the last thirty years, but it always feels right when I'm with Ismail.

"For real. Who would have thought? Maryam is a nice girl. Zaid would have asked to marry her years ago, but he wanted to wait until he could provide for her."

"He's a good kid. It's a good match. Can you imagine our grandchildren though?"

Ismail laughs. "They'll be bouncing off the walls."

Mahmoud walks in. I haven't seen him in a couple of years, not since the wedding of his youngest daughter. He's completely gray now.

"Assalaamu alaikum. What's so funny?"

"We're imagining our future grandchildren. How have you been?"

"I'm good, alhamdulillah. In two more years, I'll retire. Haleema and I plan to return to Pakistan."

"That sounds good. I have some news, too. Aisha and I are moving to Kentucky."

"Zaid mentioned that. Kentucky?" says Ismail. "Why would you want to go there?"

"Have you ever been there? You might be surprised. Fresh air and rolling hills. It's beautiful. I'm starting a new job down there at the beginning of June."

"I'm happy for you," says Mahmoud. "But don't forget about us."

"Never. We'll come back to visit. And of course, we'll be here for the wedding, insha Allah."

Ismail laughs again. "Hey, maybe when you come for a visit, you can stay at my place and play video games."

"Are you kidding, dude? Have you seen the video games these days? I don't have the energy."

≈

Later, after we've eaten, Zaid and I each say a few words. So does the imam. Then Zaid and Maryam sign the marriage contract. They're married now. They won't live together until after the ceremony, but I feel better doing it this way. When Aisha and I are in Lexington, during the month of June, I won't have to worry so much.

If it were up to me, they would have had the wedding ceremony in June, but Maryam insisted on planning something big and that takes time. I couldn't say no to my baby girl.

I've spent most of the evening with Ismail. Before we leave, though, Umar comes over. "I'm concerned about Luqman."

"Why? Has he said something?"

"No, and I wouldn't expect him to. Something's not right, though."

I close my eyes and rub my forehead. Umar is usually right. What could be going on with Luqman, though? His behavior has been great. "What do you mean?"

"Simply by looking at him, and picking up on his body language, I believe he has some very important secrets."

Luqman has been quiet tonight, except for an animated conversation with one of the waiters. He has friends. What's so strange about that?

"I don't know, Umar. This time you may be wrong." I don't know what else to say. I walk over to talk with my brother. Brad and Beth came last night, too, but I didn't spend much time with them.

"Assalaamu alaikum. Are you almost ready for your trip?"

"We're leaving next week, insha Allah. Emily graduates on Tuesday, and we'll fly out on Thursday."

"I'll come to see you before you go. The next time we meet, I won't be living in Chicago anymore."

Brad just nods.

~

Aisha and I struggle out of bed in the morning, worn out after two big nights. We make the prayer downstairs and sit on the floor, looking at each other.

"Are we really going to drive to Lexington this weekend?" she asks.

"We need to find a place to live. Would you like to wait until next weekend?"

"That would be easier. Why don't we spend the weekend packing instead? Mom is here and she'll help us."

"Maybe I should ask Hanif to help us find a place."

"Of course, you should. I'll see what I can do by phone and computer. At this point, I'd rather move into a place sight-unseen than make that long drive."

"It's not that long."

"It is after a graduation and an engagement party."

"Do you want to go back to bed?"

She smiles. "I should get to work. Don't tempt me."

I take her hand. Sharon walks into the family room. "Aren't you two going to eat breakfast before you leave? You'd better hurry."

"We're not going, Mom. Are you ready to help me get organized?"

"Not until after breakfast. Come eat."

Sharon is livelier at ninety than I am at fifty-eight. I groan, pulling myself off the floor, and follow my mother-in-law into the kitchen.

Luqman: Part One

Uncle Psychologist has been busy. For the last two nights, he's watched me and whispered to my father. Whatever he's trying to say, Dad's not buying it, but I'd better be careful. He's in his sixties now, but the guy's still sharp. And, unlike Dad, not much gets past him. I used to hang out with his son, Ahmad, and he couldn't make a move without my uncle questioning him. Ahmad moved to Seattle after he graduated. I don't blame him.

Rasheed was serving dinner tonight. He was able to get on at the hotel without a problem. The last piece of the puzzle has fallen into place. We have two more weeks until D-Day.

I'd better keep an eye on Uncle Psychologist though. Dad won't be at the dinner because of the alcohol which will make my job a little easier. I hope my uncle didn't buy a ticket.

~

It's nearly midnight by the time Rasheed and I get over to the lake to meet the boys. We have to talk fast because the cops come out after midnight.

"Here's the list of demands. What do you think?" I pass the sheet of paper around as we huddle under a street light.

Aziz nods. "This is good, man. Very good. You know what you're talking about."

"How are we gonna tell them our demands, though?" says Abu Bakr. "You gonna walk into city hall and request a meeting with the mayor?" Everyone laughs.

"Something like that. This is what I plan to do." I give them the details.

"Sweet," says Aziz.

"We'll hold the entire city of Chicago hostage," says Hakeem.

"That's the idea. By the time we're done, FOM will rule."

Mustapha starts to chant, "FOM." Rasheed hits him in the arm. "What do you think you're doing?"

A police officer is headed our way.

"Two weeks, brothers." I remind them.

We scatter.

The next time I see them will be the night of the fundraiser.

~

My parents were supposed to go out of town this weekend, but they changed their minds. It doesn't matter. The plan is in motion.

They want to spend the day packing. That's all they talk about these days. All day, I dutifully carry empty boxes up from the basement.

Last night's meeting went very well. Aziz is with me now.

I haven't seen Malek since the night we ran him off. He must still be licking his wounds.

Kyle's Family

We celebrated Emily's graduation on Tuesday. She said she didn't want to make a fuss, and we all worried that a big celebration would tire Dad. He slept all weekend after going to two events in a row for Maryam.

Dad stayed home from the graduation ceremony because Mom didn't want him going out in that crowd. The rest of us went to cheer for Emily. Afterward, Grand Caravan catered dinner at their house. Emily's parents came too. It was just as good as going out to eat but without the hassle.

~

Our plane leaves at 11:00 AM. We need to get to the airport soon. Gameel will drive us there in a rented van so we won't have to worry about leaving our cars at O'Hare.

All our suitcases are packed and in the van. Faiqa and Emily sent some baby things ahead last week. They should be waiting for us at the house in Flagstaff.

I help Dad into the front seat of the van. He turns to Gameel. "If we have time, I'd like to stop at my brother's house on the way."

"We have time. Everyone climb in. Let's go."

Hannah is in back with Emily's mother, making a fuss over their grandchildren. "I am going to miss you all so much," says Hannah.

The normal response would be that we'll be back soon. But, we won't be back until we've buried Dad. That's one of his conditions.

~

Gameel pulls up in front of Uncle Joshua's house. I give Dad a hand as he gets out of the van. "Come inside with me, Kyle," he says.

Uncle Joshua and Aunt Aisha are probably eating breakfast. This is an ordinary work day for them. My uncle answers the door with a cup of coffee in his hand.

"Come on in. Sit down. Would you like coffee, Kyle? Brad, do you want cream cheese on your bagel?"

"We don't have time," says Dad. "I came to say goodbye. Take care, Joshua." He hugs my uncle tightly.

"Do you know yet when you'll be back?"

"No. You've been a great brother. I love you."

Uncle Joshua looks surprised at Dad's emotional goodbye. "I love you, too. Take it easy. Don't push yourself."

"I'll be fine," Dad says. "Don't worry." They share another hug. "We have to go." Dad pulls away.

Uncle Joshua walks with us back to the van. As Gameel drives away, he waves. Dad watches him in the side view mirror.

I wonder how it feels to know that you'll never see your brother again.

∾

Gameel takes us to a special area of the airport. We'll fly in a company jet down to Flagstaff. It's impossible to find a non-stop commercial flight and this will be much easier for Dad.

Hannah, Gameel, and Emily's mother say goodbye before we board. Gameel hugs Dad. "Take care, Brad. Let me know if you need anything."

We settle in, the pilot is cleared for take-off, and we're on our way. It will take us nearly five hours to get there. Once the plane levels off, a stewardess passes out our meals. Steak and baked potato for the rest of us. Fish and steamed vegetables for Dad.

∾

We were held up at the Flagstaff airport because they neglected to reserve a specially-equipped van for me to drive. They finally gave us a regular van at half price and promised to come up with a car for me by Monday.

Matt slides behind the wheel and laughs. "You never let anyone else drive, Kyle. How does it feel to be in the backseat for a change?"

"Wait until Monday."

The house is on the outskirts of Flagstaff, up a winding road, in a wooded area. "Perfect," says Dad.

~

Matt helps Dad out of the car. He moves slowly, his feet swollen.

I unlock the door and go inside. This is fantastic. Hardwood floors with oriental rugs. Cathedral ceilings. A large window overlooking wooded mountain scenery. A plush blue sofa faces the window.

"Look, Dad, there's your spot." Matt takes him to the couch and helps him prop up his legs. Dad stares at the beauty while we unload the van.

Thirty minutes later, the babies are asleep in their portable cribs, and everyone's luggage is in the bedrooms. Matt carries in the food we bought on the way from the airport. Emily gets busy in the kitchen.

We talked about splitting the chores. Emily and Mom will take care of the cooking. Matt and I will run errands and do the heavy lifting. Faiqa will be busy with the babies, but she'll also keep an eye on Dad and take care of his medical needs.

~

Matt brings dinner to the round oak table in the dining room. Faiqa walks out of the bedroom, carrying Yusuf. "He just woke up and now he won't stay still."

"Bring him here." Dad holds out his arms.

Yusuf squirms. Dad laughs and kisses him. "You're just like your daddy. We could never get him to settle down." Dad puts Yusuf gently on the floor. My son takes off crawling. Faiqa keeps a watchful eye.

"The food's ready," says Matt.

As Dad struggles off the couch, I move to help him. "I can do it," he says. He slowly walks across the room and takes his place at the table. "It's been a long day. This food looks delicious and I'm hungry."

~

The last couple of days have felt awkward. The place is beautiful, but I feel a tension. This isn't a vacation. We brought Dad here to die.

Dad brings up the subject during lunch. "Why does everyone look so sad? We're in the mountains. Isn't it beautiful?"

"It is, Dad, but, well, we keep thinking about why we're here."

"We're here to have some good times together as a family, Kyle." He smiles. "So start enjoying yourself."

"But we came here so you could die."

"Are you going to act like this all the time? In that case, we might as well go back to Chicago. If I want to be around a bunch of party poopers, I can go check into a hospice."

"Party poopers?" I never heard that one before. I snicker at the image. Matt and our wives join in. Soon the four of us are laughing out loud.

Mom smiles. "I don't know how your generation would say it. A wet blanket. Spoilsport. Killjoy."

We stop laughing and stare at her. Where did those words come from?

"You know what I mean," says Dad, with a stern voice and a smirk. "Now, are we going to have a real vacation, or are the four of you going to keep acting like a bunch of worrywarts?"

Worrywarts? We start up again. I laugh until I cry. After a minute or two, I get control of myself, slowing down to a giggle. That felt good. The tension is broken.

"We're in Arizona in a beautiful house in the mountains, less than forty miles away from the Grand Canyon. We're not going to think about jobs or bills, and you are not allowed to worry about my health. Do you understand?"

Dad cured the last of the giggles. We nod. "Yes, Dad. We'll have fun."

Dad grunts. "You could sound more enthusiastic. Death is as natural as life. When the time comes, no one can stop it. And tell me why we should fight to stay alive when we have the hope of seeing our places in paradise after we die."

He's right. What can I say?

Faiqa speaks for all of us. "You said it beautifully, Dad."

I decide to add my voice. "I'm glad that's settled. Can you pass the potatoes?"

Dad shakes his head. "I would like to be around to see you in twenty years, Kyle, when Yusuf is as smart-aleck as you are."

Another old idiom, but I understood that one. Dad always has the last word.

Joshua: Part Three

Before Brad left, he looked at me with an expression I've never seen before. I felt like I should say something more, but the words wouldn't come to me.

~

Lubna sent Aisha the pictures and details of several rental houses. She even volunteered to go check them out for us. When I was young, the idea of moving into a place I'd never seen wouldn't have bothered me, but now I worry about the details. How is the neighborhood? Does the basement leak? Is the yard big enough for a garden? We thought about renting an apartment, but I want to have my own yard, my own garage, and my own basement.

We've narrowed the list down to three. Lubna is going to see them today. We'll wait for her report. When we get to Lexington, one of the first things we'll do is take Lubna and her husband out for dinner.

Packing is the focus of our lives these days. I never realized we had so much stuff. The worst part is the papers we've accumulated over the years. We can leave some of it here, which is great. It would take us a year to go through it all.

Next weekend is the fundraiser. The board agreed to hire Stu as acting executive director. I hope they're so impressed with his performance that they offer him the position permanently. He will be formally introduced at the fundraiser. They're pressuring me to attend the event myself, but I keep putting them off with lame excuses. Only Gameel knows the real reason.

Tonight, our kids are coming for dinner. Sharon will make her famous beef stew. After dinner, we'll talk about who is going to live in our house. I'll feel better once we have that resolved.

The reality of this move is starting to sink in. I'm leaving my home town. Over the next several weeks and months, I'll have to change our address, bank accounts, car registration, and voter registration. This is a major transition.

~

After the evening prayer, we all sit around the family room. Jeremy and Raheema are here, without their kids. So are Jamal and Rabia. I asked Zaid to come too, now that he's part of our family. He sits on the couch next to Maryam. Luqman and Muhammad sit cross-legged on the floor.

"Bismillah. Mom and I are leaving for Lexington in two weeks, and we're concerned about who will live in our house. You need to decide this among yourselves. What do you think, Jeremy?"

"Raheema and I have our house, and we don't want to move any time soon."

"Not until the kids leave for college," says Raheema.

"But I'm sure the rest of you could use a place to live."

"We're leaving right after Maryam's wedding," says Jamal.

"So we don't need a place," says Rabia.

"I have my apartment," says Muhammad. "And this house is too big for one person."

"I made plans with my friends," says Luqman.

We all look at Maryam and Zaid. "What do you think?" I ask.

"I already have an apartment," says Zaid.

"But, we could live here, couldn't we?" says Maryam. "Your brother Yusuf wants to move out of your parents' house. He could take over your lease."

Zaid looks at Maryam. "Do you really want to live here?"

"I've lived in this house all my life. Don't you think it would be a nice place to raise our family?"

He looks into her eyes, and I know he can't resist. I never could.

"If that would make you happy. It is a nice house." He looks at me. "Is that okay with you, Uncle Isa?"

I told him to start calling me Dad. "That sounds great."

Luqman: Part Two

If Maryam and Zaid hadn't agreed to live in our house, Dad would have pressured me to do it. He doesn't know that I couldn't possibly stay.

On Monday, I go to Hope Center with Dad to help him clear out his office. We brought two big boxes. By noon, both boxes are full, and he still has more to pack. I'll never let myself get bogged down by possessions.

We've worked hard all morning, and we're about to head out when Stu drops by. He looks at the boxes and the empty desk top. "You two must be hungry."

"We're going out for sandwiches. Why don't you join us?"

"I have a better idea. Come with me."

We follow him into a large meeting room at Evans. The place is packed with people and tables full of food.

"We couldn't let you leave that easily," says Gameel.

Everyone talks and laughs, a couple of people make speeches, and we eat. I stuff myself on salads and casseroles. This is much better than a sandwich.

Just when I think I can't move, some people carry out a huge cake. There are more speeches. Dad cuts the first piece and they all clap. They sing some old song about a "jolly good fellow." Dad grins. This is my father's world and he loves it.

By the time we head back to his office, we're loaded down with gift bags. Dad sends me to Sandra to ask for another box.

∼

We're done. I just carried the last box to the car. Dad is vacuuming the carpet. When he switches off the vacuum cleaner I say, "At the luncheon, I heard someone say you won't be at the fundraiser."

"No. It won't be my kind of gathering. This is my very last day at the center."

"Volunteers get free tickets though, don't they? I would like to go and hear Hiram Johnson speak."

"If you really want to go, I won't stop you. I'm not comfortable with the man, and I won't go to any event where alcohol is served. But you're almost twenty-five, and old enough to make your own decisions. I don't have any tickets here. Go to Sandra, and see if she has one for you."

It's late. Sandra will be going home soon. I rush to the office. I need to be at that fundraiser.

∼

We're heading out the door when Darnell walks up. "I'm sorry I couldn't make it to your party, Joshua. I had a final."

Dad hugs Darnell. "Keep working hard. You're doing a great job."

"I'm really going to miss you." He looks like he's about to cry.

Dad smiles. "Stay in touch. Let me know how you're doing. You might want to check out the University of Kentucky. I hear they're good."

"I'll do that. I have another year of community college. Maybe I can come down there to finish my degree."

"I'll be looking for you." They hug again.

Darnell walks with us to Dad's car. He waves as we drive away.

I'm starting to feel rotten about what I'm about to do to Dad, but it's too late. Anyway, it needs to be done. Sentimentality kills revolutions.

Joshua: Part Four

On Monday night I collapse, falling asleep on the couch right after dinner. When I open my eyes again, it's nearly sunrise. Luqman must have overslept, too. He worked hard yesterday. I stretch, rubbing my neck before washing up and calling my family for the prayer.

When we're finished, I'm still tired. I stretch out on the couch again.

"You can't go back to sleep," says Aisha. "We have another big decision to make."

"What's that?"

"Last night Lubna sent me the information on the houses, and we have to act fast. Which one do you want?"

~

We spent nearly two hours debating the pros and cons of each house. The one we settled on will cost a little more, but it has a basement, a garage, and a nice backyard. It's close to the Islamic school and shopping. It looks great.

Aisha calls Lubna, and I send in the deposit. We're set.

Now, we just have to finish packing. That's the hard part.

Kyle's Family

Dad is getting stronger every day. It must be the air down here.

Every morning, he and Mom take walks in the woods around the house. They're gone for an hour or more. It's good that they have this time together.

~

During breakfast, Dad says he wants to spend a few days at the Grand Canyon. "We could hike down into the canyon and camp out."

"You're not strong enough for that, Dad, and you know I couldn't make it."

"What if we rode burros?"

I managed to ride a camel in Egypt, but it was rough. And that was on flat land. "Why don't we rent hotel rooms at the canyon instead?"

That's still too much for Faiqa and Emily. "I have three babies," says Faiqa. "I don't want to take them anywhere near the canyon. It's too risky."

"Zakariya is a handful just here in the house," says Emily.

"Would you mind if we went with our parents?" I ask.

Faiqa pauses just a second. "No, you should go. Emily and I can stay here. Matt and you need to spend this time with your dad."

"That sounds like a great idea," says Emily.

Our wives fix lunch while Matt and I load the car. I wonder what they're planning for their time without us.

~

Before we leave, we remind our wives to call us, and we kiss our babies. I always hate leaving them.

We take my car, leaving the van for our wives. Dad directs me to the highway that will take us north to the canyon. It's a nice drive. Very peaceful. I'll bring Faiqa back here someday, insha Allah.

We check into the hotel and go outside to look out over the canyon. I'm amazed every time I see it.

"Let's go back inside," says Dad. "I have a surprise for you." In the gift shop, Dad introduces us to a middle-aged man, not much older than me. "This is Roy, our pilot."

Pilot? At least Dad didn't go with the burros. Roy leads us to his helicopter. I haul myself in and pull my chair in after me. This is more comfortable than I thought it would be.

Dad buckles his seat belt. "I won't die until I've seen the floor of the canyon."

Roy takes off. We hover directly above the canyon for a few minutes before gradually descending. We're surrounded by the beauty. I become lost in it. There are no words.

He lands the helicopter on a broad ledge at the bottom. "You have fifteen minutes to look around," says Roy.

"Make it thirty," says Dad. "I'm a dying man."

Roy nods. "You got it."

Leave it to my father to turn dying into an advantage.

I slide into my wheelchair and look up. This is more beautiful than I ever imagined. The Colorado River trickles past us, just a stream in this part of the canyon.

Dad walks up to the edge and studies the river. Before we know what he's doing, he wades into the water. I rush to him.

"No, Dad. It's too cold. You'll get sick."

He laughs. "I'm already sick. When I first came to this canyon, I remember looking down at the river and wanting to touch it."

Mom looks resigned. Matt shrugs. Dad splashes like a kid.

I study the area. There are caves and ledges. A lot of great places to climb. I'll bring the triplets back here one day, maybe when they're in high school. They'll love it.

We stay for a full thirty minutes. Dad sits on the bank of the river and studies the sky. He's wet. We should get him out of this cool air. He's really pushing this whole fate thing.

Roy calls us back into the helicopter. Dad balks.

"Let's go," says Roy. "I'm taking you to another special place."

Mom grabs Dad's hand and walks with him back to the helicopter.

Roy takes off again, flying across the canyon to the north rim.

"I always wanted to come here," Dad whispers, examining the view. "Can we set down for a few minutes?"

Roy smiles. "You have fifteen minutes. Not a second more."

Dad sits on a rock and peers across the canyon. I think he would be happy if he died right here.

When we board the helicopter again, Roy heads back, buzzing into the canyon and taking a few frightening turns. He's giving Dad the ride of a lifetime.

When we land back on the south rim, I give Roy a nice tip. "Thanks for doing this. You can't imagine what it meant to my father."

He turns back to his helicopter. "Glad I could help."

"Let's get you inside," says Mom, pulling Dad away from the canyon. "And get you out of those wet clothes."

∾

During dinner, Dad says, "This is the second time I came to the canyon to die."

"What do you mean?" says Matt. "What happened?"

Dad tells us the story of his suicide plans that year he left us. I never knew. He describes nearly slipping into the canyon and realizing how much he wanted to come home to us.

"This time," he says, "I absolutely don't want to die. But there's nothing I can do about it."

"You could go back to the hospital. They discover new therapies every day."

"No, Kyle. I don't want to spend my last days being poked and prodded. People die in hospitals, too. Remember that."

I'm married to a doctor, and I support modern medicine, but Dad does have a point.

∾

I wake up and look out the window. The sky is getting lighter. Soon, the sun will rise over the canyon. I wake Matt up for the prayer. When we're done, we go outside to watch the sunrise. Mom and Dad are out here already.

We spend the morning studying the canyon. It's nearly June, but we're in the mountains. Mom convinces Dad to wear a jacket.

After the midday prayer, we go to the hotel restaurant for lunch.

"Do you boys know why I left?" Dad asked.

"I thought it was because of something I did wrong," says Matt.

"Same here," I say. "Was it your drinking?"

"That was part of it. Mostly, it was losing my mother, and reliving some very bad moments in my childhood. Promise me you won't go off the deep end when I die."

What do you say to something like that? I nibble at my chicken.

"It will be different when you die, Dad," says Matt, "because you taught us about Islam."

Dad smiles. I almost say, "Same here." But, sometimes it's better to stay silent.

~

We spend the rest of the afternoon at the canyon, and the next morning too. We plan to go back after lunch.

Matt glances at his phone. "Everything must be okay back in Flagstaff."

"I'm sure you're worried about your family. I'm finished eating. Do you boys want to leave now?"

"Maybe we should," says Matt.

"Thanks for doing this with me," says Dad. "Give me fifteen more minutes at the canyon, and I'll be ready to go." He offers his hand to Mom. "Are you coming?"

They walk off together.

Joshua: Part Five

Aisha and Sharon take the morning off to go visit Jamal and his family. My wife is way ahead of me when it comes to packing. I have to finish sorting through all the things I brought home from the office, and there are all those boxes still in the basement and garage. In the morning, I reserve a moving van. Muhammad has volunteered to drive it for us. Aisha and I will both need our cars down in Kentucky. I hope we can manage the convoy.

Later, I'll worry about the trip. Right now, I need to get to work.

~

My wife and mother-in-law return in the late afternoon. "That little Kamila is so precious," says Sharon. "She reminds me of you when you were a baby, Angela."

Aisha smiles. "I'll have to spend a lot of time up here in June. Between the wedding and the baby, it will be hard to stay away. Oh, I'm going to miss my grandchildren. You won't mind, will you, Isa?"

Just don't make a habit of it. I'm not moving to Lexington so I can be alone. "No. Go ahead, hon."

Sharon walks into her room and comes out a couple of minutes later with her suitcases. "I told Angela that I'm going over to Umar's house. I've hardly spent any time with him, and with all the packing, you don't need me underfoot." She gestures at the mess I've created in the family room.

"You don't need to leave."

"I'll be back in the morning, Joshua. I can't wait to hear Maryam's ideas for the house."

"What is Maryam doing to the house?"

"She wants to tell me her decorating ideas. We'll decide which furniture to leave for them and which to take with us." Aisha claps her hands. "I need to get busy packing so I can be free tomorrow to help Maryam."

I grab Sharon's suitcases. "I'll take these out for you. But, you really don't have to go."

She laughs. "Look around you, Joshua. Can you honestly tell me you need another person in this house?"

I grin. "We always need you."

She shakes her head. "Hurry up and carry those suitcases out. Safa is making biriyani, and I want to get there while it's hot."

So, that's what it is. I could make biriyani for her, too. After I clean up this mess—which will probably take me all night. "Let's go."

～

Luqman is out. Maryam is eating dinner with Zaid's family. Aisha and I order pizza.

"The packing is coming along nicely," says Aisha.

"For you, maybe. How did we ever accumulate so much junk?"

"What do you expect after thirty years? Maryam said she'll help us tomorrow."

"Today while I was carrying a box up out of storage it hit me. This is a big move. Are you sure we're ready?"

"It's too late now. You accepted their offer, and we put a deposit on the house."

"And I rented a truck this morning. I hope we can do this."

"We can do anything, insha Allah, as long as we work together."

Let's see. Luqman is gone. Maryam is with her in-laws. We're alone.

~

Maryam, Aisha, and Sharon start up right after breakfast. They go from one room to another, deciding what to take, what to leave, and what Maryam wants to change. I ignore them until they come to the family room. "Oh, here's the other blue chair," says Maryam. "It matches the one in your bedroom. Could you leave those here?"

I stop what I'm doing. "I'm sorry, Maryam. We're taking the blue easy chairs." They're the most comfortable chairs in the house, and I have a lot of good memories associated with them.

"Okay," says Maryam. She sighs, and frowns a little.

I hate when she does that. "You can have the chairs. We'll buy some in Kentucky." She always knows how to get to me. I hope Zaid is ready for her.

Revolution!

*Eager souls, mystics and revolutionaries, may propose
to refashion the world in accordance with their dreams;
but evil remains, and so long as it lurks in the secret places
of the heart, utopia is only the shadow of a dream.*

—Nathaniel Hawthorne

Luqman's Revolution

Today is the twenty-fourth of May. This is it.

The supplies are in my trunk. Last night, I went into the basement
and dug up an old tent my parents bought when my dad decided we
should go camping. One night was enough to convince us not to do
that again. After a little more searching, I found the lantern, three
sleeping bags—I don't know what happened to the others—and a
propane stove.

I didn't buy the phone yet. I'll pick that up on my way to the fundraiser.

A couple of hours before I leave, I practice reaching for my gun.
I'll tuck it into my pants, in the small of my back, the way I've seen
them do on cop shows. I draw. It works. I practice a few more times,
getting a little faster with each try. Of course, I'm not practicing with
my gun. There's no way I'd bring it into the house again. I keep it
locked up in a box in my trunk. I can't afford another accident.

Yesterday, I picked up my suit from the cleaners. It looks good. I
put it on and stand in front of the mirror. The suit coat may slow me
down a little. I practice again with my suit coat on.

I'll miss this room. Mom and Dad want me to stay here at the
house until Maryam and Zaid have their formal ceremony. They don't
know I'm not coming home tonight.

$\approx$

Dad is surrounded by boxes in the family room. He's glad to be
staying home tonight. I watch as he stumbles around, trying to organize his things. He does try. I feel a touch of regret. I almost say
something, but decide it's better to leave silently.

Mom, Maryam, and Grandma are in the kitchen talking about the wedding. Between moving and the wedding, that's all anyone thinks about these days. Tomorrow, they'll have something else on their minds.

I climb into my car and drive a few blocks, pulling into a quiet alley where I go to my trunk and take out the box. When I'm back in the car, I remove my gun from the box, make sure it's loaded, with the safety on, and put it in the small of my back. It fits nicely. No one will be able to see it.

This is it. I'm ready.

~

Stu greets me at the door. "Hi, Luqman. I'm glad you're here. Is your father coming?"

"No, he's in the middle of packing. I thought someone should represent the family."

"Great. Excuse me." He shakes hands with the couple behind me.

I survey the room. The VIP table, where Hiram Johnson will sit, is near the kitchen door. Rasheed should be in the kitchen. In fifty-five minutes, the others will pull up in Abu Bakr's work van and park in the delivery area. I'm anxious to set the plan into motion. We worked everything out to the last detail. This is the opening shot of the revolution.

The guests continue to pour into the room. It looks like a full house. So many witnesses, but no one will realize what happened.

They'll mill around for another twenty minutes. Gameel will open with a short introduction. Dinner will be served. Stu will introduce Hiram. Hiram will give his speech. He'll sit down. And I know exactly what will happen next.

~

The food is good. Dad doesn't know what he's missing. While he's at home struggling with his mess and grabbing a few bites of pizza, I'm dining on real food. They spared no expense.

I don't know anyone at my table, but anonymity is good. How many other secrets are hidden in this room?

Rasheed is serving the VIP table. He chats with Reverend Johnson. Rasheed is good at making people feel comfortable. He must have told a joke. Hiram laughs. Rasheed smiles and nods, playing the role of the docile servant. Hiram eats it up. On his way back to the kitchen, Rasheed shuffles just a little. I try to send him a signal. Don't overdo it, man. But, Rasheed knows exactly what he's doing.

Hiram is an interesting contradiction. He's a teetotaling preacher who has no problem sitting at a table where wine is served. He's a racist who pretends to be good friends with Stu, a black man. Of course, Stu knows how to play the game.

Everyone plays. I played my parents for the last month. I also played the boys who put me in charge, including Rasheed. Rasheed plays Hiram Johnson. Hiram plays his congregation. The congregation plays Chicago and Chicago plays me. We're all part of the game, spinning round and round. Until tonight. Tonight, the rules will change.

∾

The waiters brought out dessert ten minutes ago. Rasheed is chatting up Hiram again. Good job, brother.

Stu stands and walks to the microphone. "Hello. Good evening. May I have your attention?" The talk dies down.

"Good evening. I wish to welcome everyone who came out for this special event tonight. My name is Stuart Woodson. For the last four years, I have served as the director of the Jim Evans Memorial Center, where we help the homeless. Recently, the executive director of our organization, Joshua Adams, accepted another position, and I was named the acting executive director.

"That's enough about me, though." He laughs nervously. "I'm sure you will enjoy listening to our keynote speaker. Reverend Hiram Johnson, one of Chicago's most notable native sons, has led the New Pilgrims Evangelical Church for the last thirty-two years. Some of you may have heard of his father, Steven Johnson, who was one of the four founding members of the New Pilgrims back in 1974.

"Like Hope Center and the Evans Center, the New Pilgrims Evangelical Church works for the good of the community. Though the church was founded on the simple principle of providing moral guidance, it has expanded to offer faith-based services for the community. Under the leadership of Reverend Johnson, the New Pilgrims have grown to become an essential part of the social and political landscape here in Chicago.

"Since I was a boy I have admired the work of Reverend Johnson and the New Pilgrims, and I am also in awe of the reverend's gifted oratory. I know you will all agree that we are fortunate to have Reverend Johnson with us tonight. I'm sure he's anxious to share his wisdom with you, so I will step aside. Please give a warm welcome to Reverend Hiram Johnson."

Hiram approaches the podium, accompanied by loud applause. Many stand. I smirk. What 'wisdom' will the good reverend share with us tonight?

He clears his throat, his bulky figure overshadowing the podium. Using his best church voice, he shouts, "Good evening, brothers and sisters."

The audience murmurs. He smiles. "You don't have to be a member of my church to be my brother, my sister. Shall we try that again? Good evening, brothers and sisters."

"Good evening." Some reply enthusiastically.

He smiles. "My topic for the evening is 'Finding Hope in Dangerous Times.' If I were to cover all aspects of this inspirational message, I would still be talking well after midnight. The hotel won't let us stay that long, so I'll touch only on the basics.

"Dangerous times. We have only to turn on the news to realize how truly dangerous the world is today. Terrorist acts are being perpetrated not only in world capitals but here in our own backyard. The youth in my church, the Young Pilgrims, have been viciously and relentlessly assaulted by a gang calling themselves the Friends of Muhammad."

I smile. He sneers.

"You and I are in danger every single day of our lives. Will they break into our homes, taking everything we own and leaving only our bloodied bodies? Will they steal our cars at gunpoint or kidnap our children for their own nefarious purposes? From 2001, when they first attacked our homeland, until today, they have threatened to destroy our very way of life. What's worse, they are no longer holed up in caves or palatial dens of iniquity. They now hide among us."

You have no idea how close we are, Hiram. No idea at all.

"Drive down any street on the South Side and you will see the dangers we face. Obscene graffiti on every building. Gang members slouching on every street corner. Armed criminals lurking in the darkness. The danger is spreading. No longer confined to a single neighborhood, criminal activity seeps into our suburbs and waits outside our doors."

He spends the next fifteen minutes thoroughly exposing the threats posed by Muslims and other minorities. By the time he's done, even the most stalwart man in the audience must feel weak and vulnerable.

"If we were to dwell only on the dangers surrounding us, I suppose half of us would commit suicide, and the other half would hide in sturdy vaults, afraid to come into contact with the outside world. However, even the lowliest among us has hope. It is the hope of better lives that keeps us going, day after day, confronting and even conquering the surrounding dangers. Chicago's own native son, Barack Obama, aimed for the White House while buoyed with the message of hope."

I studied President Obama's speeches as an undergraduate. He has become like Martin Luther King—an icon who wasn't supported by half the people who now praise him.

He goes on for another five or ten minutes, giving examples of hope. Much of his material is plagiarized. I stare at the pattern of the wallpaper.

"Hope is why we are here tonight. The appropriately named Hope Center was established thirty-five years ago to provide services to the needy and offer them hope. Four years ago, the Evans Center was built to assist the neediest among us, those without even a place to lay their heads at night. I never had the privilege of meeting Jim Evans, for whom the center is named, but I am certain he was a man who reached out into the darkness and brought light into the lives of those he touched."

I wish I had known my grandfather. He was that kind of man, though I don't like to hear Hiram talk about him.

"In spite of personal obstacles, Mr. Joshua Adams promoted hope through these two agencies."

Personal obstacles? Like what? Being a Muslim, maybe?

"Now, Mr. Stuart Woodson stands firmly at the helm, and he will carry on the mission. However, he cannot do this without the assistance of the leaders of our community. You, Chicago's elite, have the power to perpetuate hope and vanquish the dangers we face."

He wraps it all up with an open call for donations. Darnell and some of the other volunteers go to the tables and hand out pledge forms. I'm glad Stu didn't recruit me.

Checks and cash make their way to the front. Hiram calls out the donations while the proud donors bow and beam. Isn't charity supposed to be given in secret?

I hope they hurry. We need Hiram back in his seat. My boys must be getting restless.

∿

Hiram is at his table now, and Gameel has taken over. I make a call, walk casually to the VIP table, and tap Stu on the shoulder. "Could I see you a moment?" I whisper.

He follows me out to the hallway. Rasheed comes out of the kitchen and continues flattering the reverend.

"What is it?" says Stu.

"My father is on the phone. He wants to talk to you."

Usually, I won't carry a phone because it interferes with my anonymity. I bought a cheap one just for this purpose.

While Stu talks with Dad, I peek into the banquet room. Rasheed is leading Hiram into the kitchen. *"The boys in the kitchen want to meet you,"* Rasheed says. *"We would be honored if you would take a picture with us."*

Stu is still talking to Dad. Gameel is telling stupid jokes to the laughing audience. And Hiram is being led, at gunpoint, to the back of Abu Bakr's work van.

Kyle's Family

When we check out of the hotel, I notice the date: May 24. The fundraiser is tonight. I meant to go and support the cause, but I can't be in two places at once. When we return to Chicago, insha Allah, I'll make a donation in Dad's honor.

∿

If it was up to my father, we would stay in the hotel by the canyon. But Matt and I need to get back to our families. We wait by the car while Dad takes a final look.

He walks slowly toward us, holding Mom's hand. As he gets into the car, he sighs. "I may never see the canyon again."

Now I feel guilty for leaving. "Insha Allah, we'll come again soon."

"We could stay," says Matt, "but I worry about my family."

"Of course you do," says Mom.

"But they do grow up," says Dad. "And one day you'll look at your son and be so proud that you'll wonder why everyone says raising a kid is difficult." He reaches up and puts his hands on our shoulders. "I couldn't have asked for better sons."

I don't want to get emotional. I put the car into gear and head back toward Flagstaff.

~

We walk into a quiet house.

Matt panics. "Emily didn't answer her phone."

"Neither did Faiqa." What's going on?

"Come here," says Mom. "Emily left a note. They went shopping for baby things."

"But why won't they answer their phones?"

"Settle down, Matt. I'm sure they'll be back soon." Dad relaxes on the couch. "Bring me some tea. That will keep your mind off things." He sneezes.

"Are you okay, Dad?" I ask. "You sneezed a couple times in the car, too."

"Can't a man sneeze without being noticed? Stop worrying, and tell Matt to hurry up with the tea."

As Matt brings Dad the tea, Faiqa and Emily walk in, each carrying a carseat.

"Khalil, you can go get Nathifa and Yusuf. They fell asleep in the car. This is the first time I've tried to go shopping with the triplets. I won't do that again anytime soon."

Matt rushes to Emily. "Where were you?"

"We were shopping. Did you find my note? Wait until you see what I bought for Zakariya." She puts his carseat on the floor and heads back out toward the car.

"Wait here. I'll get your things," says Matt.

She kisses him. "Thank you, sweetie."

"Why didn't you answer your phones?" I ask.

"Matt and you should try going shopping with four babies. Then you'll understand," says Faiqa.

"My phone needed to be charged, so we left it in the car," says Emily. "Faiqa's phone was somewhere in the bottom of the diaper bag. We heard it once, but by the time she got to it, you had hung up. Nashwa was fussing, and Nathifa had a dirty diaper. There were other things to think about." She sits down and puts her feet on the hassock. "I'm worn out." Zakariya fusses. Mom takes him.

Dad sneezes. "Are you okay?" says Faiqa.

"It was just a sneeze. Now leave me alone." He goes back to his tea.

"Dad went wading in the Colorado River. Can you believe it?"

Faiqa walks over and puts her hand on his forehead. "You don't feel warm. Let me know if you start feeling sick, will you?"

Dad sips his tea and smirks. "Party poopers!"

I can't help it. I laugh every time he says that.

Luqman's Revolution

Stu hands me the phone. "I'm glad your father called. It's too bad he didn't come."

"You know how he is. He cares about the centers, but he's stubborn about his principles."

Stu peers into the banquet room. "I wonder where Reverend Johnson went."

"Maybe he's in the restroom."

"That must be it. We'd better go back inside."

As I sit down, Gameel finishes his remarks.

"Now, I would like to ask Reverend Johnson to say a few closing words." He turns to the VIP table.

Stu whispers something to Gameel and goes to the microphone. "Reverend Johnson will be back in a moment. In the meantime, I would like to announce the winners of our silent auction. Gameel, do you have those names?"

They stall. After about ten minutes, Stu walks out the side door. He returns, rubbing his eyebrows and scanning the room. He goes out to the hallway, comes back in, and shakes his head. Gameel tells more jokes.

Stu whispers something to Gameel. He's visibly upset. Gameel shakes his head. Stu takes the microphone. Gameel opens the kitchen door.

As the kitchen door closes, Gameel's voice rings through the room. "What the hell happened here?"

Murmurs arise from the crowd. A woman screams. A man shouts, "What's going on?"

Stu uses a handkerchief to wipe sweat from his forehead. "Everything's fine. Calm down. There's nothing to worry about."

Gameel's voice cuts through Stu's entreaties. "Where is he? Who took him? How many were there?"

"Excuse me." Stu runs to the kitchen door and looks in. "Oh my God. Is he breathing?"

"I'm getting out of here." A woman shouts. She grabs her husband's hand and heads for the door.

The string quartet plays something calming. It sounds like Mozart. It doesn't work. More people get up and head for the door, pushing each other to get out.

"Stop. Return to your seats, please. Everything is under control." Gameel's firm voice halts the panic. A few leave. Most straggle back to their tables.

"We had an incident in the kitchen. It's nothing to worry about. The last thing we want to do is panic." He fumbles with some note cards. "Remember why we gathered here tonight. We're here to support the fine work of Hope Center and Evans Center as they strive to meet the needs of the less fortunate. We cannot lose sight of our goals.

"I would like to fill you in on a little history. Many of you may not be aware of how we started Hope Center back in 2001. It was the dawn of a new millennium. Several community leaders gathered together that April, thirty-five years ago last month, to discuss how we could meet the challenges of the twenty-first century. Hope Center was to be only the beginning of our mission, and it has remained our flagship all these years. We sought to increase opportunities for all people, expanding their educational horizons and removing the obstacles that limited them in achieving their goals. As you remember, the fall of 2001 brought special challenges for us all and yet we continued onward, until today when we stand here—."

"Holy crap!" A man in the back of the room shouts out.

Police officers are rushing into the room. Four of them run to the kitchen. Two stay in the banquet hall.

"What happened? What's going on?" a woman calls out. Some guests in the back move toward the door. There's a scream somewhere.

"Nobody move," says an officer. "Stay where you are. There's no reason to panic."

"Tell us what's going on?"

"What are you hiding?"

"What happened in the kitchen?"

"Ladies and gentleman." Gameel tries to get the crowd under control.

One of the policemen nudges him aside and takes the microphone. "I need you all to sit down and be quiet. A man has been shot, and you're all witnesses."

"I didn't see anything. Who was shot?"

"Quiet."

"Where's Reverend Johnson?"

"Sit down. You will all have to be interviewed before you can leave."

A woman in a light purple gown stands up. "You can't make me stay here. Other people left."

"Sit down, ma'am."

She marches to the entrance. Two more police officers block her way.

"The entire area is being cordoned off. No one is going anywhere."

A quiet murmur runs through the crowd. The string quartet starts playing again. This piece sounds like Bach

I hadn't expected this. I need to get over to the camp to meet with the boys. They said someone was shot. I'm glad they remembered to use silencers.

I wonder how much force the boys had to use. We hoped they could simply gag and tie up the kitchen staff. I turn to the stranger sitting next to me. "What do you think happened?"

"I don't know," he says, "but it's big."

An ambulance crew comes rushing into the banquet room, toward the kitchen. Those in front get a look at the scene inside the kitchen.

"Did somebody die?"

"I need to get out of here."

At a table near the podium, a man stands up. "Is there a doctor here? My wife fainted."

"My husband is having chest pains," says a woman in the front.

People get up from their seats and move forward, trying to get a better view.

"Sit down," says the officer. "Could the doctors in the audience please help these people?"

Three rush to those stricken. Another woman calls out, "I don't feel very well."

While the officers try to control the chaos, I wonder what's happening in the kitchen. And how does Hiram like his new accommodations?

Joshua: Part One

Luqman's call surprised me. It was good talking to Stu. He said the fundraiser is very successful.

When did Luqman start carrying a phone again? My life would have been so much easier if I could have called him to find out where he was, but he refused me even that simple peace of mind. Maybe this is another sign of his maturity.

~

I'm more than halfway done with the mess. I still need to pack my clothes and whatever books I decide to take. Jeremy and Muhammad will help us move furniture into the truck on Friday night. We should leave before noon on Saturday.

Maryam walks around with a notepad, not a book, in her hands. She makes notes on the wedding and how she wants to decorate the house after we leave. She's also written a list of furniture we're leaving here for her, including my two blue easy chairs. Maybe I should rent a smaller truck.

There's a knock at the door. "Assalaamu alaikum Isa." Umar's voice comes through the open window.

"Walaikum assalaam." I open the door, ready to hug him, but his arms are full.

"Safa made biriyani. She also sent sweets."

"Masha Allah. That's great. Do you know I haven't eaten anything except pizza for the last three nights?"

"I'm not surprised. My sister probably said she was too busy to cook."

"I heard that." Aisha calls from the kitchen. "Look around you. Do you know how much work it is to move to a different state?" I peek in. Half of the cupboards are open and bare. Pots, pans, and dishes cover the table and counters.

"That's why I brought the food. Safa said she'll cook for you all week, though I doubt it will be biriyani every night."

"Whatever she makes, it will be more than my wife cooks for me." I grab Aisha and kiss her on the cheek. She playfully pats my arm.

"Are you two working alone? I can help." He looks around. "Where are the kids?"

"Maryam is around here somewhere. Muhammad had to work late. He'll come by later. Luqman went to the fundraiser."

"Is that tonight?" Umar pauses. "Why did he go?"

"He said something about wanting to hear Hiram Johnson speak. In fact, he insisted on going. I don't particularly like the man."

"I don't believe Luqman does, either. His statements are generally racist, and from what I can tell he strongly opposes Islam." Umar strokes his beard while staring off into space.

"Is something wrong?"

"I'll be back."

He leaves without giving salaams. What's up? Umar won't tell me until he's ready. I know that much.

Aisha clears a place at the table. "Come and eat, Isa. Then we can get back to work."

I sit down and enjoy the biriyani. The mess in the family room can wait.

Luqman's Revolution

It took eight officers to get the crowd settled down. Now, we're all waiting to be questioned. Nervous murmurs continue to spread through the room.

Stu is sitting at the VIP table, his face in his hands. Gameel has gone back into the kitchen. I know where Hiram is. As soon as they release me, I'll go meet the boys and start re-educating our hostage.

～

The couple in front of me is almost finished. The police will call on me next. I'm ready.

The man in his tux escorts his wife in her long gaudy dress away from the table. An officer signals me.

They need my name, address, and phone number. An officer asks for my ID. I hand him my driver's license. They may want to ask follow-up questions later, they say. That's not a problem. By the time they show up at my parents' house, I'll be safely out of town.

"Did you see Hiram Johnson leave the room?"

"I thought I saw him go out the side door toward the restrooms, but it may have been someone who looked like him. I just spotted him from the back."

"Did you see him enter the kitchen?"

"No. He was sitting at the VIP table when my father called and asked to talk to Stuart Woodson. We went out in the hall. When we came back, Reverend Johnson was gone."

"Why did your father want to talk to Mr. Woodson?"

"They used to work together at the centers."

"Is your father's name Joshua Adams?"

"Yes. That's him."

"Mr. Woodson told us about the phone call. That's all the questions for now. We may contact you later, and if you think of anything, you need to call me." He hands me his card. Detective Arif Hussain.

"Are you a Muslim? Assalaamu alaikum." I offer my hand.

"Walaikum assalaam. And your name is," he consults his list, "Luqman. I'll be sure to remember that. I have a brother named Luqman. You may go now."

I did it. I'd like to leave, but they're holding us all here until the questioning is complete. I glance at my watch. Hopefully, everything is going well out at the lake.

~

They're finally releasing us. Now I'll walk casually to my car and drive to our meeting place just over the border. But what is my uncle doing here? I wait while he approaches.

"Assalaamu alaikum Luqman. What happened? I saw the emergency vehicles outside."

"I don't know exactly. Reverend Johnson is missing, I guess."

He nods in that annoying way of his. "Yes, I heard about it on the news. They were holding the fundraiser here, weren't they?"

"It was going very well until Reverend Johnson disappeared. I wish there was more I could tell you."

"Your father will be shaken by this. I'll come back to the house with you so we can tell him together."

"That's okay, Uncle Umar. I can handle it."

"Your father will be very upset. It's better if we both tell him. We'll take my car. I'll bring you back later to pick up your car."

If I try to talk my way out of this, Uncle Psychologist will start analyzing me. I'd better go along with him. If it gets too late, I can call the boys.

No, I can't. I gave them strict instructions not to carry phones because those things can be traced. I'm still glad I did that.

I don't need to worry. Hakeem is in charge and he knows what to do.

~

Uncle Psychologist keeps quizzing me, trying to get inside my head. He starts as soon as we get into the car.

"Tell me again what happened."

"We had dinner. Reverend Johnson gave his speech. Then there was the phone call." I'll have to remember to change my story when I talk to Dad. "I called Dad to let him know how everything was going, and Stu wanted to talk to him. Sometime while we were out in the hall, Reverend Johnson left the VIP table. Stu started looking for him. Then they found something in the kitchen. They say someone was shot. I'm still not quite sure what happened there. No one seems to know where Reverend Johnson is."

My uncle strokes his beard. "It appears he was kidnapped. Can you imagine why anyone would want to abduct him?"

"I don't know. From what I've heard, he's very popular."

Uncle Psychologist nods. What deep insights does he think he can glean from my statements?

We're stopped at a red light. My uncle looks at me and says, "Tell me about Reverend Johnson's speech."

"He spoke about hope in dangerous times. He talked about crime and other dangers, and said we need to have hope. He used the example of the Hope Center, and Evans, as ways to fight danger. Then he gave his fundraising spiel. I heard they collected quite a bit."

"Did he say anything about Muslims?"

The speech will be in the news tomorrow. "He mentioned something about caves and the FOM. That's it."

"What do you know about the FOM, Luqman?"

"Not much, really. I've heard of them. Back in high school, I knew a guy who belonged, and once, some of them hassled me at the masjid. They're in the news all the time. That's about it."

"You didn't come across them in your thesis research, did you?"

"My concentration was on events that happened over 100 years ago. FOM has been around for only eight or ten years, I think."

He's quiet the rest of the way. Even his silence, though, is a trap. As difficult as Mom is to fool, Uncle Umar is much worse. I must be very careful.

Joshua: Part Two

The biriyani was great. After two plates and a few sweets, I'm ready to get back to work.

I'm in the middle of things when Umar knocks. "Assalaamu alaikum." Before I

can get up, Luqman opens the front door with his key. Umar follows.

"Walaikum assalaam. Why did you leave? Is everything okay?"

Umar frowns. "There was an incident at the fundraiser. Luqman, tell your father what happened."

Luqman tells me something I know can't be true. It was just a simple fundraiser.

"Are you serious? Hiram is missing? Was anyone hurt?"

"An ambulance came. They say someone was shot."

"Turn on the news, Luqman. I need to see this for myself."

A reporter from Muhammad's station is at the scene. "According to the police, a waiter was killed, and two servers were injured. We don't yet know the extent of their injuries."

What am I seeing here? This makes no sense. Aisha walks into the room, and I turn to tell her, but I can't speak. I point to the screen. She covers her mouth and sits down to listen.

"Luqman, don't you want to watch with us?" says Umar. My son is out in the hallway. "Maybe they'll find Reverend Johnson."

"It's been a difficult evening. I need to rest."

Luqman can do what he wants. I need to know what's going on.

Luqman's Revolution

Here I am again, in the room I thought I left this evening. My car is at the Essence Hotel, and I won't be able to sneak out until Uncle Psychologist leaves and my parents go to sleep. I can't call Hakeem to come get me. My best bet is to stay with my uncle. I'll ask him to take me back to the hotel, and I'll be on my way.

Will they search any cars at the hotel? I'm glad I took my gun out of the trunk. It's still nestled in the small of my back, a little uncomfortable but well worth having.

~

After twenty minutes, I go back downstairs. Uncle Psychologist gives me a look.

"I couldn't relax. I'm too worried. Is there any more news?"

"Two of the kitchen workers were able to give descriptions of the kidnappers," says my uncle, "so they should have sketches of the suspects soon."

I hope the boys remembered to cover their faces. "How many were there?"

"Apparently there were anywhere from three to six. The workers are still shaken. A report has just come in that one of the kidnappers worked as a server. This sounds like a major operation."

It's only the beginning, Uncle Psychologist. "He was working there? That's eerie." I sit down and watch with them. Someone says the kidnappers were black, but someone else says they were Hispanic. I hold my breath when one guy says he got a good look at the vehicle, but he describes a tan passenger van, not a white work van. In psychology class, I learned about the unreliability of eyewitness accounts, and I was counting on that.

The reporter begins interviewing Stu. Dad stands up. "He needs support. I'm going down there."

"You weren't there, Isa," says Mom. "You can't help the police."

"No, but I can help Stu." He grabs his keys and slips on his shoes.

"I'm coming with you, Dad." I'm out the door before Uncle Psychologist can stop me.

~

On the way there, Dad asks me again what happened, even though he heard it repeated at least four times on TV. If he and Stu check their stories, the phone call won't add up; but by the time they figure that out, I'll be long gone.

"Why would they target the fundraiser? All we're trying to do is help people. Do you realize what this could do to the centers? We don't need this kind of publicity."

I don't point out that he doesn't work there anymore. "I'm sure they weren't going after the centers."

"What then? Is it Hiram? I don't like the man, but that's no reason to kidnap him. Ya Allah, I hope they don't find his dead body in the morning."

If one of my boys kills Hiram, he'll answer to me. We didn't go through all this trouble for a quick thrill. "I hope not. Does he have enemies?"

"Probably, but I don't think anyone hates him enough to kill him." Dad swerves a little. He's really upset.

"Are you okay? Would you like me to drive?"

"No, I can handle it."

When we get to the hotel, I lag behind while Dad rushes in, making his way through the news crews. He's stopped by police officers.

"I'm Joshua Adams, the director of Hope Center. I need to talk to Stuart Woodson."

After checking Dad's ID and making him wait several minutes, an officer escorts him inside. I head for my car. The boys are waiting for me.

Joshua: Part Three

Stu is sitting at a table in the front of the room, staring into space, while police and crime scene technicians work around him. I'm surprised they haven't asked him to move. "Let's go out in the hallway, Stu." I grab his arm.

He's quiet until we get outside. "My wife was planning to come tonight but, at the last minute, our babysitter canceled. Thank God she wasn't here. They're saying one of the kidnappers was serving our food. How could they let him work in the kitchen? The thought of it makes me sick."

"It's been a rough night."

"I was right there, right next to Reverend Johnson. I didn't get up until you called me."

"I didn't call you. Luqman said you called me."

"That's strange. Maybe he was confused."

"But, he told me this before Reverend Johnson was reported missing." No, it's not possible. "Hold on a minute."

I run outside and search for Luqman. He's not by my car. I don't see him anywhere. He gave me the number of his new phone. I call. A sound comes from somewhere near my car. I hang up. The sound stops. I dial again and find the phone on the ground next to the passenger door of my car.

He could have dropped it accidentally, but I doubt that. He's gone. How could I have been so blind?

∼

I can't go back to Stu, and I can't go home. I sit in my car, wondering what happened to my son. Or am I wrong? Maybe he's at home, already asleep in his bed.

And maybe one day I will walk on the surface of Mars. That's just as likely.

Just to be sure, I call home. Umar answers.

"Brother, could Luqman have something to do with this? He hasn't come home, has he?"

"No. If he's not with you, I imagine he's on his way to see Hiram."

Luqman's Revolution

How long will it take Dad to figure it out? Has he compared stories with Stu yet? It doesn't matter. They'll never find us.

Aziz suggested this place. He has a great aunt who lives near here, and he used to come every summer for family reunions. He described the lake and the campgrounds. It sounded perfect.

No one will think to look for us in Peony Lake, Indiana.

∼

They picked a nice secluded campground, surrounded by trees and right next to the lake. As I drive in, Rasheed comes running. "Where were you, man?"

"I couldn't get away. First, I stalled them. After the police came, they questioned everyone. Then my uncle showed up and started hassling me. He made me go home and watch the news coverage with my parents. It is everywhere. We're famous."

"Have they mentioned the FOM yet?" Hakeem asks.

"Not on the news, but my uncle brought it up. He asked me what I knew about 'them.' What did you guys do in that kitchen?"

"We were able to get most of them tied up but a cook, a waiter, and one of the busboys resisted," says Rasheed. "I pistol whipped the cook. Hakeem put a bullet into the waiter and the busboy, but it was just to stop them. No one got killed."

"They're saying the waiter died."

Hakeem winces. "Believe me, there was no other way"

"How's our guest of honor?"

Rasheed laughs. "He's sweating like a pig in there. Did you know he could curse? I should have recorded that. Mustapha gave him something to make him sleep because we got tired of listening to him."

"Rasheed, you need to lay low. Some of the kitchen workers are giving the police your description. Tomorrow, they'll start working with the sketch artist. The rest of you wore masks, didn't you?"

"What d'ya think we are, man?" says Hakeem. "'Course we did."

Aziz is roasting hot dogs on an open fire. "You should have brought us some of that banquet food, man. You're eating steak, and we're stuck with these."

"It was chicken. You didn't miss much."

"Yeah," says Rasheed. "Only our man Hiram got the steak. Go around thinking he's better than everyone else. You aren't so hot now, are you, big man." Rasheed shouts into the van.

"Settle down," I warn him. "You don't want the other campers to hear you. I brought the tent. Let's get it set up. We need to make everything look as normal as possible."

Rasheed grins. "Yeah, it's completely normal for six Muslim guys to go camping with a fat racist evangelist."

"Why not? Come help me with the tent."

When we're done, Hakeem softly makes the call to prayer. Three of us line up to pray while the others watch Hiram. After the prayer, we switch.

~

Aziz, Hakeem, and Mustapha are asleep in the tent. Abu Bakr snores in the front seat of the van. Rasheed and I keep watch over our hostage. In an hour, I'll wake Aziz and Abu Bakr so they can take over.

Hiram is still passed out on the floor of the van, bound and gagged. His breathing appears normal. We'll kill him if we need to, but I don't want him to die on us. That sedative Mustapha gave him was too strong. Hiram relieved himself in his clothes, and the smell is nearly unbearable. I'll tell Mustapha to ease up on the dose next time.

Hiram will be surprised to see me. Or, maybe he won't be so surprised. A few years ago, I went to one of those center functions with my parents, and I saw the way Hiram glared at my mother. I've hated him since that day.

That's not why we kidnapped him, though. Hatred isn't a strong enough motive for something this big.

The New Pilgrims have been a problem for Chicago for the last thirty years. They were founded back in 1974, as a reaction to the legalization of abortion and other moral issues, but they minded their own business, for the most part, until the second Bush administration started funneling them money through their faith-based programs. They grew stronger and more powerful each year. For the last fifteen years, they've had a stranglehold over Chicago.

As leader of the New Pilgrims, Hiram is the most influential man in the city. Members of his church hold a majority on the city council, blocking every motion that might benefit the people. The deacon of the church owns the Chicago media, including the news station that won't give my brother a break. And two years ago, they tricked the people of Illinois into voting one of their own into the United States Senate. Amos Edmonds has already proposed four bills restricting the rights of minorities. So far, none has passed, but that hasn't stopped him.

All of the trouble in my family can be traced back to Hiram Johnson and his church. They've restricted funding of the public schools even while raising millions for their own church-sponsored schools. They've taken over the best jobs, forcing the rest of us into menial labor. Because there aren't enough menial labor jobs, the rates of homeless and unemployed in this city have skyrocketed. That's why my father had to keep bringing people home with him. Everything starts with Hiram.

I close my eyes. It's been a very long day.

Rasheed nudges me. "Hey man, stay awake. We got another forty-five minutes."

I rub my eyes and train my gun on our hostage. I would like nothing better to shoot him and be done with it, but we have bigger plans.

Meeting Demands

Success demands singleness of purpose.

—Vince Lombardi

Kyle's Family

Dad woke up coughing this morning. He coughed all during the prayer. Now he's sitting on the couch. Usually my parents take their morning walk after the prayer, but Dad just leans into the couch and closes his eyes.

Faiqa runs to our room and comes out with her medical kit. "Open your mouth, Dad, so I can take your temperature. I need you to unbutton your shirt, too, so I can listen to your chest."

Dad shakes his head. "It's only a cough. Kyle, why did you have to marry a doctor? A man can't cough without being bothered."

I'm glad he's protesting. That means he's still feeling well. "Do what she says, Dad. She's trying to help."

"I don't need my daughter-in-law listening to my chest."

"Then let her take your temperature. Will you do that?"

"You'll keep bothering me if I don't."

Faiqa checks. "It's 99.1. That's not too bad, but you are a little warm. Can I give you some aspirin?"

"Just bring me my morning juice."

"Hold on, Brad. It's almost ready," Mom calls from the kitchen.

"Hurry up. Let me know when breakfast is served." He stretches out on the couch.

∼

Dad is looking better. After lunch, Mom and he took a short walk. Right now, he's sitting on the floor, playing with the babies. Nathifa lets him hold her. Zakariya and Nashwa squirm away. Yusuf has gone exploring, under Faiqa's watchful eye.

Dad still has a cough, but he sounds better than he did this morning. My wife will keep a close eye on him. I wish Dad would make it easier.

He's been strong and independent most of his life. This whole sickness and dying thing can't be easy for him. He will hold on to his strength and independence for as long as he can.

Joshua: Part One

Umar didn't leave until 2:00 AM. Aisha and I barely slept last night. We didn't talk much, either, after Umar left. We have to figure out what all this means.

After the morning prayer, I review the facts. Hiram Johnson is missing, the victim of a kidnapping. One of the kidnappers is Rasheed Muhammad, who worked as a server at last night's dinner. I study the composite sketch released by the police. He looks familiar. Is he one of Luqman's friends? Luqman didn't come home last night. We have no idea where he is.

I'm tired but anxious. I stumble into the kitchen to start the coffee. Aisha is sitting at the table.

"What's happening, Isa? Do you really think Luqman could be a part of this?"

"He disappeared after Daud was shot. Then he came home and acted like the perfect son. Have you ever known Luqman to do everything we wanted him to do? He offered to volunteer at the center and showed special interest in the fundraiser. He lied to Stu and me about the phone call, and apparently that's when Hiram was kidnapped. Now he's gone. What do you think?"

Aisha puts her face in her hands. "What did we do wrong?"

"I don't know." And I'm tired of trying to figure it out. "Let's eat breakfast. Then we can get back to work."

"How can we leave when everything is up in the air? Are you going to turn your back on your son?"

"Don't give me that. I have tried everything with that boy. I'm here. Where is he?"

"It's our fault, Isa. We didn't love him enough. We didn't protect him from the bullies when he was little. We—I don't know what we did, but it was wrong."

"We have four children, Aisha. Three of them are doing great. What's so special about Luqman? Why should he be treated differently?"

"He is different. He always has been. Don't you remember how much he cried when he was little?"

"And we gave him more attention because of it. If anything, I'd say we spoiled him."

She throws her hands in the air. "I can't deal with this now. I'm going upstairs."

I'm not hungry, but I force a cup of coffee down my throat. We need to keep packing.

～

The mess in the family room is taken care of. Everything is either boxed up or in the trash. I'd better go check the basement to see if we're missing anything.

What happened down here? It didn't look like this a few days ago. Stuff is thrown all over the place. I start cleaning it up.

This is our old gear from that time we tried camping. It was cold and rainy, and we never did that again. I fold up the tarp and find an axe under the mess. Where is the tent? We'll never use it again, but I could give it to someone.

I wipe away the sweat from my forehead. Everything is boxed or on the shelves. But the tent, a lantern, and three sleeping bags are missing. Oh, and the propane stove.

This mess wasn't here three days ago. Someone did this. Who else, but Luqman?

Luqman's Revolution

Everything went according to plan yesterday, in spite of my uncle's interference. Now, it's time to put the second phase into action.

I climb out of my sleeping bag and look around. No one in sight. Aziz knows how to pick a camping spot. He's frying eggs on the propane stove.

"That smells good. I'd like some, but first give me two for our visitor. We have to keep the man fed."

Mustapha and Hakeem are watching our hostage. "Assalaamu alaikum, how is our fat evangelist this morning?"

"He thinks he can get himself loose. He must have watched too many spy movies." Hakeem laughs.

I kneel next to Hiram. "Settle down. If you try to escape, my boys will have to shoot you. You don't want that." He's staring at me. "Yeah, you've seen me before and you know my father. Dad wouldn't approve of this, but there are things about you that he doesn't know."

He mumbles behind his gag. I crouch over him.

"When my brother brings your breakfast, I'll remove the gag. You can scream if you like, but there are two guns pointed at you, so that wouldn't be smart. Do you understand?" He mumbles angrily. "I didn't ask for a sermon. Do you understand? Just nod."

He nods. Rasheed brings the eggs. I don't want to untie his hands, so I'll have to feed him. I pick up the fork. "Open your mouth. Here it comes."

He eats a few bites and starts coughing. "Water," he says gruffly.

Rasheed brings a bottle. I hold it for him. Then I feed him again, like a big baby.

When he's almost done, he says, "Why are you doing this?"

"You've spent the last fifteen years cheating the people of Chicago. Isn't that reason enough?"

"I need water."

When he's done, I put the gag back on and pull a piece of paper and a pen from my pocket. "I'm going to untie your right hand now so you can write something for me. Don't think about trying to escape. My two friends here are ready to shoot you, and I have another friend right outside the van. If you cooperate and the New Pilgrims fulfill our demands, you'll be home soon. If you and your New Pilgrims refuse to work with us, you will die in this van, lying in your own filth. Do you understand?"

He nods.

I hand him the pen and put the paper in front of him. "Write these words: *'Give them what they want.'*" I watch while he slowly writes down my dictation. "Good. Now sign it." When he's done I say, "Good job. This is my proof that we have you. I didn't want to cut off your fingers." I laugh. We wouldn't have done that, but I need to keep up the fear.

I leave the van and go to Aziz. "Forget my eggs. I have the evidence. Now I'll make the call. Can you get him cleaned up? It's rancid in there."

"Sure. The five of us can handle him. Go get the message out."

Kankakee, Illinois is a small town a little south of Chicago, surrounded by much smaller towns. Driving winding two-lane roads, it takes me nearly an hour to get there.

First, I buy another phone. It's a necessary expense. I locate a fast food place where I order a late breakfast. I'm the only customer in the place. While I eat, I call my brother. "Assalaamu alaikum Muhammad. Are you ready to boost your career?"

"Is this Luqman? Where are you?"

"Listen carefully. This is what you need to do. Bring a cameraman. Make it Brett, the guy you usually work with. Come to River State Park in Kankakee, Illinois. You'll find my car by the concession stand. It's 10:30 AM now. Meet me at noon, and I'll give you the hottest story in Chicago."

"What are you talking about?"

"There is one question on everyone's mind this morning. I have the answer. Noon. River State Park. Come with Brett, but nobody else. I'm armed." I hang up.

No wonder my brother is still doing animal stories. He's too dense. Or maybe he just couldn't believe I had really done it.

He'd better not do anything stupid like tell the police. Or even Dad. I don't want to shoot anyone, not even Muhammad, but I have to defend myself.

We never had a normal brother relationship because he always looked at me like some kind of weird alien. Now, he'll respect me. It's about time.

Muhammad

He hung up on me. What's going on? Is he really involved in this? It's possible, but I never imagined Luqman would go that far.

I have ninety minutes to get there. It will take me at least an hour, maybe longer in midday traffic. Dirk just sent Brett and me to report on a dog show, but I'm sure he won't mind if we come back with the story on Hiram Johnson instead.

I take the next exit south. "What are you doing?" Brett asks.

"I just got word on a breaking story. If it pans out, we're headed for the big time."

"What is it?"

Should I tell him or wait? "Trust me, it's big."

"Listen, Muhammad, Dirk is expecting some footage on the dog show. If we go back without that, he could fire us."

"Let another station cover the dog show. We have an exclusive."

Brett continues badgering me. He'll thank me later.

I check the GPS. River State Park. We can be there before noon, insha Allah.

~

I pull into the park at 11:50 AM and follow the signs, but I take a wrong turn. By the time I get to the concession stand, it's 12:05 PM. Luqman is here.

He steps out of his car. "What took you so long?"

"I got lost."

"That figures. That had better be Brett in the car. You didn't tell anyone else, did you?"

"No, I didn't talk to anyone."

"There are two reasons I called you, Muhammad. One, I'd like to see you report on something besides animals. Two, I can always tell when you're lying. Tell Brett to get out of the car. We're going for a walk."

Where is he taking us? This feels dangerous. But he is my brother.

Luqman's Revolution

I lead them down the wooded path to a secluded area, then stop and turn around, pointing my gun.

Muhammad and Brett both jump. I smile. "Relax. I'm not going to shoot you. Yet." I laugh. This is fun.

I put my gun away. "Let's get serious. I know where Hiram Johnson is, and I need you to help me make my statement. I'll list our demands. You'll take the story back to the station. You'll be famous, and I'll have what I want. Sounds good, doesn't it?"

"Are you really part of this?" Muhammad asks.

"I have proof that we have Hiram. I'll show you that in a minute."

"Why would you confess to the kidnapping? Don't you know you'll go to prison?"

"Maybe. Many great leaders were imprisoned. I'm not worried. Brett, turn on the camera. Let's get this interview started."

Muhammad looks uncertain as he holds up the microphone. "Relax," I say. "Think about how famous you'll be after this airs."

"But what's going to happen to you?"

"Don't worry about it. Ask me why I wanted to meet with you."

Muhammad begins slowly, getting a little more confident with every question. I won't answer when he asks how many of us there are or who they are. I won't tell him where Hiram is. But when he asks for proof, I pull it out of my pocket and hold it up.

"Hiram Johnson wrote and signed this note this morning. You can have it. Take it back, and let the police analyze it. They'll find Hiram's fingerprints on it. They can study the signature. It's genuine."

"Why did you and your group kidnap Reverend Johnson? What are your demands?"

"I thought you'd never ask." I pull another paper from my pocket. "This is what we want. After our demands are met, we promise to return Hiram Johnson unharmed.

"1. We're asking for the immediate resignation of all New Pilgrims who currently sit on the Chicago city council. Khalif Amin, who has tried unsuccessfully for years to pass laws helping the poor and minorities, will be made head of the council. New and fair elections will be held as soon as possible.

"2. The New Pilgrims will begin hiring non-members in the environmental industries. Currently, 90 percent of the middle and upper level positions are held by New Pilgrims, while those not belonging to the church receive menial jobs such as garbage collection. Every project in wind turbines and alternative fuels, along with waste management and recycling, will hire new staff comprised of minorities, and no more than 50 percent of the employees will be New Pilgrims.

"3. The Young Pilgrims will be disbanded. If they cease all activities, the Friends of Muhammad will also stand down.

"*4. Senator Amos Edmonds will draft and propose a bill calling for reparations to be paid to all victims of the War on Terror, from 2001 through 2008, as well as all American political prisoners of the last 28 years.*" Including my father.

"*5. For our trouble, my boys and I are asking for a ransom of $6 million.*

"These are our demands. The city of Chicago has one week to fulfill these and bring about the safe return of Hiram Johnson."

"How could a representative of the New Pilgrims or the city of Chicago contact you to discuss these demands?"

"First, there's no negotiation. Second, all contact will be conducted through my brother, Muhammad Adams. I will be in touch with him on a regular basis."

"Is Reverend Johnson being held somewhere in the Kankakee area?"

I frown. "You know better than to ask that. This is the end of the interview. I will wait for Chicago's response to my demands." I turn my back to the camera until Brett stops filming.

"There's your scoop, Muhammad. You'd better rush back to the newsroom."

"When will I hear from you again?"

"When I'm ready. Soon, everyone will know my face, so I'll send one of my boys out to call you." I start walking back toward the concession stand. "I'm looking forward to the next newscast."

"The camera's off now, Luqman. Where are you staying?"

"Somewhere. Don't worry. I'll be in touch."

He pulls out his wallet. "Here. You might need this." He hands me some bills.

"Thanks." Those phones are getting to be expensive. "Tell Mom and Dad I'm okay. I know they won't like what I'm doing, but tell them it's for the greater good. The New Pilgrims have tyrannized Chicago too long."

"Do you think this will work?"

"I wouldn't be doing it if I didn't."

They get into Muhammad's car. I stand by the driver's side. "I'll leave five minutes after you do. Don't try to follow me. You don't want to get involved with this."

"I think I'm already involved."

"You're just the messenger. Next time, let me know how many networks have contacted you. You too, Brett."

Brett nods. "Muhammad is your brother, but how do you know you can trust me?"

"I've heard some good things about you. Besides, I know where you live. Now go on. And don't tell anyone where you met me."

"I'll see you, Luqman. Assalaamu alaikum."

"Walaikum assalaam."

I watch them drive away. After a minute I laugh. I had to kidnap someone in order to finally get Muhammad's respect.

I know he'll tell the police about meeting me in this park. Muhammad can't stand up to pressure, and he never lies. That's okay. There's no way they'll find us.

Joshua: Part Two

Muhammad just called and told us to watch the news. There's a special bulletin about Hiram Johnson.

"Have they found him?" I ask.

"Not yet. Watch the bulletin, and don't be shocked. I did what I had to do."

What is he talking about? I call Aisha and turn on the TV.

It's Muhammad. And Luqman. Aisha stops in the doorway of the family room and gives a little cry. Umar was right.

∾

The phone starts ringing before the interview ends. First it's Umar, Jeremy, and Jamal. Then Ismail, Stu, and Gameel. Sharon comes and sits with Aisha at the kitchen table. I stare at the TV.

There's a rap at the door. I get up slowly. The rap becomes a pound. "Police."

I never told them that Luqman had returned. He had changed, I thought, and I could cover for him. I won't make that mistake again. "Come in."

Sharon brings them tall glasses of juice while they ask us questions about our son. Where is he? Where has he been? Can they search the house?

"No," says Aisha. "If you want to walk through my house, you'll need to get a warrant."

I disagree. Aisha and I have nothing to hide, and I'm done protecting Luqman. I won't contradict her, though. "When you come back with a warrant, you can conduct your search."

They leave with promises to return. I don't doubt them.

"What should we do?" says Aisha. "Luqman is in serious trouble."

"He's been in serious trouble for months now, and we haven't been able to stop him. I'm done with it."

"But Joshua, he's our son."

"Is he? Does our son lie and kidnap? Did we raise our kids to carry guns and join gangs? He's not a child anymore, Aisha. He needs to be responsible for his actions."

"Of course he does, but does that mean we have to open our house to the police?"

"Yes, if it will help them find Hiram. Allah told us not to be distracted by our wealth and our sons. I can't let my love for Luqman keep me from doing what's right."

She puts her arms around me, her head on my chest. "You're right, Isa, but what should we do?"

I kiss her forehead. "Don't worry. We'll get through this."

〜

Jeremy says we have to let the police come in if they have a search warrant. "I'll come over as soon as I can."

Sharon comforts Aisha in the kitchen, I pace in the hallway. When will they return? What will they find? Will they be able to use the evidence to find Hiram in time? What will happen to Luqman?

In five days, we need to finish packing up and move to Lexington.

I sit on the front steps, my head in my hands, and wait for the police.

Muhammad

The response to my interview with Luqman has been tremendous. Dirk cut into regular programming to air it. The police showed up within the hour to question me. I told them honestly that I don't know where Hiram is being held. Luqman knows I don't lie. That's why he wouldn't answer some of my questions.

Luqman will call again sometime in the next day or two. Dirk wants me to wear a wire. I refuse. Brett will come with me. That will be enough.

Everyone in the news room knows my name today. They congratulate me and give me the pats on the back I've always craved. But one guy, Riley, asks me if I'm part of the plot. I ignore him. He's always been a jerk.

My fame is at the expense of my brother, but that was his choice. I hope he stays safe.

~

I'm getting ready to leave for the night when my phone rings. Could that be Luqman?

"Assalaamu alaikum Brother Muhammad. My name is Malek Abdul-Kareem. I'm a good friend of your brother."

"Walaikum assalaam." That name sounds familiar. Wasn't there a Malek in our school? "Why are you calling?"

"Do you have any leads on your brother's location? I would like to help him."

"I don't know where he is. Why are you calling?"

"Luqman is my friend. I'm concerned about him."

Who is this guy? "I can't help you." Five other people have called saying they want to help Luqman. And two girls said they're in love with him. We live in a crazy society.

~

In the morning my phone rings while I'm eating breakfast. "Assalaamu alaikum, this is Malek. Did your brother say anything about camping?"

"You saw the tape. That's all he told me."

"Is he with a guy named Aziz? Did he mention the other members of his gang?"

"No, he didn't give me any names. Please stop calling." I hang up. I hope I won't have to put up with this all day.

Joshua: Part Three

Jeremy stops by in the evening. "Why didn't you call me?"

"They haven't brought the warrant yet. I guess they'll come sometime tomorrow."

He hugs us both. "I know how hard this is for you. Luqman made his own choices."

Yeah. Is that supposed to make me feel better?

≈

The police arrive early in the morning with the warrant. I let them in and go back to my coffee and bagel. Aisha sits at the table with me, clutching my arm. My heart beats hard while I say silent prayers.

After a few minutes, I remember to call Jeremy.

"I'll be right there, insha Allah. Are you watching them?"

"No, we're eating breakfast. I can't do this anymore, Jeremy."

"Don't worry. I'm on my way."

They started upstairs in Luqman's room. We hear them banging around up there. Jeremy had better get here soon.

≈

For the last three hours, our home has been dismantled by police officers who rummaged through our things, wearing their shoes in our house. They made me open every packed box, even as I explained that my wife and I are in the process of moving. I glanced at Jeremy. He nodded.

They've started taking bags out to their cars. I'd like to know what they're taking, but Jeremy tells me to stay quiet. It occurs to me that Aisha and I could also be under suspicion. Guilt by association has never died.

One officer, who seems to be in charge, sits with us at the kitchen table. Jeremy also sits down. "Can you give me any more information about your son?" he says. "Are there any items you've noticed missing?"

Aisha knows about the camping gear. She closes her eyes.

"Give me a moment." I consult with Jeremy by the stairs. "They could use that, couldn't they?"

"That's valuable information. You don't have to tell them. It's up to you."

"What would you do?"

He looks at the carpet and sighs. "Luqman's gun injured my son. I forgave him for that, but we can't let him continue to hurt people."

"What would you do if we were talking about Daud?"

"I would cry and pray. Ultimately, I hope I would choose the greater good." He puts his arm around my shoulders as we walk back into the kitchen.

Sitting down at the table, I say Bismillah and tell the officer what I know. He takes some notes and thanks me for my cooperation.

After he leaves, I lay my head on the table and weep. Jeremy comforts me. Aisha is quiet.

~

Umar just called. The police will hold a news conference sometime in the next hour. "I'll be there as soon as I can, insha Allah."

They left our house only five hours ago. What could they have discovered in five hours?

~

We huddle together on the couch and wait. After a few brief comments, the officer we spoke with presents the evidence against our son.

"After the release of the interview yesterday by Muhammad Adams from WCST, we concentrated on learning more about Luqman Adams. A search of his home has turned up possible leads as to his whereabouts as well as his motive. We have reason to believe that the suspect could be detaining Reverend Hiram Johnson at a camp site. We are asking all citizens in the viewing area to keep their eyes open. Currently, we are searching for two men, Rasheed Muhammad and Luqman Adams, although we believe there are others. The department is releasing these pictures—a composite drawing of Muhammad and a video of Adams. Call us at once if you spot either of these two men. Do not approach them. Alert law enforcement officials immediately. The men in question are armed and presumed dangerous."

He fields a few questions. I stare at the ceiling. How did everything become so complicated? Where did I go wrong as a father?

Limbo

The quest for certainty blocks the search for meaning.
Uncertainty is the very condition to impel man to unfold his powers.

—Erich Fromm

Luqman's Revolution

The boys are hauling Hiram, still bound and gagged, out of the lake. They stripped him down to his boxers. I wince at the sight.

"Assalaamu alaikum Luqman. We got him a little cleaner," says Rasheed.

"That's good. Now put a towel or something around him. I can't stand to look at his fat flesh."

"Be glad that's all you have to complain about," says Hakeem. "I had to strip him. Abu Bakr washed his clothes. They should be dry soon."

"How did it go?" Aziz asks. He's cooking hot dogs for lunch.

"It was excellent. I met my brother and his cameraman at an empty park and gave the interview. They have our list of demands. I didn't mention any of you, but they've IDed Rasheed from the sketches, so the two of us will have to lay low."

"When do you think we'll hear from them?" Mustapha asks.

"One of you will have to go call my brother in the morning. We'll see what he says."

"I'll do it," says Hakeem.

"My brother gave me some cash. That will help cover our expenses until we can claim the ransom. I put that last on the list. They need to concentrate on the injustices done by the New Pilgrims."

"You're right, brother," says Aziz. "But I need that cash." Everyone laughs.

"We prayed already," says Hakeem. "You can go on ahead."

I find a spot near the lake and bow down. This is the right time and place for praying.

～

In the morning, Hakeem takes off in my car. I give him last minute instructions.

"Drive over the Illinois border. I don't want them to know we left the state. Ask Muhammad if they're meeting our demands. If he wants to meet with me, tell him I'll be at the northwest tip of Lake Metonga at 4:30 PM and remind him to come alone. No cameraman this time."

"Is that safe? What if he tips off the police?"

"He's my brother. If the police ask where he met me, he'll tell them, but he won't tip them off."

"All right. I'll be back soon, insha Allah."

The game is getting a little more dangerous, but we're still in good shape. Hakeem will keep his eyes and ears open. If we have to, we can always break camp and move further south into Indiana, or north into Michigan. I'm not worried.

I decide to visit our hostage. He's eating breakfast while Abu Bakr and Mustapha guard him.

"How are you today, Hiram? They have our demands. I hope we hear from them soon. If they act fast, you could be home tomorrow."

"What do you want?"

"We want justice. Is that too much to ask? The New Pilgrims have ruled Chicago long enough. We demand equal opportunity and fair treatment for all."

"All you needed to do was ask. Why did you go to all this trouble?"

I laugh. "All I needed to do was drive out to your fortress in Oak Park and walk into your office? How long before you would have had me arrested for trespassing? I heard your speech, Hiram. The black man, the brown man, the Muslim. We're all dangerous. We decided to show you just how dangerous we can be."

"You will be punished. *Vengeance is Mine, saith the Lord.*"

"I wouldn't talk so tough if I were you. We can end your life in a second."

"*Dear Lord, do not forsake me.*"

"Go ahead and pray. We're praying too."

"Chicago would be lost without the guidance of the New Pilgrims. We have brought the blessings of God upon the city and made her what she is today."

"And that's the whole problem, Hiram. Don't you understand?"

He spits eggs into my face. The boys prepare to fire. I raise my hand and replace his gag.

"You're not in Chicago, Hiram. We're in charge. You should have told us you don't like the food. We don't have to feed you." I throw the rest of his eggs on the ground. "Do you hear that, brothers? Hiram wants to fast. No food or water until sunset."

The anger in his eyes becomes fear. I'm sure Hiram has never fasted a day in his life. This is a good time for him to learn.

~

Hakeem pulls up in the early afternoon. I rush to the car. "What's going on?"

"Man, your story is all over. So is your face. You'd better stay underground."

"What did my brother say?"

"They haven't responded to the demands. The police went to your house this morning with a search warrant. He'd like to see you, but he'll understand if you don't show. I don't think you should go."

I have a couple of hours to decide. Meeting with Muhammad probably won't help our mission, and it will put me in danger. I'm getting restless, though, just hanging around the campsite. "Let's have lunch, and I'll see what the boys say."

"How's Hiram?"

"He spit out his breakfast at me, so I think he wants to fast."

Hakeem smiles. "With all that extra weight he's carrying, fasting will be good for him."

~

We discuss the options during lunch. Everyone says I should stay here.

They'd better come up with an offer soon. This wait is eating at my nerves.

Kyle's Family

Dad's cough is nearly gone. The home treatments worked. Along with the juice, he drinks tea with honey. A couple days ago, I went out to track down some black seed, finally finding a small Muslim grocery store that sells it. Faiqa is amazed from a medical standpoint that he's still able to fight. I'm just very, very grateful.

∼

Gameel called. He wants me to go to Phoenix. "I'll be there too. We'll review the data on our new product lines and make marketing decisions. Also, Phoenix is hosting a Natural Foods Convention this weekend, and I'm depending on you to represent our company. I'm sorry to cut into your time with your family."

"Don't worry about it."

"Bring Faiqa and the babies to Phoenix with you. I miss them."

"I'll see what she says."

"Good. I'll see you in Phoenix."

∼

After dinner, I tell Faiqa about the trip and ask her to come.

"I don't think so, Khalil. Can you imagine traveling with the triplets? You'll be in meetings all day, and I'll be stuck in the hotel room. Ask Baba to come up to Flagstaff to see us."

"I'll miss you." I stroke her arm. Nathifa cries. Faiqa jumps up to get her. The babies always come first.

∼

Gameel wanted me to fly down, but I decide to drive. I'll get there in three hours or less and have a chance to enjoy the scenery.

This morning, Dad took his usual walk with Mom. Right now, he's sitting on the couch, holding Nathifa. If he lives long enough, those two will have a great relationship. Nashwa and Yusuf are too active. Nathifa contentedly sits on Dad's lap, sometimes pulling his beard, and babbling. Dad smiles and babbles back. I grab the camera, trying to capture another moment that can never be replaced.

∼

Fifteen minutes ago, I kissed my wife, hugged my parents and children, and said goodbye to my brother and his family. The sun is shining. The land stretches out before me, mountains and desert. As my red rental car zips south on Highway 17, I breathe deeply and take in the beauty of it all.

By the time I get to Phoenix, it's rush hour and I'm stuck in traffic, but I don't mind. These last two hours have relaxed me.

I have been tense since the night Dad was rushed to the hospital back in January. Now, it's nearly June. He's still hanging on, but I never know how much longer Allah will give him. The stress is wearing on me.

For a few days I'll be productive, out in the business world where there are fewer uncertainties. When I return to Flagstaff, I'll be ready for whatever comes next.

Joshua: Part One

Today is Wednesday. We're supposed to be moving to Lexington on Saturday, but we can't seem to do anything these days.

During breakfast I ask her. "Should we forget about the move? Should I call Hanif and tell him I need another week or so? We have to do something, Aisha." Every time we try to talk about this, one or both of us ends up crying.

She stays calm this time. "We don't know where Luqman is or how this will turn out for him. We can't just leave him."

"But he turned his back on us."

"But parents don't do that. You'd better call Hanif, and tell him what's going on."

That's not a phone call I'm looking forward to. "What if I just turn down the job, and we stay in Chicago?"

"How are we going to do that? We've already quit our jobs here. Zaid is ready to move out of his apartment in July. We promised the house to Maryam and him. Besides, after all this, I'm not sure I could show my face in the masjid."

"You're right. Lexington will be a fresh start. No one knows Luqman." Where am I going with this? The tears start again.

Aisha comforts me. "We have to take care of ourselves."

~

Some Muslims I've met would have taken back the job offer after learning what my son did. Alhamdulillah, Hanif is not one of them. "I saw the story on the news, but I didn't realize that was your son. I can only imagine your stress. Why don't you plan to start on June 16? Will two extra weeks be enough to work this out?"

"I hope so. My wife and I are both anxious to come to Lexington. We've tried to be good parents," I stammer. "Our other children have all made us proud."

"The father doesn't pay for the weaknesses of his grown son. Don't worry. We're anxious to have you work for us, and we can make accommodations. I'll keep the reason for your delay confidential."

"I can't tell you how much I appreciate that. After everything that's happened, we're looking to Lexington as a chance to make a fresh start."

"Please keep me posted, and let me know if there's anything I can do."

That's taken care of, and it's a huge burden off my shoulders. It's good to know there are still Muslims who are forgiving.

Now all we can do is to wait. I hope and pray that Luqman comes out of this alive.

Luqman's Revolution

It's another morning at Camp Hiram. Our fat hostage was much more cooperative after his imposed fast. He was so happy to be fed yesterday at sunset that he'll probably do anything we say now. Food is a more powerful motivator for him than guns. To be safe, though, he's still being guarded.

Hakeem just left to call Muhammad. We need to know if they've agreed to our demands. If they refuse, we can stay here as long as is needed. We're well-stocked on food and water, the weather is nice, and I'm starting to enjoy camping. Yesterday afternoon, I went for a swim in the lake.

My biggest concern is that the campground may soon be full of summer vacationers. We were lucky to find this spot during the Memorial Day weekend, but I'm not sure how long we'll be able to keep it without being detected. Aziz said the operator of the campground is an old man, and as long as we pay our weekly fee, he won't come around giving us trouble. I'm counting on that.

~

Hakeem just came back. "There's no word. They're going to make us sweat."

"Tomorrow you'll tell Muhammad we have an ultimatum. Unless our conditions are accepted, we'll start the countdown. If they still haven't agreed to our terms by Friday morning at 8:00 AM, Hiram Johnson is a dead man."

"Will you do the job?"

"Hopefully, it won't come to that. They should realize we mean business."

"I hope so. I never killed a man."

He killed that waiter, but I'm sure he didn't mean to. "Neither have I." And I'm not looking forward to it. But if it's necessary, I will do what I have to do.

Joshua: Part Two

A detective shows up in the afternoon. He offers his hand. "Assalaamu alaikum. May I come in?"

"Walaikum assalaam. You're a Muslim?"

"Detective Arif Hussain." He flashes his badge and hands me his card. "I would like to ask you and your wife a few questions, if you don't mind."

"Go ahead." We sit on the couch. Aisha brings him a glass of juice and sits with us.

"I met your son on the night of the kidnapping. He was very self-assured. If not for the taped interview, I wouldn't have thought to look at him as a suspect."

That's one way to put it. He's a good liar. "What is your question?"

"Do you have any information about your son's friends? What about his habits? Anything you can tell me that will help us find him. He just delivered an ultimatum."

"How did he do that?"

"You know your son Muhammad went out to interview him. Luqman is making daily contact with his brother through a surrogate—another member of the gang, we assume. Luqman has threatened to kill Reverend Johnson by 8:00 AM on Friday unless we meet his demands."

I can't believe Luqman would murder Hiram, but there many things I once couldn't believe about Luqman. "Luqman is very intelligent." But, not very smart. "Wherever he is, it's probably somewhere you would never think to look."

"Would you say your son considers himself to be a revolutionary?"

"Maybe he does."

The detective looks at Aisha. "Do you have anything to add?"

"I don't think Luqman will kill Hiram Johnson, but he may be feeling desperate. He expected his demands to be taken seriously. If you show that you respect him and his concerns, he's more likely to cooperate with you."

Detective Hussain smiles. "I'll see what we can do. Are you familiar with someone named Malek Abdul-Kareem? He claims to be a close friend of Luqman's, and he's offered to help us in our search."

Aisha answers. "I once had a student by that name. He's in his mid-twenties now. He and Luqman were never friends, though. In fact, he bullied my son."

"That's interesting." The detective writes some notes. "When was the last time you saw Abdul-Kareem?"

"I teach his niece. He came to see her perform in a school play last fall, and we talked for just a moment. Sometimes I see him before school in the morning, dropping off his daughter who is in our kindergarten class."

"When was the last time you saw Luqman interact with him?"

"Throughout elementary school, Luqman complained that Malek bullied him. They had a fist fight when Luqman was in sixth grade and Malek was in eighth. Other students reported that Malek had been taunting Luqman. Both boys were suspended. It was near the end of the year, and the teachers made sure they stayed far apart. The following year, Malek attended a high school in his neighborhood on the South Side."

"Do you think Abdul-Kareem could be trying to use this crisis to get back at Luqman?" He makes more notes.

"He was only 14 years old when they fought. He seems to be a mature young man now."

"I'm sure he is, though I wonder why he's so adamant about wanting to be involved with this case." He writes a little more before closing his notebook. "That's all the questions for now. I appreciate your time."

"We tried to raise our son to be a good Muslim," I say.

He nods. "I'm sure you did. Assalaamu alaikum."

"Walaikum assalaam." I don't know what else we could have done.

Muhammad

Soon after I reported on Luqman's ultimatum, the police came to question me. They asked me to describe the man I spoke with on the phone, but I couldn't give them much information.

Luqman is getting out of control. The next time his friend calls, I'll tell him I need to see my brother. I need to stop him before it's too late.

〜

Malek calls me up to five times a day. He keeps pressing me for information about Luqman. Even if I did know more, I wouldn't tell him. He is the one I knew in school. Two years younger than me, he was always making trouble. Luqman was his favorite target. He may have changed, but I won't take that chance.

This morning, Malek asked me about Luqman's favorite camping sites. We only went camping once, and Luqman was the biggest whiner. I know he took lots of gear from our basement, but I can't imagine my brother sleeping in a tent. When I told Malek that, he called me a liar. He's still a bully.

〜

My role in the Hiram Johnson kidnapping story has changed my status here at the station. Dirk has assigned someone else to the animal stories, an excited new graduate who is happy to be in front of the camera. The kidnapping is my only assignment. I attend police press conferences, conduct interviews, and make pleas for more information. Yesterday, Dirk said that after this is over, he'll put me on the crime beat.

I'm finally starting to get somewhere with my career. But, I don't like doing it on the back of my brother.

Action

Force is all-conquering, but its victories are short-lived.

—Abraham Lincoln

Luqman's Revolution

When Hakeem came back from calling Muhammad, he said, "Your brother needs to talk to you. He'll be at Lake Metonga at three."

"Thanks for the message."

Muhammad can tell me why they haven't said anything about our conditions. We have less than twenty-four hours before the deadline, and I don't want to kill Hiram, but I have to follow through. It's the only way they'll take us seriously.

~

I arrive at ten after three. Muhammad is standing outside his car. There's no one else. He wouldn't betray me.

"Assalaamu alaikum. How's it going?"

"Walaikum assalaam. You have to put an end to this, Luqman. Muslims don't go around kidnapping people. There are other ways to make our voices heard."

"Do you think those other ways work? For years, we've tried boycotts and petitions. Oh, and meeting after meeting. They're laughing at us, Muhammad. They need to know that Muslims mean business."

"But what are you accomplishing? You're on the run. Mom and Dad are torn up over this. I don't see how any good can come from it."

"There are always some sacrifices in the beginning of the revolution, but these are necessary in order to achieve the greater goal. Muslims have been oppressed far too long, and Hiram Johnson is one of our oppressors. This is only our first step. We can return Islam to its former glory."

"Muslims are oppressed, in some cases, but Islam was never tarnished. And tell me how you can promote Islam by going against

Islam? You may call yourself a friend of Muhammad, but this is not the way of our prophet."

"That's what they want you to think. Misinformation is the greatest tool of the oppressor."

Muhammad shakes his head. He doesn't understand. "Forget theory. How can you make an ultimatum like that? Are you serious?"

"They have to respect our conditions."

"You're challenging the city of Chicago. Do you seriously expect them to give in to your demands?"

"They're working on an agreement, aren't they?"

"Of course they're not. They're doing everything they can to find you before the deadline, and I think they're closing in. Send another message. Extend the deadline. Say you're willing to negotiate. At least buy yourself some time. Better yet, release Hiram and disappear somewhere. I'll give you more money."

"Surrender means weakness. I made an ultimatum, and I can't give in."

"They already think you're weak. Don't you get it? The city of Chicago is bigger than the New Pilgrims, and the New Pilgrims are bigger than Hiram Johnson. It's going to take a lot more than this to break them."

"Then I'll come up with something bigger."

"No, Luqman. Listen to me. You have to rethink your whole mission. If you don't, by this time tomorrow, you will be dead or in prison."

"Let them put me in prison. Many revolutionaries have spent time behind bars. And if I die, I'll be a martyr. No one can say I didn't try."

"I don't believe you. Sometimes you're too smart for your own good. Stop fighting for a lost cause, and start worrying about saving yourself."

"You'll never understand me. That's okay. I appreciate everything you've done for me these last few days. It makes up for all those years of bullying." I smile.

"Yeah, well, we've both grown up. Talk about bullies. Malek Abdul-Kareem is trying to find you. He calls me several times a day, and he's gone to the police. I think he was following me today, but I lost him. He keeps telling everybody he's your friend, but it looks like he's out to get you. What's going on?"

"A couple of months ago I made him look like a fool. You should have seen it."

"Keep your eyes open, okay? He's out for revenge."

"Don't worry about me. I know how to take care of myself."

"I need to get back. We don't need anyone to come looking for me. Take care of yourself, and don't do anything stupid." He reaches for me.

"Thanks." I reach for him, too. We hug. Probably the last time we hugged, I was five or six.

"Be careful. I'll talk to you later. Think about what I said, okay?"

"Thanks for the warning about Malek."

"That's what brothers are for."

I watch him drive away. It's too bad it took us this long to be brothers.

∽

By the time I get back to camp, I have a plan. After dinner, I call the boys together. We meet in the van. It doesn't matter if Hiram hears. He doesn't look so good. His face is pale.

"They're not taking our demands seriously. The police are doing everything they can to find us before the deadline. I don't know how close they are, but let's assume they're on the other side of the lake.

"Also, my brother told me that Malek is out for revenge. He keeps saying he's a friend of mine, but you brothers know I wouldn't associate with an adulterer. Is there any way Malek could find us?"

Aziz speaks up. "Once or twice Malek came with my family and me out to this lake. We were kids, and I don't know if he remembers how to get here, but if he does, we're in trouble."

"That's good to know. We'd better pull up camp. Rasheed and Abu Bakr, guard the entrance. If Malek shows up, call me. Aziz, do you know of another place we could go around here?"

"No. This is the best place in the area."

"We'll drive up to Michigan then. That will at least give us some distance. Let's break camp. Hurry."

Mustapha and I pack up the tent. Aziz gathers the eating supplies. Hakeem keeps watch on our hostage. We're just about to pull out when he calls me.

"Hiram doesn't look so good. What do you think could be wrong?"

His skin is clammy, and his breathing is labored. "No, Hiram, don't die on us. Hakeem, go keep guard. Mustapha, come here. Hurry."

Mustapha quickly examines Hiram. "He could have had a heart attack. He was making some noises earlier. What should we do?"

"We can't let him die on us." I step out of the van to find Aziz. He can direct us to the nearest emergency room. We'll drop Hiram off outside the hospital. He's become a liability.

Hakeem shouts. A second later, a shot rings out.

"Where are you, Luqman? Stop hiding like a coward." Malek is here.

I duck back into the van. "Take care of Hiram, will you? We don't need a dead body on our hands."

"Where are you hiding?" Malek yells. "Did you know you're a wanted man?"

I slide out, go behind the van, and pull out my gun. The sun is setting. I clean my glasses with my shirt, but all I can see are shapes and shadows. He's too far away.

Aziz is standing next to me, his weapon drawn. "Go on. I have you covered."

Now I know I can trust Aziz. I slowly creep toward my car, about ten feet from the van.

"What are you doing here?" calls Aziz.

"My business is with Luqman. Come out, you liar. You hypocrite. Did you think you would get away with it?"

He still sounds like a bully. I feel the rage of a twelve-year old. Malek will not torment me again.

"Brother Malek, take it easy," says Aziz. "You don't want to fight a fellow Muslim."

"A fellow Muslim? Luqman's no more a Muslim than Hiram Johnson is. Where are you hiding, hypocrite? The police are on their way."

Peering over the hood of my car, I can barely make him out. There's a tree about mid-distance between the two of us. If I can get over there, I'll have a clear shot. I creep out from the cover of my car. A shot whizzes five or six feet in front of me.

"Stop this, Malek." It's Aziz again. "Put the gun down before somebody gets hurt."

"He fooled you, brother. He fooled all of you. Luqman's the one you should have thrown out, not me."

"Put down the gun, man, and we can talk about it."

I pick up a handful of stones and throw one. It lands a few feet in front of Malek. He fires at it. He's wired.

I throw more stones, one at a time. While he's trying to figure out where they're coming from, I run faster than I ever thought I could and make it to the tree.

He still doesn't know where I am, but I can see him clearly. One bullet and it's over.

"You know what this is about, Luqman. Face your punishment."

I don't want to kill anybody, but this is self-defense. Malek would approve of that, wouldn't he?

"You're still a coward. Come out and show yourself, mama's boy."

Aziz tries again. "Malek, listen to me. You do not want to do this. Think about your family."

"Don't talk to me about my family. My wife walked out after she heard the rumors. She won't let me see my kids." He trembles.

"Put the gun down, Malek. I'll talk to your wife for you. We can fix this, but you have to put the gun down."

"Let me tell you something about Luqman. You think you know him, don't you? Did you know that he was still wetting his pants in fourth grade? You should have seen him, snotty-nosed and weak. Did you know he always ran away from a fight? He went crying to his mommy. That's your leader." He laughs.

I ran away then, but not now, Malek. I aim carefully. But, I don't know if I can do it.

Muhammad told me I'm too smart for my own good. If I keep standing here, debating and analyzing, I'll be dead.

"Where you hiding, mama's boy? Where did you run to? Are you still afraid of the dark? Come out, so I can punish you."

Malek won't bully me again. I aim, close my eyes, and fire.

Joshua

The doorbell rings at midnight. We weren't sleeping anyway.
Detective Hussain gives his salaams. "May I come in?"

I lead him into the family room. Aisha asks him if he wants tea.

"You'd better make it coffee, and you'd better make a lot. It's going to be a long night."

We sit. I don't want to ask. Will he tell me my son is dead, or that he's a murderer? Maybe it was all a mistake, and Luqman is waiting outside in the detective's car, sorry for all the trouble he caused and ready to ask for forgiveness. I like happy endings.

Aisha brings three cups of coffee, along with sugar and milk, and sits in the blue easy chair. We wait, not really wanting to know.

"Luqman is in custody. Tomorrow, he will be arraigned."

"Is Hiram dead?"

"No. He had a heart attack. Some of the gang members claim they tried to save him. Anyway, he's being treated in an area hospital."

"The charges will be kidnapping then."

"It's more serious than that. Do you remember when I spoke with you about Malek Abdul-Kareem?"

Aisha puts her hand to her mouth. "What happened?"

"Malek found the campsite. He called local police, but by the time they arrived, it was too late." He takes a long pause. "Malek has been flown to the hospital in critical condition. Your son shot him."

"No! " Aisha shouts, jumping to her feet. "Luqman is not a murderer. Don't tell me he shot that boy. My son wouldn't do anything like that."

My body feels numb. I can barely move. "No. Not Luqman. He couldn't."

The detective continues. "Pray that Malek lives. Your son's friends claim it was self-defense. In the morning, we'll conduct a thorough investigation of the site."

"Of course it was self-defense," shouts Aisha. "Just like that time on the playground. Where is Luqman? Where did you take my son?"

"He's at the Cook County Jail. In the morning, he'll be arraigned."

"You let him out of there. Luqman tries to be a good boy. You have to understand." Aisha wails. I should reach out to her, but I can't. She throws herself into the blue chair and sobs.

The detective is calm. It's not his son. "Do you have anyone you can call? I'm sure you don't want to be alone."

Aisha is hysterical. I still can barely move. After I moment I say, "We'll call our kids. Um, thanks for coming by."

Maryam runs down the stairs in her nightgown, hair flying. "Mom, what's wrong?" She stops when she sees the detective.

"You can come to the courthouse in the morning." He finishes his coffee and studies us. "Don't blame yourselves. I have three kids of my own, and I know how difficult it is." He pats me on the shoulder. "Assalaamu alaikum."

He lets himself out. Maryam runs to Aisha and puts her arms around her. "Is it Luqman?" she asks. Aisha moans.

I sit.

∼

After a while, Aisha's sobs turn to whimpers. I stare at the phone. I should call someone.

When I finally get the courage to pick it up, I call Umar.

"Assalaamu alaikum. Isa, is that you? What's wrong?"

"Luqman."

"I'll be right there."

∼

Jeremy and Jamal are here. Umar called them. Muhammad is out conducting interviews.

Sharon, Maryam, and Aisha huddle on the couch. The rest of us are in the kitchen.

I fiddle with a spoon. "He said it could have been self-defense."

"But Luqman was playing with fire," says Jamal.

"Maybe it was self-defense," says Jeremy. "I remember when that Malek kid beat him up."

"It's possible. But he could spend the rest of his life in prison," says Umar.

"How could he have done that?" says Jamal.

"I don't know." My hands are shaking. "I wish I knew."

Hakeem

I've been quiet all this time because even when I didn't agree with Luqman's methods, I thought he had the right intentions. I should have stopped him before it ever got this far. He trusts me. I could have talked him out of it. But last night, Malek was talking crazy, egging Luqman on, and I didn't know what to do.

It's all over now. Malek may live, though I doubt it. And that bullet ended more than one life last night.

∾

Every time I close my eyes, I see it. Malek is taunting Luqman. A shot rings out, and he crumples to the ground and doesn't get up. Luqman drops the gun and doubles over, sobbing. Aziz goes to Malek. The rest of us don't move, not even when the sirens get closer.

When the police pull into the campground, Aziz runs toward them. "We need an ambulance," he shouts. They draw their guns. He stops and puts his hands in the air. While they cuff him, Abu Bakr and Rasheed run away, toward the woods. Police officers run after them. I can't move.

An officer throws me to the ground, takes my weapon, and puts me in cuffs. Mustapha comes out of the work van with his hands raised. Two shots ring out from somewhere in the woods. Abu Bakr walks out, a few minutes later, in cuffs. I don't see Rasheed until paramedics carry him out on a stretcher. It's too late to save him.

And Luqman? He lies on the ground, hands behind his back and his face in the dirt, and he won't stop wailing. Our brave leader.

He still won't stop. His screams echo through the jail.

∾

I walk into the courtroom feeling like crap. Mama cries out. Jasmine is sobbing so loudly that they may put her out. Aunt Denise sits next to Mama, holding her. She glares at me. I look away.

The arraignment is quick. I'll be locked up in the federal prison until the trial. Hiram had something to do with sending me there, I'm sure.

Right now, the only charge is kidnapping. They may have figured out that I was the one who put the bullet into that waiter. He was big, and he came at me. I didn't think I killed him.

None of that matters anymore. A man is dead, and I shot him. Either I'll get life in prison, or I'll get the chair.

I want to scream, like Luqman. I want to fight. I want to escape. But I can't move. One way or another, my life is over, and there is nothing I can do about it.

~

Everything is dirty—the cell, my clothes, my body—but I need to pray. I try hard to concentrate, but my mind is blocked. My prayer is no good anymore.

Why did I do it? I had my wife and my little boy. I had a steady job and the brothers at the masjid. But I got greedy, and I thought I could have more. That's why I went along with Luqman. I helped him get rid of Malek. I killed that waiter. I even bought that gun for Luqman. Another charge piled on top of the others.

Luqman made me believe we could make a difference. All we did was put Malek in the intensive care unit and ourselves in separate jail cells. Astagfirullah, I should have known better.

I need to pray. I stand up and try again. Allah, don't abandon me. Oh Allah, I need you. Forgive me, forgive me, forgive me, Allah.

Luqman is still screaming.

Time

By (the Token of) Time (through the ages),
Verily Man is in loss,
Except such as have Faith, and do righteous deeds,
and (join together) in the mutual teaching of Truth,
and of Patience and Constancy.

—Qur'an: Surah 103

Kyle's Family

For the last five days, I've sat in meetings and conferences. Over the weekend, I hawked our company at the convention. This morning, I presented new product ideas to other executives. It's been exhausting. It's been great.

Tomorrow, Gameel and I are driving back to Flagstaff. He's anxious to see Faiqa and the babies, and so am I. Faiqa and I talked every night, but I can't wait to hold her in my arms again.

∼

Gameel puts his suitcase in the trunk of my rental. "What is it with you and red sports cars?"

"They make me feel young. Climb in. We can be there in two hours."

When we're out of Phoenix, I push down on the accelerator. The scenery speeds past, taking us closer to my family.

"Do you always drive this fast?"

"I can get you there in record time."

"If we get there alive. Slow down a little, Kyle. My heart can't take it."

His heart is as strong as mine, but I take it down to sixty-five. "Is that better?"

"That's much better. I want to enjoy the desert. It's beautiful out here."

"Do you see why I didn't want to fly?"

"Yes, although as fast you drive, we practically were flying. Do you speed like that with my daughter and grandchildren in the car?"

"Of course not." Not with the babies. I don't tell him Faiqa likes it when I drive fast.

He leans back. "This is nice. It's such a beautiful part of the country. It's almost enough to make me want to leave Chicago."

"You can understand why my father loves to come out here."

"Your father's a smart man. I wonder if Hannah would be interested in moving."

I can't imagine Gameel leaving Chicago. I wonder if he would consider transferring me to Phoenix, though. I could get used to this.

∼

We're halfway home. Gameel says, "I keep thinking about Joshua and what he's going through."

"Is there something wrong with Uncle Joshua?"

"He didn't tell you? I suppose he didn't want to disturb Brad. Luqman was arrested last week for kidnapping and assault."

"What? Are you talking about my cousin?"

Gameel tells me the story. "That's as much as I know. They have Muhammad reporting on it, which can't be easy for him. I didn't expect that from one of Joshua's sons."

"I never would have expected that from Luqman. He came to see my father every day when he was hospitalized. They have a good relationship. Luqman? He's a little mischievous, but he's also kind of nerdy."

"Your father will be surprised to hear what happened."

"Don't tell him," I say quickly. Then I hesitate, not wanting to give away Dad's secret. "It will only upset him. He'll find out when we get back to Chicago."

"Do you think you'll go back soon?"

"My cousin Maryam's wedding is in July. I know Dad would like to be there."

We're quiet for a moment. Gameel says, "You should call your uncle, at least. He'd appreciate hearing from you."

"I'll do that."

∼

I pull into the winding driveway leading to the house. "This is very nice," says Gameel. "Didn't I say your father is a smart man?"

The door is unlocked. "Assalaamu alaikum. Where is every-body?"

"We're in here," Mom calls. "You're just in time for lunch."

We remove our shoes and go to the dining area. Dad stands and hugs Gameel. "I didn't know you were coming. It's good to see you."

Gameel studies Dad. "How are you feeling?"

"I'm great. Haven't you noticed the air here? I can really breathe."

I bring another chair for Gameel. "Sit down. You must be hungry."

My father-in-law frowns. "Faiqa, do you know how fast your husband drives? I may have left my stomach back in Phoenix."

She squeezes my hand. We'll kiss later. "He's careful, Baba. Don't worry."

"Where are my grandchildren?"

"They're taking naps. They should be awake in about an hour."

"I can't wait."

∼

In the morning, Dad suggests another trip to the Grand Canyon. "We can all go. There are enough of us to watch the babies, and I'd like to share the experience with my brother here. Can you believe he's never seen the canyon?"

"Never took the time," says Gameel.

"You'll make time now. Faiqa, pack up the triplets. Matt and Kyle, help your wives. We'll leave in three hours and have lunch at the canyon."

It's been weeks since Dad's had this much energy. His drive stuns us into action. By eleven, the van is packed and everyone's ready. Since there are so many of us, Gameel and I will go up in the sports car.

Dad grabs the van keys from Matt. "I'm driving. Get in back with your family." He glances back at the four car seats. "Are we ready, Nathifa, Nashwa, Yusuf, and Zakariya? Let's go."

∼

Dad insisted on taking Gameel on the helicopter tour. Faiqa, Emily, and our children stayed behind. Mom, Matt, and I went with them.

If possible, Dad was even giddier. When we got to the bottom, he
waded into the river again and splashed around. The day was warmer
than last time, but I still worried. I moved to stop him. Mom shook
her head. By the time we got back into the helicopter, my father was
soaked, but as happy as I've ever seen him.

∼

We decided that, with our wives and children here, it would be
easier to have breakfast in our own rooms. We're supposed to meet at
ten outside the gift shop.

Gameel is waiting. Matt and Emily come a few minutes after we
do. After fifteen minutes, though, Mom and Dad still aren't here.

I run back into the hotel and call from the lobby phone.

Mom answers. "Kyle, is that you?"

"Assalaamu alaikum, Mom. Is everything okay?"

"Walaikum assalaam. Your father's sick. He didn't want me to call
anyone."

"Faiqa and I will be there in five minutes."

Faiqa makes a quick stop at our hotel room for her medical bag. I
didn't know she brought that.

Dad is coughing. Faiqa takes his temperature. "It's 101.8. Did the
fever start last night or this morning?"

"He didn't feel well last night," says Mom, "but he said he was just
tired."

Faiqa touches his arm. "Dad, you have to let me listen to your
chest. Don't think of me as your daughter-in-law. I'm just another
doctor."

"I don't go to the doctor anymore." He still has his spirit.

"Brad, unbutton your shirt, and let her listen." Mom sits on the
other side of the bed and holds his hand.

We wait. Faiqa has him sit up and cough while she listens to his
chest and back. "Breathe deeply now. Good. Can you breathe deeper?"

Dad starts coughing again.

My wife lets the stethoscope hang around her neck. "It doesn't
sound good. You could have pneumonia. I would like to take you to
the hospital to have you checked out."

"I won't go to the hospital. People die there."

"Not usually. I know you don't want any more treatment, but it's practically suicide to let yourself die of something so treatable. I can't let you do that."

"You can't stop me."

Mom squeezes Dad's hand. "Do this for me, Brad. You won't have to stay there unless it's absolutely necessary, but you need to get checked out."

He reaches up and brushes her cheek. "First, I want to see the canyon again."

Mom and Faiqa join the others while I help Dad get dressed. He's weak.

I walk with him to the door. He stops and goes back to sit on the bed. "Check with the front desk, Kyle. They have wheelchairs."

Kyle's Family: Part Two

Dad has pneumonia. Alhamdulillah, my wife caught it before it got worse. After some tough negotiations, Dad agreed to spend a few nights in the hospital for treatment and observation. When he came home, he was confined to bed rest. So far, he's obeying the doctor's orders.

Gameel left two days ago, while Dad was still in the hospital. It's just us again. We spend our days taking care of Dad and watching our children grow.

∼

After the morning prayer, Dad walks over to the couch and stares out the window.

"Brad, get back in bed. You're still sick."

"I'm sick and tired of staring at four walls. It's like a prison in there. At least I can sit out here and enjoy my grandchildren."

"You can do that," says Faiqa, "but you have to rest. No taking walks or getting on the floor with the babies. Will you promise?"

He sighs. "Bring me my pillow."

He tries to get comfortable on the couch, twisting this way and that. By the time he finds a position he likes, he's worn out.

I go to our bedroom and make a call.

~

Dad is resting, drinking his juice, and eating fairly well, but he's not getting better. He still has the hard cough, and he's weak. Faiqa takes his temperature regularly. It hovers between 99 and 100.

At night, after the babies are asleep, she confides in me. "His body may be too worn down. His immune system can't fight this anymore. If we put him in the hospital, I could get him on an IV and oxygen. That would buy him more time."

"Are we talking about months or years?"

"No. It's probably a matter of weeks."

"That's what Dr. Wilson said over four months ago."

"It a miracle he's made it this long. He was already in poor health, before the leukemia was detected, from all his years of drinking, and yet, he came through chemo and was in full remission for over ten years. Look at what he's done since January—the garage, the weights, soccer, the Grand Canyon. It's amazing."

"But it won't last, will it?"

"He'll continue to get weaker. We can talk to him about going back into the hospital. He may live another few weeks, even a month or so. Or, we can keep him here and watch him slowly slip away."

"You know what he wants."

"He would be miserable if we forced him into a hospital. When will you tell the others?"

"Not yet."

"They need to know."

"They will, at the right time. And I'm sure Dad already knows. Let him tell them."

~

After breakfast, there's a knock at the front door. The delivery arrived. I race out to meet them. After I sign, they carry in Dad's old green couch. Gameel, who agreed to watch the house, took care of the details on the Chicago end.

When Dad sees his couch he doesn't say a word, but his face says it all.

Matt moves the other couch and puts Dad's green couch near the window. "Would you like to try it out?"

He lies down and settles in. "This is more like it." He closes his eyes and falls asleep with a smile.

Uncertainties

Every area of trouble gives out a ray of hope,
and the one unchangeable certainty is that
nothing is certain or unchangeable.

—John F. Kennedy

Joshua

For the last two weeks, our lives have revolved around courtrooms and the Cook County jail. And the hospital. Luqman was taken to the psych ward after his arraignment and put under twenty-four hour observation. He's still on suicide watch.

Malek died three days ago. My son has been charged with his murder.

I haven't talked with Luqman since his arrest. At the arraignment, when he broke down in front of the judge, I wondered how a son of mine could sink so low.

When he was in the hospital, Aisha barely slept or ate. She tried to see him, but they wouldn't let her. She visits the prison twice a week. She says they talk. She wants me to go see him, too. She tells me he's sorry.

I would like to believe that, but he lied, and he kidnapped, and he murdered. How can I call him my son? His breakdown at the arraignment wasn't an act, but it was a pitiful example of a spoiled young man who played with fire and got burned.

~

We're moving on Saturday. On Monday, I start my new job. During breakfast, I remind Aisha that we have only three more days left for packing. "We need to get busy."

"I know, Isa. I'm not blind."

"Then why do you keep going out? You need to stay here and help me."

"Don't start with me about Luqman. Don't you realize how much he needs us? Yesterday, his lawyer said that the prosecutor's office has mentioned the death penalty. How can I sit at home when our son's life is in danger?"

"He used us, Aisha." I slam my coffee mug on the table. "And I have no more use for him."

"You're his father. He needs you more than ever. Don't turn your back on him."

My mug shatters when I throw it against a cabinet. I stomp out of the kitchen.

"What are you doing?" she screams.

She doesn't deserve an answer.

～

Umar is with a patient. My stomach twists and rumbles. I flip through a magazine, toss it on the table, and pace.

After twenty minutes, his receptionist calls me. "You may go in now, Mr. Adams."

Umar meets me in the hallway and pulls me into a hug. "We'll use this office." He leads me through a door to my left.

"Do you have patients waiting?"

"My next hour is free. How are you, Isa?" He closes the door.

"I'm confused. I can't sleep. Sometimes I hurt all over. Aisha and I don't talk anymore. We fight. She goes to see him all the time. When she's not at the jail, she's talking to the lawyer or giving interviews. Why won't she leave it alone?"

"She's his mother. You saw his distress in the courtroom. Aisha can't turn her back on him. It would be against her nature."

"But she needs to realize what this is doing to us. We're not ready for the move. If I ask for another delay, I'll lose the job. And we have to leave. Aisha doesn't mind telling our story to the world, but I can hardly show my face in public." Since Luqman's arrest, I haven't even attended the Friday prayer.

"Calm down, Isa." He puts his hand on my shoulder. "Sit down, and tell me what's actually bothering you."

"He lied. All those times when he volunteered at Hope Center. He used what I told him to pull off the kidnapping." I stand and pace again. "And he killed a man, Umar. A fellow Muslim. He could go to the electric chair, and I can't even imagine his punishment beyond the grave."

"Are you planning to help throw him into the fire?"

I stop. "What do you mean?"

"Will you help Luqman when he needs you most, or will you continue to ignore him?"

"What do you want me to do?" I shout.

Umar grabs my arm and guides me to the chair. When I sit down, he kneels next to me. "Do you think you can still be a father to him?"

"No. I can't. Could you? What he's done is too awful."

"I'm not asking you to accept his actions. Can you still accept *him*?"

"I don't even know who he is. When he wanted something from me, he was a perfect son. But behind my back, he was plotting. I can't get past the lies."

"You saw him in the courtroom. Do you think his hysterics were an act?"

"No, but why did he have to do that, right there in front of everyone?" It was embarrassing. "Either he's lying and plotting, or he's screaming hysterically. Is that all there is to Luqman?"

"When the police arrived on the scene, Luqman was sobbing. You know his condition is precarious. Aisha understands his despair. Won't you try?"

"We always had to love Luqman more. He's a grown man. Why won't he snap out of it?"

"Luqman was born with a sensitive soul, and he has suffered for it. This revolution meant everything to him. Muhammad told us he was ready to go to prison or even die for his cause, but he was trapped in an unrealistic fantasy. Malek revived the childhood hurt, and Luqman retaliated. Now, he's unable to deal with the consequences. Do you realize he may still take his life?"

"What do you want me to do about it? Everyone has thoughts like that. He needs to get over it. I did."

"Did you 'get over it' on your own, or did you have help?"

Umar's expression stops me from answering too quickly. We both remember that night. My new wife, Aisha, had thrown me out, with good reason, and I thought about ending my suffering. Thoughts of suicide had plagued me since I was thirteen. By the mercy of Allah, I stopped myself and went to Umar's apartment that night. He helped me deal with my despair and reunited me with his sister. "You know that answer, brother."

"Luqman needs you. Visit him."

"What will I say?"

"You'll know."

"We still have to leave on Saturday."

"Go to Kentucky, but first go see your son."

"I can't do it, Umar. The shame. You can't imagine."

He puts his hand on my shoulder. "Stop worrying about what people think. Go see your son."

"Maybe. I'll think about it."

"If you don't go, Isa, I know you will regret it."

He glances at his watch. I need to leave. "I'll think about it." I rush out of his office and sit in my car and cry.

∿

Aisha doesn't come home until early evening. She can't spend all that time visiting Luqman. Where is she?

Her eyes are red. "They moved him," she says softly.

"What do you mean? Where is he?"

"He's off suicide watch. They took him to the federal prison."

I swear my heart stops for a minute or two. But I'm still breathing, and I have to face this. Twenty years ago last month, I was released from that prison. The place still haunts my nightmares. While driving around Chicago over the years, I have gone out of my way to avoid the place where Clark and Van Buren Streets meet, the place where I spent those hellish months.

Umar is right. I'll visit my son. But I wish he was someplace else.

∿

I haven't gone to the Friday prayer for two weeks. Prophet Muhammad said, "Whoever misses the Friday prayer three times, Allah will set a seal on his heart." Today I must go.

When I walk into the masjid, no one talks to me. Some turn away. I sit in the front row and read the Qur'an, ignoring everyone. When we stand up for the prayer, the brother next to me moves. I pull him back. The imam turns and motions for the brother to move closer, reminding everyone, "Shoulders to shoulders, feet to feet."

After the prayer, I sit and pray silently. No one approaches me. As I leave, I give my salaams to the imam. He replies, "Walaikum assalaam." Then he turns away from me.

Everyone in Chicago knows that Luqman killed a Muslim. They don't care that it could have been self-defense. Luqman is guilty and, for many, so am I.

~

The prison has visiting hours at 6:00 PM. After the prayer, I eat lunch and do a little last-minute packing. No matter what happens, we must leave tomorrow, insha Allah.

For a second, I think of bringing Jeremy or Jamal with me. It's not that I don't want to face Luqman. I simply don't want to go to that prison. We made the mistake once, though, of including Muhammad when we confronted Luqman. I won't do that again.

Aisha doesn't know I'm going. We barely talk these days. I find a parking place and look up at the skyscraper prison. My heart beats faster. I sweat. Putting one foot in front of the other, I walk inside.

I show my ID. They check Luqman's name. He put me on his list of visitors. I wasn't sure he would.

They pat me down and tell me to walk through a scanning machine. The guards frighten me. I don't recognize anyone and, thankfully, they don't seem to recognize me. It has been twenty years.

They lead me through a hallway. Doors slam behind me. I jump and touch the wall, trying to shake a flashback. The guard waits. I step forward, still disoriented, still expecting him to shove me. He doesn't. I'm a father, not an inmate. But I can still imagine myself in sandals and a jumpsuit.

By the time I get to the visitors' room, I'm shaking. But, I know what I will say to my son.

Jamilah Kolocotronis

Luqman

When I first bought a gun, I knew I might have to use it, but I never wanted to hurt anyone. When they knew I was armed, other guys feared me. That helped when I was in the middle of a fight. It also helped on the night we kicked out Malek.

Malek kept taunting me. He asked for it, like he wanted to die. But when he went down, I lost it. I didn't really want to shoot him.

After I shot Malek, and even in the courtroom, I wanted to die, too. For days I kept seeing him go down, especially when I tried to sleep. Visions tormented me.

Later, I regained my senses and realized that if I acted crazy they might go easy on me. My lawyer could use a temporary insanity defense. It didn't work. They knew I was out of danger and sent me over here to medium security.

Two seconds after I got here, I realized I had to act tough. The other inmates had to know I had killed one man, and I could do it again. In spite of my size, the bigger men left me alone.

∼

They tell me I have a visitor. Mom comes as often as she can. They're still planning to move to Kentucky, though. When she's gone, no one will remember me.

Dad is waiting for me, not Mom. His name is on my visitors' list, but I never expected to see him here. He looks nervous. I know he's ashamed of me.

"Hi, Dad." I sit down. "Assalaamu alaikum."

"Walaikum assalaam. How are you? Are you feeling better?"

"I'm okay."

"Do they treat you well? Is anyone bothering you?"

"Don't worry. I can handle myself."

He nods. The rest of the room buzzes with conversation while we sit in silence.

"Mom and I are moving to Lexington tomorrow."

"Don't worry about me."

More silence.

"Do you remember when I was in prison? You were still little. This is the place where they sent me. I hope the food is better now."

"They're probably serving us the same food they gave you. It's awful."

"Make sure you eat, even if it is bad. You don't want to get sick."

"Yeah."

Another long pause.

"Luqman, I have to ask you something. Are you a Muslim?"

"What kind of question is that? Of course I am."

"Do you pray?"

"That's my business."

"Listen to me. The prosecutor may seek the death penalty, and prison itself is dangerous. I nearly died here. You have to be ready to answer the questions."

"What questions?"

"After you die, Allah will send angels to your grave. You'll be asked four things. Who is your Lord? What is your religion? Who is your prophet? What is your book? Will you be ready to answer?"

"Why does it matter? I'm alive and healthy."

"I'm serious. While I was in this prison, I was nearly beaten to death. My lawyer was stabbed. My cellmate was murdered. Can you answer the questions?"

"I'm a Muslim, okay? Why should I have to prove it to you?"

At this point in the conversation, he usually gets up and walks away, or he screams at me. This time he closes his eyes and takes a deep breath. I wait.

He reaches over and grabs my hand. I try to pull away but he won't let go. "Whatever else you do in your life, Luqman, I need you to be a Muslim. And I want to know that even though things are bad now, I can hope to see you in paradise."

What do I say to that? This isn't how Dad usually acts. Did I have to kidnap and kill before he decided to treat me like an adult?

Am I a Muslim? Like Muhammad said, Muslims don't usually go around kidnapping people. I know Islam, but I haven't studied it in years. Can a Muslim kill another Muslim? Malek and I were never friends, but he practiced Islam better than most people do.

"You won't see me in paradise, no matter what I do or say. People like me don't end up there."

"'*Oh my servants who have sinned against their own souls! Do not despair of the mercy of Allah; for Allah forgives all sins for He is Oft-*

Forgiving, Most Merciful.' This ayah saved me, Luqman, years before you were born. None of us is perfect."

Dad's crying. What has he done that was so bad? I know about his time in prison and his shotgun marriage to Heather, and his alcoholism. Is there more?

"This isn't the time to confess my sins to you, but I want you to know that Allah will forgive you if you turn to Him. Paradise is within reach, if you make the effort."

"Do you still want to know the answers to those questions?"

"Go ahead."

"My Lord is Allah, my religion is Islam, my prophet is Muhammad, and my book is the Qur'an."

"Is that what you believe in your heart?"

I've never been very religious, but I have studied different systems of belief. None measured up to Islam. "I don't believe anything else."

"There is no god except Allah. That's all you need to believe. And make sure you pray. Talk to the chaplain. He can help you."

"Maybe."

He grasps both my hands and lowers his head, like he's praying. I look down, too. It seems like the right thing to do.

After a few minutes he looks up. "Our time is almost over. Tomorrow morning we'll leave for Lexington. We'll be back in a couple of weeks for Maryam's wedding. Insha Allah, we'll see you then."

"I wish I could be there."

He sighs. "You should have thought of that a few weeks ago."

"Yeah."

"They won't let me hug you." He holds tight to my hands and looks into my eyes. "I love you, son. Remember that."

I look away. "Yeah. Me too." The last thing I want to do is let anyone see me cry.

~

That was the deepest conversation I ever had with my father. If I'd known I had to get arrested to get his respect, I might have done it sooner.

He never said he loved me. He complained about my messy room and yelled at me for staying out too late. He interrogated me and walked away when the situation got too intense. He must have loved me all those times, but I wish he would have said it just once.

~

My lawyer, a public defender named Cody, tells me I should plead guilty. He'll try to bargain with the prosecutor. If I'm lucky, I'll get twenty years. Then, when I'm forty-five, I'll be free to go about my life.

That's not great, but it would be better than the death penalty. Hiram could personally request the electric chair for me. He has the clout to get it done. The prosecutor is a New Pilgrim. The governor was elected with Hiram's endorsement. I don't stand a chance.

But if I plead guilty, I will never get my day in court. Kidnapping Hiram didn't expose the corruption of the New Pilgrims. If Cody puts me on the stand, every word will be in the public record. That would be worth dying for.

Dad told me I should pray. Sometimes it seems like a meaningless ritual to me, but the rest of my family seems to get something from it. Maybe they're right. Besides, there's nothing better to do. I go to the sink and wash up. There's no way to tell which direction points to Makkah, so I pick a corner and bow down.

Struggles Ended

Every soul shall have a taste of death;
In the end to Us shall you be brought back.

—Qur'an: Surah 29.57

Kyle's Family

Life with Dad has become a series of ups and downs, good days and bad. On Saturday morning, he and Mom took the triplets for a walk. Dad returned and asked me to go into town to buy a barbecue grill. We had his famous hamburgers for lunch.

Today he woke up and went straight to the couch. He spent the day there; looking out the window, and watching the babies play on the living room floor.

∽

On Monday morning during breakfast Dad says, "Let's go to Sedona."

"Are you well enough?" says Faiqa.

"Take my temperature. If I have a fever, we'll stay home."

I think he likes having a resident physician. And, because Faiqa is family, he gets to boss her around just like he does the rest of us.

"What will we do in Sedona?" says Matt.

"They have art galleries and interesting places to shop. There's an African safari park nearby, and we might even want to ride in a hot air balloon."

"That sounds like fun," says Mom.

"I won't be able to do all that," says Emily. "Zakariya will get too tired and fussy."

"We'll drive there together and get hotel rooms. You and Faiqa and the babies can sit out some of the activities if you like. It will be nice to have a change of scenery."

Isn't that why we left Chicago? Does my father get bored too easily, or does he just want to experience as much as he can before he dies? Actually, a change of scenery sounds good to me, too.

∽

Dr. Faiqa cleared Dad for travel. We're almost finished packing. It's only thirty miles away, so we don't have to rush.

With the babies and their carseats, the van is too crowded to be comfortable. Dad wants to come with me in my sports car.

We head out into incredible beauty. The mountains and beautiful rock formations surround us. Dad gazes out. "Don't drive too fast, Kyle. I want to enjoy this."

We arrive in Sedona right before sunset. Dad makes me pull over to the side of the road so he can watch the sun go down. "I don't know how many sunsets I have left, but that was one of the best." He looks around. "Let's pray here."

The land is rocky. "It would be safer if we wait until we get to the hotel."

He sighs. "Go on." As I drive away, he glances back before raising his hands in private prayer.

Our hotel has a tremendous view of the red rock. In the dusk, I can see only the shadows. Sunrise should be spectacular.

After dinner at a local restaurant, we go to our rooms. "We need to get an early start tomorrow," says Dad. "Everyone sleep well."

Faiqa falls into our hotel bed. "I don't know how your father does it. Sometimes I can barely keep up with him. The triplets wear me out."

"I'll help you tomorrow. You've been great throughout this whole Arizona adventure, and I really appreciate it. This is something we'll remember all our lives."

"That's true. Remember what you said. Tomorrow, you're taking care of Yusuf."

"No problem."

The triplets are asleep. First we pray. Then I reach for her.

~

After a nice breakfast, we start our tour at the Out of Africa Wildlife Park, going on a savanna safari and riding the tram. We even watch a tiger show. Emily holds Zakariya tightly during the show, and Faiqa keeps the stroller close to her. I let Yusuf watch, though I'm not sure how much he notices. He laughs anyway. That's my boy.

By the time we're finished with the park, Faiqa and Emily are exhausted and the babies are all either asleep or fussy. We take them back to the hotel. Mom, Dad, Matt, and I continue our Sedona adventure.

Mom wants to go to an art gallery. I find a beautiful painting representing the Southwest. It will look perfect in our living room.

Later, I realize that the painting will remind me of the time we came to Arizona with my dying father. We can put it in storage and take it out later. The kids will like it.

We also stop by a few souvenir shops. Dad buys Mom a turquoise necklace. He gently places it around her neck. She fingers the turquoise.

Dad consults the local map and directs Matt to one more destination. We end up at a hot air balloon rental place. Dad looks at Mom. "What do you think?"

"I have always wanted to try that."

My brother and I stay on the ground and watch their multicolored balloon soar into the sky and drift away. The owner made sure Dad knew how to use the controls. They'll be okay, I hope. I can understand why Dad wouldn't mind death-defying acts, but Mom is incredible, staying with him every step of the way. He'd better not decide to go skydiving.

They're gone for nearly an hour. When they come back to earth they have their arms around each other. All the way to the hotel, they're grinning and signaling each other with their eyes. I'm a grown man, and I still feel strange watching my parents act that way.

One day, when our kids are older, I'll bring Faiqa here. It will be just the two of us. That will be nice.

～

We leave in the morning. Faiqa and Emily are glad to be going back. Mom and Dad haven't said much since their hot air balloon ride. They all squeeze into the van. I drive alone. I'm sorry to leave the red rock beauty behind. Later, I'll talk with Gameel about a transfer.

～

On the day we returned from Sedona, Dad asked Faiqa to get him something for the discomfort. "You know I want to go naturally."

"I learned about some natural remedies in med school. What exactly do you want?"

"I've read about the benefits of medical marijuana."

"Yes, so have I."

"Be sure to control the dosage. I need to keep my mind clear for the prayers."

"Don't worry. I'll take care of it." She patted his arm.

"I don't want to smoke anything."

"There are different methods. Why don't we put it in your tea?

"Yes. That sounds good." He smiled. "Thank you, Faiqa. For everything."

Kyle's Family: Part Two

For the last three days, Dad has hardly left his green couch. That trip wore him out. Mom sits with him much of the time, and every time I look at him, he has a smile on his face. As long as he's happy, I'm not complaining.

∾

After Sedona, Dad never bounced back. He spends his days on the green couch, and sometimes sleeps there at night. Faiqa keeps a watch on his temperature which hovers between 100 and 102. "His body can't fight any longer," she says.

When Gameel calls and asks me to drive down to Phoenix for another series of meetings, I tell him I can't make it. "Dad's health is declining. I need to stay here with him."

He's quiet a moment. "That's why your family went to Arizona, isn't it?"

"You didn't hear it from me."

"I understand," he says. "I've known your father long enough. Don't you think his brothers would want to know?"

"Dad told us not to call them."

"He didn't tell me."

"Hold off for a little while. They have busy schedules, and it won't do any good if they're just hanging around waiting. It might irritate Dad."

"Let me know. Is he seeing a doctor?"

"You know my dad. He's seeing Dr. Faiqa. She's the only physician he trusts."

"I'm glad she can help. Your father is a special man, Kyle, and I will miss him. Please give him my strongest salaams."

"You're welcome to come out here again."

"No, this is a time for family."

"You are family."

"Not in that way. I'll make sure your uncles know. Call me if you need anything."

Dad won't mind, will he, when his brothers show up? It's always hard to tell with him.

Joshua: Part One

Our move down here went smoothly. Muhammad drove the truck down on Friday, helped unload everything, and drove it back on Saturday. Hanif and a couple of other brothers came to help. We're still unpacking boxes.

I'm nearing the end of my second week at Caring House. This is what I was looking for. We exchange salaams in the hallway and stop at midday to pray together. Last Friday, we shut down for ninety minutes to make Salatul Jummah. After the Friday prayer, we enjoyed a potluck lunch. This place has the Islamic spirit I've always wanted, and I'm grateful to have found that before I die.

Aisha is flying to Chicago tonight to help Maryam get ready for her wedding. She'll visit Luqman, too. I plan to see him next weekend.

~

Aisha's flight just left. For the next week, I'll be alone.

My phone rings as soon as I pull into the driveway. It's Gameel.

"Assalaamu alaikum. How are you? How is everything up in Chicago?"

"We're good, alhamdulillah. Reverend Johnson is recovering from his heart attack, and the centers are recovering from all the publicity. That's not why I called, though. There's something very serious I need to discuss with you."

"Okay." I try to think of what I overlooked at Hope.

"It's your brother. Do you know why he took his family to Arizona?"

"He said it was for a vacation. They're back now, aren't they? I'm looking forward to seeing him at the wedding."

"Listen to me, Joshua. Brad went to Arizona because that's where he wants to die. Knowing your brother, I'm sure you understand why he didn't tell you. He made the boys promise not to say anything, either, but I worked the truth out of Kyle. He just called. Brad is in bad shape, and you should go there as soon as possible. Chris plans to take the next flight out."

"Brad is in bad shape?"

"He's dying, and this time, I don't think there will be a reprieve. You need to fly out to Flagstaff. Kyle will pick you up from the airport."

"Thank you for letting me know. I'll get there as soon as I can." I hang up, too stunned to say goodbye.

∾

Hanif's number is on my speed dial. He answers on the second ring.

"Assalaamu alaikum, Hanif. Um, my brother is dying, and I need to fly out to Arizona right away."

"How long do you think you'll be gone?"

"I don't know." This time, I think, it's for real. "Um, I haven't made a good start here. After this is over—" I choke on the words. "When I can, I'll work harder to make it up."

"Don't apologize. Things happen, and sometimes they happen all at once. Have a safe trip, and keep me posted."

Now I need to find a flight to Flagstaff. And I'd better call Muhammad. He'll tell Aisha when he picks her up from the airport.

∾

Last night, I slept for two hours, and not well. At 5:00 AM, I caught a flight from Lexington to Cincinnati. From Cincinnati, I flew to Phoenix, with a one-hour layover in Denver. During my flight from Denver, I realized that I might have been at my brother's side all this time if I hadn't lied to the organization in Flagstaff.

I have a two-hour layover in Phoenix. Aisha calls while I'm waiting. "Call me, will you, and let me know?"

We left a lot unspoken. It's easier that way.

After hanging up, I take time to think about what this means. Brad is really dying. Somehow, I thought it might not happen. I go to the restroom, lock myself in a stall, and cry.

～

Kyle is waiting for me. "Gameel called and told me your schedule. You must be tired."

"Don't worry about me. How is your father?"

"It's good that you came."

"Is Chris here yet?"

"He got here a couple of hours ago. Where's your luggage?"

I hold up a travel bag. "This is it."

He takes it from me and leads me to his car.

"Your father didn't want to tell us why he was coming to Arizona? Why not?"

He shrugs. "That's how Dad is."

～

He's lying on his old green couch in the living room of the rental home. When we walk in, Matt greets me with a hug. "Dad's sleeping," he whispers.

Brad looks frail again, like he did in January. "Does he sleep a lot?"

"He's very weak," says Kyle. "Like he was in the hospital, but this time he's not going to get better. The last few days have been especially rough."

Chris touches my shoulder. "I'm glad you're here."

I hadn't seen him when I came in. "Did you know that's why he came to Arizona?"

"I asked him, but of course he denied it. Brad has always been a good actor."

"He's been a lot sicker than he would admit," says Kyle. "Even to me."

We all watch as his chest rises and falls. How much longer?

"You must be tired," says Kyle. "Go freshen up. Your room is down the hall."

"Are you boys planning to attend the Friday prayer?"

Kyle looks at his watch. "Yes. We need to leave soon."

"Give me five minutes, and I'll come with you." I need to pray for my brother.

～

Brad is awake when we get back from the masjid. I put on a smile. "Assalaamu alaikum brother. How are you?"

He winces. "Not so good."

Where are the sarcastic remarks? The complaints? He's very sick. I hold his hand. "Would you like me to recite for you?"

"Yes."

I read the Qur'an, and he closes his eyes. When I stop, he opens them again. "Go on. Please."

I continue, saying silent prayers for him between each verse.

While I'm reading, Matt comes over with a bowl. "Dad," he says. "Dad, you need to eat." I stop and watch.

Brad opens his eyes. Matt picks up the spoon and feeds him soup. When the soup is gone, Matt helps him drink water. "Would you like your tea?"

"Yes."

Emily hands the cup to Matt, and he spoons the tea into Brad's mouth. My brother's body relaxes.

"He's asleep," says Matt. "You need to come eat, Uncle Joshua." He leads me to the dining table where Emily serves me chicken and vegetables.

"How long have you been feeding him?"

"Since last Tuesday. Up until Monday, he was taking walks almost daily, hiking through the woods around the house. He started running a high fever on Monday afternoon and went quickly downhill. His body can't fight anymore."

"Has he seen an oncologist here in town?"

"You know how he feels about doctors. He'll listen to Faiqa, but he's afraid of dying in the hospital."

The image of our father, dying alone in the hospice, never left him. Brad has been haunted by Sam all his life.

～

After lunch, I took a nap. Kyle woke me up at sunset to pray.

After our prayers, Matt helps Brad make tayammum, a dry ablution. Brad moves his lips, saying his prayers with a voice so weak I can't hear him.

≈

Beth is incredibly strong and patient. Chris and I talk with her at the kitchen table.

"You're very brave," says Chris. "How can we help?"

"Don't worry about me. Keep praying for Brad. That's all I ask."

I wish Aisha and Melinda were here to support her. She has her daughters-in-law, and I can see how she relies on them.

≈

I can't sleep. The house is quiet. I pull on my sweat pants and walk down the hall toward the living room to check on my brother.

Kyle is washing him. My nephew wipes my brother's face, neck, and hands. He massages as he cleans Brad from head to toe. He removes an adult diaper and cleans that area, too. I look away. After a minute, I go back to the room and pray for my nephews.

I'm drifting to sleep when I hear a moan. It continues for a couple of minutes. I walk out again and watch Kyle helping Brad drink his tea. My brother relaxes and falls asleep. Kyle keeps his watch over his father.

≈

Matt is making the call to prayer. I struggle to open my eyes.

When I walk into the living room to pray, Brad is sitting on the couch. "You don't look very good, Joshua." He smiles. "You'd better take care of yourself."

Kyle leads us in the prayer. Afterward, Brad asks for a copy of the Qur'an. He sits and recites for thirty minutes. I sit with him.

Matt touches my shoulder. "Go eat breakfast, Uncle Joshua. Dad, I brought your soup."

Brad finishes reading and closes the Qur'an. "I'm tired of soup. Bring me a soft-boiled egg and toast. And a cup of coffee." He pauses. "I'll come over to the table to eat. Help me, Joshua."

We walk together. He needs my support, but he's stronger than I expected. "I need to start running," he says. "I'm out of shape."

He talks and even laughs a little during breakfast. "You're in Lexington now, Joshua? I can't picture you down there. Are you going to start speaking with an accent?"

"You never know."

After breakfast, he tells Kyle he'd like to take a shower. The boys find a chair he can sit on. Beth follows him into the bedroom. Forty minutes later, he walks back into the living room. "That felt good. There's nothing like a nice hot shower."

He naps until the next prayer. At lunch time, he comes to the table and picks up a hamburger.

"Wait, Brad." Beth calls from the kitchen. "Your fish and rice are almost done."

"Thanks, but I'd rather have a burger."

When we're finished he says, "Let's take a walk. Come on. I'd like to show you around."

We all walk with him. Beth stays by his side. Matt is ready to catch him if he falls. After a minute or two, he pauses to catch his breath, but he won't go back into the house until he's shown us his special spot. "Look here. It's completely secluded. Sometimes, I come here to think."

"Dad," says Matt, "we need to go back to the house."

"Go on. I'm not done yet." He sits on a fallen tree for a moment before continuing.

∼

He's asleep now, back on his green couch. That walk wore me out, too. I go to the room for a nap. The house is quiet.

When I wake up, it's dark outside. I wash up before standing in the hallway to make the call to prayer. While waiting for everyone else, I check on Brad.

He's still sleeping. I touch his shoulder. "Brad. It's time for the prayer."

He opens his eyes and stares at me.

"You have to make tayammum, Brad, so you can pray."

"I can't," he whispers.

I move Brad's arms for him, helping him perform the ritual cleansing. I say the words. He follows me with his eyes.

Faiqa walks into the room. "Come here," I call her.

She sits next to Brad and holds his hand. "How are you, Dad?"

"Help me."

She gets her stethoscope, listens to his chest, and without a word, goes back to her room.

Kyle comes running. He holds Brad's hand. My brother opens his mouth but doesn't speak.

"What is it, Dad?"

"I need to pray," he whispers.

Kyle goes to the hallway, and calls everyone for the prayer. The tone in his voice brings them running.

"Let's pray before it's too late. Line up." Kyle takes his place in front. We follow him.

After the prayer, Beth sits next to Brad and holds his hand. "Dinner can wait," she says. "Let's sit together. Get your Uncle Chris, so he can pray with us."

We form a casual circle next to the green couch. Some of us read silently. Beth reads aloud. Some of us pray. Chris folds his hands.

Brad begins to recite Surah al-Fatihah. Halfway through, he coughs, and lies back into the couch. We stop.

"Go on," he says.

We continue reading and praying. Beth grasps his hand.

Brad speaks again, reciting Surah al-Ikhlas. He completes the verses and calls out, "La illaha illa Allah."

Beth strokes his face. "I love you, Brad."

Brad whispers Kyle's name.

"What do you need, Dad?"

"Take care of your mother."

It happens so quietly, I almost don't see it. Beth is holding his hand. It goes limp. She lays her head on Brad's chest and softly cries.

Kyle takes hold of his father's hand. After a moment he says simply, "We all belong to Allah and to Him we all return."

Matt whispers, *"Inna lillahi wa inna ilayhi raji'un."*

Joshua: Part Two

Kyle took a couple of hours to mourn, and then did what he had to do. First, he called the mortuary and arranged to have Brad's body transported to the masjid. Then he called the imam. Though he was grieving, he hid it well.

The hearse arrives a little before 11:00 PM. They come in and take Brad away. We watch in silence.

After they've left, each of us retreats. The babies sleep while we read and pray.

～

Early in the morning, we drive with Kyle and Matt to the masjid. The imam meets us with few words and great compassion. He leads us to a special room. Chris and I step aside while Kyle and Matt wash their father's body.

When they're done, Kyle talks with the imam. Matt goes back to the house to get Beth, Faiqa, Emily, and the children. Chris and I pray, each in our own way.

The janazah is after the midday prayer. I stand behind my brother's body, with Kyle leading. Even though I was with him when he died, it's hard for me to believe this is happening. Some brothers from the local community stand with us, praying for a man they met only at Friday prayers. In Islam, he is their brother, too.

Kyle leads the convoy to the cemetery. Matt, Chris, and I ride with him. Faiqa and Emily drive with Beth back to the house.

At the cemetery, the imam says a prayer. Brad is lowered into the ground of the place he loved so much.

As Kyle drives back to the house, I look out the window and see kids playing soccer. Today is June 30. Brad didn't make it to July.

～

Aisha says she'll call Beth later. Right now my sister-in-law seems to need time alone. Through the window, I spot her walking on the familiar paths she shared with Brad.

I call Hanif. We don't talk long.

I sit on the bed and read the Qur'an, pausing often to pray for my big brother. May Allah bless his soul.

Brad lived for sixty-five years, and he had a full life. As he said, he accomplished everything he set out to do. Including beating me at soccer. And he died in the way he chose, surrounded by beauty and the love of his family.

But it's still so hard to have him gone.

Kyle's Family

My uncles flew out of Flagstaff today. In spite of what Dad said before we left Chicago, he was glad they were here. So was I.

Before they left, we reminisced about my father. They told me stories I had never heard. How Uncle Chris followed him around when he was little. How he took care of Uncle Joshua. They smiled just a little when they told me about the time Dad and Uncle Chris tried to talk Uncle Joshua out of being a Muslim. They cried about time wasted, when they fought with each other or were just too busy. While they talked, I sometimes glanced at my brother. We're close now, and we have to make sure we stay that way.

Before he left this morning, Uncle Chris took me aside and told me how much my father loved me. A little while later, Uncle Joshua said the same thing. While he was alive, he depended on me. Now, I have to do what I can to honor him. I pray for him all the time, hoping he'll be rewarded for the love he gave me and the million things he did for me, good deeds I could never repay.

∽

Mom doesn't cry much, not around us, but she seems lost. She spends hours out in the woods every day. Tomorrow she wants to go to the Grand Canyon "just to think." Matt and I will go with her.

We should go back to Chicago soon, but it will be hard to leave. This afternoon, I called the owners and asked if they would consider selling me this house. They said they'll get back to me. We had happy times here along with the sad ones, and we had Dad here with us in the final days and moments of his life.

Matt and Emily plan to go home in August. Faiqa and I may stay here. I don't know yet if Mom wants to leave. There will be time to talk about that when she's ready.

Sometimes I miss my father so much that my whole body aches. He was a good man. I hope I can be like him one day.

Truth

I never did give anybody hell.
I just told the truth and they thought it was hell.

—Harry S. Truman

Joshua: Part One

Less than a week after saying goodbye to my oldest brother, I publicly consent to the marriage of my youngest daughter. Poets talk about the circle and cycle of life, the strange twists and turns of fate. No wonder I feel dizzy.

While the imam gives a speech on marriage, I gaze at my youngest child. Happy and self-assured, she's the woman I always hoped she would become. I look at the man who will leave with her tonight. I couldn't ask for a better son-in-law. Insha Allah, they'll have a blessed life together.

The circle and cycle and crazy spiral of life. A few days ago, I watched my brother being lowered into his grave. Today, I celebrate my daughter's new life with her husband. As Maryam stands before the ummah, a new bride, her life flashes through my mind. I picture the moment when I held her, newly born, on the side of the expressway, and I can almost believe that is the reality, and this is only a dream. Endings and beginnings both lead me to tears. I swallow hard and wipe my eyes before anyone notices.

~

The celebration is ending. Maryam and Zaid will leave soon. He's taking her on a Mediterranean cruise. In three weeks, they'll return to Chicago and build their marriage in the same house where Aisha and I built ours.

Our family is gathered together near the front of the hall. We've been closer since Luqman's arrest. Maryam and Zaid talk with guests a few feet away.

"We're all planning to spend the day at Jamal's place, Dad, and help him finish packing. How soon do you have to leave tomorrow?" Jeremy asks.

"We should take off by early afternoon. I'll go see Luqman in the morning. We can come by Jamal's apartment on our way out of town. When are you leaving, Jamal?"

"We're hoping to take off on Monday morning, insha Allah."

"Call us when you get there," says Aisha. "We'll need to visit soon."

Maryam and Zaid walk over. "We're leaving," says Zaid. They plan to spend the night at Zaid's old apartment and fly out tomorrow for Barcelona. This man is about to take my daughter with him, and suddenly I don't like it. She's my little girl.

Aisha hugs them. "Have a safe trip."

Maryam looks at me. "I'm leaving, Dad."

I throw my arms around her and don't want to let go. But she doesn't belong to me anymore, and she never really did. Before releasing her, I kiss her cheek.

She smiles. "You're not losing me. Don't worry."

Zaid hugs me, too. "I'll keep her safe, Uncle Isa."

How many times have I told him to call me Dad?

~

They're gone. Ismail and Amal invited us back to their house for tea.

"It was a nice wedding," says Amal.

"Nearly everyone came, too," says Aisha. "I was afraid—" She leaves the thought unfinished.

"Everyone knows your family," says Ismail. "Isa and you are highly respected."

"Even though our son is in prison." I sigh.

"Luqman is trying to change," says Aisha. "He wants you to know that he prays regularly."

"That's good. If only he had stopped to think about what he was doing."

"Don't you remember, dude?" says Ismail. "Being a Muslim doesn't mean being perfect. It just means that you try."

Ismail can always make me smile. "But, dude, this is more serious than anything I ever got into."

"Your problem was you were still hung up on Heather. That boy was trying to change the world. He just didn't know how to do it."

My face turns red. After all these years, the incident with Heather still embarrasses me. Aisha got over it, though.

She smiles. "You have to admit he's right."

I kissed my ex-wife a few days before I married Aisha. My son set out to end the tyranny of the New Pilgrims. My act nearly ruined my marriage. Luqman's act took the life of another Muslim. Both of us were young and foolish. Luqman may pay with his life.

~

We had planned to spend the night at the old house, but Ismail and Amal convince us to stay with them. "It's late," says Amal. "We have plenty of room."

It is late. At 2:30 AM, we finally struggle into bed. I put my arms around my wife, and thank Allah she's stayed with me all these years.

Joshua: Part Two

Luqman is waiting for me. "Assalaamu alaikum. How was the wedding? And how's Uncle Brad? Was he there?"

Aisha didn't tell him. "Uncle Brad died in Arizona last week, on June 29. I was with him during his last days."

He shows just a flash of emotion, but quickly hides it. "Why didn't anyone tell me? I wanted to talk to him again before he died." He pauses. "Did he know what happened?"

"No, he didn't." Kyle called soon after the arrest and said he would keep it from his father. When he said that, I should have realized why Brad left town. "You remember they went to Arizona back in May. He went there to die."

"He was the only person who always treated me like I mattered."

That hurt. "I tried to be a good father to you. You demanded so much from us."

"When I was little, I did. Later you always yelled at me. But I talked with the chaplain about it, and I think I understand." He looks up. "How was the wedding?"

"Your little sister looked beautiful. They left for their honeymoon in Europe this morning."

Luqman looks past me and quietly sighs. "I'll never go to Europe, will I?"

He'll never get married, either, or do anything that takes place outside of these walls.

"It's easy to look back with regret. Have you tried looking forward?"

"I am looking forward to the trial. That will be my chance to speak out. They can't deny me that. Who knows? I might have a shot."

"How do you figure that?"

"I killed Malek in self-defense. If you were there, Dad, you would know. He's the one who came out shooting. Aziz tried to talk him down, but he wouldn't listen. And we never planned to hurt Hiram. You saw our demands. We asked for ransom because we knew their church could afford it, and we thought they owed it to us and to everyone in Chicago, but we really just wanted to break the monopoly of the New Pilgrims."

"But you didn't break it, and now they're stronger than ever. Do you think they will ever let you go free?"

"We saved Hiram's life. That should count for something."

All of the gang members have said that, but news reporters say they nearly killed him. "Hiram is your biggest enemy. He claims you abused him out there. You starved him."

Luqman laughs. Is he crazy?

"One day I was feeding Hiram, and he spit in my face. So, I made him fast until sunset. You see how fat he is—and I saw him nearly naked." He grimaces. "That man should fast every week."

Hiram fasted. He would consider that abuse. "Some of your ideas are good. But you did it the wrong way, and you will have to pay for that."

He frowns. "I wanted justice. If something happens to me, Dad, will you make sure there is justice? That everything I did won't be for nothing?"

"I don't know what I can do."

"You never tried." His voice gets a little louder. He stops, looks around at the guards, and continues. "I was so angry because you wouldn't try. You knew what was going on, more than most people, but you just sat in your office and came home to watch the news, and never did anything more than that."

"I never did more? You know I brought the homeless back to our house. There were weeks when I didn't get home before seven or eight. On the evening your mother and I came back from Hajj, I was working. If I didn't do more, it's because I couldn't, not because I wouldn't."

"Are you telling me you would have stood up to Hiram?"

"No. That's not my style. And, as director, I could have lost his support for the centers. Life is complicated, Luqman. Everything isn't as simple as black and white."

He snickers. "That's a good way to put it. Is that why our family is so complicated, because we're not black or white? Sometimes I just wanted to belong somewhere."

"I grew up as a white kid of white parents, and I never belonged anywhere. Not until I became a Muslim."

"Simply being a Muslim didn't work for me. Do you know how cruel some Muslims are? The problems between Malek and me started long ago, and he wasn't the only one."

"When Malek tormented you, he was still a boy. But when you slandered Malek, you were a man."

"Don't turn against me." He whispers sharply. A guard glances over. "I had to move against Malek. His skirmishes against the Young Pilgrims weren't getting us anywhere. We needed something bigger."

"Why did you have to fight at all? I've worked with Christians most of my life, and I never had problems with them."

"You had problems with Hiram, though. He didn't respect you. And you never saw the Young Pilgrims in action. They harassed our sisters. They slandered Prophet Muhammad to our faces. And when we fought them on the South Side, that last time, one of them tore up a copy of the Qur'an and stomped on the pages."

"None of that was in the news. All I heard was what the FOM did."

"Who owns the news in this town, Dad? They do. And don't talk to me about Christians. They're not Christians, they're a sect. The real Christians are people like Sandra and Uncle Chris. Hiram Johnson is no more a Christian than I am. Ask any priest in town, or any minister. They know."

"Why don't they fight the New Pilgrims, then?"

"Because they're just like you. The New Pilgrims own this town. No one can speak out against them and get away with it."

"And you thought you could put an end to that?"

"I thought they would be so desperate to get Hiram back that they would take our demands seriously. If he hadn't returned, though, they would have put his son, Caleb, in power and moved on. To them, everyone is dispensable. Even Hiram."

"They do good work. They run several charities."

"Can't you recognize a hypocrite when you see one?"

Hypocrite is a heavy word, but I could easily apply it to the New Pilgrims after remembering all their empty promises. "So you plan to fight this? You know the odds are against you."

He nods. "If I don't make it, you need to get the message out. Don't be afraid, Dad. They can't really hurt you."

A guard interrupts. Our time is up.

"We're going back to Lexington today. I don't know when we'll be in town again."

"I hope to see you before the trial. You will be here for that, won't you?"

My job is in Kentucky, but I need to be here for my son. "I'll be here. Keep praying, Luqman. I love you."

"Yeah." He looks down. "I miss Uncle Brad."

"I do, too."

He nods, his eyes still to the floor. "I, uh, I love you, too, Dad."

The guard takes him away before I have a chance to respond. I glance back at him as I'm being led out of the room.

Joshua: Part Three

For the last month, since our return to Lexington, I've closely followed the news in Chicago. I need to know if Luqman is right.

Every night after dinner, I watch the news on a Chicago station, and I've begun noticing the New Pilgrim bias. Every broadcast has at least one positive story about Hiram, the church, or one of its members. The bad news is almost always about crime, usually involving minorities. I think back to all the negative stories I've heard about blacks and Hispanics, and how I never paused to question them. There is plenty of fluff, too, about animals and small children.

I don't remember a time when the media wasn't biased, but I never noticed this much overt propaganda before. Luqman did.

∼

Tonight, when I took my place on the couch, I expected the usual mixture of fluff and propaganda. But I wasn't prepared for the lead story. I watch, not really believing what I'm hearing.

"The New Pilgrims have gained control of Hope Center and the Evans Center for the homeless in a special merger. Hope Center board members approved the deal last night. The official unification is expected to be complete by Labor Day. Reverend Hiram Johnson called the merger a 'great and glorious blessing for all of Chicago.'"

The New Pilgrims are in charge of Hope and Evans? Gameel wouldn't agree to that. I search for his number.

"Yes?"

"Assalaamu alaikum Gameel. I just heard about the merger. Is that true?"

"It wasn't a merger, it was a takeover. They have my resignation. There's a limit to how far I will go." He sounds tired and tense.

"What about Stu?"

"Hiram has Stu in his back pocket. We shouldn't have put him in charge. He's too young. It's done now. I was planning to call you later."

"Isn't there anything we can do?"

"It's all perfectly legal." He pauses. "Listen, Joshua, I'll call you later." He hangs up.

This is a nightmare. Luqman was right. I should have listened to him sooner.

Courage I

The Qur'an is the infallible weapon
which destroys the cunning of the conspirators,
shakes the hearts of enemies, and fills the believers
with courage and steadfastness.

—Syed Qutb

Luqman

"Oh my son! Establish regular prayers,
enjoin what is just, and forbid what is wrong;
and bear with patient constancy whatever happens to you:
For this is firmness of purpose in (the conduct of) affairs.

—Surah Luqman, verse 17

Last week, I turned twenty-five. Our family never celebrated birthdays, but I always bought myself a treat. All day, I thought about a banana split. No one tells you that when you set out to create a revolution, you have to give up banana splits.

Most of the time I stay to myself, watching my back, especially in the dining hall and recreation area. The prison is in downtown Chicago, so there is no yard. We go up to the roof once a week and stretch out a little. Some guys play basketball. I watch. Sometimes I stand and jog in place, enjoying my few minutes of sunshine.

As soon as I got here, I let them know not to mess with me. When they asked me what I did, I leaned back and told them the story.

"There was this guy who was older and bigger, and when I was little, he beat me up. But I never forgot. When the time was right, I put him down. Then, I put a bullet into him. Everyone knows not to mess with me."

I looked around to make sure of the identities of my listeners. "I don't go telling everybody this, but I took the biggest man in Chicago and turned him into a whining fool." I paused dramatically. "Those were two of my victims. It's hard to remember them all, you know?" I said it slowly and confidently, and it made me sound bigger than I am. They leave me alone.

There are some Young Pilgrims here, and I keep a close eye on them. Their leader put a few of our guys out of commission last winter. During the Evanston fight, I came face-to-face with him, and I managed to break his nose. What did he do to get himself in here?

The dude is well over six feet tall with the biceps of an athlete. Most of the guards call him Charles. The white guys call him Charlemagne. The rest of us stay out of his way.

My friends are few. There's Duke, who's waiting for his trial on arson. They say he burned his house down for the insurance money, but his little boy died in that fire, and I know he didn't set it. Emad is guilty. He beat his father nearly to death during an argument about curfew. Manny got into a fight with his best friend and pushed him to the ground. The guy never got up. His lawyer hopes to reduce the charge to manslaughter. Hakeem is here, too, waiting for his murder trial, but he won't talk to me. Jasmine is divorcing him, and somehow that's my fault.

Hakeem

How could I ever have called Luqman my friend? He ruined my life. Now he goes around bragging about what he did. Malek was my friend, and I don't care what happened when they were in grade school. He had no right to kill my Muslim brother.

My lawyer is telling me to take a plea bargain, so I can avoid the electric chair. I'll have to serve at least twenty years. My son will be twenty-one when I get out. He won't know me. Jasmine will make sure of that. She couldn't get the divorce papers drawn up fast enough. She brought them last week for me to sign. That's the last I'll see of her.

Now, Mama's the only one who comes, and every time she starts crying. "I tried to raise you to be a good Muslim. What I did I do wrong?" The whole hour is like that. I almost wish she wouldn't bother. She just makes me feel worse.

I don't belong in this place. My first night here, some inmate tried to hit on me. I fought him off, but I never feel safe. How will I be able to survive the next twenty years?

Luqman isn't safe either, but he doesn't seem to notice. Those Young Pilgrims are waiting for the right time. They were probably planted in this prison just to get rid of him. He thinks he's gonna fight Hiram in court. Didn't he learn anything out at that campsite? There are some people in this world you don't mess with, and Hiram Johnson is one of them. We should have killed him when we had the chance.

Every Friday, I talk to the chaplain. He's helping me keep my faith. Without that, I would lose my mind.

Luqman had better watch his back. Sometimes, I think I should warn him. But he's such a big man. Let him take care of himself.

Luqman

"And swell not your cheek (for pride) at men,
nor walk in insolence through the earth:
For Allah loves not any arrogant boaster."

—Surah Luqman, verse 18

Today after the Friday prayer, I talked with the Muslim chaplain, Brother Syed. We were alone, so I told him about myself. He didn't act surprised that I had gone to an Islamic school for eight years but could barely read the Qur'an in Arabic.

"It's a matter of intention," he said. "If you want to learn, you will."

I thought about that for a while. Then I wanted to talk about Malek.

"I didn't mean to kill him, but he was there, shooting at me and badgering me. You have to believe me when I tell you it was self-defense."

"I'm not the one you need to convince," he said. "If your conscience is clear in front of Allah, you have nothing to fear."

"I never liked him, but other people didn't know him the way I did."

"Why are you arguing? I didn't accuse you of anything."

"People talk. Everyone in Chicago hates me for what I did. You might hate me, too."

"I'm here to help you, Luqman. That's all."

"Do you think I'm going to hell? My father says he wants to see me in paradise."

"Allah is the Most Forgiving, the Most Merciful. Turn to Him."

"You know prison isn't safe, and some guys are out to get me for what I did to Hiram Johnson."

He's quiet for a moment. "You're right. Keep your eyes open, and ask Allah for help. Would you like me to say something to the authorities?"

The warden is probably a New Pilgrim too, like all the others. "Don't bother. Thanks for talking to me."

We'll talk again next Friday. If I can get through this one week at a time, I'll be okay.

Hakeem

My lawyer came through with the deal. I'll confess to killing the waiter and my role in the kidnapping. I'll also agree to testify against Luqman and the others. In return, the charge of murder will be reduced to manslaughter, and the gun-buying charge will be dropped. My maximum sentence will be twenty years. It's not great, but it's a lot better than the electric chair.

I hope the other guys take plea bargains. None of them killed anybody, which is why, I guess, they're still in the Cook County jail while Luqman and I are over here in federal prison. Aziz carried a weapon and helped with the kidnapping, but he also surrendered before the rest of us. Abu Bakr drove the van across state lines, but he wasn't even armed. And Mustapha practically saved Hiram's life.

Luqman is determined to go to trial, just like he was determined to kidnap Hiram. This guy's a loser. I can't wait to sit there in court and testify against him. By the time I'm done, he'll be fried. Someone like that deserves the chair. If they let him out, he'll ruin more lives.

Rasheed is dead and buried. They might have come down harder on him because he was the first one they were able to ID. But, I wish he hadn't resisted. He was a good guy.

Six months ago, everything was good. We were skirmishing with the Young Pilgrims, and each time we gained a little respect. Luqman was just one of the boys back then. He was a good fighter, and we were happy to have him. There was a time when I would have done anything for Luqman. He was my Muslim brother.

Not anymore. He had to push the FOM to "the next level." It sounded good when he said it, like we were making progress. We made it to the next level, all right, in the medium security section of the federal prison. And he keeps pushing.

I keep trying to pray. It doesn't always work. I can't get my mind past the bars and the concrete. Some nights I dream I'm with Jasmine. That just makes it worse.

More than anything, I miss my son. By the time I get out, will he want to know me?

Luqman

"And be moderate in your pace, and lower your voice;
for the harshest of sounds without doubt is the braying of the ass."

—Surah Luqman, verse 19

I'd rather be anywhere else, but I'm surviving, one day and one week at a time.

Charlemagne worries me. They say his father is one of the leaders of the New Pilgrims. Whatever Charlemagne might have done, his dad could have kept him out of here. What's the story?

～

On a Thursday, I'm shuffling to the dining hall for lunch. Charlemagne and his disciples are up ahead of me. When they slow down, so do I.

Suddenly they stop. I stop, too, and lean up against the wall. I'd rather miss lunch than try to get past them.

Hakeem walks past me, staring down at the floor like he has since the night we were arrested. We don't exchange salaams. He refuses to talk to me. He doesn't see Charlemagne up ahead, and I don't dare say anything. I want to live to see Friday.

He keeps plodding along, his head down, getting closer with every step. Charlemagne steps in Hakeem's path and waits. I nearly yell out a warning, but my own sense of survival keeps me quiet.

Everything seems to slow down. Hakeem walks, step by step, toward Charlemagne. Charlemagne's followers gather behind him, their eyes on Hakeem. They look restless, like animals waiting to pounce. I close my eyes and say a prayer for Hakeem's life, and my own.

Hakeem is only a few feet away from them now. Something makes him look up. He backs away. The Young Pilgrims swarm over him with Charlemagne leading the charge.

They attack silently without hesitation. I press myself against the wall and watch their hunger with curiosity and disgust. A guard stands at the end of the hall, looking the other way. A few other prisoners pass the slaughter without comment.

Hakeem has stopped screaming. I keep my eyes on his body as I continue to back down the hall. The predators, having satisfied their need for blood, leave the battered carcass and proceed to the lunchroom. Only Charlemagne remains. He glances at me, briefly making eye contact, and turns away toward the cafeteria.

I keep backing down the hall. After a minute I vomit. While my stomach empties, so does my bladder.

Charlemagne and his minions are out of sight. Only Hakeem's remains give testimony to their brutality. I turn away and rush to the safety of my cell, hoping nobody witnessed my weakness.

Luqman

"And We have enjoined on man (to be good) to his parents.
In weakness upon weakness did his mother bear him.
And in years twain was his weaning: (hear the command),
'Show gratitude to Me and to your parents:
To Me is (your final) goal.'"

—Surah Luqman, verse 14

Hakeem's murder keeps flashing in my brain. The vicious animal brutality makes me sick. The cruelty makes me afraid. I shiver on my bunk and close my eyes. The images won't go away.

I can't do this anymore. There must be something in this the cell I can use to hang myself. If I'm going to die, I'd rather do it by my own hand than wait for the brutality of Charlemagne's gang. I take off one of my socks and stretch it. How am I supposed to do this? Would it work, or would I just prolong my agony?

Before I shot him, Malek taunted me for wetting my pants in fourth grade. Sometimes I got so upset, I lost all control. It made me weaker and more vulnerable. I've worked hard to build my image here, but I lost it there in the hall. They might rape me before they kill me. I can't imagine the horror.

Prisoners do manage to kill themselves. There have been two in the time I've been here. I envy them. They're free of the pain. But, how did they do it? I don't think I have the courage.

I have to do something to get my mind off the massacre. Brother Syed gave me a copy of the Qur'an. I haven't touched it yet. For some reason, I never could learn the Arabic, and after a while I stopped trying. But, I could read it in English, I guess. Maybe it will help.

I flip through the pages until something catches my eyes. There's a surah named after me. Of course, I'm named after the surah. I knew my name was in the Qur'an, but I didn't know it was a whole surah. I start reading.

Some of this sounds like what my dad says. Be grateful. Be good to your parents. Don't be boastful. Maybe that's why he kept lecturing me. I keep reading. Am I one of those people who reject faith? I'm not sure what faith is, actually. I keep reading.

There's some science in here. No one ever told me that. Or maybe they did, and I wasn't listening. And look at this verse. "… fear a day when no father can avail aught for his son, nor a son can avail aught for his father." That old English is one of the things that always turned me off, but I'm smart enough to understand the meaning. We're on our own, both Dad and me. That's why he was talking to me about paradise. He knows he can't do anything to get me there. But he has faith, and I think he'll be there.

My father wants to see me in paradise. If I kill myself, he'll never find me there. I've disappointed him in so many ways. I have to give him something left to hope for. I'm tired. Too much has happened. I set the Qur'an aside and close my eyes.

∼

"Time to pray, Luqman. Wake up." My father raps on my door.

I open my eyes. But, I'm not home. It probably is time to pray. I won't go down to the showers; I want to live. Instead I go to the sink and wash myself the best I can, cleaning up the last evidence of my panic when Hakeem was killed. I should have done it earlier, before I picked up the Qur'an. I knew better than that, but I wasn't thinking straight.

Brother Syed told me which direction to face. I stand up and raise my hands. Quietly, I recite the only two surahs I ever bothered to memorize.

∼

After the prayer, I read Surah Luqman again. Look at this last verse. Allah knows everything. I thought I knew everything, but it turns out I didn't know much at all. There are even some things my father knows more than me, like how to recite the Qur'an.

What did Allah say in the beginning of the surah? "These are Verses of the Wise Book—A Guide and a Mercy to the Doers of Good—those who establish regular prayer, and give regular charity, and have the assurance of the Hereafter." Then, a little later, Allah said, "But there are, among men, those who purchase idle tales, without knowledge, to mislead from the Path of Allah and throw ridicule: for such there will be a humiliating penalty." The one time Hakeem spoke to me, after our arrest, he said I had misled them. He was right. I did it intentionally because I wanted the leadership. I wanted the power.

I'm already being humiliated here in prison. But it doesn't have to last forever. Dad says that Allah forgives. The question is if I believe in Allah.

My Islamic school experience was one of the worst times of my life, until I was sent to this prison. The other kids made fun of me. Some of the teachers always got upset with me. My mom tried to protect me, but that just made it worse. By the time I finished eighth grade there, I didn't want anything to do with Islam.

Most of the people I knew in high school thought religion was outdated and mind-numbing. Some of my university professors were atheists. They mocked the idea of any supreme being. I laughed along with them and my like-minded friends.

But I never bought their theories. There had to be someone. Or should I say, *Someone*? After my failed attempt at revolution, I realize more than ever that people are just too screwed up to run the universe on our own. There is a God. And He is Merciful.

Maybe I shouldn't base my religious beliefs on my experiences. Usually I read when I want to understand. I open the Qur'an again and start at the beginning.

≈

I'm not going to kill myself. There is no rope or knife in my cell. But I do have paper and a pen.

First, I pray again. After my prayer, I pick up the pen and write a final letter to my father. When I'm done, I lie down and talk to Allah. I don't know Arabic, but I'm sure He understands me.

≈

I wake up and check my surroundings. I'm alive. I haven't eaten since breakfast yesterday, but I'm not dead yet. I breathe deeply. How many more breaths do I have?

Hakeem is gone. I should have helped him. But if I had fought them, I would be as dead as my brother Hakeem. And for what? So Charlemagne can be more feared? So Hiram can have more power? I needed to write the letter first. Now, if I must, I can die.

My stomach rumbles. I make the morning prayer and head for the cafeteria. Hakeem's body is gone, but a spot of his blood stains the floor. I shudder and walk carefully toward the cafeteria, trying to forget long enough to get some food in my stomach.

~

After lunch, I go to the Friday prayer. This is one place where I always feel safe. But the brothers know how Hakeem was killed, and how I did nothing to save him. They watch me and make their judgments.

After the prayer, I rush to Syed. "I need to talk with you."

"I heard what happened."

"Can we talk? My life depends on it."

"Sit down." We stay in the prayer room. The other brothers leave. When they're gone, I hand him my letter.

"My life is in danger. You can't go to the administration. They're probably with the New Pilgrims. I'll accept what happens to me, but you have to get this letter to my father. It's urgent. Please promise me you'll do that."

"I'm sure you're very shaken by Hakeem's death. It was tragic—"

"It was unjust and unfair. It was awful. I was there. But the Young Pilgrims will wipe out all the FOM if they can. They're waiting for me. Pray for me, and give the letter to my father. That's all I ask."

"You don't have to die, Luqman. I want to help you."

"Everyone knows the New Pilgrims rule Chicago, but no one will admit it. No one will stop them. Charlemagne isn't a prisoner, he's a hit man. He's going to kill me. Find my father and give him this letter."

He doesn't respond. I stand. "Thanks for being here. Assalaamu alaikum." I touch his shoulder and leave.

~

It's been three days, and Charlemagne hasn't made his move. Every prayer has meaning because it could be my last. I concentrate when I pray, rather than just going through the motions. My spare moments are spent reading the Qur'an. I continue to focus on Surah Luqman, the surah I was named for. Islam is finally beginning to make sense to me.

Every time I go to the dining hall, I'm on alert. This morning I got up the courage to take a shower, remembering the joke I thought of playing on Muhammad. It's no joke now. Charlemagne and his gang are waiting.

∼

Hakeem has been dead for a week. I nearly didn't go to lunch, but as I walked down the hall, there was no danger. I ate quickly, always on alert.

I'm feeling especially restless today. In the afternoon, they take us up to the roof for a little exercise. It's good to see the sky again. I stretch a little, do a few jumping jacks, and jog a couple of times around the perimeter. When I'm done, I feel calmer.

Manny, Duke, and I lean up against the wall for a minute. Emad is off by himself.

"Look at those white guys," laughs Duke. "They think they got game."

Those white guys are Charlemagne and his disciples, and I don't dare laugh. Charlemagne has a few good moves, but the rest are sorry. They trip and fumble the ball while trying to act cool. Finally, I can't help myself. A snicker escapes.

"What's your problem?" One of them shouts.

"Nothing." I turn away and start jogging.

Before I know it, one of those little white boys is up in my face and Charlemagne is right behind him. I stay calm. One wrong move and I'm dead.

Charlemagne blocks me. "Where do you think you're going? You gonna run like you did before?"

I turn and start running the other way. Five of Charlemagne's disciples stand in front of me. "You're going nowhere," one of them says.

I'm surrounded, just like Hakeem was before they killed him. Duke stands tall behind the crowd, and if he had help he could take them on, but Manny's too small, and Emad doesn't care about anybody.

One of the guards pulls out his radio. The other one runs for the exit. I close my eyes and pray.

The knife penetrates my back. I gasp and try to keep standing. My arms flail, but I can't hit anyone. When I'm stabbed again, I go down. They descend on me. I ask Allah to forgive me.

Courage II: Patience

Patience is a type of courage.

—Hamza Yusuf

Joshua: Part One

Luqman's trial has been scheduled for the middle of September. The prosecutor is rushing the case to court, pressured by Hiram. I need to be there, but I don't know if I can get away from my job. Tomorrow, I'll talk to Hanif.

I walk into the house, put down my briefcase, and breathe in a delicious aroma. Aisha cooks nearly all the time here. Now that she isn't teaching, she actually seems to enjoy it. I love coming home to a warm meal.

I kiss her. "It smells great. How was your day, hon?"

"It was good. Dinner will be ready soon. Why don't you go change?"

~

After dinner we pray. I wash dishes while Aisha reads. The news will be on soon. I sit on the couch and edit a report while waiting.

The phone rings. Aisha gets it in the bedroom. She cries out. I rush to her.

"What happened? Who's on the phone?"

She can't answer. After a second or two, she starts crying, gasping between sobs.

I grab the phone. "Who is this? What do you want?"

The words don't make sense. I understand only a few. *Luqman. Stabbed. Dead.*

I drop the phone and hold Aisha tightly. We sink to the floor, aching for our son.

~

We have to go to Chicago. I check the house while she throws a few things into a suitcase. I drive. We barely talk. What is there to say?

At 5:00 AM, we pull into Chicago and go straight to the prison, where we wait for another thirty minutes before anyone will talk to us.

A man walks out with a clipboard. "The body will be released later this morning. At that time, you will receive his personal effects. Do you have any questions?"

"How did this happen?"

"This is a prison, Mr. Adams. You can go to the morgue at 9:00 AM. The body should be ready at that time."

"My son is dead. I want an explanation."

"Wait here." He leaves the room, the door locking behind him.

Several minutes later, another man walks out and offers his hand. "I'm a counselor here at the prison. What are your questions?"

We learn that there will be no autopsy and probably no explanation. He says the body will be ready at 9:00 AM and we can claim it at the morgue. It's all very professional. But we're talking about my son. I want answers, not dry policy statements.

When he's done, Aisha and I cry together.

≈

It's a Saturday and Umar is home. "Assalaamu alaikum. I didn't expect to see you two this weekend."

Aisha and I look at each other. Neither of us wants to say it.

"What's wrong?" Umar pauses. "Is it Luqman?"

Aisha throws herself at Umar, burying her head in his chest. I clear my throat. "They called us last night. He was attacked." I stop and breathe deeply. "Sometime yesterday."

"Did they tell you what happened?"

"They wouldn't tell us anything. We can pick up his body at 9:00 AM." The words nearly catch in my throat. "That's all I know."

"Let's go to the kitchen." He puts his arm around Aisha's shoulders. I trail behind. Umar takes Safa aside, and whispers something to her. She embraces Aisha.

He picks up the phone. "Have you told your other kids?"

"Not yet. You go ahead. I can barely —" I drop to the kitchen chair and cry openly.

≈

While I force coffee down my throat, Umar makes the calls. He notifies all the kids, including Jenny and Michael. Then he contacts the masjid to make arrangements. I don't pay close attention as he talks, ends the call, and makes another. After the ninth call, though, I start to wonder.

Umar shakes his head. "I need time to work through the issues, and that's something we simply don't have."

"What's the problem?"

He glances at Aisha, who is talking quietly with Maryam and Safa. "Luqman killed a Muslim. No one wants to offer his janazah."

"Let me talk with them," says Jeremy. "That is ridiculous."

Umar hands him the phone. "After we find a masjid, we still need permission to use the cemetery."

I check the kitchen clock. "It's after eight."

"We should go to the morgue," says Umar.

"I want to go to the prison first. I need answers.

Umar nods. "Keep making those calls, Jeremy. Muhammad, use another phone and make calls too." He looks around. "Where is Muhammad?"

"He had to go in and cover the story," says Zaid, "I'll make the calls."

"Why would they send him to cover his brother's death?" Umar asks.

Jeremy shrugs. "Muhammad wanted to go. He said he'll tell Luqman's side of the story."

"Would you like me to ask my father to help you, Uncle Isa?" Zaid asks.

"Not yet. You can let him know, though. Let's go, Umar. I need to take care of my son."

On our way to the prison, my phone rings. It's Lexington. "Assalaamu alaikum."

"Walaikum assalaam, Isa. Are you sick?"

I forgot to call Hanif. "No, I have urgent family business in Chicago. It has to do with my son."

He hesitates a moment. "I'll see you on Monday then?"

"I'll be there, insha Allah." I should have called. I can't lose this job.

Umar warns me on the way over. "They're releasing the body to the morgue. You won't be able to see him at the prison."

I shake my head. When we get there, I walk through the same door we entered this morning and wait for someone to emerge. It's the same man, still carrying a clipboard.

"Listen, my son died in this prison yesterday, and I want to know what happened. How could you have allowed this?"

"This is a prison, Mr. —"

"Adams. Joshua Adams. My son's name is Luqman. Why won't you tell me what happened to him?" My face is red, and my heart beats furiously. I stop to catch my breath. Umar touches my arm.

"Let's go to the morgue, Joshua."

Tears stream down my face. I cry out, "I want to see my son."

"I'm sure you can." Umar leads me outside and helps me into the car.

∾

A hearse is parked outside the morgue. It looks empty. I rush into the office. "Where is my son?"

"What was the name?"

How many deaths do they have at that prison? "Luqman Adams."

"Fill out these forms and sign here."

I finish the forms and wait. When they wheel out Luqman's body, I peek under the sheet. He's cut and bruised and his body has already started changing, but he still looks like my son. I kiss his check. The hearse driver steps up. "Where would you like us to deliver the body?"

"Here's the address." Umar hands him an index card.

"Where is that?" I ask him.

"They provide burial services for Muslims in the city. You can wash his body there. Hopefully we'll find a masjid for the janazah soon."

I nod, overwhelmed by it all. Someone hands me a box with his personal effects. I'll look at it later.

∾

We stop at Umar's house first. "I found a masjid," says Jeremy.

"What about the cemetery?" I ask.

"This masjid can get us a spot."

"Why didn't you call us?" Umar asks.

"I just made the arrangements. There is so much hostility. Let's go."

Aisha looks up. "Where are you going?"

Umar touches her shoulder. "We need to arrange for the janazah. Safa will bring you. Derek went to get Mom. She'll be here soon."

In the car, Umar calls the mortuary and arranges for the transfer.

∾

We're greeted by Samir, a young brother who works for the burial service. First he talks about finances, which is the last thing on my mind. Then he takes me to Luqman.

"I've never washed a body before." But I need to do this. "How do I start?"

Samir walks me through the process, step by step. I lovingly touch my son, feeling closer to him in death than I did when he was alive. Silently, I count the many wounds on his chest. They brutalized him. My tears mingle with the water.

∾

Samir tells me they'll transport Luqman to the masjid. Umar and I drive there.

I've never been to this masjid. It's small, a renovated house on the South Side. A brother meets us at the door. "Assalaamu alaikum. I'm Brother Arqam. I'm sorry for your loss, brother."

The hearse arrives soon after we do. Maryam, Aisha, and Sharon are here too, and they insist on seeing Luqman. They cry when they do. Aisha caresses his face, kisses him, and whispers a few words in his ear.

Sharon and Maryam huddle together. Sharon is shaking. Maryam holds her tightly. After a minute or two, they walk up to Luqman's body. Sharon reaches out, putting her palm on his chest. Maryam studies his face. When Sharon breaks down, Maryam leads her away, glancing back at her brother.

vBrother Arqam wants to hold the janazah after the Friday prayer. Brothers file in. When Brother Arqam asks them to stay for Luqman, some walk out. More get in line.

Brother Arqam asks me to lead the prayer. "The father is the best one to lead the janazah," he says. I nearly refuse, but this is one last thing I can do for my son. With a shaky voice that grows stronger with the remembrance of Allah, I stand in front and raise my hands. My heart hurts in a way I never knew it could.

$\sim$

Aisha and Sharon come with us to the cemetery. Maryam walks with them. The imam says another prayer. Umar, Jeremy, Jamal, and Muhammad all lower Luqman into his grave. I feel like taking him in my arms and holding on. But he's on his own now.

We go back to Umar's house. Others come. Ismail and Amal are here. So are Gameel and Hannah. Isaiah walks in and hugs me hard. Matt walks up, his own eyes red. Kyle and his family are still in Arizona. Gameel says he'll call.

They offer words of comfort. I have no words. Losing a child is bad enough. My son died in prison, alone. Prison officials won't tell us what happened. Muhammad and Jeremy say the New Pilgrims are behind it. The trial was coming, and they didn't want Luqman to testify. He had to be silenced. He had so many wounds.

Muhammad tells me about the other deaths. Luqman's friend Hakeem was killed last week. A man named Duke died trying to defend Luqman. Too much blood spilled, and for what?

In the evening a man comes to the house. When Umar answers the door, the man asks for me.

"What do you want?" I've never seen him before.

"Assalaamu alaikum. I'm Syed, the prison chaplain." He hugs me.

"Walaikum assalaam." I want to hold on. What can he tell me about my son?

"I can't stay long, but I have something for you. Before he died, Luqman gave me a letter and asked me to make sure you get it. May Allah help you with your loss."

I take the letter and hold it tightly. "Thank you, brother."

He pats my shoulder. "Call me." Then he disappears into the night.

I put the letter into the box so I can read it later, when everything is quiet.

$\sim$

Umar asks us to stay with them for the night. When everyone is gone and Aisha and I are in bed, I open the box.

These are all of Luqman's possessions. He didn't have much. A little cash. A pen. A notebook. A copy of the Qur'an. His glasses.

The clothes he wore on the night they arrested him are also here. I finger the blue shirt. It was one of his favorites.

I carefully open his letter. His handwriting always was messy. I turn on the overhead light so I can see better.

Aisha moans. "Turn off the light."

"Were you asleep?"

"No, I can't sleep."

"Look at this." I hand her the box. "And this is a letter from Luqman. I'm having trouble reading his handwriting."

"Give it to me. I know how he writes."

"Can you read it out loud?"

She puts on her reading glasses.

"Assalaamu alaikum, Dad. And Mom, too. I want you to know that I'm praying regularly now, and I go to the Friday prayer here in prison. I read the Qur'an a little. The chaplain, Brother Syed, has helped me. I asked him to give you this letter.

"Hakeem was killed today. I saw the whole thing. It was brutal. I think I'll be dead soon, too. Brother Syed keeps saying he can alert the authorities, but I know they're all New Pilgrims. It won't do any good.

"The New Pilgrims arranged for Hakeem's murder. He was killed by Young Pilgrims, but the parent organization was behind it. Their assassin is Charles Edmonds. His father is a New Pilgrim. Could that be Senator Edmonds? I saw Charles at some of the fights. Whoever his father is, he's powerful enough to keep his son out of prison. Hakeem and I are both members of FOM, and he's here to kill us.

"Please warn Aziz, Abu Bakr, and Mustapha. They're still in the Cook County jail, as far as I know. Aziz can give you the names of the other FOM members. They're all in danger. If I had tried to save Hakeem, they would have killed me before I could write this letter. I have to do what I can to save the others.

"I know your life is in Kentucky, but you have to stop the New Pilgrims from destroying Chicago. Let my death be worth something."

Aisha stops and cries quietly. After a few minutes, she continues reading.

"I'm sorry for all the mistakes I made. Now, I'm facing the consequences. Forgive me for the times I talked back to you or disobeyed you. I've read Surah Luqman, the surah you named me for, and now I understand. But it's too late for me.

"Contact religious leaders. Work together to get rid of this sect. They are very dangerous. If I'm dead when you read this, you know how treacherous they are." Aisha pauses and shakes her head.

"I love you both, and I'm sorry for all the trouble I caused. Please forgive me. Tell Jamal, Muhammad, and Maryam that I'll miss them. Tell Jeremy I appreciate the way he stood up for me. Take care of Daud. He's a great kid. Tell Grandma I love her, and tell Uncle Umar he's a challenging opponent. I think he'll know what I mean. Give my salaams to Michael and Jenny too.

"Tell Kyle and Matt that I'm sorry about Uncle Brad. I miss him every day.

"I know you're both worried about me. But don't worry, Dad. I know the answers to the questions.

"Love, Luqman."

I take the letter from Aisha and put my arms around her. Another small paper falls out of the envelope. *"Call me. Syed."* He wrote his phone number.

My wife looks up. "What questions?"

"Give me a minute, and I'll tell you." I wipe my eyes.

Joshua: Part Two

We're still talking when Umar makes the call to prayer. After the prayer, Aisha shows him the letter. "I think you'll want to read this."

He reads silently, smiling a little at the end. "What do you think we should do?" I ask.

"Everything Luqman says about the New Pilgrims is true. They're corrupt. They're also very powerful. It would be suicide to oppose them."

"There must be a way."

He's silent for a moment. "Senator Edmonds does have a son named Charles. If this news were to reach the national level, it would cause serious damage."

"Could Muhammad do that?"

"He would have to quit his job and leave Chicago. He would probably be blacklisted, and his life could be in danger."

"How do we fight them, Umar? Don't tell me it's impossible."

Aisha grabs her brother's arm. "We have to do this for Luqman."

Umar nods. "We need to start with Muhammad. Isa, call him and tell him to come here." He looks at Aisha. "You didn't sleep, did you?"

"How could we? Our son died."

"I'll put on the coffee. We must be alert for the task ahead."

$\sim$

We were energized all weekend. Jeremy found a way to let me talk with Aziz, Abu Bakr, and Mustapha. After I had the names of the other gang members, Jeremy warned them. I also spoke with Detective Arif Hussain. He seems to be one of the good guys.

Muhammad ignored messages from the station and sat with us. He agreed to work on the exposé. We formed a plan. It felt good not to be sitting still.

$\sim$

On the Monday after my son died, I was back behind my desk. I've tried to keep up with my work, but my concentration is lagging. I haven't said anything to my coworkers. My son died in prison. What does that say about me?

It's been nearly a month. Luqman's trial would have started today. I try to stay busy. At work I walk the halls, chatting with colleagues. I'd like to work late, but Aisha is alone. At five, I leave the center and call her. We're going out for dinner. She couldn't gather the energy to cook today.

We go to an Italian place. Usually she likes the food here, but tonight she only nibbles. I try to cheer her up, but I don't feel very cheerful either. We ask for carry-out containers, our food barely touched.

Instead of going home, I take a drive out along Highway 25. We pass horse farms and rolling hills. She usually enjoys the scenery. But she just closes her eyes and leans against the headrest. I turn around and head back toward Lexington.

I still don't want to go home. The house is too quiet. We'll think too much. But there's nowhere else to go, and we can never escape it. Our son is dead.

∼

"Let my death be worth something." Luqman's voice comes to me, so clear that I think he must be standing next to me. I open my eyes. The room is dark.

Muhammad found an independent news station in Minneapolis. They're small but growing. When he offered to do an exposé on Chicago politics, they gave him a good salary and his own office. He's working day and night to put the story together. They expect it to air in the beginning of October.

What can I do? I've lost the energy of that first weekend. How can I honor Luqman and carry on his mission?

∼

It's Saturday. In the morning, I work in the garden. We grew a lot of tomatoes and zucchini this year. The cantaloupe didn't do well.

At lunchtime, we heat last night's leftovers and sit at the kitchen table to eat. "I miss him, Isa."

"Me, too."

We keep eating. I don't enjoy the food, but going hungry won't help anyone. We eat in silence. Aisha and I have been married so long that words aren't always necessary.

∼

In the afternoon, I stretch out on the couch, close my eyes, and drift off.

I see it so clearly. Luqman took a plea deal. After twenty years, he receives parole. We drive back to Kentucky together. After all these years, I'm not sure what to expect.

In the morning, he makes the call to prayer. We stand side by side.

After the prayer, he makes my tea and toast. "I want to make it better," he says. "For the last ten years, I've sent half of my pay to Malek's family, even the little I earned in prison. I hope it helps."

"You lost so much, Luqman."

"I know. I'll never get married or teach at a university. But I'm trying to be good. I hope you'll give me a chance to prove myself."

"I haven't seen you pick up the Qur'an since you came back."

"I read in my room last night."

"Go get your copy. Let's read together."

I finish my breakfast and sit with him on the living room floor. He begins to recite. I close my eyes and listen to his beautiful voice. After a few minutes, I join him.

I wake up crying. According to his letter, Luqman died as a Muslim. Only Allah knows if I'll see him in paradise. But I can repair the damage he caused and carry on the good he tried to do.

～

Aisha is outside, working in her flower garden. I slip on my shoes and join her.

"Did you have a nice nap?"

The dream disturbed me, but I feel refreshed. I saw my son again. "Do you know how to contact Malek's widow?"

"I think she's staying with her mother. She was expecting the last time I saw her in early May. The baby must have been born now." Aisha sighs. "How will she manage with three small children?"

"We need to visit her. Do you think she'd see us?"

"If you want, I can call her mother."

"Do it today. We can drive up next weekend if that would work."

"I don't know if she'll talk to me, but I'll try."

"Thanks." I kiss her cheek and go to work in my vegetable garden.

～

During dinner, Aisha says, "I called Madhiyah. Malek's mother-in-law. We haven't spoken since it happened, but she was polite. I've taught every one of her children. When I told her we would like to come, she said she would talk to her daughter."

"I hope she'll see us. It can't be easy for her."

"Can you imagine, Isa? She's only twenty-five. Malek didn't live to see their youngest." She puts down her fork. "I'll always love Luqman, but I hate what he did to Malek. Two young men are dead, and they've left so much pain behind."

I pat her hand. "I dreamed about Luqman during my nap. We read the Qur'an together."

She hides her face in my shoulder and cries. How long does it take to get over the death of a child?

～

Aisha calls me during my lunch hour on Monday. Malek's widow wants to see us. We're going to Chicago on Friday.

I hang up and take Luqman's letter of out of my briefcase. I carry it with me wherever I go. Setting aside my sandwich, I read his words again. *"Let my death be worth something."*

Muhammad is working on the exposé. Aisha contacted Malek's widow. What can I do?

Joshua: Part Three

On Wednesday morning, when I'm between dreams and waking, I hear Luqman's adhan. It's so clear and beautiful. Only Luqman made the call to prayer that way.

I keep my eyes closed and listen. After the adhan I hear him whisper. *"If I don't make it, you need to get the message out. Don't be afraid, Dad. They can't hurt you."*

I lie in bed a moment longer, comforted by his voice. When I open my eyes, I see the dark night sky turning to gray. It is time to pray.

In my office, I take out his letter and read it again. In a few lines, he answered all of my questions. Each time I read this letter, I feel at peace.

Others need to know who Luqman was and what he wrote. I need to get the message out, as he said. Right now, I need to do work for the center, but when I get home I'm going to help my son.

~

I walk into the house, give Aisha a quick kiss, and go to our office. As I type furiously, she stands in the doorway.

"What are you doing?"

"Let me finish and I'll tell you. It's for Luqman."

Later, she brings my dinner into the office. I type and eat, taking care not to get the letter dirty. "I'm nearly done, hon. Give me a few more minutes."

She waits, leaning up against the desk. I double-check my work, send it out, and lean back in the chair.

"What was that about?"

"I typed up Luqman's letter and sent it out to every Muslim leader in Chicago, along with my personal note. When we go there this weekend, I'll check back with them, especially those who refused to offer his janazah. I also sent the letter to Chris and asked him to contact his Christian friends in Chicago. The last time I saw him, Luqman asked me to get his message out. It's time we stood up to the New Pilgrims and took back our city."

"Do you think that's possible?"

"We have to try."

Joshua: Part Four

Aisha picks me up from work on Friday afternoon, and we hit the highway. My car will be safe in the center parking lot.

She drives. I doze. It's nearly 2:00 AM when she wakes me. "We're here, Isa."

Umar left the porch light on. I grab our suitcases and walk up the steps. He meets us at the front door.

"You didn't have to wait up, brother. Weren't you going to leave the key under the mat?"

"I had to make sure you arrived safely." He hugs us both. "You must be exhausted. Go rest. We'll talk later."

~

Umar's adhan wakes us. We slept only a few hours, and I'm still tired, but we have no time for rest. After the prayer, Umar puts on the coffee.

"What time is your meeting?"

"We're visiting her at 10:00 AM," says Aisha. "I hope I'm ready for this."

"You're both grieving," says Umar. "Make that your common ground."

"But, Luqman took away the father of her children. I have trouble forgiving him for that."

"Luqman and Malek allowed themselves to be ruled by the primitive emotions of jealousy and pride. Each is guilty. What you must do, Aisha, is begin to heal that wound."

"You make it sound so easy."

Safa walks in and puts her hand on Aisha's shoulder. "If anyone can do it, you can."

Aisha grabs her sister-in-law's hand. "Thanks for the encouragement."

"You also need a good breakfast. Umar, didn't you make them eggs or toast? They can't get by on coffee, especially not today."

He smiles. "You're the master cook."

Safa gets to work. Aisha asks, "Is Mom still here, or did she go back to Moline?"

Umar sits across from her. "Mom's having a very hard time with Luqman's death. She keeps saying no woman should outlive her grandson. She's here. I've talked with her, but she's different now. Would you believe she doesn't get up until nearly 10:00 AM?"

"Maybe I can help." Aisha sighs. "No woman should outlive her son, either."

~

After breakfast, Aisha goes into Sharon's room. I pick up the phone and start making calls.

"Assalaamu alaikum Imam Iyad. This is Isa. Joshua Adams. Did you receive my email?"

"Walaikum assalaam Isa. Why did you send that to me?"

"My son was a Muslim when he died, but you refused to perform his janazah. You need to know who Luqman really was."

"He killed another Muslim man. That's all I need to know. I don't want to discuss this. What good will come of it?"

"Luqman recognized the corruption in this city and tried to do something to stop it. Don't you think it's time that the Muslims of Chicago spoke out?"

"Chicago has always been corrupt. Our job isn't to delve into politics but only to spread the message of Islam."

"Islam covers all aspects of life, including politics."

"You're not a scholar, Isa. Leave it to the learned men to interpret Islam. You need to go back to Kentucky and forget about your son."

I'm tempted to say many things. After a moment, I simply hang up. I take a few minutes to regain my composure and make another call.

~

Aisha spent an hour talking with Sharon in her room. They just walked out together. I hug my mother-in-law.

She looks at me with red eyes and goes with Aisha into the kitchen. Kids aren't supposed to die. But they do. Allah gave him a lifespan. I have to remind myself of that.

I've made seven calls in the last hour. One, like Imam Iyad, refused to discuss Luqman with me. Two pledged their support. Four said they will have to think and pray about it.

I didn't know it would be this difficult. They should understand. Instead of hiding behind words, they should reach out and offer to help. But change never comes easily. It took me a while, too, to listen to Luqman's message. I can't expect more from those who barely knew him.

Later today, I'll visit some of the masajid and talk with the imams. They must be convinced that this isn't only about Luqman. Stopping the New Pilgrims will be good for Chicago.

I stretch and walk into the kitchen. Umar and Aisha sit with Sharon. I go to the other side of the table and pat her hand. "We all miss him, but we have to leave these things up to God. He knows best."

She nods. This isn't the right time for words.

Joshua: Part Five

Malek's wife and mother-in-law live on the South Side, not far from Hope Center. I drive past. The building looks the same, except for the New Pilgrims logo next to the name. I wince and look away.

"Her name is Henna," says Aisha. "She's a nice girl—one of my former students."

This is the house. We brought food and diapers. Aisha helps me carry the bags up to the door.

An older woman answers. Aisha offers her hand. "Assalaamu alaikum Madhiyhah. It's nice to see you again."

The woman embraces Aisha, hugging her long and hard. She cries. "How are you? I miss you."

I wait. Madhiyhah releases my wife and opens the screen door wider. "Come in. Both of you."

I look around. "I can stay on the porch if that's more proper."

"Come in. My son is home. Imran, come down here," she calls.

We walk into a dimly lit room. A woman sits on the couch, holding a baby. Other children run through the room. Aisha puts down her bags and goes to the woman.

"Assalaamu alaikum Henna. How are you?" They hug. Aisha pulls back and looks at the baby. "She's sweet. What's her name?"

"Malekah." Henna cradles her baby, holding her close.

"Sit down," says Madhiyhah. "You didn't need to bring anything. We're just happy to see you. Imran, where are you? Come down here."

Aisha sits next to Henna. "I'm sorry for what my son did. There's no way I can make it up to you."

Henna says nothing. Madhiyhah scoffs. "That boy was old enough to know what he was doing. Both of them were. It's so hard to raise them these days." A young man bounds down the steps. "Isn't that right, Imran? You know what I'll do to you if you go anywhere near a gang."

He grins. "Yeah, I know."

"It wasn't just a gang," says Henna. "Malek thought he was doing the right thing. He wanted to spread Islam. That's all." She holds the baby tighter and cries. "I should have believed him. That's what set him off. He would never have gone out there if I hadn't listened to the gossip."

One of the imams I talked with today mentioned the rumor Luqman started. I'd only heard whispers and references until today. "Luqman was wrong, and I hope he realized that before he died. But why was it so easy for people to believe the lie?"

"You know how people are," says Madhiyhah. "They latch onto bad news and won't let it go. Malek was a good man and an excellent husband and father. I tried to tell folks that, but my own daughter believed the lie."

"It's my fault," says Henna. "If I had believed Malek, he would still be alive."

"We've been through this, honey," says Madhiyhah. "It was the will of Allah."

"I'm sorry for what Luqman did to Malek, and to your family. He'll have to answer to Allah for that now."

"Abu Bakr's mother told me that Malek was acting crazy out there. I don't think Luqman had much choice. Anyway, it's done now." Madhiyhah sighs. "We've lost too many young men. Don't you go near a gang, Imran, not even if they tell you they're doing it for Allah. There are other ways to change things."

We stay and talk for nearly two hours. Henna is still very sad, but I think her mother's love and strength will get her through this. I wish it could have been different. Several months ago, though, Daud told me it's wrong to wish. We must accept what Allah gives us.

Joshua: Part Six

When we get back to Umar's house, we all sit with Sharon and talk it out. Being with Madhiyhah made me stronger, and I think it helped Aisha too. Before we're finished, we're all crying. But I hope Sharon can learn to live with this, just as we must. Not even the loss off her own husband shook her as much as Luqman's murder.

In the evening, I go to a masjid to pray and talk with the imam. "I hope you understand what I'm trying to say."

"I hope you understand, Isa, how hard this is for our community. We knew some of our boys were in trouble, but we never expected it to go this far. Why didn't you come to me before, when Luqman was still living at home? I'm sure you were concerned about him then."

"I knew he was lying, but I couldn't predict what he would do. If you had told me five months ago—"

He nods. "That's how the community feels. It's still a shock. Luqman wrote a powerful letter, and I agree we must fight the corruption. We won't let him down this time."

～

Before we leave Chicago, I call Syed. He agrees to meet me at the masjid.

We talk first about the New Pilgrims and Charlemagne. Then I ask him, "Tell me about my son. Was he a Muslim when he died?"

"As far as I know, he was." Syed shares some of their conversations with me.

Each word gives me comfort. I know what Luqman told me the last time I saw him, and what he wrote in his letter, but I needed to hear it again. Whatever Luqman did wrong, I have to hold on to the hope that I'll see him in paradise.

Joshua: Part Seven

We drive into Lexington on Sunday night, exhausted but more hopeful than we've been since the night of the kidnapping. Instead of just mourning our son, we're working to make a difference.

On Monday morning, I call for a meeting. In front of my coworkers, I stand up and confess, "I had a son named Luqman. Last month he was murdered in prison. I thought you should know."

"Why?" says Munir. "Are you looking for sympathy?"

"No." I scan the room. "We have no greater resource than our youth. They can slip away so easily. What can we do for them here in Lexington?"

Marwa, a young mother of two, raises her hand. "I'm interested in developing programs for young women."

"I'd like to help the boys," says Tawfiq, a recent college graduate.

"Good. Start writing some proposals and get back to me. And don't be shy in asking for help."

A few laugh. Neither one of them is very shy.

"That's all. You can get back to work."

Some stop to give words of compassion. That really isn't why I told them. Luqman's death has to count for something, and maybe it will inspire us to help the youth of Lexington.

Joshua: Part Eight

Muhammad's exposé on Senator Edmonds and the New Pilgrims aired nationally last month. The response was overwhelming. The president seized the moment, promising swift justice, and won reelection by a wide margin. Edmonds was forced to resign and is facing indictment. His son has been charged with murder, and several prison guards were fired. The New Pilgrims have come under federal investigation for violations including unfair labor practices and tax fraud. Hiram may soon be spending time in the federal prison where he had my son assassinated.

The faith community of Chicago is adding to the pressure. Twenty-four imams have openly condemned the corrupt practices of the New Pilgrims. Sixty-three priests, ministers, and rabbis did the same.

Khalif Amin is the head of the city council now. Special elections will be held in two weeks to replace indicted members. The Department of Labor is actively investigating hiring practices in the environmental industries. Next week Congress will hold hearings.

Luqman's revolution is succeeding. I wish he had believed that it is still possible to work within the system.

It will take years to reverse the effects the New Pilgrims had on Chicago. Unemployment is still at 30 percent and homeless shelters are bulging. Hope and Evans nearly became casualties of the purge, but faith communities and some business leaders, including Barnett, came to the rescue. Stu is being investigated. If necessary, I'll testify on his behalf. We don't really talk, though. Too much has happened.

◇

I always thought of myself as a good father, but I failed Luqman. When he was a child, I should have been more patient. When he complained about the bullies, I should have protected him. As he grew older, I should have taught him how to be a man. But I was busy. My time with him is gone and can never be reclaimed. Sometimes I sit alone and cry for lost opportunities.

I didn't do enough for Luqman while he was alive. We're making great strides, but I must carry on his mission. Not through armed revolution. Using a measured approach, I'll continue to use the resources available to me to fight the many injustices of our society. Daud says it's wrong to wish, but I can't help thinking I should have started doing this twenty years ago. Imagine the suffering that might have been avoided.

Joshua: Part Nine

A year ago, Brad had just died. Luqman was in prison. It's been a rough year, but we survived.

Aisha and I are spending part of my vacation time in Chicago, giving talks on parenting and warning signs. The first time we stood up, at a small church in Lexington, it was difficult to admit our failures, but we hope to help other parents avoid our pain. She's decided to write a book about our experiences.

We also talk with city officials and faith community leaders, urging them to provide support for our youth. The feedback has been positive. Khalif Amin is working with the mayor to rebuild the neighborhoods. Unemployment rates have inched down to 24 percent. Much work remains to be done, but Chicago is slowly recovering.

I've spoken with Stu. Unlike Hiram, he avoided prison time but remains on probation. The board hired a new director from St. Louis. The centers appear to be thriving.

≈

On a Saturday, Umar invites everyone to his house for a barbecue. "We don't know how long we'll be together," he says.

Umar, Derek, and Ahmad stand by the barbecue grill. How many years before Umar gives his master barbecue apron to his sons? He takes medication for his heart, but his health is good.

Marcus and Hafiz coach Daud and Mikhail on soccer's finer points. Daud's leg healed well. His voice is deeper and he's grown six inches since last summer.

Kyle flew in from Arizona for the barbecue, along with Beth, Faiqa, and their children. Right now he's everywhere, chasing his triplets. Zakariya, Kamila, and Bilquis join the game.

Isaiah, Matt, Jamal, Muhammad, and Jeremy sit at a picnic table, eating watermelon and holding an animated discussion. Yesterday, Muhammad told us he plans to get married. Aliya is another reporter at his station. Aisha and I will fly up to Minneapolis next week to meet Aliya and her parents.

Maryam and Zaid sit together, holding hands. Last month they learned that Maryam is pregnant. She hopes to teach one more year before taking time off to raise their children.

Raheema and Safa run into the kitchen to get the pies. Aisha sits with Sharon, Beth, Emily, Faiqa, Becky, and Melinda. Amir wiggles on her lap. He wants to play. I scoop up Kamila and take her to Aisha, releasing her big brother.

Chris walks up and hands me a root beer. We're closer than ever now. The rest of our birth family is dead and all we have is each other.

"Are you okay?" he asks. "You're quiet."

"I'm just thinking."

I should have known Luqman. He always had too much energy, too much curiosity. He didn't know what direction to go, and I didn't know how to help him. His energy became a negative force because he lacked the focus his father should have taught him.

I should have just let Luqman be Luqman and loved him for who he was. I did that, toward the end, and I'll always treasure the conversations we had in prison. His letter has a special place in my briefcase, and his memories are always in my heart.

With Luqman's help, we brought down the New Pilgrims. Chicago has a fresh start. That is his legacy.

ABOUT THE AUTHOR

Silence is the final book in Jamilah Kolocotronis's *Echoes Series*. Other books in the series are: *Echoes, Rebounding, Turbulence, and Ripples.* In addition, Jamilah has written the novel *Innocent People* and the non-fiction book, *Islamic Jihad.*

As the mother of six sons, Jamilah Kolocotronis is anxious for the availability of quality Islamic literature for young Muslim adults. This prompted her to write the *Echoes Series*. Her sons have also helped her develop the characters of Joshua Adams and others in the series. Through them, she has learned much about the challenges facing young Muslims in America.

Jamilah and her family live in Lexington, Kentucky.

Islamic Fiction Books

Muslim Writers Publishing is proud to have published *Silence*, a quality Islamic Fiction book for older teens and adults. You can learn more about the availability of Islamic Fiction books and Muslim authors by visiting: www.IslamicFictionBooks.com

Islamic Fiction books: This refers to creative, non-preachy, and imaginative fiction books written by Muslims and marketed primarily to Muslims. Islamic Fiction may be marketed to secular markets, too. The content of these books incorporates some religious content and themes, and may include non-fictionalized historical or factual Islamic content with or without direct reference to the Qur'an or the Sunnah of the Prophet (pbuh). The stories may also include modern, real life situations and moral dilemmas. Islamic Fiction may be written in many languages. Islamic Fiction books do not include any of the following Harmful Content:

- vulgar language
- sexually explicit content
- unIslamic practices that are not identified as unIslamic
- content that portrays Islam in a negative way

Linda D. Delgado, Publisher
Muslim Writers Publishing
www.MuslimWritersPublishing.com

CPSIA information can be obtained at www.ICGtesting.com
Printed in the USA
LVOW11s1634160216

475338LV00001B/205/P

9 780979 357794